DATE DUE

JUN 20 '08			
FEB 16 2012			

F
Blew Mary Clearman
Jackalope Dreams

FLYOVER FICTION

Series editor: Ron Hansen

Jackalope Dreams

Mary Clearman Blew

May 21, 2008

UNIVERSITY OF NEBRASKA PRESS | LINCOLN AND LONDON

F
Blew

19.96 Barnes+Noble

For Cali
who sat on my lap as I wrote

Jackalope \\'jak-el-lop \ *n, pl* jackalope or jackalopes [ME, *jacke*, male, ME *antelop*, fabulous beast, prob. fr. MF *antelop* savage animal with sawlike horns, fr. ML *anthalopus*, fr. LCK *antholop-antholops*] 1: offspring of a small long-eared mammal (*Oryctolagus cuniculus*) and a ruminant mammal (*Antilocapra americana*) exhibiting the bodily conformation of the former and the pronged antlers of the latter 2: an omen or threatening force; cf. MONSTER 3: an anachronism.

Monster, loved for what you are
Till time, that buries us, lay bare.

Robert Lowell, "Near the Ocean"

Acknowledgments Many people were of great help to me in writing this novel. My cousin Ted Murray gave me detailed information I could not have gotten elsewhere, and my old friend Brad Parrish, Fergus County High School Class of '57, advised me on legal and other aspects of the novel. My heartfelt thanks to the members of my writing group, especially Joy Passanante and Kelly and Pamela Yenser, who read and reread drafts of my novel. Thanks also to my sister and brother-in-law, Jackie and Bud Rickl, and all the robbers of the Charlie Russell Chew Chew Train.

1

She's what, in her late fifties, and that's the kind estimate. Truth is, she feels older and she knows she looks older. This afternoon, with the long June sunlight steaming through the streaky schoolhouse windows, she feels the lines burrowing into her face, the flesh sliding down her neck. She's been facing the weather too long, she's got a temper like a bad windstorm, and she's too old to be starting over. She knows what the neighbors are wondering, and she wonders, herself. What the hell is Corey Henry going to do with herself, now that the Mill Creek school has finally closed, and how much hell is her old dad liable to raise with her for it?

Still doesn't seem possible to her. She has to say it to believe it. The school's not just closed for the summer, but closed. Closed. Down.

Hardly seems worthwhile to sweep the schoolroom floor before she leaves for good. None of the usual June chores seem worth doing. She's erased the chalkboard, that was automatic, and she's put dust covers over the three computers, she's done that much Hailey

Doggett's been talking about holding a schoolyard sale in a week or two, get rid of the small stuff that way, he said. Probably he'll buy up some of it himself, seeing as he's going to be home-schooling his girls, Ariel and Rose, from now on.

Until Hailey started talking about the sale, it hadn't occurred to Corey to wonder what became of schoolhouse gear when a school closed down. Had to have happened often enough, beginning after World War II, fifty years ago, when the highways started getting paved and the schools started to consolidate. It's a new world now, the beginning of a new century, and all the country schools are long gone, sold for salvage lumber or hauled off and turned into granaries with a clutter of folders and abandoned textbooks and construction-paper cutouts bleaching in sun and dust or buried under tons of bushels of wheat. In all of Murray County, only the Mill Creek school has withstood the years of consolidation by being incorporated into a private school by a community resisting change, then trapped in some kind of goddamn time warp, and Corey Henry with it. But now it's done for, and so is its teacher.

She thinks this clutter will likely stay where it lies.

The handbell. She guesses she could take it home with her, to remind herself how many recesses she's rung in. Hailey probably won't care if she takes it. And what if he does.

And so she walks out the schoolhouse door for the last time with the handbell clanging in pure air until she puts a finger on the clapper to silence it. Turns the key in the door, on account of the computers. Hides the key under the steps for Hailey. The world has changed, after all, even up here at the head of Mill Creek, and who knows which new neighbor or carload of kids from town might come snooping around.

The schoolhouse sits on what some would call view property, but was nothing but a useless knob of pine pasture in 1912, when the neighbors pitched in to build their children a school overlooking foothills that would have receded then as they recede today, from green to blue in serrated ranks of pines rising to the long white crest of the Snowy Mountains. It's the familiar that's giving Corey pause, the way the hills roll as they always have. Her next step will be into the unfamiliar, and she's afraid to take it, afraid she's losing her balance.

But from the patch of fresh grass, the young mare raises her head at the end of her picket rope, sharpens her ears against the blue and whinnies. Corey comes alive again, tells herself to quit her lollygagging. She's got to get home, face her old dad, get it over with. So she goes to get the feed bucket from what once was a coal shed, is now a crazily leaning structure of boards, probably soon will be a bonfire. Holds the bucket for the mare and watches her dip her muzzle into the oats and lift, munching, with faraway eyes.

"You going to miss your ride every day, Babe?" Corey asks her, and winces at the sound of her own voice interrupting the summer sounds of grasshoppers, the swish of wind through pine needles. "We'll have to think of something," she mutters.

Babe ripples her hide at a deerfly. Corey pulls up the stake of the picket and leads her to the shed, throws the blanket across her back and then the saddle. Bridles her, bit first through wet flakes of grain, then the headstall over soft black ears, the buckling of the throat latch.

You going to give me another wild ride, Corey starts to ask, but thinks it instead, so as not to disturb the silence. She leads Babe a few paces in a semicircle, until the hump in the mare's back flattens and the cantle of the saddle settles. Then she flips her braid over her shoulder, pulls down her hat, bunches the reins and a hank of mane in her left hand, saddle horn in the right hand, and toe in the stirrup for the quick swing up and astride. Corey's face may show her age, but her body is limber from years of riding. Babe snorts and takes several quick stiff steps, but she doesn't try to bog her head and buck.

Good girl, you're getting better, Corey says silently.

She remembers the handbell, left on the schoolhouse steps. Hesitates, thinks about riding young green Babe and ringing the bell at the same time, tells herself what the hell, and spurs Babe clattering across the gravel road to the verge, where her shod hooves are muted on grass and white clover.

Mill Creek starts at a spring high in the foothills above the schoolhouse and, freshened by other small springs, some mere bubbles of water, winds down its steep bed below the county road, glints through the aspens and chokecherries that glut the ravines, sparkles briefly over gravel, and froths through the last rotting timbers of the sawmill that give it its name. Along this road the past is creeping back, overgrowing the old Ballard hay meadows with scrub pine and aspen saplings, choking the roads and trails with grass and hawthorn brush, calling bears and cougars down from the mountains like advance scouts into last-ditch human settlement.

Riding this road, it's possible to believe that sky is still sky and air is still to breathe, that satellites aren't winding their invisible skeins through the blue, and fate in the form of Hailey Doggett can't suddenly snip a thread and change everything. Ahead is the Tendenning gulch, deepening and widening to accommodate log sheds and corrals and a sidehill cabin. Ranching in the foothills is too marginal to make a living, although the Tendennings still try. The gravel road cuts below their cabin, then crosses Mill Creek over a culvert and follows the natural curve of the gulch until, after five hairpin miles, it levels and turns to asphalt.

Here's where change becomes too obvious to overlook. Mill Creek widens and flows under the bridge at the bottom of the Reisenaur Hill, where Reisenaurs no longer live, and spreads itself behind the beaver dams, deep enough for trout to hover and dart under the shadows of grasses. The Reisenaur barn still stands back of the meadows where the pines have thickened and cast their cones in a widening circle of seedlings, but the house, and a poor shack it was, no bathroom, two cramped bedrooms, and a kitchen so shaded that it stayed dark even during summer afternoons, has been bulldozed away, and a new roof rises above the aspens, a redwood-and-glass A-frame with a deck and a satellite dish, belonging to the retired veterinarian who bought the place from Annie Reisenaur five years ago.

Just beyond the veterinarian's fancy gate, the road divides at the county cattle guard. Its main fork, the asphalt fork to the right, runs west past the subdivided Reisenaur meadows where Hailey Doggett has built his huge house behind his barricades of rail fences and transplanted cedars. The left fork, gravel again, turns east up the Henry Gulch.

It makes about an hour's ride for Corey, five miles from the school down to the cattle guard and another two miles back up the gulch to her old dad's place. She could shorten her ride by three miles if she'd turn past the school and open the wire gate, then cut across the old Ballard meadows and follow the trail along the ridge, but she seldom takes the shortcut. Talk is that the consortium of doctors who now own the Ballard ranch for its hunting rights are planning to padlock the gates, but while that hasn't happened yet, Corey hates feeling like she's trespassing on land she's known all her life.

So she rides the long way, past the high serene of Hailey Doggett's twenty-first-century luxury. At least the longer ride, the hour every weekday morning and the hour every afternoon, is good for Babe.

Keeping her saddle blanket wet, as her old dad says. Her old cowboy dad, Loren Henry.

This afternoon Corey remembers how many saddle blankets she's kept wet for Loren on so many colts over the years, colts sold and forgotten or grown old and died. Pepper. Tango. Pet. Polly. Remembering their names, struck by sadness at so many good and faithful horses dead and gone to bones, she wells over with tears, then shakes her head angrily and yanks what's-her-name's, Babe's, head back from snatching a mouthful of timothy that has escaped the meadow and grown over the embankment.

God damn it to hell. She guesses she needs something to bawl about. Hears herself explaining to her old dad. It wasn't my fault, Loren. Wasn't my fault we lost the school. It was that sniveling little weasel Hailey Doggett, who isn't worth the powder and shot it would take to blow him to hell. I'd wring Hailey's neck myself if I could get my hands on him. I'd walk away from his cooling corpse and never look back.

And yet, at this time of year the ride ought to be a pleasure. The sun warm on her shirt, then the cool shade of pines where the road bends to the south. The sharp tang of pine needles and just the faintest reek of mud and rotting roots at the lowest dip where Mill Creek is likely to flood over the road and freeze during spring snowmelt, if only those fools moving out from town onto their twenty-acre lots knew it. Wild geraniums bloom along the old Reisenaur barbed wire fence, paintbrush reddens the sunny hillsides. Corey thinks she'd like to resurrect her old paints and easel and try to capture these June hillsides, but the goddamn tears well up again at the thought of coloring those deep pinks and valiant scarlets, and she lashes her leg with the ends of the bridle reins until she feels the sting through her Levi's and Babe shies at the sound of the slap.

But now the creek forks, and the Henry Gulch road, as warm and worn as Corey's own skin, follows a mere trickle of water. The sun is at its hottest, the shadows of pines just beginning to lengthen and point toward home. Stone barn, stone house in the deep fold of meadows and hill pastures. Babe breaks into a spontaneous trot, anticipating her own corral and manger.

At the pole gate beside the barn, Corey eases Babe alongside with a touch of spur, reaches for the chain that loops it shut, misses when Babe snorts and side steps.

"Whoa, dammit!"

On the second try, she catches the chain and spurs just a little to push the gate open ahead of her and the mare, then spurs and neck-reins Babe around in a tight circle so she can replace the chain. Babe hates the maneuver, which runs contrary to all she's learned so far. She fights the bit and slobbers but finally pivots, with a clatter of shod hooves on gravel, until Corey can drop the chain over the pole.

"Good girl, you're catching on," Corey tells her, and Babe flicks back an ear at the tone of praise. "By the time school starts this fall, you'll be perfect."

School. Won't start again. God damn it to hell, she has to start remembering. Not that Loren is going to let her forget.

Later she will remember how, unsuspecting, she unsaddled Babe in front of the stone barn. How she rolled back the wide door on its iron track, hung her saddle on its rope and the bridle on its nail, then brushed down the sweaty mare and let her lip up a scoop of oats before she led her across the road with a twine string off a hay bale around her neck and turned her into the small pasture below the corral where Baldy, Loren's old thoroughbred stallion, lived until he died last winter. How she watched as Babe ambled a few paces and shook herself until her wet withers rippled. Babe, a dark bay, not a white hair on her. Shows her Arab blood in the slight dish of her face and the arch of her neck, and in her gentleness, but she has the long legs and stride of Baldy, and she's fast enough for racing, if Loren wasn't dead set against racing any of his horses. Wouldn't hurt Babe, though, to be worked some on the barrels this summer, as long as nothing is said in front of Loren about competition barrel racing.

Corey drags up the barbed-wire gate, sets its pole in the bottom of the two wire loops on the gatepost, then braces herself with her arm around the pole and leans into it to slide it under and then through the top wire loop. You got to hug a wire gate, Loren instructed her years ago, and Corey at age ten or eleven went around all summer with fine red blisters like stitches sewn into her right arm and shoulder from hugging hard gates closed. Now she straightens from the gate and looks down the slope of road past the log springhouse, the outcropping of sandstone boulders, and the hawthorn brush that crowds the old root cellar with its door hanging off its hinges. Doesn't matter, the root cellar hasn't been used for years, and neither have the three long log chicken sheds, collapsing in the shade of pines that overgrow the hill behind the house.

The springhouse door scrapes a half-circle on the gravel as she drags it open. The dark cool is like walking into a refrigerator with wet log walls. Sunken into the dirt floor are ancient pine two-by-twelves, rough-sawed at the mill long before Corey's time and nailed together into a square bottomless box filled with spring water that trickles over the sides and through a gap in the logs to become the creek. The box smells of saturated wood and creosote and chill, and moss grows in its cracks. Corey takes down the tin dipper from its nail, dips it full, and drinks and remembers her grandmother's wrinkled hand on the dipper. She barely believes she's seeing her own hand, scarred and spotted with her nearly sixty years.

She guesses it's an afternoon for memories. Hangs up the dipper, steps back into the late afternoon sunlight. Drags the heavy door shut and looks at the familiar scene as, she supposes, a real painter might see it. The house, heavy as a fortress with its sandstone walls and picket fence and ring of firs. Blue sky and masses of clouds floating over pale aspens in the distant draw and dark points of pines on the ridge above the hay meadow. Farther still, the outline of mountains, the blue frame of the world.

A painter could gloss it over. Smooth out the cracks in the sandstone, park the old Farm-All somewhere out of sight, trim the grass along the picket fence and get rid of the empty motor-oil cans that Loren drops wherever he gets done with them. Loren might not care if she got out her paints again, if she painted him a picture of the house and maybe some old-time cattle herds and cowboys.

Loren's red truck, gone from its usual place by the log shed. Gone to town, Corey supposes. Loren likes to drive to Fort Maginnis in the afternoons and park behind the old Majestic Hotel, where he'll limp through the service entrance and across the lobby to the coffee shop and find cronies from the stockyard crews or other old ranchers with nothing to do but sip coffee and worry about the weather and curse the federal government. But he also likes to be home for supper by five.

Corey digs her watch out of her pocket, thinking Loren should have passed her on the road home. She'd been later than usual leaving the school, and yes, it's almost five-thirty, although the long June afternoon still seems endless. She'd better get on up to the house and put her potatoes on, or Loren will be home and sulking about his late dinner, and she doesn't need that.

Eighteen-inch sandstone walls, high ceilings, and deeply recessed windows keep this house cool and dim even in June heat. Corey throws her hat on the washing machine and feels the hair lift on the back of her neck. Smells the horsehair and grime on herself. At the sink she turns the faucet on, cold, soaps her hands and uses them to scrub her face, cowboy-style, then rinses and dries herself on the blue towel. Hangs up the towel, looks around the kitchen for signs of Loren.

There's Loren's coffee mug on the kitchen table. There's his book, facedown, and his ashtray, full of butts. And, through the arch into the front room, on his rug in a corner, is Loren's old dog, Sonny, half-blind and smelling like rotten meat but thumping his tail at the sound of her steps. Sonny has water in his dish, yes, he can wait.

Corey goes back into the kitchen, thinks about emptying Loren's ashtray into the garbage under the sink. But her knees feel weak, her arms heavy.

"Too goddamn long a day," she says aloud. She pulls out a chair and drops into it. Holds her head in her hands.

After a few minutes she looks to see what Loren has been reading. One of his old Louis L'Amour novels. Anybody would think he'd know them all by heart. Her feet feel hot and swollen in her boots, but she can't work up the energy to lean over and yank them off. She thinks about heating up a cup of the cold coffee left in the pot, decides it's too much trouble to move from her chair. What a day. What a day. She knows she should forget about it, but the noises buzz, a whole angry hive of neighbors' and children's voices, clamoring, quarreling, screaming good-byes, and every scream an accusation.

What has she done, what has she done.

If only the school had closed thirty years ago, when all the other country schools closed. Or if the school board had fired her twenty years ago. Or ten, even. Ten years ago she would have been forty-eight. Loren would have been seventy, and plenty able to get by without her. He would have been angry, but no angrier than he is now, and she might have escaped as far as Billings, say, where she could have taken art classes at the state university and lived in an upstairs apartment in one of those hundred-year-old houses on a leafy street where Loren, or the likes of Hailey Doggett, would never look for her.

Knows she shouldn't, but lets herself imagine a dark hardwood floor polished and flickering with the shadows of leaves, and a single bed with clean white sheets and a white blanket, no, a white down comforter, one of the expensive ones, and a down pillow in a linen case where she can lay her head and listen to nothing but the rustle of passing time.

When her eyes snap open, daylight still shows at the window, but its edge has filtered away, leaving the sky whitish, and she knows her daydream has spun away the time. Or has she slept. Her vague anxiety feels like the leftovers of a real dream. And oh hell the time, it's nearly seven, she must have slept for over an hour in the chair, no wonder her neck feels broken. Something dark has just run past the window, and yes she has been dreaming, but no this is real, and there runs another and another.

Yearling calves, running loose, along the picket fence.

Corey leaps up, snatching her hat from the washing machine as she runs. Yes, the yearlings, the Angus yearlings or most of them, seven or eight anyway, spilling down the road from the upper pasture. Damn them, damn them. Next they'll be in her garden. She'll take the red truck—but the red truck is gone, Loren hasn't come home at nearly seven o'clock, nearly twilight, and Loren never drives after dark.

Corey sprints for the barn, her braid batting behind her. Snatches the bridle off its nail and whistles in Babe with a few flakes of oats, bridles her and swings up, bareback, which surprises the young mare, who takes an uneasy sidestep, but Corey has no time for her nonsense and kicks her into a lope.

Even so, all the yearling calves are hurrying toward the yard, and the three leaders are sinking their hooves deep into the tilled soil of her garden. They turn in mild bovine astonishment, onion sets and early pea vines trailing from their mouths, to stare at horse and rider.

"Out of here, God damn you all!"

She flaps her hat at them and screams, and the calves break into a lumbering gallop through the rows where she has planted corn in hopes that for once it will mature before the fall frosts. But between the calves' unwillingness to be driven and Babe's ignorance of working cattle, she sees that her garden is doomed. She would have been better off on foot. Woulda shoulda, woulda shoulda. Still she shouts her throat raw. Lashes Babe back and forth with the ends of the bridle reins until Babe, plenty smart enough to make a cow horse, starts to catch on and pivots and dives to head the calves and drive them back through the broken pickets.

The calves trot to the middle of the road, stop, and look back.

"And if I could keep a decent goddamned fence!" Corey screams at them.

Then feels stupid. Look at her, the old harridan, her hair pulling out of her braid in wild gray hanks, screeching at cattle that stare back at her.

It takes her another twenty minutes, riding Babe bareback, to drive the calves off the road and back through the upper pasture gate, which, she now sees, has been pulled back and left open deliberately.

She slides off Babe and walks, bridle reins trailing over her shoulder, across the double dirt ruts of the hay road. Knows she wears an outline of horsehair and horse sweat on her butt and the inside legs of her Levi's from riding bareback. Picks up the gatepost to drag it shut. Stops.

Stunted wild roses in full pink bloom along the fence, plush purple heads of Russian thistles, a distant ruckus of crows from somewhere in the aspens, and the scent of ripe grass freshly crushed where someone, as recently as this afternoon, drove through the gate and off the hay road to disappear over the ridge where pines filter the last of the daylight.

It takes Babe's hard nudge at her shoulder to remind her how long she has stood there, minutes at least. Not wanting to go farther along these tracks. Waiting for what, advice from the crows?

She leads Babe through the gate and closes it, puts the reins over Babe's neck and gathers herself a handful of mane, vaults on and gets her balance with the heels of her boots in Babe's warm sides. Reins Babe to follow the truck tracks along the fence and up the sidehill where the soil thins and orange mallow holds on by its roots. Babe's shod hooves loose tiny landslides of dirt and gravel as she stretches her neck and exerts herself. Corey hangs on, hears the sound of her own breathing and Babe's.

At the crest, simultaneity. The red truck parked in deep grass and pine seedlings, facing east into the red reflection of the setting sun from the west. The gunshot crashing over Babe's head and Corey's head into reverberating echo, bouncing back and forth between ridge and ridge as though it will never die, and Babe's convulsive snorting, fighting the bridle, bucking until she is reassured by automatic hands on her reins and legs that clamp her sides into a shivering standstill. Crows rise from the aspens in the draw below the truck, flap, and settle again as the echo of the gunshot finally, finally dies.

Corey nudges Babe with her heels. Babe takes a shaky step but refuses another, so Corey slides off and coaxes her far enough to tie her by the reins to a pine seedling.

Fifty yards away, the truck sits to the top of its tires in the gently blowing grass. The only sign of damage is to the rear window. The red-dyed spiderweb of shattered glass, the centered hole. Corey takes off her hat. She approaches the truck on the passenger side, wills her hand to the door handle, opens the door, sees what she has known she will see.

Corey sits beside Loren in the cab of the truck. Silence, their old familiar. She and Loren often have gone hours without speaking, and not necessarily in anger but in absorption, he lost in his paperback Westerns, she in her wandering mind. So little needed to be spoken, after all. Want more coffee? Want to keep those yearlings on grass over the summer? It'll be dark in another hour. That wind's picking up, it'll blow in rain by morning. What did you do, watch in the rearview mirror until you saw me ride over the hill?

If she glances sidelong at him and looks away quickly into the deepening twilight, she can almost imagine him unaltered behind the steering wheel with his head just a little off-kilter, concentrating on the barrel of the .22 in his mouth. He had rolled down both windows, maybe for comfort, while he waited for her in the heat of the afternoon, and now the wind blows through the cab and disturbs his heavy white hair, ruffling it, tugging at strands that blood has matted to his skull.

His hat hangs on the gearshift. He had taken off his hat.

The curious thing is how young it's making her feel, sitting beside her father while the wind raises goose pimples on her bare arms. It's almost dark. A current of warmer air rises from the lower pasture. Along the ridge the pines have bared themselves like jagged teeth at stars beginning to wink through night-driven clouds. A dark shape wings past the windshield, an owl on the hunt for small terrified soft flesh. Corey feels her blood stir, as it did long ago at a change of season or fall of night or smell of rain. The smell of death, yes, more dis-turbing than a stockyard smell or an outhouse smell, but eased by the flow of cool air through the cab. So dark that she need not avert her eyes from the face under the pure shine of white hair.

Her skin tingles. Sooner or later it'll sink in, she supposes. For now, she's out of body. She's let Loren down, all right, living in her head and dreaming her subversive dreams. Imagining another life in which she might have raised children, run marathons, learned foreign tongues. The thought raises the ghosts of the unborn and unknown, the wind carries their chatter, and she feels herself swell and expand to the bursting point, beyond truck and mountain pasture, pine ridges and stars. The sting of tears. The need to call out, to cry.

Corey comes back to herself. The cab of the truck, the bite of torn padding and wire coil into her shoulder, the junk at her feet, wire pull-ers and buckets of staples from the last time Loren thought about fix-ing fence. The whinny from yards away, Babe still tethered and lonely in the dark.

She finds the door handle, stops.

What now.

She watches a shadow of herself leave the truck and flit the fifty yards to the waiting mare. Feels the stiff bristle of needles on the pine seedling, the pliant leather of the bridle reins. Sees herself pull the reins out of the slipknot Loren taught her to tie when she was what, six, maybe. The warmth of the mare when she mounts, bare-back, and rides—where, anywhere—because the moment she gets out of the truck and merges with her shadow and mounts the mare and rides away, Loren will have made his point and punished her for losing her job and her paycheck, and something giant and new will have begun its slow roll.

Or she could—no she can't, can't move Loren far enough to reach the ignition and the gearshift and the brake pedal and drive, no, no, she can't, can't even think about it, can't stop thinking about it, no.

Or she can sit here all night. Sit until she turns to stone.

She imagines the night passing. Dawn lighting the east before Loren's unseeing eyes and hers. Babe, more and more frantic, jerking at the bridle reins as the sun rises.

Babe whinnies again, and Corey opens the door and slides out of the cab into the dark depth of invisible grass and sod that tips under her feet and then steadies as she walks away from the truck.

2

From their nest in the hawthorns, the children also hear the shot. The crashing explosion freezes what they're doing, the boy with his hand on his zipper, the girl on her knees. Then the racketing back and forth of the echoes until a long silence seems to hold the rest of their lives.

"What was it?" says Ariel Doggett, her voice tiny in her own ears.

"Gunshot," says Bobby Staple. "Sount to me like a twenty-two. Wonner whut sumbody's shootin at, thes time a year."

As he turns to look through the hawthorn branches, late sunlight falls through the leaves and dapples his face gold and green, reddens the transparent rims of his ears, and shines on his nostrils, which flare as he cranes his neck to see better. Ariel has to repress a shudder, tell herself she hasn't fallen in with an alien, just a clod. A year ago she wouldn't have paid any attention to him, wouldn't have had to. Even a breath ago she was thinking how glad she was she couldn't see his face for shadows, and now she's worried that he's distracted. He's supposed to be totally engrossed in what she's about to do to him, otherwise what's the point of her kneeling on roots and hard dirt and what must be a stone that feels like it's cutting right through her good Gap jeans, and when will she ever get another pair, not in this awful place her parents have dragged her to live.

"Oh, ouchie," she can't help saying, and eases her weight off her knees. In the dragging warmth, the air hardly stirring the leaves, she sits cross-legged and remembers when she was younger and could play all summer without worries or suspicion. She finds a forked twig, twirls it between her fingers. Wishes she was still her sister Rose's age. Well, not really, but.

"Loren Henry's truck's parked up thur. I wunner whut he's doin."

"Hunting a deer, maybe."

"This tima year?"

Ariel cringes at the tone of his voice, which implies that she or any retard ought to know that people don't shoot deer in June (and why not, it can't be that the deer are scarce, the deer are everywhere, at the sides of the road, materializing out of the trees, venturing down to the edges of lawns in the early evenings and eating people's flowers until even her mother has stopped marveling at them.) From his tone, anybody would think he's not the one who's a clod! Bobby Staple, farmer boy! And what is she, Ariel, doing with a farmer boy, having to take his thing in her mouth? Even though she's thirteen, Ariel can almost sympathize with her little sister's reaction: *Oh ick, that he goes to the bathroom with!*

But hey, Ariel can get used to anything, and her mouth is what she's got. Her mouth and the rest of her little bod. She looks down complacently, likes her small self now that she's starved off the baby fat. She even likes her feet in her Skechers sandals, pretty high-arched feet with straight toes and perfectly painted sea-green toenails, like tiny green seashells landlocked here in the heavy air and hard-baked dirt under the hawthorn leaves. Ariel sighs and settles herself as comfortably as she can with her back against spiny branches while she waits for Bobby Staple to lose interest in whatever Mr. Henry is doing and remember what they came here for. Tells herself that in a year or two, with any luck, her boobs and butt will shape out and she'll look even better. She won't stay that way, of course. She's got six years before she's out of her teens, and she'll go downhill from there.

Not that she has to worry about downhill. She can't possibly last another six years, not with her horrible father in charge of her. Still, what she can do, she will. She'll hold out as long as she can. Meanwhile she looks at plants she doesn't know the names of, heart-shaped leaves and five-petal whitish-violet blossoms in the shade of brush and bending grasses. She watches an ant scurry past her foot on his way to do whatever ants do. A spider has spun a web across a patch of sunlight, and Ariel worries about the ant, but he knows to dodge the web, and then she can no longer track him into the darkening undergrowth.

With the ant gone, she looks to see what Bobby's doing, but he shows no signs of losing interest in the great grown-up world of gunfire. He has shoved branches out of the way and tramped down a patch of grass where he can crouch without being seen. Ariel observes his back and shoulders, the strong lines of his muscles on either side of his spine. Tells herself he isn't that bad-looking. Montana girls may even think he's cool. He thought he was cool until he met Ariel and found out what cool was, she reminds herself with a triumphant inner smile.

"Dunno whut's goin on," he says in a low voice. "Sumpen, from the soun a them crows. En now Corey's up there, with her saddle horse."

"Corey the borey whorey!" she jeers, and sees Bobby's shoulders twitch. He has no sense of humor, she knows that by now. Especially he doesn't think there's anything funny or brag-worthy about Ariel's success in getting the school closed and the dumb old teacher fired.

"We oughta leave," he says.

"Why?"

"Jes not a good place for us if sumpens wrong."

His mumbling speech annoys her. All Montana kids mumble, as though they're afraid to let their words pass their lips. Ariel considers reaching for Bobby's zipper, getting him hot and hard again just to remind him that she can, but something of his tension has infected her. When he holds out his hand, she allows him to pull her to her feet and lead her back down the deer trail into the coulee and up the other side of the hill.

"You're going too fast," she complains. They are deep in the pines now, and her sandals slip on layers of rusty needles, and a bough slaps at her face.

"I'm sorry."

Bobby pauses, turns back to free the strands of her hair that have caught in roughened pine bark. He glances over her shoulder, but there has not been another gunshot. Next he'll want her on her knees again. But no, his fingers are soft in her hair and she sees an expression in his golden-green eyes, tenderness, she guesses it is, as though he really cares about her, and at this appalling revelation she jerks away, leaving curling strands of black hair in the pine bark like a blazed trail of where she's been.

"You're the one who wanted to leave," and she's almost running along the hill trail, away from him, stubbing her bare toe on something that hurts, really hurts, but she pushes her foot back into her sandal and keeps running. Through the pines below the trail, she gets a glimpse of the stone house and peeling picket fence at the Henry place with the creek and the barn farther down.

"Hold on, Areyul, did I say sumpen wrong?"

And then she does slow, reminding herself how much she needs him and his father's pickup, even now hidden off the road in the grove of aspens. At least Bobby can get to town now and then, even if he is a clod.

At least he doesn't try to touch her hair this time, although he stands so close that he shadows her vision. Another, deeper shadow falls from above their heads, from the remains of somebody's old tree fort in the branches of the huge pine that overhangs the trail and holds three strands of barbed-wire fence with rusted staples driven into its bark. No, not my fort, Bobby had told her when she first noticed it, I dint build it, I dunno who.

Ariel has never tried to climb the frayed end of rope. The fort is too elevated, too exposed, for her purposes, but now she feels it looming over her, threat or shelter, she doesn't know which. "It's getting dark, I have to be home or my dad'll kill me!" she pants, and she knows Bobby knows it's true, because he reaches for her hand but doesn't stop her when she lets her fingers slip out of his.

"Walk yuh furs yur fence."

She can hear the sound of his breathing and the scuff of pine needles under his boots. Other night sounds, the gurgle of current in the creek, a strange call from the timber that she hopes is only a bird. A dog barking, far away. The sky glows orange above the dark tips of trees, but even as she registers the color, it begins to fade. Her dad really is going to kill her, he'll never believe she just went for a walk. She breaks into her shambling run again, slowed by her sandals. The trail is downhill now, pitching her forward. Branches grab at her, but she claws them away from her face. And now she's running on level ground, past the faint parallel tracks where Bobby drove his pickup through the deep grass to hide it in the bushes. She's run into her dad's new rail fence almost before she sees it.

"Go back!" she hisses.

Bobby's fingers, warm on her shoulder. "Kiss?"

Why not, she's dead anyway. She flings herself at Bobby, kisses his mouth with her mouth open and wet for him to remember her by, twists out of his arms. Hopes he's got sense enough to stay out of the light falling from the windows. Doesn't dare look back as she dives out of the wild underbrush and through the fence rails and lands on her butt on her father's well-watered fresh lawn.

She runs across the wet grass and almost into a strange vehicle parked under the security light behind her father's Blazer. A dark truck-camper with dirty mud flaps and California license plates. So he's got company from home, whether that's good or bad, and the man closing the camper door and walking around the corner of the garage must be the company, a man so tall and lanky that Ariel thinks he must be a giant. Even his shadow is so long that it has to follow him out of sight.

Ariel lets out a yelp as the freezing spray from an automatic sprinkler hits her in the chest and almost knocks her down.

Not that she expected to get inside without being caught, but no way he won't have heard *that*.

Shuddering in her wet clothes, she pauses to listen. Was that the door of a pickup slamming? A drift of music from a rolled-down window?

Top forty, how can Bobby stand it.

Ariel lets herself through the carved doors with the key she carries on a chain and leaves a trail of mud and pine needles across the Mexican tiles in the foyer. Her mother's dream house, here in the foothills of Montana! Even after almost a year of living in the house, Ariel doesn't quite believe it's real. New everything, carpeting, wall coverings, crystal, leather. But no way of getting to town, except in Bobby Staple's father's pickup, and town when she does get there is crappy old Fort Maginnis, that doesn't even have a mall.

She glances through the archway and sees her little sister, scab-kneed Rose, sprawled on the leather sofa and watching television. Satellite TV, at least they've got that.

"Where's Mom?"

"Playing cards up at Tendennings," says Rose. She's chewing her hair, doesn't look at Ariel.

And then the door to the den opens, the sacrosanct door, and her dad's head pokes around it. Slime shines on his upper lip, not a good omen. He's been doing the nose candy too much, Ariel has heard her mother say.

"And what do you think you've been doing, young lady?"

Ariel lifts her chin and stands straight in her wet shirt. Leaves and bits of grass on the knees of her blue jeans, mud on her toes. Ariel's baad, she's a baby bitch, she's a brat, but she never backs down. Whatever he says about her, even her dad has to admit she's brave. He's tried, but he's never been able to make her cry.

However, tonight he's controlling his temper. She sees the effort in the tight lines around his mouth as he glances over his shoulder and forces a laugh.

"My daughter," he says. "See what I mean?"

And Ariel sees a bald head craning on its neck. A face like an anxious turtle with its bulgy eyes magnified by glasses. She takes an involuntary step backward, hears something snap, just a twig from the wild woods that she's tracked in, but she almost expects the sound to reverberate, like a demarcation of all that has passed in her life and all that lies ahead."

Ariel," says her dad, "you remember your Uncle Eugene, right?"

Five miles away, in the cabin on the main fork of Mill Creek, Ariel's mother sits at Val Tendenning's kitchen table, playing cards by lamplight. Val's kerosene lamp is an affectation, because she could always switch on the electric light in the ceiling, but Rita knows that Val and Barb Staple and even seventy-year-old Annie Reisenaur, who can remember what it was like to have to use kerosene, enjoy the ambience of the sparkle in the bowl and the clear flame in the glass chimney. At nine in the evening the long June light still lingers outside the uncurtained windows, where dark trees loom and peer like voyeurs and make Rita uneasy.

"Hearts," says Val.

"I knew you were going to call hearts," says freckled Barb Staple. Her husband is mostly wheat and alfalfa, up on the benchland toward town. She and Val have known each other forever, went to the Mill Creek school together and then to high school in Fort Maginnis. Barb fans her cards, shakes her head. "I don't know what the heck I'm going to pass you."

The other women look at their own cards. "We'll set 'em this time, partner," says Annie Reisenaur to Rita. Annie, who always partners with Rita, has a face as brown and deeply wrinkled as old tree bark, with a frizz of white hair like a dandelion gone to seed. Annie has been playing a hand in this card game since her own mother gave up and died, fifty years ago. Rita, on the other hand, has been playing for a few months, and she's pretty sure she was asked to join the card club only because Barb Staple's mother moved to Arizona last fall and the other women didn't want to play three-handed.

Barb groans, rearranges what she's got. Slowly pulls one card out of her hand, another, another. "Sorry, Val, I can't help you any better than that."

"So did Amy get home with all her school stuff?" asks Rita.

"She did," says Barb. She picks up the four cards Val passes back to her, pulls a face, and arranges them in her hand.

Val lays out her meld.

"You bid three hundred and thirty on that?" says Barb.

"Seventeen to pick," says Val, and leads with the queen of hearts.

"So is she looking forward to school in town next fall?"

"I don't know that she's ever exactly looked forward to school," says Barb, carefully. She's waiting for Rita to remember it's her turn.

"Oh, sorry," says Rita, and sees that she holds only one heart, an ace. She's got no choice but to lay it down and take the trick.

That puts Rita in the lead, which she hates. If she and Annie don't set Val and Barb, it will be her fault. She looks across the table to Annie for help, but Annie's old tree-bark face looks benign and gives away none of her thoughts. None of these women wear their thoughts on their faces, these ranch women with their tough, sharp names—Val, Barb—as though the extra syllables, *Valerie, Barbara,* stretch their mouths too far.

She will never, ever understand these women's bitten, abbreviated ways of conversing. Not one of them picks up on her carefully phrased openings. Their children's summer plans, their plans for fall, their thoughts on schools in town. She knows there has been a strong minority feeling in the community against closing the Mill Creek school and getting rid of that teacher, and she suspects that she is playing pinochle in the midst of that minority.

Play one, look at the rest, one of the women is likely to say if she hesitates too long, so Rita lays down a queen of diamonds, and of course

it's a mistake, because Annie has to follow with a ten, Barb with a king, and Val scoops up three points with the ace of diamonds.

At least this is the last time she'll play cards. Val and Barb will be too busy over the summer, haying and driving grain trucks or whatever ranch wives do, while Rita supposes she'll spend her days driving her girls back and forth to swimming and tennis and library, back and forth over the bumpy miles to Fort Maginnis. And planning a fall curriculum for Ariel and Rose, now Hailey has set his heart on homeschooling them. Perhaps she'll have to provide more elaborate dinners now, with Eugene apparently planning to stay with them for some unknown length of time—Eugene and Hailey like to have the table set, candles lit, plates warmed—but will she also be cooking for that young giant Eugene brought with him? If she was told the giant's name, she can't remember it. But surely he won't expect to eat with the family, surely he won't sleep in the house!

Oh a house in the country, Hailey had argued. It will be a new beginning, you'll see. New everything. The girls will be out of the city and safe, *we'll* be safe, and we can stockpile, we'll have plenty of room. We'll be totally self-sufficient, and you can plant a garden, and everything.

If it just weren't so remote. She looks about her, at this room in the log cabin that Val and her husband have been building by themselves for much longer than Rita has known them. Lamplight and bare sheets of wallboard to hold the wind at bay. Windows framed in raw wood in what could, at best, be called a kitchen of sorts: rifles on a rack above a row of sweatshirts hung on nails, rough-sawn planks for a sink counter, a board floor, a fifty-year-old refrigerator with a domed top, and a teakettle steaming on the wood stove to keep a little moisture in the resin-scented air.

Night finally has fallen on the foothills outside Val's cabin. The trees have vanished into textured dark, and the windows are sheer black mirrors that reflect the lamplight and Rita's face, her horn-rimmed glasses and straight blonde hair held back with a barrette, her neat blouse and denim blazer, like a little urban moth drawn to a dangerous light. You'll get used to it, Hailey has promised her, but Rita believes she will never get used to the sullen roar of the wind in the ridge pines or the distance between the lights of houses.

And then the phone rings, and Val gets up to answer it.

"Yes," she says, after listening for a moment, and then she turns and looks at the women at her kitchen table as though she wonders how they got there.

She listens for another long minute. "I know that," she says, "but I'm on my way."

She hangs up the phone and stands by it longer than she should have. The lamplight polishes her face back to a younger Val who has just been handed a complicated knot to untie.

"What?" says Annie.

"Loren Henry's dead."

A pause.

"His heart?" says Annie, at last.

"No," says Val. Her face works as though it is the knot being untied. "Gunshot. Apparently."

"Shot?"

"Himself. Shot himself. Apparently. I'm going over there," says Val. She's pulling a sweatshirt over her shirt. Her face emerges, her fair hair tousled in spikes. "I wish James and the boys hadn't gone to Ryegate."

"I'll come with you," says Barb. "Well, no, Bobby's out somewhere with the pickup, and somebody has to stay with Amy. I'll tell you what. I'll go home and send Nolan."

"I'm coming," says Annie. She's getting into her gray coat, tying her scarf. Brushing fiercely at her face.

Rita hesitates. "So will I," she says. She suddenly cannot contemplate even the short drive home by herself in the dark; she needs to be within the sounds of voices, even these women's voices. She's seen Loren Henry only once, a fierce old man in a pearl-gray Stetson who had walked out of the school board meeting. She would have thought him likelier to have shot Hailey than himself.

Val blows out the lamp and turns on the yard light, which sets the pups yapping from the kennels back of the house and illuminates the junk around the back steps, old tires and feed buckets and overshoes still caked with dried mud and James's anvil and a shovel, an archery target and part of a rope hung for some reason from the branch of the enormous pine tree that overshadows one corner of the house. The same trees that frighten Rita are friends of Val's, every pine carefully preserved when she and James were planning their cabin, although Val has said she well knows they really should be cutting away the undergrowth and even the trees as protection against wildfire.

As for the junk, it's nothing but ordinary ranch litter, Rita has learned, although it worries Hailey. The ranchers up here in the foothills are regular hillbillies who never put away a thing, he complains. They just leave it lay. As soon as Hailey and Rita's house was built, Hailey poured a concrete sidewalk and driveway and installed an underground sprinkler system and laid strips of sod for an instant lawn. He doesn't even want shrubbery cluttering his clear expanse, which amuses their neighbors. Been out there with your tweezers lately, they like to ask Hailey, grinning.

She and Annie climb into the old Suburban with Val, who fires it up and backs around to follow Barb's taillights down the ruts to the county road. Pine trees lean toward the headlights, hawthorn brush festers up from the gully and scratches at the windows. Rita shivers in her jacket. Another thing she can't get used to is the way the foothills cool off at night, hardly ever a warm night, not even in summer. She thinks of Loren Henry's daughter, Corey Henry, with her hag's hair and brilliant eyes and seething anger that startled Rita the first time she met her. Is *that* the Mill Creek teacher? Rita had asked. What in the world is the matter with her?

What are you talking about, everyone had said. That's Corey Henry, nothing's the matter with her.

"How old was Mr. Henry?" she asks.

"Eighty?" says Val. "Must have been, at least."

"He was one of the big boys when I was a little girl," says Annie Reisenaur with a strange wobble in her voice. She swallows back to steadiness and says, "Did she tell you anything else, *why*, or—"

The Suburban's heater kicks in, blowing stale air and dust.

"Just that he did it," says Val. "You know Corey. Only reason she called me was to find out who—how to—well, to call the mortuary or what. I told her to call the sheriff."

The kitchen walls close in on Corey. The refrigerator tilts, the table revolves, the ceiling light hammers down at her. She's got to breathe, so she stumbles through the junk in the lean-to and casts herself into the dark, where the stars find her, and also the slow glow of the evening Horizon Air flight out of Fort Maginnis on its way to Billings, until its drone and its lights vanish over the ridge. If she could change shapes, she would change into air current and follow the flight.

If she can block out the sound of the gunshot with the sounds of night, maybe she'll keep breathing. The oblivious gurgle of the creek, the growl in the wind as it tortures the ridge pines, the hunting call of an owl. The mice are in trouble tonight. She thinks of all those separate bits of furred flesh, all those tiny terrified hearts pounding in the dark, and then without warning, *simultaneity: the red truck parked in deep grass and pine seedlings, facing east into the red reflection of the sun from the west. The rifle shot cracking over Babe's head and Corey's head into reverberating echo. Simultaneity: the red truck parked in deep grass and pine seedlings, facing east into the red reflection of the sun from the west. The rifle shot cracking. Simultaneity: the red truck—*

Oh, stop! I'm sorry, Loren, I should have tried harder. Please, please stop!

She has to call the sheriff. Tell him what. That she always supposed Loren liked his life, which never varied from one week to the next, or at least varied only in details as obscure and trivial as mice in the woodwork. He liked his books, his cup of coffee always at hand, a cigarette constantly being lit or being stubbed out, and a swallow of whiskey last thing every night. Every day or so he'd drive his truck up the ancient ruts to the butte pasture to look at his horses or down the gulch to Fort Maginnis to visit with the other old men in the lobby of the Majestic Hotel, where strangers never checked in at the marble-topped desk, where a black-and-white TV talked to itself in a corner, and where traffic on Main Street rumbled as slowly as it ever had. Life without change was what Loren liked.

Now she thinks back for clues. Had he, for example, given up his weekly bathing in the wooden tank of cold water in the springhouse? When had she last seen him walking back to the house in his clean clothes with his towel over his arm and his face private? Had he, no he had not asked her to heat water to bathe, as she herself did, in the galvanized tub on the kitchen floor, and no he had not, as far as she could remember, neglected to heat his own small basin of water and shave at the mirror by the light from the kitchen window.

No. There's only the loss of the school. What she has done. What Hailey Doggett has done.

Globes of light shine in the road ahead. Val slams on the brakes. The eyes of trees, is Rita's first thought. She's always known the trees are watching her. Then she sees the shape behind the eyes before it disappears into its own world of the night.

"Deer," says Val. "Sorry. You okay, Annie?"

"Val, you went to school to Corey. You know she was a good teacher," says Annie from the back seat. She sounds choked, and Rita winces, although she knows she shouldn't be feeling guilty, she knows Hailey did the only thing he could do. That teacher slapped, actually slapped, Ariel, and not that Ariel doesn't have a mouth on her, but still! To assault a child! Rita hopes Ariel and Rose have sense enough to be home on the dot tonight, because Hailey's going to be fearful enough when Rita herself isn't home on the dot.

Val slows and stops. They have come to a pole gate across the road. The Suburban idles in gear for a moment before Rita realizes what Val is waiting for. Belatedly she opens her door and slides down to uneven gravel under her good leather shoes. Picking her way, she opens the gate in the beam of headlights, waits while Val drives through, then closes the gate while Val's taillights wait for her. The air feels even colder here, and it smells of coal smoke and horses. So this is the famous Henry ranch.

Rita climbs back up to her seat, and Val drives down a narrow road that dips to a plank bridge over the creek, then ascends steeply to the square indistinct bulk of a house sequestered by a picket fence and a dense surround of fir trees. When Val turns off the ignition, the quiet is absolute. At first the house seems dark, unoccupied even, but gradually Rita makes out a light, dimmed by the firs and the thick stone walls.

"Well," says Val.

The wind has blown the night clouds to the east and lighted the stars. Rita follows a walk of old boards nailed to boards that creak under her feet. She smells lilacs—lilacs in June, up here in the foothills!—and sees wavering shadows, the heads of late peonies, she thinks, and long-stemmed columbines beside stone steps.

Then a light on a pole outside the picket fence bursts on and the stars vanish.

Val opens the door without knocking and leads through a dim room smelling of apples and saddle soap and crammed with the obscure: dark clothing on hooks, stacks of crates in corners, tools, some kind of appliance gleaming white under a pile of old magazines, no, paperback books that slide off when Annie Reisenaur bumps into them. A second door opens into what appears to be a kitchen, at least it holds an electric range and a newish refrigerator and Corey Henry, talking on the telephone.

"Up in the pasture," she's explaining. "I wouldn't want to see him try it with anything less than four-wheel drive."

She listens for a moment. "I don't know. Must have been a little after seven."

Another pause. "No," she says, and hangs up.

Turns, looks at the three women.

She's in her stocking feet. Without her boots she seems not quite so tall to Rita, and her face looks much younger, its lines washed away, although that could be the effect of the bare light bulb in the ceiling. Her braid is coming unraveled, ends of gray and brown sticking out as though she has faded grass in her hair—well, yes, she does have grass in her hair, like a middle-aged maenad.

She killed him. Or else she drove him to kill himself. It wasn't anything Hailey did. The unexpected insight warms Rita with relief and makes her realize how anxious she had been feeling.

She would have expected—what—embraces, at least. Corey Henry in Val's arms and then in Annie's. But no.

"All of you. Should have known you'd be playing cards on a Friday night. Guess we can sit in the front room."

So they all troop through an archway that leads to a square room with a sagging sofa, a piano, and a stench. An ancient dog rises from a blanket on the floor, white muzzle and milky eyes straining for a clue to who they are.

"Hello, Sonny," says Val, and offers her hand for a ritual sniff, which the old dog performs with grave and perplexed dignity on his uncertain legs. "It is Sonny, isn't it?"

"Yep, but not for much longer. He's too damned old. He's getting put down on Monday."

A silence. The old dog sways. He must have been a large dog once, maybe a collie, but now his shags of hair are loosening in handfuls and showing scabbed skin and knobs of bones. Rita is not sure she can go on breathing in his rotten aura. As she watches, he folds and sinks back on his blanket.

Annie makes a small sound from the top of her throat.

Val pushes back the hood of her sweatshirt. She's four inches shorter than Corey, but she faces her with her chin up and her thumbs hooked in the loops of her Levi's. "I can take him home with me," she says, "and give him a warm place to sleep, if that's your only problem."

"He's not my problem. At least, he's not going to be."

The old dog lifts his head and looks from Corey to Val, following the sounds of their voices.

Rita could not have imagined such a conversation. Who could believe this house, this *smell*, in the year 2001? Desperate for a reason, any reason, to back away from the dog's stench, she casts her eyes around the room and notices the oil painting above the piano, of a man's head and shoulders, positioned frontally, and so large that his face takes up most of the canvas. Naive or post-modern, she can't decide which.

"Is that your father?" she asks.

"What?" says Corey. "Oh. No. That's Charlie Russell. I painted it for a contest one time. Didn't win."

Rita looks from the grim face in the painting to Corey's face, a wild night hag with her mass of hair and grass. Wasn't it the maenads who tore apart their own father?

"Somebody's coming. I hope it's the coroner," says Corey, and strides out of the room.

She wishes to God she'd never called Val.

Headlights pass through the pole gate, sweep the gravel road, and stop at the fence. A short-bodied white Ford Bronco with bubble lights on its roof and the county sheriff's insignia in gold on its doors. Out climbs a young woman in uniform, squinting against the yard light.

"Miss Henry?"

"You've come to the right place!"

She's trying for heartiness, so these people will do what they have to do and leave her alone. She hears her grandmother's voice, *for heaven's sake don't dah-de-dah fuss over me.* At the funeral she'd half expected the old woman to sit up and say it in her casket.

Val, though. And Annie Reisenaur. And Hailey Doggett's wife, of all people. How is she going to get rid of them? She'll give Val the dog, if that's what she wants.

The deputy girl rattles. "Gosh, it's been a long time since I've been out here on Mill Creek. They sent me ahead because I knew where you live. When I was in high school and all, we kids used to drive out here and park, and well. It was a favorite place. Probably still is. I wouldn't know. It's been a long time since I was that young. You don't have to listen to me jabber if you don't want to. The team ought to be along any time, now."

"That's fine," says Corey. In spite of the brown-and-tan uniform with its holstered gun and encrustation of epaulets and badge, the girl looks very young to Corey. How could she ever have been younger?

"We just wanted to make sure you weren't alone."

Loren's voice playing in Corey's head: *Does she think you can't turn around twice by yourself without somebody holding your hand?*

He's settling into his long spiel. *That's the trouble with kids today. They don't know what's tough. They whine about their lives when they're not talking filthier than I ever heard in four years in the Pacific. Take them foul-mouthed Doggett girls. The little one, Rose, maybe she ain't so bad, but Ariel. What kind of name is that to give a kid? A smack across the mouth is what she'd get, if she ever talked that way to me.*

A smack across the mouth. Corey's hands tingle with the feel of it. A smack across the mouth was what Ariel Doggett got, all right, and then one thing happened after another, right up to tonight.

"The one back of you is a C. M. Russell," says Val. "A print, anyway. This ranch wouldn't sell for enough to buy the original."

"*Riders of the Open Range,*" reads Rita from the small gold plate on the frame.

"Half the old ranchers in Murray County have that print hanging on their walls. Loren loved it. He always said he was born fifty years too late."

Rita is standing too close to the print. When she backs away, the pink-and-yellow brush strokes change into cowboys riding over the crest of a hill at sunrise. She has always supposed that such art represents a romanticized myth, but the closest cowboy could be the flint-eyed man in Corey's painting. Or Loren Henry himself, with his eagle nose and eyes like drill points.

The kitchen smells of cigarette smoke, which she can stand better than the smell of the dog, but her hair and clothes will smell of smoke when she goes home, and Hailey, hating second-hand smoke as he does, will probably send her straight to the laundry room to strip and wash. Rita remembers Loren Henry lighting a cigarette at the school-board meeting and smoking it right there in the schoolroom.

"Where do you think he is?" she whispers.

"Upstairs, maybe? Wherever he did it?"

"And accident, had to be a terrible accident," laments Annie.

"They don't have a bathroom, just an outhouse. Maybe—"

"—in the *outhouse*?"

Rita's eyes meet Val's. Another word out of either of them, and they'll both be giggling. It's the closest Rita has ever felt to Val, and she wishes she could hold on to the moment.

Abruptly, hugely, the deputy girl yawns.

"Whew. Excuse me. I should be used to the night shift by now. What time is it?—wow, almost one, that's why I've got the yawns. Normally I'm four to midnight."

"You don't have to hang around on my account."

When the girl winces, Corey realizes she must have snarled and immediately regrets it. Who would want to hurt this deputy girl, so young in her stiff serge uniform that so obviously was tailored to fit a man? Oh, the jobs a woman can get these days! All dressed up in her cap and her badge and her gun, carrying out her assignment in the dark and windy foothills of keeping company with a bad-tempered old woman! Corey the crosspatch, sit by the fire and spin. Corey can't remember the rest of the rhyme, something about inviting the neighbors in. Damned if she will. She didn't invite Val. She called her out of habit was all, because Val's father had been one of the old boys, like Loren, who knew how to cowboy up and never shed a tear.

"Maybe that's them now," says the deputy girl in relief.

Pulling up at the pole gate is a pair of headlights, and another pair of lights and another. Corey feels a yoke being lifted off her shoulders, freeing her for she doesn't know what. She feels the urge to say something ridiculous, to laugh, to float. Decisions will be made about what's left of Loren, but not by her tonight.

And here comes the first vehicle, a Suburban like the one Val Tendenning drives, but much newer, roaring up to the picket fence. Right behind it comes a black sedan, and behind the sedan a ton-and-a-half truck with its grain box rattling. Nolan Staple, climbing out of the truck in his coveralls and dirty cap. His kid must have taken his pickup tonight and left him with nothing but the grain truck to drive. The coroner and the two guys from the mortuary and Nolan Staple, talking in reverberating boom-boom voices to each other, to the deputy girl, to Corey. It's sinking in that one more task will be required of her tonight.

But no.

"No, I think I can find him," Nolan booms. "If I can't find him, Val Tendenning can. Val's ridden horseback over every inch of these hills."

But Loren's truck, she has to—but there's Nolan again. "Don't worry about his truck, I'll drive it home for you."

"Drive it into town where we can clean it up," booms one of the mortuary guys.

"We'll take care of it for you, Corey." Boom, boom.

Hands guide her through the gate and along the planks to the house. The hands of the deputy girl, so determined for one so young. Corey wants to fight her off. Doesn't. Lets herself be pushed through the lean-to past the shadowy presences of coats and washing machine and feed buckets and the mop and room. The light in the kitchen hits her in the face. Val Tendenning and Hailey Doggett's wife are talking in voices like the beating of drums.

Take. Care. You. Rest. We'll get the dog. Sleep. Pill.

And yet her body vibrates, she's ready to levitate. A secret, subversive Corey is about to smash through the ceiling, float out of the commotion into the silence of air currents, float and float and float.

3

Corey is explaining to the deputy girl that she should just steal into Seattle if she wants to live there so much. Pretend every one of those big glass buildings downtown is another tree, she advises. You can hide behind trees. That's what I did in Minneapolis.

Don't know if I'd like police work in the city.

You'll like it, Corey assures her.

"I loved Minneapolis," she wakes up saying, and instantly the voices buzz around her head: *You did not! You did not love it!*

Her dream is gone. Her bedroom walls have taken back their four-square sameness. Wallpaper so old that her mother must have picked it out, its pattern faded to ghost morning glories over nine or ten layers of still older wallpaper pulling away from the corners of the room. A dresser and a closet contrived by a curtain hung from a shelf. Two windows, one to the west and one to the north, deep with light and the tips of her mother's firs. Good God, what time is it, and when has she ever slept until full daylight?

Why had she said she loved Minneapolis when she had hated it? Hated art school.

I wish I could draw, the deputy girl had said last night, trying to fill silence with words. But it's the truth, I almost flunked kindergarten. I couldn't get beyond finger-painting.

Finger-painting. Corey's seen enough in her life. Forty years of it. Sheets of watercolor paper pinned to a clothesline strung between the schoolhouse porch and the old coal shed, dripping reds and blues into autumn grass or winter snow. And the arguments.

It's mine! No mine! So why didn't you put your name on the back? No fair! No fair!

She rolls over on her back and kicks off the limp sheet. Raises her bare legs in the air. They're still shaped the same, long and thin, and if they look different than they did forty years ago—and she supposes they must—she can't see it. Maybe some loose skin around the knees is all. She's still feeling yesterday's sensation, that she's suddenly much younger than her years. Except for the din in her head. She's always carried the voices around with her, but they seem louder now. Which does she really hear, which does she dream, which does she merely recall? Forty years ago, *five* years ago had she argued that they ought to plumb the house—wouldn't you like an inside toilet, Loren, wouldn't you like to have a shower—and had he said no, or had he said sarcastically, *what do you think we're going to pay for it with, my good looks?* Or had he merely raised his eyebrows, astonished because he'd never wished for modern conveniences, so why should she?

She'd been as much an extension of himself as the boots he wore, and now here she is, worn-out empty boots without Loren.

Andreas speaks. *You could have stayed in Minneapolis. You could have enrolled in another year of art school.*

"No I couldn't have," she answers him aloud.

You might have stopped listening to the old man if you'd stayed away. Is that why you ran home? Afraid to wipe your own pussy without him telling you when?

"Shut up," she tells Andreas. She hates to be reminded of him, hates to think she ever was so foolish that she, well, *cavorted* would be Loren's word for what she did with Andreas.

Yesterday happened. Last week happened. The crack of the slap through the schoolroom, and the sudden silence from the children at their desks. Surprise that washed the impudence off Ariel Doggett's young face. The red mark of Corey's hand rising like a brand on Ariel's cheek.

Corey lies back under the weight of it and lets her eyes follow the familiar water stains on the ceiling that had looked to her, when she was a little girl, like a map of the world that waited for her. Now she notices for the first time where plaster is crumbling, ready to fall. That will be the next thing, she supposes. The ceiling falling down on her.

Sounds from downstairs. Somebody walking across the kitchen, running water at the sink. So she isn't alone in the house after all. One of the women must have spent the night on the couch.

"Where's your hairbrush?" says Annie. "You've got such nice thick hair. You ought to brush it a hundred strokes every night."

Annie's hands look wrinkled and soft, as though they've been soaked in dishwater all her life, but her fingers are as tough as old tree roots. Corey leans back in her chair and allows the occasional bump of her head against Annie's stomach as Annie untangles the snarls with her fingers and brushes them out. The weight of her hair draws Corey's head back until she feels the blood rise in her face.

"—get you cleaned up," Annie is saying, "so you can go into town."

She can smell Annie. Annie's clothes come from yard sales in town. Elastic-waisted pants that bag in the seat and a long-sleeved skewed blouse fraying in the armpits from other old women's secretions that never can be laundered out of the polyester.

Corey's grandmother speaks up. *Well, you wouldn't expect her to spend extra money on clothes, would you? Like some city woman?*

The odor of horses, however, could have been washed out of Corey's clothes, if she'd bothered. But no, she's pulled on yesterday's shirt and yesterday's Levi's with their layer of horsehair from riding Babe bareback, and now she sees she's shedding horsehair on the oak seat of her chair.

"—and Tim at the mortuary will want to know about his clothes, you know, what clothes you want to bring for Loren to wear at the viewing."

"Viewing."

"In the little parlor, the night before the funeral. Or maybe two nights. So many will be wanting to pay their respects."

Corey pulls away from the insistence of the hairbrush. "People will want to go and look at him?"

"Oh, yes! Don't you remember when your grandmother died? And when Nails died? I remember Loren went in and sat with Nails for a couple hours, just to visit with him. You'll want to take Loren's good boots. And he'll want his hat with him."

Annie's voice breaks, and Corey looks away, embarrassed for her. Annie's one of the old staunch women, and her roots are tough and deep. She never shows her feelings or tells what she knows, but tightens her mouth until the permanent furrows make her lips look sewn shut. Better that way, doesn't hurt as much, doesn't hurt hardly at all as long as nothing's said aloud. But now Annie's crying over Loren's hat, and Corey can't even remember whether he had changed out of his old clothes into his town-going Levi's and pressed shirt for his last drive. The good hat had been hanging on the gearshift, she remembers that.

Simultaneity—no!

"Sure is clouding over," says Annie in a tight voice. She lays down the hairbrush. Sits, picks up her coffee cup and looks into it. Sets it down again. "Sure hope the rain holds off. Nolan was saying how close he is to cutting alfalfa on the bench, if it just don't rain. Corey. The coroner was asking me and Nolan last night, and we didn't know. Loren. Didn't leave a note, did he?"

"No. Not that I saw." The room swims. Didn't need to leave a note, did he. Because he waited. Waited until he saw her in his rearview mirror. Made his point like he always did, without saying a word.

"Corey?"

She opens her eyes. "No. No note."

A pause.

"Corey, have you decided on pallbearers?"

And Corey realizes what she's in for. Sees the mortuary chapel reeking of carnations, and everybody who's ever known Loren or bought a horse from him or heard of him, even, crammed into folding chairs or standing in the back. Everybody's boots polished. Pallbearers carrying Loren's casket to a horse-drawn carriage—half the crowd following on horseback, the other half in pickup trucks. Herself riding Babe—no, walking at the head of the procession and leading Babe, with Loren's boots backward in the stirrups.

Damned if she will.

"I was thinking cremation," she says.

Annie gasps. "You can't cremate Loren Henry! Loren Henry of all people has to have a casket and a funeral!"

Annie knuckles away a fresh overflow of tears. Blows her nose. "I had to run away to marry Nails. My dad was ornery, you know. If it hadn't been for Loren and Nails, I don't know what I'd have done. But it turned out all right. Nails and I raised a good family of boys. Corey, you're not worried about the money, are you? About losing the school? You don't have to worry. There's room on my corner for another double-wide, and it's so nice and quiet, just once in a while somebody driving by on their way to town. There's no reason why you shouldn't have indoor plumbing, and a TV—why, the reception at my place is just fine. I get seven good clear channels, and once in a while I can get the public station, all the way from Billings. You can put your feet up and watch all you want and just twiddle your thumbs. But you can't cremate Loren. We just have to get through the viewing and the funeral, is all."

Money. Corey adds in her head. She has her last pay warrant coming, which will be enough for groceries until fall, if she's careful. Not enough for the bills, of course. Not for taxes coming due in the fall. Or for Loren's funeral. Whatever a funeral costs.

"I can get by for the summer," she tells Annie.

Loren had taken care of her grandmother's funeral. Corey hadn't gone with him, but she can imagine him driving to town at his stately twenty miles an hour and parking in front of the mortuary. Removing his Stetson in the old well-mannered way as he entered the door. Taking his checkbook out of his hip pocket and flattening it out on Tim Mc-Clanahan's desk to write his careful check for what he owed Tim for burying his mother.

She knows Tim will wait to be paid for Loren's funeral. Tim's is an old-time Fort Maginnis business, run by handshakes, with none of this touch-tone, poking in one set of numbers and then more numbers without ever talking to a real person, which used to make Loren so apoplectic with rage that he'd slam down the phone and make Corey poke through the menu of options. Tim McClanahan, unlike the options menu, knows he'll eventually get his money.

It can't be easy for Tim, though. The way things used to work in Fort Maginnis, Tim could run up bills at the Power Mercantile and the Ford garage and the Chevron station and the florists and wherever else a mortician had overhead. When he eventually got paid, he'd go around and pay his bills, or part of them, and that was all right, because all the businessmen understood about running tabs until the cattle checks or grain checks came in the late fall so the ranchers could pay their bills and everybody else could get paid down the line.

Not any more. Power's had closed its door for good the year Corey was studying in Minneapolis, and eventually so did all the little groceries, even the Fort Maginnis Market at the high end of Main Street and the Olympian Foods at the other end of town. First a dry cleaner had moved into the building where the Olympian had been, and then a coin-operated laundry, and then a copy shop, and now it's a tattoo parlor. For groceries there's a Safeway with carts to push up and down its aisles and out through the checkout stand with a cashier who asks for a phone number on a check, no matter whose check or how long he and his family have lived and done business in Murray County, which enraged Loren to the point where he got in the habit of stalking past the ATM and cashing Corey's pay warrants at the bank and carrying rolls of twenties that he could peel off and slap down in front of the cashier. The bank isn't even the First National any longer, it's been several different banks during the past twenty years and currently is a branch of Seafirst, but the tellers have been trained to recognize their customers and call them by their first names, which appeased Loren.

By God, the way this country was going to the dogs, he'd tell Corey when he got home from town, why he was sorry he'd lived to see as much of it as he had. Things had gotten to the place where he couldn't blame that old boy over in eastern Montana who'd holed up in his Freedom Township, which was the fancy name he called his ranch, or what had been his ranch until the goddamned banks foreclosed on him. It wasn't that Loren held with them Freedom Township boys pointing their rifles and firing at federal agents, no by God, he'd tell Corey, slamming down his coffee cup and pausing rhetorically before he expounded on his main theme for the twentieth or thirtieth or hundredth time.

No by God. He'd take a fierce drag on a cigarette, grind out the butt. What was wrong was treating a man like he was a number! Like he was one sheep in a whole goddamn flock of sheep! Like he had to be herded along by the numbers boys as if he didn't have wits enough of his own, herded along in a goddamn flock instead of being treated like a man with a name he was proud of and a word that was good. Loren Henry had put on a uniform and gone to fight the Japs in New Guinea so he and a lot more like him could be treated like men, not numbers, and by God he'd just about as soon he'd died in that uniform as lived to see what was happening to this country.

You let him cash your paychecks? Andreas again, talking in her head.

Of course she always endorsed her pay warrants over to Loren. Just like her grandmother endorsed her little social security checks over to him after she started getting them in the 1950s. It made sense. Loren was the one who went to town, bringing back what they needed.

Andreas snickers.

Maybe—no, Loren wouldn't have. Wouldn't have shot himself over the loss of her pay warrants. It was the school. It was Ariel Doggett.

It was Hailey Doggett. Corey wills herself back into the familiar stale kitchen, shutting off Andreas for the time being. But she wonders what Andreas would have thought of Ariel Doggett. Probably he would have thought she was a pretty little girl. The son of a bitch probably would have thought she was just his type. Like what's-her-name, that really young girl at the art institute he was shagging at the same time he was shagging Corey. Shagging. Andreas's word for it.

Annie speaks out loud to Corey, startling her. God! Has she gone so far over the deep end that she can't remember who's with her in the body and who's merely in her head?

"Just think of raising your girls to sass a teacher," laments Annie. "Corey, at least you'd still have your pay warrants coming in, if it weren't for them Doggetts."

In the late afternoon Nolan Staple drives up in the red pickup, with his son Bobby following far enough back not to breathe road dust in Nolan's own pickup. Bobby will drive his dad home again, and also drop Annie at her house. Nolan had had the red pickup washed cleaner than Corey can ever remember seeing it, and somehow he's persuaded A-One Glass and Tinting in Fort Maginnis to stay open late enough on a Saturday afternoon to install a new rear window. Shine of wax, swept-out box, and Nolan in the driver's seat with the window rolled down, Nolan's healthy face under the bill of his cap and his deeply tanned forearm showing just a line of white where the sleeve of his T-shirt is rolled up. Loren always used to sneer about Nolan, and it's true he is more farmer than rancher, satisfied to wear short-sleeved shirts and eat dirt and hear the roar of heavy machinery all day long.

"Sure do thank you," says Corey.

"Wasn't nothin. Least I could do for Loren. Didn't know if you were goin into town to be with him tonight, but I thought you ought to have the wheels so you could if you wanted to."

"They thought it'd be tomorrow before they'd have him ready," says Annie. Annie looks exhausted. She's carrying her gray coat over her arm, ready to catch her ride home.

Nolan squints at the chokecherries behind the log shed, at the weight of purpling afternoon sky over dusty leaves. "Sure hope it don't rain. My alfalfa's thirty, forty percent in bloom."

"When are you going to start to cut?" says Annie.

A grasshopper flies up, lights on the windshield. Nolan studies it as though he expects to have to pass a test on the way its legs work. The grasshopper turns its wide and staring eyes on the new surface it has found itself on, then crawls awkwardly to explore a windshield wiper.

"Hoped I'd get started by Wednesday. If it don't go and rain on me."

Corey finally hears what Nolan is not saying. If he has alfalfa in bloom, he's going to have to cut it, unless he has to wait for a funeral, in which case he'll go to the funeral but end up losing leaves and a lot of his tonnage.

"Tuesday," she says, "if we can get the notice in the paper."

"Tuesday."

Bobby Staple roars up the incline in his dad's pickup and brakes a few feet from the picket fence in a scatter of gravel. Music thunders from his rolled-down window with a drumbeat so loud that the pickup seems to levitate.

"Shut that goddamned stuff off!" screams his father from the other truck.

"What?"

"Turn it off!"

Bobby looks annoyed but turns down the volume. He's grown so much since Corey taught him in eighth grade, two years ago or was it three, that she wonders if she would have known him. Wonders if he still hangs out with the Tendenning boys. He's a good-looking kid, as tanned as his dad, with sun-lightened hair that curls down his neck and a big pair of shoulders that are still so lean that his shirt hangs from them.

Nolan gets out of the red truck, hands the keys and Loren's .22 over to Corey. Shakes his head—"That kid's driving me crazy."

That kid looks like a girl! First thing I'd do is take a pair of sheep shears to that hair of his! What's the matter with Nolan, letting his kid go around like that?

"Shut up, Loren," Corey starts to say. Catches herself. The hell with Loren, anyway, still laying down the law as though he weren't dead. But he is dead, and the pulse of the music, like a living thing that wants to explode on its own, lends her a rebellious spirit.

"Nolan," she says. "If you and Bobby would be pallbearers?"

Nolan looks surprised, and so does Annie. The Staples are good neighbors, yes, but they're not exactly old Murray County, and there's nothing glamorous about them. Nolan's not a cowboy or a veteran of foreign wars, he's not the man to carry an old war hero and rodeo rider to his final rest. And Bobby's what, fifteen? Sixteen?

"Be honored to," Nolan manages.

If Nolan is surprised, Loren is outraged.

You're asking that dirt farmer and his hippie kid to be my pallbearers? Do you know what you're doing?

"Damn right," says Corey, and then realizes that she's done it she's answered him aloud.

As dust settles on the road beyond the pole gate, Corey carries Loren's .22 into the house and replaces it on the gun rack over the washing machine, between his shotgun and his deer rifle. Empties the cold coffee, unplugs the coffee maker. Here it is, late afternoon, and she still hasn't put on her shoes. She walks barefoot to the kitchen table, sits with her back to the window in the chair that has always been hers, and waits for the day to die.

To her left, Loren's empty chair at the head of the table. To her right, the empty spindle-backed oak chair that had been her grandmother's. Across the table from her, handy to stove and sink, the chair she supposes had been her mother's.

No one now but her and the rattle of voices in her head.

Now what, says Andreas.

What was I supposed to do? Stay in Minneapolis when he needed me home? Not that you'd understand. And not like the world lost a great artist in me. As you'd be the first to remind me.

Corey Cowgirl! he taunts. *You'll never be an artist if you can't tell the truth, and the truth is, you were too scared of getting outside your corral.*

"Go away!" she shouts at the kitchen ceiling. "Go away!" And then wonders if she's wakened Loren's dog.

Andreas is right about one thing, she might have had to come home from art school, but she hadn't had to put up with all Loren's notions. She could have insisted—but on what? Loren hadn't been stingy. Her grandmother had sniffed about girls who thought they were too good to make do with rags, but if Corey phoned in a catalog order, which was how she supplied herself with pads during the years she needed pads, all she had to do was say, as Loren was getting ready to go to town, "Made a catalog order," and he would nod, and it would be all right, he would stop in at Sears on his way home and pick up the brown paper parcel from the desk at the rear of the store. Never said a word about it.

Ariel Doggett, thirteen years old, sat on the school swings at recess and argued with her mother on her cell phone. Riding the rag was what Ariel said she was doing, although of course she wasn't wearing a rag, but a tampon. I'm outa tampons, Mom, so bring some up here! Mom? R-i-i-ta? *Now!* I'm bleeding in my pants.

Had Ariel's mother sat her down and explained, or had Ariel been born knowing what Corey had learned the hard way?

So of course Loren could be difficult, not because he demanded obedience, but because his surprise was so painful when he found out she didn't necessarily want what he wanted. About her getting a regular allowance out of her pay warrants, he had been bewildered. "We get what you need, along," he kept saying. "Why would you need some set amount?" until she finally dropped the idea.

And now she's forgotten to feed his dog, to soak the dry pellets in water until they are soft enough for Sonny to gum them down then carry the dish to him and stick it under his muzzle so he can smell where it is. Carry him out behind the house afterward and help him squat to do his business.

The silence strikes her. The undisturbed air.

She pushes back from the table and takes three barefoot strides through the archway and looks at the empty space back of the piano where Sonny and his blanket had been. Had Loren—he'd been talking about taking Sonny to town on Monday, Sonny was just too god-damned old, it was time to have the vet put him down.

Had he? Had she somehow not noticed?

No. She's forgotten Val Tendenning, and whatever she must have said to Val that Val would take Loren's dog home with her.

Her face feels hot. Tears threatening, and over a dog.

What else has she forgotten, what has she left broken or undone? She counts on her fingers trying to remember, but in truth most of the ranch chores have been abandoned over the years. The milk cow sold, the few remaining chickens killed and eaten after her grandmother died. The hay meadows grown over with wild grass and pine seedlings when Loren got to where he'd rather sit all day and dream over his paperbacks than go out and tinker the aged mowing machine and buckrake and hay baler and Farm-All into operation. She supposes she could ride up tomorrow and check the pump in the brood mares' pasture, make sure their water trough is full.

She looks at the backs of her hands. The wire cuts, the deep scar where she caught her hand in a lariat loop years ago. The broken fingernails. Andreas would never recognize her now. And without Loren to cook for, without his dog to feed, with the mares and the yearling calves on pasture and Babe turned out to graze, she might just as well, as Annie advised her, sit and twiddle her thumbs.

Ariel Doggett, no twiddler of thumbs, has a plan for herself. She's in serious pain, and she's lurking in the cranny where her father's garage attaches to the house and where, she has long known from careful reconnaissance, she cannot be overseen from any window. She also knows that any minute now her mother will activate the automatic system that closes all the draperies in the house against the reddening sun, and Ariel won't be seen from the house when she makes her dash across the long wet expanse of open lawn to the protection of the underbrush along the creek.

But there's a complication. Her Uncle Eugene's camper, which he and her dad and the Giant levered off the back of Uncle Eugene's pickup and, at her mother's insistence, set on a level spot far up the slope behind the house, is almost but not entirely hidden by a screen of hawthorns. Ariel guesses the camper is where the Giant is going to be living for a while, because he's been up there all afternoon, in and out, doing whatever giants find to do, and occasionally glancing down at the silent house and parked vehicles. Not that Ariel hasn't checked him out pretty carefully, all six foot eight or so of him, but she's reluctantly decided he's too old to trust. He's thirty, at least. His real name is Albert, but whoever heard of anybody called Albert? So when she heard her mother complaining about *that giant* Eugene brought with him, Ariel glommed onto the tag.

So now she's got just what she could do without, another watcher! If Ariel's mother had been *trying* to post a lookout, she couldn't have found him a better spot. Ariel isn't sure the Giant can see her in her cranny, but he'll for sure see her when she runs for it. Unless she waits until he makes one of his brief trips inside the camper, and then she sprints for the creek and just hopes she makes it.

The sky reddens and, right on schedule, all the curtains slide shut. Ariel imagines the swish and the faint electric hum, imagines her mother's hand falling from the switch, imagines her mother's sigh as she sinks back into the leather divan. Now if only the Giant—*yes!*

Stay in your camper! she wills him, as she bolts out of her cranny with her head down and her arms cramped close to her sides. What do you want to be outside for, anyway? Why do you want to watch me? Her eyes are streaming, the lawn is a blur, the pulse in her ears a thunder, and her poor, poor butt a scream of pain. Faster, faster, faster, faster over endless wet grass, faster, faster, faster, faster and at long last the rail fence. With bursting lungs she dives and rolls.

From the shade of weeds she looks back and oh shit, shit, shit, shit. The Giant has come out of the camper and paused. He's looking right at her.

Ariel hardly dares to breathe. But after a long curious moment, he seems to lose interest in her. She watches the lanky body turn, watches late sunlight redden the stubble on his skull as he bends and picks up something, a sleeping bag, and shakes it out. What he's not doing is reaching for a cell phone to call her dad or Uncle Eugene, and at length

Ariel squirms down the bank as far as the trail, where she picks herself up and pads the few hundred yards through dust and briers to the old pine that holds the tree fort.

Farther west is where Ariel wants to be, where the sun teeters on the unfolding hills and blinds her when she tries to stare it down. But here is where she's stuck for now, under the tree fort, where the grass is saturated with ruddy heat and the pine needles stilled, while the sky overhead looks pinkish and fragile. Something's coming, she can feel it in the lack of wind, the weight of the air, more punishment maybe, and she leans her cheek into pine bark until it hurts, thinking one pain perhaps will pay for another. When she listens hard enough she can almost imagine that she hears a drift of music from a pickup radio, but knows she doesn't really, knows Bobby won't drive so close but will pull off the road into the poplars. If he's coming at all. If Rose kept her promise and got the phone call through to him. Of course her dad had taken Ariel's cell phone, that was the first thing he did.

Then she does hear the scuff of boots on the trail, and a spasm of pure fear vibrates through her. What if it's the Giant. What if it's her *dad*, and he's found her room empty, window unlatched.

But it won't be her dad, she reminds herself. The whole reason why she and Bobby meet up here on the Henry place is because her dad would never, never set foot here. No, it's got to be Bobby. And it is.

Panting after the steep hike, Bobby finds a warm seat on a sandstone boulder and grins at her in the heavily pine-scented air, where the late day hums and tiny insects rise and fall. He's so good-looking with his lightened hair and gold-flecked eyes in the red sunlight that Ariel's heart turns over. If only she could trust Bobby, with his long arms and legs, his shoulders that hold the promise of the grown man. But she's stern with herself. The last thing she needs is to get attached to him; what she needs isn't Bobby, but what Bobby can do for her, which is getting her back on good, dependable, solid concrete pavement.

Bobby, of course, is oblivious of her swirling desperation. "Wassup?"

"Took you long enough to get here."

"Hey, I hed to help my dad move trucks."

He smiles at her, placating. "En I can't jes walk off with these pickup keys. My mother had a fit last night—where'd I been en all that—and did I know Mr. Henry kild himself? I hef to be a pall bear. Er yer folks goin to the funeral? Mebbe we can—"

"It won't happen." Ariel makes her voice firm, allowing Bobby no hope that he and she can get together in town. As if a few minutes with Bobby Staple in stinking old Fort Maginnis could matter to her now! Not that her mom and dad won't go to the funeral, because one of them probably will, it'll be part of her dad's plan of fitting into the neighborhood, but what they certainly won't do is take her along. They might even—no, oh please they won't, her stomach shrivels at the thought—leave her and Rose with Uncle Eugene.

Ariel knows, of course, that Mr. Henry put his rifle in his mouth and used a string to pull the trigger (as though anybody could care, he must have been a hundred years old!) The details of how he'd offed himself she had heard during last night's ruckus—her dad mad at Ariel for arriving late and wet and guilty, her dad frantic over her mother—ten more *minutes* and I'd have got a gun and come looking for you—and her mother in tears, oh Hailey, it was just awful, that awful, awful house, and that woman's blighted life—it's 2001 and they've been living like it was another century—please don't, Hailey, let go my wrist, I know you've been frightened, but you're hurting me. And her dad, trying to toss it off to Uncle Eugene as a joke. Geno, you can see for yourself what happens when you let the women have wheels. And young girls, well.

Yeah, Uncle Eugene had said, and Ariel had watched the old turtle lick his lips. There's a way to teach young girls to behave themselves.

Ariel tries to breathe, but the air feels too thick, the smell of grass and hot sandstone too intense under the canopy of pine needles. The sun has gone, the sky darkened to a purplish blue, even the insects stilled. Bobby reaches for her, but suddenly she can't stand him, can't stand for him or anyone to touch her. She takes a crunching backward step, blurts out her need.

"You have to get me some money!"

"Money?"

At the blank look on his face, she feels like flying at him with her fists. Why does he have to be so fumbling? So dumb? If she could pound some awareness into him, she would. But he says nothing, and after a desperate moment, she adds, "You must have a way. Your folks have credit cards, don't they? ATM cards?"

Steals a look at his face. Hates what she sees.

"What do you need money for?" he asks, finally. *Whudyoo need munny fer.*

"A bus ticket. Back to Santa Monica. Where I can—"

But she can't finish. What she'll do, once she gets home to blessed, blessed Santa Monica, boggles her. She can imagine only the relief of arriving in the noise of the downtown bus station, the familiar reassurance of solid pavement under her feet, mountains that keep their distance, an ocean that minds its own business, and herself walking, walking, walking with her shoulder bag until she recognizes the street signs, the bougainvillea that grows over the security walls, the disciplined palms that know their places along the boulevards, the driveway that leads to their old house where, a year ago, a century ago, a breath ago she was as young and careless as Rose. Whether she still has friends she can trust not to tell their parents, whether she'll be better off panhandling at the bus station, well, she'll worry when she gets there.

In the meantime she's stuck here in the middle of Montana where the pines bristle and the mountains get in her face and this clod is the only one she can turn to. In the crackling stillness, his words hang between them—*what do you need money for*—until she cries, despairing, "All right, I'll show you why!"

Turns her back, drops her pants, bends over. In the silence, the warm air heavy on her bare skin, she sees the old pine tree in close focus, its rough bark a landscape of deeply gouged cracks and wounds that ooze resin like beads of blood along a welt. She hears Bobby's gasp, knows the red stripes he sees across her butt, and then hears the crash of thunder. It's going to storm, all right.

4

By nine o'clock on Saturday night, Hailey Doggett's party is in full swing. He's planned it for months as part of his plan to show his neighbors that while he may have come from California, at heart he's no different than they are. He wasn't expecting Eugene to show up, and he sure as hell wasn't expecting the Henry suicide, but he wasn't going to cancel his celebration because of his brother, much less because an ill-tempered old rancher put his gun in his mouth. The weather is against Hailey, though. His fairy lights, strung in the aspens below the deck, have just begun to glow in the fading daylight of the high latitudes when the sky suddenly turns the dark purple of a bruise. Thunder crashes and everybody jumps.

Rain gusts—"Oh, hell, these mountain showers never last very long!" cries Hailey—but some of his guests flatten themselves against the side of the house, under the shelter of the eaves, while others hurry through the sliding-glass doors to the safety of the living room. Hailey, being Hailey, goes right on prodding the steaks on the grill, grinning in the rain, but Rita runs to roll the portable bar inside.

"—main problem has been keeping the deer out of my garden," somebody complains as she wipes raindrops off her glasses.

"—commercial sprays you can buy, they hate the smell—"

Eugene can't contain himself. "Whitetail deer! You'll never get rid of whitetail deer! They're the weeds of the animal world. Read that somewhere. After the big bang, it'll be them and the few of us that got ready for it."

"Anyone need a towel?" Rita asks, hoping to distract Eugene, who glares at her but takes one of her thick chocolate-colored towels and sops rainwater off his bald head. Rita has known him as long as she's known Hailey, since college, and he's a lovable dweeb, just a computer nerd, really, but prison wasn't good for him. His twitching is a bad sign, and he never seems to notice when his listeners become quiet and polite.

"—anybody thinks he can take what food and water I've got stockpiled, he'll be looking up the barrel of my—"

"Beauty!" shouts Hailey, who has misheard the living room conversation over the drum of rain. "Those deer are pure beauty, which is what we're after here. We could have bought at Big Sky or Whitefish Lake, but even at a half-mil for a view lot, what you're going to see is other people's condominiums. Or one of those gated communities? Not for us. We want to talk to our neighbors."

"—wool," says old Saylor Lambert, who can't hear Hailey. "It's letting the wool touch the carcass when you're skinning your sheep that gives your meat that mutton taste."

People are discussing wool and sheep at her party? It's a dream come true, the authenticity she and Hailey have found. Somebody makes the obligatory sneer about sheep, starts to say something about thinking this was cattle country, but somebody else cuts in with the original thread of the conversation, which is about adjusting to life in the country.

"There's a black bear been seen down by the Georges' carport. They keep their dog food in a garbage can, and so of course the bears—"

Rita edges between an analysis of somebody's option to buy—"ranchland with private trout water only fifteen minutes from a jet-capable airport, easily worth the five-point-mil asking price"—and a discussion about upland game birds—"I wouldn't walk that far for a chukar, I'll stick to Hungarians—" and continues to the antique walnut wardrobe, where she restarts Hailey's favorite Miles Davis CD on the sound system. The warm notes begin again, as serenely as though rain were not pouring down and thunder grumbling overhead.

She and Hailey had looked, but lakefront lots at Whitefish were overpriced, and then too, Whitefish was getting overpopulated. The realtor had let it drop that land around Fort Maginnis, down in Murray County, was undiscovered and still unspoiled and therefore still affordable, and she and Hailey had left the girls in the motel and rented a car and driven five hours out of the mountains and across high prairie and finally into the sheltered valley where the little ranch market town had kept its main street and its stately courthouse with its clock tower and watered lawns, its historic hotels and shop fronts and sleepy residential streets in the spreading shade of cottonwoods along the boulevards. Rita's and Hailey's eyes had met, each knowing what the other was thinking, although in Rita's daydream she had seen herself living in one of the old two-story clapboard mansions, walking along cracked sidewalks and being greeted by neighbors from their porch swings. If Eugene wanted to move to Montana after his release, couldn't he and Hailey talk their collapse-of-civilization talk in town as well as not? No no, said Hailey. Space and privacy were what they were going to need. A house in the country with new everything, that would be the ticket.

For all the rain, the party seems to be going well. Laughter getting louder, just as it should. A stain where it shouldn't be on the Navajo rug, somebody's spilled drink. Tons of food, of course. Some of their guests, especially the long-time residents, are still in the covered-dish habit, and bowls of potato salad and three-bean salad crowd her perfectly arranged buffet, with her silver candlesticks shoved over to make room on the Mexican wedding chest.

"—I told John I loved him, but I wasn't in love with him, if you understand what I mean," says the big blonde who came to the party with the new attorney.

"No. What do you mean?"

"—everybody knows about the black helicopters, and everybody knows who's flying them and *why* they're flying them."

"We'll be hearing about blue helmets next."

"I know it's a helluva time to be asking," she hears the new attorney assure James Tendenning as she passes on her way to the deck with a platter for Hailey's steaks. Rita had worried about inviting the Tendennings, worried they would feel out of place, but James seems to be holding up his end of the conversation with the attorney, and Val is somewhere, Rita has lost track. Out on the deck the rain does seem to have let up, although streamlets still ooze through her hair and down her scalp, and Hailey is soaking wet. Rita holds the platter and watches it bead with rain as Hailey forks on the steaks.

Dr. Mackenzie, the retired veterinarian who lives in the glass A-frame across the creek, lumbers out on the deck. He's a ruddy-faced bear of a man, with a big grizzle of mustache, and he's known to have money. "By God, I'd rather get rained on than listen to any more of that black helicopter bullshit."

"Bullshit?" says Hailey. "You think it's bullshit?"

"—the sewage these twenty-acre lots drain into the water table, it's irresponsible—"

Rita glances back, apprehensive. That was the attorney's girlfriend, starting to steam.

"—and if anybody thinks I'm gonna put up with a bear in my backyard, they've got another think coming. Not with my kids playing under those trees. It'll be *gone bear!*"

Dr. Mackenzie holds out his empty glass. "Is there any more of Hailey's great scotch to be had, or does he save it for the first round of drinks? Yum, yum."

"She slapped her!" Hailey shouts, and Rita jumps, then realizes he's talking to Eugene, who has wandered out into the lessening rain.

"Slapped?" says Dr. Mackenzie.

"Right across the face. Ariel, our thirteen year old. You bet she did."

"Grounds for a lawsuit," says Eugene.

"No, the hell of it was, the school district was us. They'd turned it into a local private school, all incorporated. Hell, I was on the damned board. I'd have been suing myself."

"What about the teacher?"

"No, that was another thing. We found out she owned nothing. All that property is in her father's name?"

"Won't she inherit now?"

"That's true," says Hailey, thoughtfully.

Thunder crashes again, an enormous crash like boulders being flung across the sky, followed by a bolt of lightning that illuminates guests, glasses, deck and grill with a greenish sheen. At that moment every light in the house goes out.

As daylight faded, Corey had roused herself and switched on all the downstairs lights for courage. She had turned her back on the ghosts that peered through the window and scratched at the glass like the boughs of firs, turned her back on her own painting of Charlie Russell, although his drill-point eyes followed her along their two separate sight lines, and faced the empty space where the old dog's odor still hung, where Loren's rolltop desk sat closed and smug.

Now she pulls the chain of Loren's brass reading lamp. Sits in Loren's swivel chair, yes the dent of his butt in the scratched leather cushion. Opens the rolltop on the papers, the stacks, the crammed-full pigeon-holes that she has seen in glimpses but never asked about—be quiet, Andreas, none of your goddamned business why I never asked, okay I let him run my life for me, does that satisfy you—looking for the ancient black account book with its corners thumbed to gray, the checkbook—is Loren's checkbook here in his desk, or had he carried it for the last time in the rear pocket of his Levi's? No, here it is, bent to the shape of an old man's hip.

Touching it feels as taboo as touching Loren would have been. She has to dissociate herself and watch her hands find her reading glasses in her shirt pocket and stick them on her face and fold open the checkbook and flip through the register to its most recent entries in Loren's neat pencil.

Electricity bill, $115.32. The pump in the butte pasture must have been running overtime, she really will have to ride up there and check it out. Groceries at Safeway, $47.53. Loren must have been short of cash that day. Check to self, $50, which would have been his walking-around money. Check to Saylor Lambert, $7,500.

She has to read the last entry twice to be sure of the amount, the placement of the decimal.

Then she nearly jumps out of her skin. No, not a gunshot this time, but thunder breaking over the ridge behind the house. Another electrical storm, well, it's that time of year. Pity about Nolan's alfalfa. Thunder crashes again, sounding like it's right over the house, and yes there's the flash of lightning filling the windows. Rain pummeling the roof. Then another lightning flash, so close that she hopes it hasn't hit a tree and started a fire somewhere, and there goes the power in the house. Off.

Seventy-five hundred dollars. It's as though the numbers glow in the dark. Where had Loren gotten his hands on that kind of money, and what the hell was he buying from Saylor Lambert?

Ariel sits dripping in the rain on the terrace wall where the fairy lights cast just enough glow for her father to know if she tries to slip away. Of course he couldn't keep her locked in her room during the party, but *I'll have my eye on you every minute, young lady,* and she knows he's watching her, even while he flips steaks in the downpour, which is one of the dumbest things Ariel has ever seen him do. Ariel has lost her sandals somewhere, fallen out of them perhaps, on one of her mad dashes for her life, and now the tips of the young lilacs her mother has planted along the terrace wall are tickling her bare insteps and sending sensations up her ankles, reminding her that she still has legs to run with.

Wanting more, she locates a rough patch in the masonry under the wall to dig at with her heel. She'll dig at it until her heel bleeds, if she has to. As long as she has control of it, pain is a friend. And while she hopes Bobby will bring her at least five hundred dollars, she'll settle for any amount over $133, which is the price of a bus ticket to Santa Monica.

Ariel has never traveled on a bus, knows about bus travel only from certain made-for-TV movies, but she believes it's slow, hopes it's anonymous, hopes she can sleep most of the way. For a moment she allows herself to imagine the depths of a plush seat, herself curled and safe with her cheek against the chill of the night window to remind her of the unnamable beasts out there on the dark unspeakable plains and mountains that are being left behind as the dear intrepid bus rumbles westward and lulls her into sleep.

Actually, she can't remember when she last slept. She's taut as a guitar string, rigid in her effort not to turn her head or move in any way that would draw her dad's attention, although her heel keeps worrying the rough patch on the masonry and her eyes scan over the puddles on the terrace to him and his grill, to the lighted living room, to the grove of trees where her little sister, Rose, and Amy Staple have been drinking Cokes stolen from the extra ice chest in the garage and holding a burping contest. The little twerps haven't had sense enough to come in out of the rain, because Ariel can still hear their burps and the sounds of their voices, but not (as though she cares!) what they are saying to each other.

Bobby Staple, of course, is not at this party. The Staples weren't invited, although Ariel did hear her mother and father arguing over the guest list—you want us to fit in, so why not—because *they* wouldn't fit in, they'd feel humiliated, and it would be cruel of us to invite them— but Amy Staple is always hanging around. She hikes what must be a million miles just to play with Rose, well, two or three miles, anyway, up the creek from her farm. She pops out of the underbrush just when she isn't expected, with her scraggling hair the color of a bad penny and her big front teeth shining out of her smile, as though everybody ought to be glad to see her. Bobby got all the looks in that family, just as Ariel got all the looks in hers. Much good her looks have done her, though. Here she is, *captive*, while her heel, slippery now and really painful, digs away at the masonry.

But it's at that moment (one thing Ariel is learning about the world, just when she thinks it will never change, it turns around and wallops her with a real surprise) that thunder rumbles a threat along the ridge and then explodes like a thousand gunshots right over her head, followed by a forked bolt of lightning that splinters the sky and sears her vision and (the truly amazing part) turns the world black.

At first she thinks the lightning has struck her blind, and she has time to wonder which of the many bad things she's done, when, turning, clutching her face, she sees the red glow from her dad's gas grill and realizes no, they've lost their electrical power, that's all.

The jazz died, of course, when the power went, and for a breath or two the only sound is the driving rain. But then somebody laughs in the living room, somebody strikes a match. Candles are being lit. A patter of conversation resumes, and Ariel's vision clears, and she sees her chance and without thinking of consequences she rolls off the wall into the lilacs.

The newly transplanted shrubs snap under her, not that her mother will do anything but whine about the ruin of her landscaping, but her dad will kill her. Too late to worry about that now. She finds her footing on wet grass and slips and runs, runs for the indistinct mass that is the grove of trees, runs and plunges into its scrape of twigs and drip of leaves where startled squeaks tell her she's fallen over Rose and Amy.

Mock fear: "Eek! It's a bear!"

"No, it's my stupid sister."

Ariel disentangles herself from squirming wet arms and legs, eases herself against a tree trunk, and wrings out her hair. Her scalp feels alive with crawling water. She still can't see a thing, although the afterglow of the lightning still spins and whirls when she closes her eyes.

"So what are you guys doing, sitting out here in the rain?" she hisses.

They seem to confer. "You're supposed to be grounded," says Rose.

"Yes, and this is stupid. There has to be somewhere drier than this."

The rain has settled into a sullen steadiness. Ariel listens as it falls through the invisible branches above her head. These trees have leaves, unlike the pines on the ridge above the house, and Ariel supposes they have names, although she's never bothered to learn the kinds of trees. Well, *palm* trees, but these certainly aren't palms, and anything is better than sitting under their drip. She clambers to her feet, staggers to find her balance, starts walking toward what isn't exactly light, but a little less darkness. She hates to think what her bare feet are walking on, mud and slimy leaves and worse, worms probably. Hates where she is, hates it, hates it. But she can see a little now. That's her dad's supply shed, behind the grove of *leaf* trees so it won't be an eyesore on the property, and strictly off-limits to kids.

Ariel gropes her way around the side of the shed as far as the door, which creaks open on (biggest surprise yet of the evening) the ripe sweet smell of burning bud.

"Who's in here?" she demands. She can tell it's at least two people from their slight startled scuffle and also from the red tip of the joint as it moves from hand to hand.

"Yeah, and who are you?"

It's a lazy, insolent voice, but it's also a kid's voice, and Ariel has her bearings now. "I live here," she says. "And I know who you are. You're the Lamberts. Travis and—" she can't remember the other boy's name.

"Our name's not Lambert."

"Your grandfather's name. Same thing," she says, "and the least you can do is give me a hit."

A hesitation, then the tiny glowing tip moves her direction. Ariel fumbles for it, feels the touch of strange fingers. Finds her mouth with the joint, drags deeply and inhales. And o-oh it's so good, it's been so long, she's been trying to get Bobby to bring her some, but the clod has strange ideas, plans to play football in the fall and says the weed won't help his hustle at all.

One of the boys flicks a lighter, and its pale wavering flame illuminates his free-floating face, strands of unwashed hair hanging over pits for eyes and a mouth gaping at the shelves and shelves of containers— "What all's your dad got stored in here? Lookit all this shit!"

The other boy looms over her shoulder, casting a giant shadow against the canisters stacked on the farther wall. "Hey, gimme it back, don't suck all ours!"

"Here," she says reluctantly, handing back the joint.

His hand goes down the front of her jeans. "Here, fair trade! Just lemme—"

"No!"

Ariel shrinks back. She hates to be touched, can stand to be touched only if she's the one making the moves and calling the calls. She can smell this boy, even through the rain and the pot and the acrid flame of the cigarette lighter. He's got *pimples,* she remembers. His brother is closing in behind her, she can sense him from the flow of air.

Ariel yelps, she can't help it. And suddenly the door of the shed bursts with the beam of a powerful flashlight. Ariel freezes. The boys freeze, except for the hand that slithers out of her jeans and disappears into a pocket.

"What's goin on in here?"

It's the Giant, it has to be. She'd forgotten all about the Giant, but of course his camper, Uncle Eugene's camper, is practically next door to the storage shed, and now she can make out his dark outline behind the flashlight beam.

"Not a place for you kids. Better stay outa here," he says, and the Lambert boys, through some unspoken signal, break for the door and dodge under his arm and vanish.

That leaves Ariel. She knows she must look a sight. Leaves in her hair, muddy clothes half torn off. Be brave, she tells herself, but she's trembling.

"Yur Aryul, right? Whur you sposed to be, Aryul?"

The way the Giant swallows his words makes her think of Bobby Staple. Who *is* he? Where did Uncle Eugene find him? In *prison*?

"Whur you sposed to be?"

"Home," she whispers.

"Better git, then."

The flashlight clicks off as Ariel flees into steadily falling rain that whispers into grass and disturbs the leaves for miles around like millions of tiny voices telling her that she's stranded in the middle of an exposed bare lawn and now that they've got the Giant watching her, she'll never get away. Then she hears the high-pitched, mocking laughter from the terrace. The Lambert boys. The worst part is, she knows they're laughing at her. They think she's a clod.

Total dark, well, semi-dark as Corey's eyes adjust. She feels her way into the kitchen and finds matches. While the rain pours on the roof, she takes one of her emergency candles out of a drawer, melts its end, and sticks it to a saucer. Lights the candle and watches as familiar surfaces, wainscoting and wallpaper and cupboard doors lose solidity in that wavering illumination. Through such fluid walls she could easily walk. She could merge with her memories, her selves at eighteen, at twenty-four, at forty, and all the other selves who live inside her head but—unlike herself—are stuck at the age she remembers them best.

Like Andreas, condemned to repeat and repeat and repeat his endless charges against her. *Hey, you!* he shouts in chorus with all the other ghosts. *You, Corey Henry! How dare you go on living?*

How odd to think of Andreas, perpetually stuck at age twenty-four and perpetually scolding Corey, when in some other place, on some other level, another Andreas has split from his shadow self and gone on living, older than Corey, decrepit maybe, maybe even dead. If he's still alive, maybe a shadow Corey still flickers around the edges of his memory, the girl he knew and slept with and made fun of in art school and forgot about, except when he happens to notice a catalog reproduction or an advertisement for an auction of western representational art.

Andreas had hated Minneapolis. She wonders if he ever made it to New York.

Seventy-five hundred dollars. Where had Loren gotten his hands on that kind of money, and what the hell was he buying?

She opens a cupboard door and gropes through its contents. Her fingers recognize shapes, box of toothpicks, sticky syrup bottle, ketchup bottle with crust growing out its cap. Loren's whiskey bottle. Loren kept whiskey to ward off colds, took one sip from his bottle every night before he went to bed, made a fifth last him most of the winter. This bottle sloshes, three-fourths full, when she lifts it down. She pours herself three fingers in a water glass and screws the cap back on the bottle and puts it back in the cupboard. By candlelight, carrying her glass of whiskey, she makes her way around dim obstacles and sits, not in her chair on the far side of the table, but in its opposite, the empty fourth chair, the chair always slightly ajar from the table as though its ghost occupant might at any moment push it farther back and continue her old duties between stove and sink.

Corey is their one hope, whether the ghosts like it or not. She raises her glass to them. Then comforts herself with straight whiskey.

Ginger ale is Rita's tipple. When the power went out, she had reached for her glass, but the taste was scotch and melted ice, somebody else's unfinished drink, and she felt for a surface to set it back down. Somebody had lit her taper candles, in her silver candlesticks, and by their flicker she now can make out the shapes of her guests and her furniture and the thing over the sliding-glass doors that Hailey thinks is so funny, the taxidermed rabbit with antelope prongs attached to its head like a parody of a unicorn.

"—for chrissake I *told* the county commissioners those power lines were overloaded!" That's Hailey, furious.

"And I told you to get a generator, first thing you did." That's Eugene.

"The school was going to be closed, years ago, when the board couldn't find a teacher—" that's Val Tendenning, explaining to whomever she's sitting beside on the sofa, the new attorney, from his shadowed bulk "—except that my dad and some of the neighbors got together, the Reisenaurs and the Ballards and some others, and they took up a collection. The county had pulled the funding, so they privatized the school and sent Corey away to Minneapolis to study to be a teacher. It was the only way they could figure to keep the school open and the kids away from town. And Corey was always super-bright."

A commotion at the sliding-glass doors, noise and a scuffle and giggling, the little girls coming in from wherever they've been playing. Hyper from sugar and the excitement of the power outage, dripping wet of course, Rose and her friend Amy Staple shove each other and bump into people and upset somebody's drink, Eugene's drink. Rita recognizes him by the shine of his bald head in candlelight. Eugene turns, annoyed at the girls.

"Rose!" scolds Rita. "You, too, Amy! Calm down!"

At first she almost doesn't recognize Ariel. Draggled as a drowned kitten, scratched and barefoot, trying to slink around the edges without being seen, and no wonder! Rita has to laugh at the sight of vain little Ariel, who can spend hours in front of a mirror, playing with her hair and admiring her own face. Ariel is the pretty one of her daughters, certainly prettier than Rita was at thirteen, prettier than Rita has ever been. Ariel has inherited her father's sweet, even features along with his luxuriant dark curls and dark sloe eyes and a grace of movement that at the moment seems to have abandoned her. Perhaps she's outgrowing the worst of her rebelliousness, Rita hopes. At least this time when Hailey locked her in her room, Ariel had had the good sense to sit quietly without hammering with her fists or screeching or weeping, until Hailey told Rita she could let her out to watch the party as long as she sat quietly on the terrace.

What in the world has she been up to this evening? Hailey worries too much about Ariel, he's her father, after all, fussing over a firstborn daughter, but Rita wishes she herself had more than textbook experience to draw on. Textbooks and vaguely remembered snippets, her own mother grumbling about *girls these days*—but when had Rita ever been rebellious, except in marrying Hailey? And if Ariel seems always to walk on the edge, if a storm cloud of hazard seems always to emanate from her, she's no more than her father's daughter in her love of risk as well as her beauty.

And where was she last night? Ariel will never tell.

"Don't worry," says the attorney, lurching off the couch with his glass. "These things happen out here. The lights will come back any minute."

He's so large and warm that just for a breath Rita wants to nestle against him. Perrine is his name, she remembers. John Perrine. A big mustached man with shoulders like a linebacker's and the beginnings of a soft belly. He had towered over Hailey when they'd shaken hands, but then Hailey has the slight figure of, say, a world-class male figure skater. Hailey had been the handsomest boy Rita ever met, with his neat dark curls and close-set ears, and always that sense of dangerous venture that drew well-brought-up, timid young Rita like a moth to flame.

How Rita loves Hailey! And now she lives with him in the newness of an authentic past, a constantly renewed newness that belies the passing of days and years. Rita first saw Hailey's kind of newness when he made his first big killing, day trading, and took her on a vacation to Jackson Hole and, later, to Aspen, where paint was freshened overnight, as though by magic, and the pavement was rinsed, and the glass polished, and the very expensiveness of silver jewelry and fringed leather skirts and leather vests and leather jackets dyed red and purple and turquoise, the prohibitive prices of the hand-stamped saddles and boots and belts, the exclusiveness of the galleries that displayed bronzes and watercolors and oils of wolves and trout and grouse beside carved oak furniture and birch twig furniture, whole suites of rustic furniture, promised that the moment would be endless for anyone who had money enough, and Rita had known she was safe at last.

Rita loves her house. She loves her life, yes she does. She just wishes it didn't have to be so far out in the country.

"You've got a beautiful little girl," says the attorney.

Rita turns as Ariel slips past her, sees that whatever her daughter has been walking in has left dark heel prints on the white carpet, in a little series of crescents that by candlelight look almost like, but of course cannot be, blood.

Corey has brought the candle upstairs with her and finally blown it out, and now she lies in bed in the dark, full of whiskey and listen-

ing to Loren. It's as though the loss of electric power has strength-
ened his voice, which rattles through the rain on the shingles above
her bedroom:

*Oh sure, Corey could always draw pictures. From the time she was a lit-
tle bit of a girl. One time she was supposed to be helping me fix the side of
the shed, handing me nails and such, and damned if I didn't look around
and there she was, drawing a horse on a sheet of plywood with that big
flat carpenter's pencil. Hell, that horse is probably still out there on the
shed, nailed under the batting.*

*She used to draw a lot of horses. Or she'd cut them out of newspa-
per, freehand. Lifelike! She could get their manes and tails to look like
the wind was blowing through them. She could get the arch in the neck
like some old mare had just smelled coyotes and was about to put up a
fight for her colt. I should have kept me some of them freehand newspaper horses so I could get 'em out and look at 'em. But they all got burned
in the stove, I suppose.*

*No, I wouldn't have none of that goddamn modern art around! What-
ever they call it. Told her so. Cows jumping over the moon and women with
three faces and eyes sticking out every which way. Why, Corey could draw
better than that when she was five. I told her, I said. If she thought she was
going to paint that kind of crap, she could by God go down the road and
paint them somewhere else. I wouldn't have them on the ranch.*

Andreas asks, *why?*

Corey rouses, puts her arm under her head to hear better. This is
new, her voices talking to each other.

*We used to tell women they couldn't paint because they didn't have any
balls, Andreas adds.*

*Enough of that language! Don't want to hear it. If it comes to balls, I can
tell you that little girl's got more than you ever hoped to have between your
legs. You should have seen how she'd break a green colt.*

It's one of Loren's favorite topics. She's heard him often enough in life. Now his voice fades in and out of the rain, like a flawed frequency.

Corey, now, she'll start with a yearling colt and halter-break him. She'll rope and throw him, get a hackamore on him, snub him up to the hitching post. He'll fight that post all day, find out he can't win. By sundown, when he's good and thirsty, she'll ride another horse, take a couple dallies around the saddle horn with the lead rope in case he's still got some fight in him, lead him to water. A day or two like that, and he'll be broke to lead.

Andreas is trying to talk about abstract expressionist art.

Loren explodes. *Some of them goddamn pictures nowadays, why, they ain't pictures of anything! Just a bunch of paint dripped on a canvas. I seen them in that book she got out of the library. Told her to take it back.*

But Corey's a hell of a hand. She can ride anything with hair. Let 'em buck and be damned. She's in that saddle and raking with her spurs, shoulder to flank, oh hell, she's pretty to watch on a bronc. On any horse. She's got the legs and the back and the hands and the balance.

I maybe should have let her ride cutting horses. A good cutting horse, the way it swaps ends, it's as hard to ride as a bucking bronc. Ride a cutting horse and you'll rub the skin off the insides of your legs, even when you're wearing chaps. I maybe should have let her ride some cutting competition, and maybe she'da felt like she was getting some glory.

But rodeo? Real rodeo for Corey? No. I wouldn't have stood for it.

Why not? says Andreas.

The language them rodeo women used. Hollering and cussing, worse than the men. Filthier mouths than I heard in three years fighting in New Guinea, and their behavior was worse. Nowadays they've got their all-girl rodeos, and I guess that's all right, but those girls are probably just as foul-mouthed. Just like them kids raised in town nowadays. Damn town kids! Such words as I heard coming out of them little Doggett girls' mouths, I knew I'd outlived my time. I should have died when there was still such a thing

as decency. I should have been put down for being too old, just like I'm go-
ing to put down that goddamned old dog on Monday.

What does he mean, language, asks Andreas.

Foul language, Corey tells him. Cunt. Fuck.

You old cunt, Ariel Doggett had said to Corey. You old bitch. You
old bull-dyke cunt bitch.

I never heard such words myself until I went to art school and met
people like you, she tells Andreas. Goddamn and son of a bitch were
the worst I ever heard growing up. Jesuschrist, maybe. I once heard
Loren say cocksucker to a milk cow, when he thought I couldn't hear
him. When I said cocksucker, my grandmother told me that was man's
talk.

Andreas is silent.

Virgil told me about riding horseback with Loren. Loren's horse
farted, going uphill. Virgil said Loren laughed and laughed. A farting horse and a farting hired man, he told Virgil, them are the best
kind. I'd never in my life heard Loren say anything like that, and I felt
hurt, that he'd tell Virgil things he wouldn't tell me.

You thought you were going to marry Virgil, says Andreas. *Didn't
you.*

I thought about it. He'd have been a man Loren could talk to. Maybe
he'd have helped fix the fences, got the meadows growing alfalfa again.
Don't know whether Loren ever knew I slept with him or not, but—

But Virgil wasn't the marrying kind, laughs Andreas. *He had other
ideas.*

At least Loren never knew I slept with you, Andreas.

Rita and Hailey and Eugene sit in a room of shadows and uninter-
rupted patter of falling rain. It's nearly dawn, and still no electricity.
Their guests had felt their way to their cars and departed in a stream

of headlights, and the girls wandered off to their rooms, even Ariel, even Amy Staple, who apparently invited herself to sleep over. The taper candles have burned halfway. From where she's curled in the velvet armchair, Rita can smell Eugene, a sharp tang that reminds her of old aluminum-cooking pots.

"Gene, more scotch?" says Hailey. "We may as well drink while the ice is still frozen."

"A generator will run off gasoline," says Eugene, "so you never have to worry about electrical power going off like this. Or having your lines cut. They'll do that, you know. Try to starve you out. So of course you have to have plenty of buried gasoline tanks. Buried plenty far away from the house."

"Tanks, generators, it all costs money."

"Should we worry about money?" Rita asks, startled.

"No, no," says Hailey. "Where did Ariel run off to?"

"Forget about her," says Eugene. "I told you the way to deal with her."

The candles splutter and go out. The rain has stopped, and a gray light grows in the east, delineating sky and ridges. They've sat and talked and drunk the night away, and Rita's throat and eyes are scratchy with fatigue. She can't see the face of her watch, but she knows it must be nearly five a.m.

Eugene tastes the last of his watery scotch and makes a face.

"You want something different?" says Hailey. "I've still got my famous dollar bill. You, Rita?"

"No."

Hailey makes space on the glass-topped coffee table to lay out the lines as Eugene wipes his lips and Rita yawns. The night is passing, and she can make out the long-saturated sweep of lawn down to the dripping dark clumps of underbrush along the creek. She catches the stealthy movement of pale color, a deer, slipping out to browse in the gauze between night and dawn, the dreaming space between the human and the wild world. She yawns again, thinks of checking the girls' rooms, of going to bed and leaving the two men to talk their little boys' talk and plot their plots. What are they on about now?—"Can you imagine elk grazing here, instead of those whitetails? Trout in the creek? Everything restored to what it was?"—that's Hailey.

"We can get Albert on a backhoe, start digging trenches—trenches will slow down anybody who comes looking around—"

"How'd you meet up with that guy, anyway? Where's he from?"

Oh, surely the girls are asleep, surely Ariel is asleep with her face softened, her arms flung out, her small bones still pliant as, perhaps, she dreams.

But no, Ariel's not asleep, she's on her knees at her door with her ear pressed to overhear the living-room conversation. Are they talking about her? But no, as far as she can make out, they're talking about Saylor Lambert.

"Lambert's angry—yes, very angry—also he's respected, and he has money."

"That's good, that's good, you don't know how good to get out and get here and be able to lean back—"

"—Doc Mackenzie has money—"

"We just have to be certain we're safe."

Ariel had watched Saylor Lambert as he drank more scotch and then walked carefully to his Cadillac, then leaned on the horn until his horrible grandsons oozed out of the dark and got in with him. Mr. Lambert was so old that he looked transparent, and Ariel wondered why her father had been so ecstatic to get him on his guest list. Wondered how long those grandsons would let him live.

Try some of the bitch.

Ooh, Hailey, don't do any more. You promised!

You were attracted to him, Rita. If you'd just admit it. You're always attracted to those sloppy, overweight men.

I wasn't! And he has a girlfriend. The big blonde with the braids, the one who was yelling about septic tanks.

What is wrong with the woman? Her dad won't let up until he has Rita in tears, which is when they'll go to bed together. Ariel hears their bedroom door close, leans against her own locked door in disgust. Somehow, somehow, she's got to escape from here—which is when she hears the key turning in the lock.

It's Uncle Eugene.

"Out of bed, are you? Awake? Good!"

Corey knows by the fading darkness outside her window that the storm has blown through. She wishes it would blow through her. Her head, at least. The way it circles back to Loren's check, stubbed and dated June 2, 2001, in Loren's careful way. Eight days ago, a Friday. Loren wouldn't have known eight days ago that Hailey had convinced the school board to close the school, or that there would be no more pay warrants for Corey.

Simultaneity: the red truck parked in deep grass and pine seedlings, facing east into the red reflection of the sun from the west. The rifle shot cracking over Babe's head and Corey's head into reverberating echo.

Corey rocks back and forth, her hands locked over her ears.

Simultaneity: the red truck parked in deep grass and pine seedlings, facing east into the red—

Stop it. Please stop it.

Simultaneity: the red truck—

If she had ridden home earlier. Seen the red truck parked where it belonged, beside the wreck of the log shed. Known that after she had unsaddled and grained the mare, she would walk up from the barn to the house and find Loren in his chair at the kitchen table with his cigarettes and his cup of reheated coffee and his paperback. Worrying only whether he had locked himself into an offended silence that might last for days, or whether, the minute he heard her boots on the walk, he would start carping about the school. Them damn town kids! Them spoiled goddamn Doggett kids! It was letting them Doggett kids into our school that did it! And what are we going to live on, now Corey's out of a job?

Loren's checkbook. The check to Saylor Lambert had been the last one he wrote, leaving a balance of just over five hundred dollars. Figuring in the checks for the electric bill and his walking-around money, he must have been carrying something like ten thousand dollars in his checking account.

Had he left the taxes unpaid, had he sold some of the mares? She can think of nothing that's missing.

She wonders what else Loren's desk holds. Had he made a will? Is the ranch hers? Does a legal tangle lie ahead? To pay for his funeral, can she withdraw his last five hundred dollars, close out his checking account? Is it the whiskey, she wonders, that's making everything seem so complicated?

Let it be. Let her drift. Let somebody else worry. In the dawn, in the silence after the rain, she finally sleeps.

5

Annie Reisenaur wakes as always at first light. She lies under her blanket and quilt in the bedroom at the rear of her trailer, watching her ceiling emerge and wondering why she feels so sad. Gradually the pink stain in the window fades into ordinary daylight, and the strange shapes of the night return to their familiar selves, the alarm clock she never has to use, her old wrapper hanging on the back of the door, the framed school pictures of her sons' children. She listens, but all is still, the rain must have stopped in the night. She wonders if the power has come back on.

Her eyes sting, and her throat stings, and her sinuses feel stuffy, and she wonders if she's coming down with something. A dratted summer cold, she tells herself, before she remembers how long she cried last night. She had surprised herself, she would have supposed she'd have been cried out years ago. Loren Henry. Yes. She'd known from the moment she woke up that there was something she didn't want to remember.

She loves this bedroom she has all to herself. Loves the trailer, or modular home as they call them nowadays, that she picked out on the dealer's lot the day she closed with Doc Mackenzie on the ranch and had it set up on the corner she'd reserved. A trailer would feel cramped, her sons had warned, but Annie knew it couldn't be as cramped as the house she'd lived in all her life, child, wife and widow. She loves the trailer's bright windows, its beige carpeting, its unscarred imitation walnut paneling with its odor that reminds her of a new car. For the first time in her life she's living with new everything—except for her clothes, well, and kitchen utensils and dishes and bedding. She hadn't wanted to throw everything out, although, feeling pleasurably guilty, she'd gone out and bought new sheets for her bed, the kind with a fitted bottom that doesn't forever have to be tucked back in, patterned with lilacs and roses, 240 thread count.

Wasting money on sheets! She can just hear the old folks.

The pressure on her bladder gets her out of bed, into her wrapper, and through the sliding door into her very own, private bathroom with its brand-new almond-colored fixtures, tub and shower, sink and toilet. She reminds herself how fortunate she is, at her age when all her parts seem to ooze and seep into her underwear, not having to walk through weather to the little house that smelled bad no matter how much lye was poured down it. The first time she'd sat and flushed, she'd bragged to the scandalized ghosts of the old folks, *and no spiders, either!*

The sun has risen over the Henry Gulch and warmed her kitchen by the time Annie gets around to rinsing out her percolator and filling it and measuring the one scoop of MJB that she likes, none of that strong stuff, lattes and such, tasting to her like they've been stewing all day in a pot on a wood-burning range. She sits as she always does by her window, waiting for her coffee to perk and warning herself, no more bawling, because she will feel so bad later, her whole head swollen and raw.

She watches a dozen deer slip back into the aspens at the edge of the beaver meadow, fugitive taupe shapes taking delicate steps through the stems of willows, as wary and yet as constant as anything in her life. She's been watching deer at the edge of that meadow for as long as she can remember. Beyond the aspens she can just see the peak of Doc Mackenzie's steep roof, and if she walks out on the small deck her sons built for her and stands on her tiptoes and looks west over what used to be the cow pasture, she can see the glass and fieldstone house, big enough for royalty, that Hailey Doggett built, the fool, and two or three other huge houses belonging to people who fly in to Montana to spend their holidays and then fly off to wherever they really live. For some reason they all like to build their houses as high on the hill as they can get, where they have to look right into the teeth of the wind. They all seem crazy to her. Like last night, driving their cars up and down the road, back and forth at all hours, no wonder Annie couldn't sleep.

Well, she'd hated to sell out, it was like selling her parents and grandparents, and yet none of her sons had wanted to stay on the ranch, no way they could see to make a living on it, not with the short mountain seasons and falling cattle prices and everything costing so much nowadays.

Maybe that was why Loren did it. He could see himself having to sell, and he couldn't face it at his age. But why hadn't he left Corey a note, or at least given her some warning?

Maybe it was something else. Maybe it was his heart.

The Loren she'd had a crush on when she was ten years old and he barely in his twenties, blue-eyed Loren who rode the saddle broncs all the way to National Rodeo Finals and was called out the next day with the rest of the Montana National Guard, Loren who fought in the jungles of New Guinea and saw his friends and cousins killed but came home in one piece and never even broke a bone until after the war, when he drew that bad horse that fell down and trampled him in the chute at the Calgary Stampede—fifty years ago and more, where did the time go—Loren who was still wearing plaster on his right leg when he told her father that if he didn't sign so she and Nails could get married, he'd take him out behind the barn and work him over with the oak spoke out of a wagon wheel. Annie had been fifteen, and Loren had lived long enough to become an old cowboy, and now she would be going with Corey to his viewing in the afternoon.

Some song she's heard on the radio, lyrics stuck in her head. A wild bull rider who loves his rodeo better than he loves his girl—something, something, something, about the money and the show. She can't remember how the rest of it goes.

Annie finishes her coffee and sets down her mug. It's seven o'clock in the morning, and the sun has lit the raindrops across the beaver meadow, and it shines on the narrow leaves of willows and the trembling leaves of aspens. June, her favorite month. She can smell snowmelt from the mountains. Frosts and snow are still possible in the foothills, but unlikely. Here at the bottom of the Henry Gulch, violets will be blooming in the shade of grass roots. Chokecherries and serviceberries will be setting on, and wild raspberries about to ripen like jewels in the deepest underbrush where Annie knows to crawl with her bucket. She can't think constantly about Loren Henry's death.

Gramma, what if you had three wishes, her youngest grandson had asked her. What three things do you want most in the whole wide world? Really really most?

Can't think of a thing, Annie told him. She'd had to smile to herself. Her grandchildren are town kids with no notion of life. Yes, and she hopes they'll never know what she knows. Never will, if she can help it.

Gramma! Everybody wants something.

Well, I might wish for a garden.

She's kept a life interest in the five-acre piece for her trailer and her pine-shaded deck within easy walking distance of the creek or across the meadow in berry season. But her sons had stripped and graded through a wide swath of mountain grass and pine seedlings when they poured the concrete pad to set the trailer on, and now Annie lives inside a moat of mud when the weather is bad and dust when it's dry. She could wish for grass seed, she had thought at the time, and a good deep bed to transplant her irises and her clematis vines, white and purple, to trail over her deck rail.

Now she wonders if planting a garden is worthwhile. If anything is worthwhile, she feels so tired and worn out. And she has so much to do.

From habit she counts her tasks. Carrying food to the house of the bereaved comes first, so they won't have to think beyond the next meal. Of course Corey won't have a crowd to feed. Annie tries to remember which of the Henry relations are still alive. A few cousins in California is all. Still, she'll cook a beef stew. She'll take a round steak out of her freezer this morning and brown it and simmer it with vegetables, and even if Corey doesn't have company, she can always heat and reheat it for herself.

A loaf of homemade bread out of her freezer. A chocolate cake that Corey can pass around if company does drop in. That much Annie can do for her, though it seems so little.

Val Tendenning wakes at first light but pulls her pillow over her face and falls asleep again, dreaming and half-waking and dreaming. Thunder rumbles in her dream and punishes the clouds to hazy purple. She smells plums in the distance, as though the rain bears rotting fruit, and she thrashes, kicks free, and realizes it was the red flannel bedsheet that entangled her.

"Holy smokes," says James. "You were making so much noise, I thought something was chasing you."

Val wrenches her eyes open. God, what time is it? *Nine?* Why had she thought something awful was happening? She's not used to drinking, and whatever else was going on at the Doggett party, she knows the weed when she smells it, and something she can't identify, something nastier. But now the sunshine filters through James's spider plants in the uncurtained window and falls in squares across her twisted sheets and blanket, across her sewing machine stacked with the boys' blue jeans, across the boxes of James's books that he intends to build shelves for, one of these days. Illuminates James himself, still wearing his winter whiskers he usually shaves off at the beginning of every summer, offering her a mug of tea with one hand while the thumb of his other hand keeps his place in whatever book he's been reading, something with a long title, *The Assassination of Jesse James by the Coward Robert Ford.* Val guesses it's a gunslinger novel, which James doesn't normally bring home to read.

She takes the mug and gulps thankfully. What had she been dreaming about?

"Have you got to do anything today?" she asks. It's Sunday, but they went to mass last night, before the crazy party, so they don't have to go again this morning.

"I want to move the sheep, once the boys finish the fence. What are you planning to do with Loren's dog?"

Val sits up. "I knew I forgot something. Is he all right?"

"He wouldn't eat. Lapped up a little water. I helped him outside to do his business, but he was too scared."

"She was going to have him put down."

"Have they found a note?"

"No. But it had to be over the school. What other reason would he have? Without her job, how could they have hung on to the ranch? How's she going to hang on?"

Val's own life suddenly seems good. She and James bring in enough cash from their jobs to buy what staples and groceries they can't raise themselves, and they can afford some of the junk their sons set their hearts on, and they have the sheep that pay for their own feed and the horses' feed and the taxes on the ranch.

James breaks a piece of toast, gives half to Val and takes a bite from the other half. "Well now," he says. "Are you awake enough to hear what John Perrine's got planned?"

"What?"

"Robbing trains."

Val stares at him.

"The tourist train. The train where folks buy tickets to ride from Fort Maginnis out to Eberle and back, and they get a catered dinner and entertainment? John's got it all worked out. He's going to pay me and the boys each a hundred dollars a holdup. We'll trailer the saddle horses out to Eberle, a couple nights a week, and we'll dress up like old-time train robbers and jump out of the bushes to hold up the tourists. That's why I'm not going to shave off my whiskers."

"*Grown men* are going to do this?"

James chortles as he gathers up their mugs and toast plate, and Val shakes her head. Alone, she stretches in the sunshine and flicker of leaves. Sunday in the summer. No need to get dressed and drive to work. Rain last night, no gardening to do. But she might as well get out of bed and make something of the day. She and James will have to go to the viewing, tonight or maybe tomorrow.

Val tries and fails to imagine her father and Loren Henry and old Des Ballard playing shoot-'em-up games in front of a tourist audience. Train robbers!

Corey wakes at first light with a hell of a headache. When she can't get back to sleep, she throws off the sheet and feels her way downstairs, wincing at the dazzles of sunlight through the windows that strike her poor head like hammer blows. No more whiskey-drinking for her, not if it's going to make her feel this bad. She makes herself a pot of coffee and drinks down a cup as though it's a dose of medicine. Another cup and a half, and she thinks she might live, after all.

The dog. She has to do something about the dog, but first she thinks she might take a ride up to the butte pasture to check on the pump and count Loren's horses. So she finishes her coffee, pulls on her boots, and hikes over to the barn to catch Babe and saddle her.

Ariel sleeps late, wakens in full light with her eyes so matted that she has to pick them open with her fingers. Her thighs are stuck together, it hurts to move her legs, but she does, and she turns over to find that she's in her own bed with the strange ceiling of this strange Montana house looming over her. Knows good and well what happened to her last night, but resolves not to think about it. When she sits up and swings her legs over the side of the bed, the bottom sheet lifts and follows her, and she sees that it's become glued to the congealed blood on her heel.

Little Rose, on the other hand, had watched daylight paddle through her room while Amy Staple slept beside her. Rose, tough knot of a little girl, listened to the sounds from her sister's room and drew up her knees and pulled the bedsheet over her head, even though no one was there to recognize her blunt forehead, her insignificant nose. Nobody, that's Rose. She practices invisibility.

But Rose doesn't live in California now, she lives in Montana, and she knows ways that never existed in Santa Monica, in particular a certain trail under a screen of wild bushes and narrow leaves between the lawn and the creek, where she's Rose, the princess warrior! The princess warrior, in search of the new world, has learned to scoot herself down the deep bank and hop from rock to unsubmerged rock, where the current laughs at her but where she can get all the way across with dry feet.

Last night in the dark she had heard her mom crying and her dad's voice, *I love you, you know I love you—oh I love you too Hailey, you know I do*—and then Uncle Eugene's voice in the next room, *you think I can't make you cry*—and Rose had counted the rocks on the surface of the creek like a rosary flung across wavering reflections. The safe rock with the smooth surface. The rock with the treacherous tilt that spilled her into cold ripples the first and only time she stepped on it. Once across the creek the princess warrior can dart through the aspen grove that borders the county road, she can hide in the green protection of dappling leaves until the creek narrows and deepens into the big culvert just below the Staple place, where she can walk in full disguise as her ordinary self.

The Staple house is what Rose's mom calls your basic added-on ranch house. It draws dust and light from the alfalfa fields, and it smells of laundry, and Amy Staple's mom is just as likely to dash out to the sheds and fire up one of the monster machines and wheel it out to the big gas tank to service and refuel it as she is to dash back inside and throw frozen pizzas in the oven, and now Rose, the princess warrior, commands a monster machine of her own. Red with gold trim.

Massey-Ferguson! *No! No!* scream her enemies, but the princess warrior presses a button. Zap! Pow! Blood and guts! They're all goners.

The house is silent, everybody sleeping late. But sometime around noon Rose hears the soft slide of her sister's window opening.

The tall grasses spill heavy droplets that darken Babe's legs and the toes of Corey's boots. Babe snatches a bite, and Corey reins her sharply. Bad habit for a horse, grazing while under saddle, and a kid's bad habit of letting them, which Loren had broken Corey of before she knew how to read. She supposes Loren will always ride with her, in her half-breed saddle with the high bronc-rider's pommel and the flat roper's cantle, in her flat cowboy's posture with her heels well forward in her stirrups and her reins held low. Time was when she had consciously imitated him, the line of his shoulders, the angle of his hat, even the way he had of bracing himself with both hands on the saddle horn, which had to do, she'd learned only a few years ago, with a hernia which in the old cowboy way he'd simply put up with rather than having surgically repaired.

And yet Loren is further from her this morning than he was in the night, when the rain went on raining without him. This morning is washed with color, from the aching clean blue of sky above the pale buff sandstone ramparts of the butte, down through the shades of green, the pines infiltrating down from the ridges into the pastures and dropping their cones and sprouting their third-growth seedlings, the lighter aspens rising out of the draws into sunlit patches of quivering leaves, an invasion of saplings into what, fifty years ago, had been cleared of brush and trash trees for summer grazing. Loren had talked about bulldozing the saplings or maybe spraying them chemically to restore the grass, but he had never gotten around to it. Couldn't afford it, or so Corey had thought.

Corey follows the double ruts of what once had been a wagon road and then a road for four-wheel-drive rigs and sometimes in winter a tractor road when a tractor had been the only way to get back and forth between the Henry place and the Ballard place. Sometimes the ruts are buried so deeply under grass that Corey notices them only when Babe puts a hoof wrong, stumbles, and regains herself. But on the shale hillside the ruts reappear, as deep as ever. The pastures may be ruined, but it will be years before every trace of foothill ranching is erased.

At the crest of the ridge she sees the chimney and shingled roof of the Ballard house. Annie has said that the doctors in the hunting consortium are having the house torn down or burned down. Way, nobody knows—sound logs and a sandstone chimney with a good wood stove, why wouldn't the doctors want it for a hunting lodge? But that's the way, tear down the old and replace it with the imitation-old. Corey shrugs off the thought, which feels like one of Loren's, and reins Babe to the east, where she can look across the miles and miles of grassy slopes and pine ridges gradually bluing into the long line of the Snowies, another blue just deeper than the sky.

Babe throws up her head and whinnies, and out of the empty grass and the fringe of aspens at the foot of the ridge appear the horses, like boulders coming to life, dark heads and sorrel heads with stars or blazed white faces and sharply pricked ears. Two or three of the colts break into a hard trot to meet Babe and Corey, until they halt at the line between curiosity and fear. They are fine colts, their arched necks and lovely heads and liquid eyes showing their Arab legacy, trembling now with the tension between standing their ground and fleeing back to their mothers on their long thoroughbred legs inherited from poor old Baldy.

And now the mares are stirring themselves, heavy-bodied and un-afraid, walking with their mouths full of grass to see what's going on. Sorrels and bays, shades of brown and red among the aspens and slick in the sunlight except for a shaggy patch or two of unshed winter hair on the ribs and flanks of the oldest mares. Corey counts them—eleven, twelve, thirteen—where is old Lucy, has she not made it through the winter?—no, there she is, ambling out of the thicket, back swayed and belly sagging but a fine sorrel foal at her side.

Only seven foals, though, Baldy's sad final best get.

Corey and Babe are circled by horses now, nickering horses smell-ing of grass manure and sweat and warm hair. Colts stretch inquisi-tive noses toward her fingers, flinch from the human touch, and run, bucking and snorting in long arcs that always head back into the cir-cle. Most of the mares never have been broken to saddle, some never even halter-broken, their main human contact having been Loren's voice and Loren's hands bringing them blocks of salt and buckets of grain. But they are unsuspicious and replete with early summer grass, and they call to their foals in the grunts and whickers and murmurs by which mares immemorial have called to foals, and with squeals and nips they warn away the three or four hovering geldings that Lo-ren had broken to ride but was unable to part with and, instead of sell-ing, turned them out to pasture with the brood mares. There's Perry, for example, a line-back buckskin. Perry must be, let's see, coming six years old this spring, just into his prime and fleet as a deer. There's old Paint with the splash of white across his back, Paint who was Loren's favorite saddle horse. In previous Junes, sixteen or seventeen previous Junes, Loren had caught Paint and led him down to the home corrals to grain and occasionally ride, but what is Corey to do now with Paint, whose muzzle this summer shows more gray hairs than black?

One question is answered, though. All the horses are accounted for. Loren hadn't secretly sold any of them to raise seventy-five hundred dollars to cover his mysterious check.

Corey dismounts and unties the grain bucket from her saddle strings and passes it around to those mares who are socialized enough to stick in their noses and munch. Much crowding now, much nipping and kicking. Old Lucy takes her turn and stands placidly through the commotion, laying back her ears at younger mares and switching her tail over herself and her colt.

A mare's life. Twenty or thirty turns of the year, winter to summer, mountain snows and mountain summer pastures with a new foal at flank. Scents from the other world, the truly wild world that overlaps theirs and shares their grass and timbered shade. Occasional terrifying turmoil, when the aspens turn gold and humans, with yells and waving hats, haze the brood mares down to the corrals to be roped and vaccinated and have their foals torn away for weaning. The previous spring's encounters with the stallion are already swelling their bellies. Then back to winter pasture and loneliness in the silence of snow until spring and another foal.

Corey lets Lucy lick the last crumbs of grain from the bucket, then ties it back to her saddle and remounts. As she rides down the draw toward the water tank, several of the colts tag after her, wide-eyed and curious and vulnerable as children in their certainty that they are the centers of their world.

She pictures herself driving mares and panic-stricken colts out of the hills. Dust and frightened neighs, noses and knees skinned from falls, from charges through pine stubs, from crashing against fences, eyes wilder and wilder, milling in the corral. Loren's old truck with its stockrack on, backed up to the log loading chute, mares and colts and geldings prodded up the chute and into the trucks in groups of eight or ten for the ride into town and the auction ring. Thirty-thirty-thirty-gimme-forty—thank you! Sold to Swift! Sold to Armour! Yes, they'll go for dog food, they're too wild for anything else. She might be able to halter-break some of the colts and do a little better for them.

No. She'd be better off putting Loren's gun to her own mouth. At least she wouldn't have to watch.

The pump at the bottom of the coulee is on automatic shut-off, but the water tank is full and spilling into the muddy tracks of horses and deer and the tiny prints of quail. Corey rides down into the shade of chokecherries in white wet bloom and lets Babe drink deeply from the greenish water. Magpies squawk and squabble from farther along the coulee, and Babe lifts her dripping muzzle and points her ears. Something dead down there. Corey checks the electric box on the pole to be sure of the setting of the pump—it had shut itself off during the power outage, but it's all right now—then follows the spur wire down-hill toward its junction with the main power lines along the county road down the gulch beyond the Henry Gulch.

The trail Loren cleared when he strung the wire to run the pump is still passable, although crowded by chokecherries and aspen seedlings that snap back and shower Babe's head and shoulders and Corey's legs with rainwater and wet petals. Yes, something dead down here. She can smell it now. A few more yards and she sees the rising scatter of black-and-white magpies and the fence wires where the yearling fawn tried to jump but caught its hind legs on the top wire. Nothing much left but its stench and the bundle of bones and tendons wrapped in the picked-over hide. The magpies, interrupted, scold Corey and Babe from the branches.

"I'm not dead yet, so you can forget about me," she tells them. Babe flicks back an ear at the sound of her voice, while the magpies look down ravenously.

And here, where the trail rejoins the wagon ruts, is the gate in the old line fence between the Ballard ranch and the Henry ranch, its staples rusted into the twisted cedar posts and its wires overgrown. The gate isn't chained and locked or even posted against trespassing, and it occurs to Corey that the doctors of the hunting consortium may not be aware of this road or this gate. Why would they know about it? Nobody has crossed through here in years, nobody ever has, except for visits or exchange of work between long-gone neighbors. On impulse she dismounts and opens the gate by hugging it, drags it back and leads Babe through, hugs the gate closed, and remounts and rides down the ancient grade that somebody, old Des Ballard probably, had long ago cut out of the side of the coulee with a blade and a drag and a team of horses.

The grade leads upward where the pines lean in, skinny and starved and stretching for light. Babe's hooves crunch on layers of dead needles where nothing grows, and bare pine stubs catch at the saddle strings and at Corey's hair. In the occasional rays and dazzles from the sun, Corey feels herself in dream territory, as if she's riding backwards in time. How long since she last rode through these pines, since adolescence at least, because the Ballards have been gone for years.

And now the pines open into a clearing so unchanged that the years might not have passed. The house with its logs and shingles weathered gray, fenced in woven wire topped by gray poles. Sawed-board sheds and granary, log barn askew on its sandstone foundation, the grass uncut and rippling.

In her dream state she dismounts and wraps Babe's reins around the log rail. Pushes at the gate until it finds its old groove in the gravel under a growth of bindweed and opens enough to let her through. Absences according to a dream's logic. Paths erased by grass, ropes vanished from the clothesline poles, buckets and egg cartons and cream cans swept off the empty porch. Voices silenced.

Howdy! Mrs. Ballard would have called through the screen door as soon as she heard company ride in.

Mizzy, everyone had called Mrs. Ballard.

Corey half-expects the door to be padlocked, but it opens at her turn of the knob, and she finds herself in Mizzy's kitchen.

The room seems dark after the out of doors, although the sun casts a gold oblong through a window that once was curtained. As her eyes adjust, Corey recognizes the chimney and the wood stove where they ought to be, but the room is far smaller than it once was, and the round oak table is gone, the high-backed chairs gone.

Bare stairs lead upward into gloom. Corey hesitates. The kitchen, yes, the many times she's sat at Mizzy's table on a chair made higher for her by stacked catalogues. The time—how old had she been, seven or eight—looking for horses and caught in a downpour, she'd ridden here for refuge, and Mizzy had fed her cookies and taken her wet clothes and dried them in her oven. She cannot remember ever being upstairs. And yet she's drawn now, one step after another, letting down the heels of her boots as silently as possible for the sake of the ghosts.

At the top of the stairs, a landing with a window through which light falls and dead cottonwood twigs tap like fingers looking for a way indoors. Corey looks out the window. The old tree must have died from lack of watering or old age. Cottonwoods are short-lived trees, but this one had propagated its sprouts across the yard like foreshortened, green-headed dancers through the tall grass.

Ahead, two open doors, one for each bedroom. Corey glances into the first. Empty. In the second, an iron bed stripped down to its springs of bedclothes and mattress. And now her boots crunch on mice leavings with every step, and she can smell mice, like the smell of the dead fawn, hide and bones. She feels her gorge rising. This is no place for her; she's trespassing against graver claims than any consortium of doctors, and she backs away, setting her feet down in the prints her boots left in dust and mouse droppings. Down the stairs with her eyes on the landing to keep other eyes at bay, other feet from creeping after her. Backward through the kitchen with her eyes on the floor, feeling behind her for the doorknob, letting herself into the relief of sunlight.

Babe yawns when Corey unties her. Ghosts are no concern of Babe's. Corey sees that Babe has dropped a pungent pile of dung behind her, green as the grass she grazed, and steaming fresh.

"What did you do that for? Now they'll know we've been here," she says, and nearly jumps out of her skin at the man's voice, like a corroboration.

"Hello?"

He's straightening, unloading a sack of feed from the tailgate of a dark green three-quarter-ton truck, too clean to be a ranch truck, parked in the shade of the old shop. A big man, in his forties, she guesses, and overweight, wearing an expensive black Stetson that hides all of his face but his dark bandit's mustache. One of the doctors, has to be, although his Levi's fit him as though he's used to wearing them. How had she not seen him, how could she not have noticed his truck when she rode into the yard? Had he driven in while she was mooning around the house, trying to visit the past?

Toe in the stirrup, hand on Babe's mane, and she's in the saddle. She can be away and gone up some trail, lost in brush and pines before he can get his fancy truck started, because she's goddamned if she's going to apologize to him or admit she's trespassing on land she'd ridden when he was in diapers and probably sucking on the silver spoon he'd been born with in his mouth, from the looks of him.

He's walking toward her, pushing back his hat with his thumb.

"I'm John Perrine," he says, and reaches up to shake hands with her. Aggression is in the gesture, he's within his rights after all, but mostly it's curiosity in his brown eyes that belies the ferocity of the mustache, and what can she do but reach down and shake the offered hand, a firm shake from a warm hand that's too soft and clean and fleshy to be a rancher's hand.

"Corey Henry," she says, and adds, "I knew the Ballards. Just wanted to see the house one more time."

Then is furious with herself for offering the explanation when she doesn't owe him a goddamn thing, but he doesn't seem to notice. No, only a heightened interest in his eyes.

"Corey Henry," he says. "I'm glad to meet you, and I was real sorry to hear about your dad."

"Yeah well things happen," she says, brusquely, to warn him off.

"We're neighbors now," he says. "I just bought this place. Closed the paperwork last week."

"You're not one of the consortium doctors?"

"No, worse than that," he says. "I bought this place from the doctors. I'm an attorney," and fishes a business card out of his shirt pocket and hands it to her.

It's the last thing she would have expected to see in the foothills, the small white pasteboard rectangle with expensive engraved letters, John Perrine, Attorney at Law, just as he said, and a street address in Fort Maginnis, phone number, e-mail address. She has no idea what to do with the card, she can't just hand it back to him, so she drops it into her shirt pocket and resnaps the flap.

"It's a privilege to meet you, Miss Henry," he says. "I only wish I could have known Loren. I've done some rodeo myself, nothing like Loren of course, a little bull-riding is all, but I surely do admire him and what he accomplished. I'd like to have a chance to talk to you about him, not for awhile of course I understand, but one of these days?"

The warmth in his eyes embarrasses her. "Yeah well," she says. "Probably we could do that. I don't want to hold you up now," and touches Babe with her spurs and wills herself not to glance back, not to look and see whether he's watching. It isn't like she cares.

6

Loren J. Henry, recipient of the Purple Heart and the Bronze Star for action in New Guinea during the Second World War, died from a self-inflicted gunshot wound on his ranch near Fort Maginnis on Friday evening. He was 81.

Henry was born July 14, 1919, to Sylvester J. and Alice Corinne Henry in Bottineau, North Dakota—

Corey looks at what she's written and wonders how it could be right. Loren always let on that he was born in Montana, right here in the stone house. But it said Bottineau, North Dakota, all right, on the center leaf of her grandmother's Bible, in her grandmother's handwriting—

—and was brought to Murray County, Montana, by his parents in 1921. They ranched in the Mill Creek area near Fort Maginnis until their deaths. Henry attended rural schools and graduated from the county high school in 1937. He managed the family ranch at Henry Gulch until—

The clipping that her grandmother saved from the *Fort Maginnis Democrat-Star* shows forty or so young women gathered on the high school steps in their best rayon dresses, smiling bravely in lipstick that looks black in the photograph. Rain puddles at their feet; it would have been June, after all. Behind the girls stand the young men of the class of 1937, fifteen, sixteen, no seventeen of them in suits with high collars and ties. Which is Loren? The tall one in the center back row, Corey thinks, the one whose slicked-back hair has caught a glancing ray of sunlight that must have broken through the cloudy day.

Such a somber face, and so young.

Back then it was a luxury for a man to graduate from high school. Corey can just hear her grandmother. *What, when there's work to be done!* The very idea of big overgrown louts sitting behind school desks while their parents scrape and slave to feed them! Nobody but a pansy would want to stay cooped up in school! No, the boy goes to work on the ranch after eighth grade, unless his dad's got no ranch for him to work on, in which case he finds a job in town, and until he's twenty-one his father is by God entitled to his wages, can collect the boy's pay every week and give him back a little pocket money if he feels like he can spare it. A boy is supposed to be an asset, otherwise why would anybody go to the trouble and expense of raising him?

And yet Loren graduated, and her grandmother saved the clipping in her Bible. Corey shakes her head, another mystery with no answer.

A girl, now. A girl can be spared from ranch work easier than a boy can. She's likelier than a boy to sit still at a desk and pay attention to some dah-de-dah teacher. Then too, a girl who quits school won't find much in the way of jobs, not respectable jobs. Clerking at Woolworths, maybe, or telling at the bank. Or working at the laundry for a dollar a day. But if she finishes high school, she can go out and teach in a rural school for, oh, forty dollars a month until she gets married.

Corey remembers her grandmother and Loren talking it over.

What? They're paying $250 a month at the Mill Creek school? That much? Yes, I know it's not 1939, it's 1959, but all that money! Why, Corey could live right here at home and save most of her—what? She needs a teaching certificate? She has to go to college to get one of those? How long is that going to take?

What, she wonders, had Loren expected her to become? A schoolmarm like those schoolmarms in his favorite paperback westerns, only in boots and blue jeans instead of the calico gowns those fictional ladies wore?

More likely, he'd never expected her to age. Never expected himself to age.

I stayed in school out of damned orneriness, Loren might have said, if asked. Or, I was too dumb to quit. I wanted to be an educated fool.

Ask a stupid question, get a stupid answer.

—in 1942 he married Paula Cleveland, who preceded him in death—

Corey thinks it sounds a little abrupt, put that way. Eight words for the whole of Paula Cleveland's life, marriage, and death. Oh well, it isn't Paula's obituary. But wait—that's a thought. Paula would have had an obituary, wouldn't she, in the *Fort Maginnis Democrat-Star?*

But there's no obituary for Paula tucked among the slips of paper and brittle newsprint in the back of her grandmother's old leatherbound King James with its corners chewed by mice, used not for spiritual guidance that Corey can remember, but as a family catchall, an untidy record, out of order and arbitrary and falling apart.

—survived by his daughter, Paula Corinne.

Okay, that's all. That's enough.

No. There are the damned trophies. Her grandmother had probably saved the clippings. Yes. Here they are, in a box that Russell Stover chocolates came in. Corey slips off the rubber band. Yes. Fourth of July, 1937, and he still wasn't quite eighteen, but he won day money for saddle bronc riding all three days of the Fort Maginnis Stampede and won a belt buckle for overall cowboy. From the clippings, he rodeoed the rest of that summer. Won another buckle, that was in Lincoln. Helena. Great Falls. She wonders who was doing the ranch work while he rode broncs all over Montana. Her grandmother, more than likely.

The next summer he got as far south as Cheyenne. The summer after that, Lewiston and Pendleton, where he won the hand-tooled saddle with the silver conchos and the silver saddle horn, too good to use, that he kept in his bedroom ever after. The photo in the clipping shows him standing hipshot with the prize saddle, grinning under a beat-up Stetson.

Maybe she should just list the big ones. Pendleton for sure. And Calgary. And the year he got as far as Grand Nationals, was in the running for National Champion Saddle Bronc Rider, yes, 1940, just before the Montana National Guard was called up. He spent the next year that he'd hated so much on the West Coast, training and waiting for war to start.

Just put the good things, Annie had said. His trophies, and how he fought in New Guinea, and be sure to tell what he enjoyed doing. You don't need to give a reason why he died.

Corey goes back to the beginning of her obituary, crosses out *self-inflicted gunshot wound*. Lays down her pencil and leans back against the old piano to get the crick out of her neck. She tries to imagine New Guinea. Jungle, she supposes, tropical forest, dense undergrowth, darkness and vines and dripping water. Then realizes she's picturing a war movie the children at school had described to her. They had been aghast to learn that she never went to movies, hadn't seen one since, oh, surely she'd seen one since Minneapolis.

Don't you have a VCR at home? asked Rose Doggett, looking concerned. We do. We've got three.

What would it be like to be a Doggett daughter? Corey once saw Ariel Doggett spill the contents of her coin purse on the schoolroom floor, a small scatter of change, pennies and dimes rolling under desks and at least one quarter, spinning, which Ariel had stepped over, tossing her lovely dark cloud of hair as she dropped her coin purse in her book bag and didn't bother to stoop and pick up even the quarter.

From her seat, Amy Staple had seen the quarter. Amy's eyes had fixed on Corey, willing Corey not to look down, as her foot slid out from under her desk and then slid back with the quarter under it.

What would it be like to be Hailey Doggett, with those daughters? Little Hailey, who had started out so expansively, trying to fit in with his neighbors and getting hotter and hotter when he couldn't. At that last school-board meeting his head had swiveled, his eyes hot for trouble in his tight pig's face, his mouth open and ready to give trouble back. With the mouth Ariel's got on her, Corey can just imagine the blue flames right back in Hailey's face, and then what does he do? Although when she thinks about it, Corey realizes she's never seen Hailey with Rose or Ariel. It was their mother, poor timorous Rita, who always dropped the girls off at school and picked them up again.

Well. At least she'll never have to think about Hailey or Ariel again. And it's time to quit her lollygagging. Time to get dressed and go pick up Annie for the goddamned viewing.

McClanahan & Goff have made no outward changes to the 1911 red brick building at the top of Main Street hill, and few in the little marble foyer, although the oak door to the left reveals a desk and a serious computer monitor. To the right, however, is another oak door with a tarnished knob and frosted glass with chipped gold lettering, Reception.

Walking through that door, Corey thinks, is like climbing into the casket itself. Heavy plush carpeting and heavy satin drapery, layers and layers of cushioning, all permeated with the odor of cut flowers. And here's Tim McClanahan in his fine dark suit and discreet necktie, advancing on her with his hand outstretched and his face suitably expressing sympathy and pain.

"Corey. Annie. We've put him in the third parlor—down the corridor here—unless you'd rather sit down here for a few minutes, Corey, be by yourself, maybe drink a cup of coffee?"

"No. Let's do it." She pulls away. The heel of her absurd shoe gets stuck in the pile of the carpet, and she catches the corner of a console table to keep from falling. Rights herself, limps down the hall behind Tim into a windowless cubicle, heavily draped, with the half-lid of the casket open to reveal the waxen face lit by a recessed ceiling spotlight.

"Oh, Loren," weeps Annie.

It wears Loren's clothes, his freshly ironed white shirt and dark necktie and the Pendleton stockman's suit in a gray shadow plaid that he bought on sale at Power's Mercantile thirty years ago, but still as good as new, and its hand holds Loren's white Stetson that Nolan Staple rescued from the gearshift. Its eyes are closed, and its white hair has been shampooed and blown back from its face in a halo that feathers over the satin pillow, hiding any sign of violence.

"The end of an era," says Tim, behind her.

Voices from the corridor—"Hadn't been sick, had he?"

"No. Healthiest eighty-one-year-old body you'd ever ask for."

Tim pulls the door shut. "Do you know," he asks in his mortician's voice, "whether there's a charity you'd prefer to flowers?"

"What?"

"Donations to a charity. Instead of sending flowers. Lots of people want to do that."

"The Cowboys Turtle Association," says Annie, "if they still have one."

"I'll find out," says Tim. "Or else the Christian Cowboys?"

Corey shakes her head violently enough to head off that suggestion, which would have sent Loren into a spasm of rage. Turns back to the casket for one last look. Maybe the waxen thing is what she will remember, maybe it's the end of Loren, the end of Loren's voice in her head.

But no such luck.

I know what you're up to. Look at you, all dressed up in your mother's clothes! You pretend you're a decent daughter, but you've got big ideas, same as she did. I know you're sneaking your filthy art books home. You're planning to start painting like them perverts, now my back is turned. And how, he finishes bitterly, *do you think you're going to support my horses?*

At the Majestic Café, Annie drinks her coffee as though she's being paid to finish it and sets her cup down, precisely in its saucer. The high school girl behind the counter leans on her elbows and watches the late afternoon traffic on Main Street, while the twelve-foot walls of the Majestic Café with its original white-painted pressed tin ceiling wait for the next hundred years to pass. Out in the lobby the television is talking to itself about suicide bombers on the other side of the world.

"Tim did a real good job," says Annie. "I thought so. I thought Loren looked real good."

"Annie, what was Paula like?"

"Who?"

Corey waits, and finally Annie says, "Oh. She was so much older than me that I can't remember all that much. She was older than Loren, too, by what, five, six years. That's part of what bothered your grandmother so much about her."

"What did she look like? Do I look like her?"

"No, no! You're pure Henry."

"Well, did she have dark hair, or light hair, or what?"

"Sort of medium-dark, I guess."

Corey thinks she remembers a dark-haired woman whose face is blurred but whose hands are clear. Plain, bitten nails and a wedding ring. Reaching down for Corey, setting a table, stirring something on the stove. Carrying buckets of water to her firs.

"What became of her wedding ring?"

"I don't know!" cries Annie. "Like as not they buried it with her."

Her eyes move restlessly, and the high school girl misreads her and comes over with the pot and refills her cup. The girl wears her hair in inch-long spikes with green frosting, like an alien cupcake, and her lip is pierced with rings in two places. Also her eyebrows are pierced, and she wears a greenish tattoo like a fetter around each forearm. Annie looks after her, is about to say something about her, but Corey is relentless.

"How did she meet Loren?"

"Well—" Trapped, Annie looks into her coffee cup as though she expects another green alien to rise to the surface. Pushes it away. "They didn't exactly meet, they just always knew each other, same as Loren and me, except of course he and Paula grew up right there on the ranch together—"

"What ranch?"

"Your ranch! The Henry ranch. Except some might have called it the Cleveland ranch in those days."

"Cleveland." With the name, something dim slides into place for Corey.

"Well, yes, Cleveland, it was Paula's dad's place. You knew that, didn't you? She was Paula Cleveland, and she was always kind of spoiled. Had to have a piano, take piano lessons. But the way we always heard the story, old Vester Henry had lost his homestead in North Dakota, easy enough in those days, the drought was so terrible. So he came out here to Montana and went to work for Joe Cleveland. He and your gran and Loren lived for a while in one of those log buildings behind the stone house."

"So it's really the old Cleveland place?"

"No!" cries Annie. "It's always been the Henry place! Or as good as."

"One thing I remember," she adds. "At the time of your mother's funeral, I came up and got you ready. Your mom had permed your hair before she died, and such snarls as you had, your gran couldn't get a comb through them. She was about to snip all your hair off, right at the scalp, but Loren wouldn't let her. He called me—we had that old telephone line that ran off the barbed wire fence in those days, and I came and brushed and brushed and finally braided your hair into a little stubby thick braid so it'd stay unsnarled. So that's how you came to keep your hair, on account of Loren."

So they're back where they started, with Loren.

Corey gets up to pay her bill and almost falls when one of her white heels turns under her. The shoes are her mother's, dug out of a box in the eaves and slit along the instep to make them halfway fit Corey, and the goddamn things are going to break her neck.

Mugsy, the mother of the pups, went on an excursion of her own in the late afternoon, and somewhere in the wet grass and pine needles she met a porcupine. In the six years that Mugs has lived, she's never gotten over her curiosity, and so she sniffed the porcupine and came home with muddy flanks and muddy tail and a nose full of quills.

Val took one look at her, turned off the burner on the stove, got out a pair of pliers, and led Mugs outside by the scruff of her neck to pull the quills out of her.

"It's your own fault, so don't cry to me," Val tells Mugs, when the dog whines and tries to squirm out from between her knees. "Keep your tail to yourself, can't you? Look what you're doing to my clothes. Now I'll have to change my jeans before I can go to town, all because of you."

She stops lecturing the cringing dog to fix the jaws of her pliers precisely on a quill, which flexes under pressure, resists, and finally lets go with a tiny spurt of blood and a yelp of pain from Mugs.

"Don't you dare bite me," says Val, and drops the quill, a pale three-inch-long hollow shaft with a black tip, into the empty baking powder can she'd brought out and set on the steps beside her, otherwise who knew which wandering livestock or barefoot son might pick it up again and need her pliers, before she starts on the next quill. In ten minutes Mugsy's poor nose and muzzle look as lacerated and bloody as raw hamburger, and Val's clean blue jeans are soaked to the knees and lashed with featherings of mud from the dog's anguished tail-wagging.

James has brought out his coffee and the newspaper to sit on the steps in the late sunlight. He watches as Val squirts antiseptic over the dog's nose and releases her to crawl under the steps to lick herself. "What's it been, a whole month since she last picked a fight with a porcupine?" Val shows him the can of bloody quills, and he shakes his head.

She should be changing her jeans, but instead she leans back against James's leg. Late lilacs hang in heavy, drenched bloom around the scrap of mowed wild grass that passes for a lawn. One of the nesting bluebirds flashes between the power pole and the old pine tree on his way to the eaves of the shed. For years there had been no bluebirds, all poisoned, it was thought, by the pesticides used to kill alfalfa weevil in the 1950s. But hardly anyone raises alfalfa in the foothills now. The big fields like Nolan Staple's are up on the bench, where the season is a little longer, and Nolan sells his alfalfa out of state, because the small dairies around Fort Maginnis that had bought Val's father's alfalfa are gone, the local creamery closed and, except for a few families like the Tendennings who keep a milk cow, everyone buys their milk at Safeway, in plastic jugs shipped in from western Washington State.

Oh, well. The alfalfa had never been a dependable cash crop in the foothills, what with the short season at this high altitude, and the hayfields are grown over or built over by the new neighbors, but the bluebirds have returned, their unexpected blue like a flash to the heart, a promise that the world will continue, and Val loves them.

"Have you got the old dog to eat anything?"

"No. I tried a little chicken, some of that white meat from last night chopped up fine. He just sniffed at it. He lapped a little water, was all."

When James doesn't answer, she says, "You think it would have been better to let her put him down."

"Hard on her," says James. "Loren might just as well have taken that rifle to her as taken it to himself."

"All my life, growing up, I've always known I wasn't Corey Henry, so I would never be perfect. Horseback riding? Didn't matter how many colts I broke to ride. How many saddle blankets I kept wet. Didn't matter if I won ribbons. Corey Henry was the queen, and I was the kid that broke bridle reins and forgot to shut gates and ran off to dances and thought she ought to go to college—"

"That's your dad talking."

"*Corey* didn't think she was too damn good for the ranch, *Corey* was satisfied to stay home and break horses for her dad."

"You got to go to college."

"That one year!"

James is looking over her shoulder toward the county road, where the sun fires its afternoon bursts through the pines. Hearing the truck, Val looks too.

It's Loren Henry's red pickup, still unnaturally clean from the wash Nolan Staple gave it. It pulls up behind the Suburban, next to the pine tree where the boys hung their swinging rope and never took it down, and out climbs Corey Henry. She's oddly dressed in a longish flowered skirt and high-heeled white sandals that are giving her trouble. As Val watches, one of Corey's heels sinks into the soft gravel and nearly upsets her, but she wrenches it loose and keeps walking toward them.

"Holy smokes," says James.

"I came for Sonny," Corey says when she's close enough.

She's a sight, all right. *Miss Henry* was what Val had to call her when she went to school to her. She had seemed ten feet tall to Val then, and she looks about ten feet tall now, wobbling on her strange high heels and blazing with her Henry blue eyes. Val gets up from the steps, quaking inwardly but standing her ground.

"I don't want you to have him put down," she says.

"He's not going to get put down."

Corey has changed. Val can't quite tell how, although the clothes are strange enough, the full flowered skirt and the puffy blouse that has yellowed from its original white and creased from being packed for years. Val can't remember when she's seen Corey wearing anything but a shirt and Levi's, even to teach in, even when most women teachers wore skirts, and Val especially can't remember seeing that expression on Corey's face, as though she's just waked up and remembered something.

"At least," adds Corey, and the twist of her mouth is almost a smile, "he's not going to be put down until fall."

Evening advances slowly. At least no rain tonight, no thunder and lightning, only a deepening intensity of light at the windows, violet and rose. Tomorrow will be scorching hot in town, the pavement will absorb the sun's rays and radiate in the faces of funeral-goers in their sweltering best clothes, but at this hour the thick sandstone walls keep the downstairs rooms, at least, so cool that Corey had thrown a blanket over Sonny once she got him settled. Now she looks around the room at the disaster she's caused, Loren's desk open and a blizzard of his papers everywhere, on the sofa, on the floor around her. Loren never threw away a piece of paper in his life. Now Corey's back hurts and her legs hurt from sitting cross-legged on the floor, sorting, and her feet hurt from the goddamn shoes she kicked off as soon as she got home but will have to wear again tomorrow—and it's getting dark in here, she's going to have to get up and turn on the ceiling light—whoa—ouch—with one hand to her back and one on her knee, she struggles upright.

"God, I'm old," she says. Guesses it doesn't hurt her to be reminded of her age, the way she's been living backward in her head the last day or two.

Sonny, in his state between sleep and coma, thumps his tail at her voice. He seemed to recognize his own familiar odor when she dragged him into his corner, and he licked her ankle and lapped up some of the gruel she mixed for him. He even managed to pee when she carried him out to the yard and propped him up. She guesses he'll live a while longer, although she'd have sworn he lived only for Loren.

She still hasn't found what she's looking for.

At the bottom of a drawer so stuffed with receipts, letters, and odd scraps that it resisted being opened until she forced her hand inside to flatten the papers and pull, she had discovered the original deed to the ranch signed in real ink in 1894 when a Joseph Cleveland had proved up on his homestead and could call it his. Couldn't have been Paula's father. More likely her grandfather. But it had started out as the Cleveland ranch, all right. Another legend gone west.

She imagines the deed being placed in the empty drawer, more papers gradually layering over the deed, encrusting it with the trivia of years, a piece of paper that looked like a shopping list, *don't forget chicken feed*, another piece of paper jotted with what looked like the running tallies of a card game, odds and ends beyond anyone's memory.

She guesses it's a good thing she found the deed, in case she ever wants to, has trouble getting her mind around the word, *sell*.

Also she had found Paula's obituary, clipped from the newspaper and stuffed into an envelope along with recipes for food, also clipped from newspapers, that Corey cannot remember ever tasting. Orange chiffon cake, twenty-four-hour salad, chicken cordon bleu. Corey can just see the expression on Loren's face at being handed a plate of chicken cordon bleu.

The obituary doesn't say much. Daughter of. Survived by. Short illness.

A canceled check floats in Sonny's water bowl, too sodden now to read. Corey fishes it out and lays it on the windowsill to dry. What to do with it? What to do with any of this mess? Just one pile in front of her contains scraps and receipts going back as far as 1932—*barbed wire and staples, $4.52*—grocery lists, bills of sale for long-dead animals.

A tight bundle of letters in a rubber band that turned out to be from Loren to his mother. She had opened one, read a line or two—*Dear Ma, nothing much going on here. We saw dolfins swim by*—and couldn't bear to read further.

Also an envelope of deposit slips for her pay warrants, going back to 1962, when she started teaching. She could trace her tiny salary increments over the years if she wanted to bother. She supposes there's a story to be read in all this paper, a hum-de-dum story of ordinary life lived day-by-day and year-by-year, interrupted only by the rodeo circuit and then by World War II.

But only the one canceled check, and she can't even tell what it was for.

Corey picks up the dog's bowl and carries it out to the kitchen, empties it and runs it full of fresh water, carries it back and holds Sonny's head so he can lap a little. When he lolls back, exhausted, she covers him with his blanket and switches off the ceiling light. Total dark. Then her eyes adjust and the window reappears, gray and shadowed with firs.

So the woman had owned the ranch but the man took the credit for it. So what else is new. *Don't dah-de-dah make a fuss over it, too late now to change an old deed.*

The hell with the paper blizzard. If there isn't any wind tomorrow, she'll sweep out the whole mess and burn it.

Then remembers what tomorrow is.

The thought of Loren's funeral drives her back to the window nervous as a wild thing shut within walls, willing herself through the panes of glass and up the hillside in the obscure shadows of grassheads, into the shadow world of the pines that creep down toward the house—and then she freezes. There had been a sudden movement under the pines, movement so sudden and fleeting that it's gone before she quite realizes it, wouldn't have believed she'd really seen it if her eyes weren't country-trained to spot and follow living movement. A deer, no. A coyote, no. Not the right shape, not the right flicker.

It's human. With the certainty comes an electric surge up her spine that charges the hairs of her neck and the hairs of her arms. It's human. Somebody watching the house. Somebody who noticed when she turned off the light, moved at that moment, and gave himself away.

She draws a breath. Tells herself to draw another, a steady one. Feels her way around the obstacles of furniture and through the arch into the kitchen, putting her bare feet down as silently as though the unknown watcher might hear footsteps from all the way up the hill. Peers through the kitchen window, sees empty gravel road in a glaze of moonlight that leads past the dark shape of the springhouse to the obscure huddle of the barn. Nothing moving out there, not even the branches of trees.

She slips back through the archway. No sound here, either, until she makes out the faint rasp of the old dog's breathing. Through this window, a few stars above a jagged darkness as calm and indifferent as though nothing has ever disturbed it.

By daylight nobody would be able to see her behind these thick sandstone walls and deep windows, but if she turns the lights back on now, she'll be completely exposed. She remembers the roller shades and pulls them down, cracked and brittle as they are. They seem a thin protection.

Nothing happens, and finally she gives up and feels her way upstairs. Leaves the lights off, because the second-story windows at the back of the house may also be under surveillance. Finds the windowsill and sits there, pushing over the books to make room for herself.

Her grandmother's books, stacked since Corey doesn't know when. Books her grandmother read again and again, preferring the familiar over the strange books Corey brought home from the school library for her. Corey knows the titles, doesn't need to see them. *David Harum. St. Elmo. Freckles. Idylls of the King. In Memoriam.* Spines worn to velvet. Her grandmother, from a time when every school-child memorized lines and lines of poetry, could have recited pages from *In Memoriam.*

> *The old order changeth, yielding place for new,*
> *And God fulfills himself in many ways,*
> *Lest one good custom should corrupt the world.*

What does it mean, that one good custom might corrupt the world? Poetry has never made much sense to Corey, although she's memorized some, herself, in school. Dim rouse of memory. Leaves moving outside the tall windows of the old high school. It must have been early fall, and the class was reading what? *Tomorrow and tomorrow and tomorrow.* That had been the assignment, memorizing the tomorrow speech.

Below the window, the moon has left the grass and hillside pines in a textured and fathomless black with a dark gray horizon. So who the hell would be watching her?

Hailey? Why would he watch her?

Should she lock the kitchen door?

Old doors and old keyholes, the keys missing for so many years that Corey cannot remember ever seeing the locks used. Maybe the keys are buried in drawers of junk, along with balls of string and broken forks and colored celluloid rings to mark the legs of chickens long since fried for dinner or picked off by hawks. Parts from a cream separator from the days when her grandmother kept cows and sold the cream. Milk filters, decks of cards, old envelopes with lists written on their backs. Detritus, debris.

Locks on all the doors, but no keys. The old dog downstairs, too old even to bark. Corey thinks about loading Loren's rifle. But she can just see herself sitting up in bed all night with a gun across her knees.

Wonders if there's enough left of Loren's whiskey for her to get to sleep on.

7

Miniaturized rage is what Corey thinks she's hearing before she opens her eyes and sees her bedroom ceiling with the familiar cracks in the plaster. She's got a bad taste in her mouth from the whiskey, and somehow today she's going to have to get away from Annie and the funeral long enough to buy another bottle. Plenty of time now, though. From the light in the window, she guesses it's only about six o'clock.

Wallpaper morning glories so faded that they might as well be dead. Dead flies shadowing the ceiling lightbulb, dead flies littering the windowsill. But something's alive and buzzing, buzzing. Its persistence stirs her to roll over and look, and she sees two wasps, clinging to the bedpost above her head, buzzing, buzzing, and copulating.

As she watches, the male wasp seems to tire. He pauses, still mounted on the female's back with his forelegs holding her thorax in position. Neither moves, although one or both continue their agitated buzzing until he seems to gather strength and goes at her again, pumping away at a rapid-fire pace for a minute or more, much longer than

Corey would have supposed wasp-sex would last. What will happen when it comes to an end? Are male wasps, like ants or bees, nothing but drones kept to service a queen? Will she kill him when he finishes? Eat him?

The male pauses again. Rests. Detaches himself slowly, backs away from the female and flies off.

Corey watches his looping flight until he vanishes through her bedroom door. The female remains on the bedpost, wings flattened and head lowered to her forelegs. Corey closes her eyes and opens them, and the female is gone.

Next thing, she supposes, she'll have a wasp's nest in her bedroom.

Virgil. Could he have looped off in faster flight?

He'd been badly torn up at the Miles City bucking horse show and, half-healed, caught a bus west until he ran out of money in Fort Maginnis, where Loren had run into him and bought him a cup of coffee at the Majestic and hired him for light summer work while his bones grew back together. Virgil had actually done a little work, but mostly chewed the fat with Loren about rodeo. When Corey thinks of him, it's always with his walking cast on. Pulling his pants up and over his cast.

Got me an old maid I'm banging, she'd overheard him tell somebody at the beer garden under the grandstand at fair time. Banging, Virgil's word for it. She had come looking for him and stopped, half in shade, half in sunlight, hoping that no one had seen her. Later she realized he must have known she'd overheard, maybe even intended it, because the next day he had gathered together what he owned, a change of clothes and his saddle, and caught a ride to town.

For the next year or two she had lived a shadow life where, all tastes flattened, odors stale, and colors run together into gray, she had felt only an occasional panic—run, hide!—that gave way to a sullen plodding, one day after another, one foot after the next, until gradually some of her old energy returned. Time of life, she had read. She'd reached the age where the hormones weakened and let her go, and now she could live in uneasy, pointless peace.

Andreas snickers.

Once in a while she still feels the urge, the leftover traces in her body of whatever holds the female wasp under the male wasp's pile-driving. The procreative instinct, lingering absurdly after the organism has shut down. At those times, less and less frequently, she uses her hand, gives herself relief so she can sleep.

What had Loren felt, what had Loren done all these years since Paula died.

Uncalled-for picture, Loren naked in the jackhammer position, buttocks furiously pumping up and down—no! Surely Loren never wanted sex, no. The dignity of Loren with his hat on his head and his eyes blazing blue. The Henry blue eyes.

He had walked like a lot of old rough-string riders with a stiff back and an odd swing of his legs from his rigid hips, from the pelvis that was smashed at the Calgary Stampede the time the bronc fell on him in the chute. With his aging bones he had stopped taking so many chances, didn't buck out the colts in the corral on the first saddling, didn't swing open the gate and head out for the high pastures on the fifth or sixth saddling. Gradually let her do more and more horse-breaking. But once astride, he regained his lost grace, as brilliant as ever, Loren Henry on horseback.

"But I'm not dead yet, Loren," she says out loud, and then feels her whole body blush, first her face and neck and then all the way down.

She throws back the sheet and quilt and finds her underwear. That's enough of that, for God's sake.

An organ plays somewhere, its volume muted, as feet pad over carpet, fabric whispers against fabric, voices murmur over the occasional creak of a folding chair. From the veiled family alcove, Corey watches the ranch population of Murray County file down the aisles of the mortuary chapel. Sunburned women in summer dresses, men in ironed Levi's and pearl-snap shirts, Stetsons held in roughened hands. A few scrubbed children, bringing with them the scent of hayfields and horses. It'll be standing room only, Annie had boasted, and Annie is right.

After her experience at the viewing, Corey has carved larger toeholes in her mother's high-heeled sandals so she can bear to walk in them, but she could find nothing better to wear than the blouse and flowered skirt. The skirt hadn't wanted to meet around her middle, and now it burrows into her. Had she worn it to her grandmother's funeral? She can't remember, and also she can't remember having bare legs like hers, white as dough from living inside blue denim all their lives, and ending in thickened toenails that stick out through her mother's shoes. Is she old or young, when she looks so ruined but feels so raw?

All the names she's been called in her life. Bumpkin, freak, old maid, cowgirl, cunt.

The organ gathers volume, changes from a drone to something more profound.

"There's Saylor Lambert," whispers Annie. "Coming through the door now, with his cane. I just hate to see how crippled-up he is. There's Cindy Graus, used to be a Ballard. There's Rita Doggett. Don't look like she brought her husband with her. The slimy little twit probably didn't have the guts to show his face here."

Rita is the designated Doggett funeral attendee, but not because Hailey lacks the guts to show his face. Rita could have told Annie Reisenaur, if she'd heard Annie's remark, that a social situation in which he might be at a disadvantage has never occurred to Hailey. What Hailey fears is boredom. Where he thinks he'll start to yawn, he sends Rita, and therefore Rita has pressed one of the dark India print dresses she used to wear when she worked in Santa Monica, and she has dragged on a pair of black panty hose and her black kid shoes. One look at the ranch folk filing into the mortuary chapel in their cowboy best and she realizes she's the most funereal-looking person present.

On the sidewalk outside the mortuary she had run into John Perrine, and he had doffed his hat to her.

"Purely warm, here in town!" he greeted her. "We're way better off in the foothills. One thing I love about the foothills is the cool nights. By the way, I want to apologize for the way Ingrid yelled at you the night of your party. She gets all het up about land use."

Ingrid, the big blonde. Rita tried to remember what she had been yelling about. Something about sewage. Het up about the land. "So you didn't grow up here?" she said, puzzling at his inflections. "Where, West Texas?"

"No. Bucks County, Pennsylvania. But I've been out here thirty years. Here in the West, anyway. My dad thought I was going to Colorado College for the skiing. He almost had a stroke when he found out what I was really doing."

"What was that?"

"Bull riding."

He had a pleasant face, deeply tanned and lined around his eyes and mouth, and he had a big man's laugh that shook his shoulders and turned the heads of people going into the funeral parlor. Rita thought Hailey was probably right, she was attracted to big men who reminded her of her father. He had been so good at getting out from under her mother's expectations, like bill-paying or child-rearing, that Rita growing up had seen little of him. But Hailey! Hailey had picked Rita out, picked *her* out, camped at her dormitory the first week he met her, walked her to class, followed her to the bookstore, took her to lunch, wanted to know every detail of what she did while she was out of his sight.

About money, Hailey was, well, maybe more like her father in that respect. For a while Hailey had seemed to sit at his computer and conjure magic money out of nowhere. But magic money—*pfft!*—and Rita at least has sense enough to want the bills paid.

John Perrine, now, would pay his bills with real money, although with his black hat and his bandit mustache, she would never have guessed he was an outsider like herself. She would have picked him out for a cowboy on any street in Montana. Perhaps she could sit beside him during the funeral, and people wouldn't look at her as if she personally had shot Loren Henry.

The girlfriend, Ingrid, had come up behind John and taken his arm. "Time to go in," she told him, and thrust her large face at Rita.

The white ribbon is being removed from the front row of seats. The pallbearers take their places facing the flag-draped casket. Annie's sons and white-haired Will Ballard, Nolan Staple and his boy, Bobby, looking stiff and unnatural in dark suits. James Tendenning with his beard and shoulder-length locks, looking profound.

"We believe in the communion of saints, the resurrection of the body, the life everlasting," everyone reads aloud from their hymnals.

Nolan Staple faces the casket but watches his son out of the corner of his eye. The kid's taller than Nolan, even slouched in his new suit.

Getting ready for the funeral, Nolan had had to scrub his hands at the sink with the potato brush, trying to get the ingrained dirt out of his pores and from around his fingernails, but Bobby's hands are long and moist, like he's never done a day's work—and he hasn't, either. Where Bobby has put his hands, the flesh and fluids he's touched, Nolan can almost smell on him. But who is the girl?

Nolan can guess when the fire got stoked between her and Bobby. In the late spring Bobby would vanish, taking the truck keys without asking, returning with no explanations but looking bruised and tender, as though an outer skin had been ripped from him. The odor of sex hangs about him, a mixture of swamp gas and heavy perfume that arouses and enrages Nolan. Why has he never heard the girl's name? In his worst imaginings, she's years older than Bobby, maybe got a kid of her own, knows what she's doing, which is jerking the kid around by the dong. Maybe she thinks the Staples have money. That's a laugh. Here he is with haying season upon him and no help except what he can get out of Bobby. God knows he should have been harder on the kid all along, should have made him work harder. Ever since Corey invited them to be pallbearers, Nolan has been worrying how Bobby will behave, but at least the kid is looking sober, like a pallbearer should. Nolan straightens his shoulders and tries to focus on what the preacher is saying about Loren.

Rita loses track of her place in the hymnal. Allows herself to slip into a daydream in which she basks in filtered sunlight. Her clothes are diaphanous, they lift her floating to a wildflower meadow or a haunted seacoast, doesn't matter which cover of which novel she's borrowed the scene from. She's young and firm again, the pleats and puckers of pregnancy erased from her abdomen by sleight of hand, and she can wreathe her hair and dance, or she can drowse without fear of—of

Eugene's grumpy face materializing out of the bushes, his eyes peering this way and that—or worse, *Albert*, that's his name, long lanky Albert with his pale eyes and his pale skull with its reddish dusting of stubble, like a skinhead who has been deprived of his razor. However did he and Eugene ever get together, she had implored Hailey.

Don't know. Don't worry, honey. Nothing to worry about.

How long are they staying with us?

Not long. I don't think very long.

Hailey, is this about Eugene's *arrest*, I mean does he *blame* you, does he think you ought to pay him back that money?

No. No. Oh hell no, Hailey had whispered last night, rocking her in his arms after she had cried and cried and he had pried her hands away from her wet face and pried her legs apart—the way they both liked it best—oh hell no. I love you. I love you. You know I love you.

"—served his country in the Pacific during World War II, seeing action in New Guinea and receiving the Purple Heart and Bronze Star for outstanding service," reads the Presbyterian minister from his slip of paper. He looks out at the mourners. "So what leads such a man to take his own life?"

Because he had a bad temper, thinks Val from her seat behind the row of pallbearers. He bullied Corey until she did everything he wanted. He signed her up to teach in that school, let her wear her life away, acted like he owned her, *did* own her. When she finally turned herself into what he wanted, which was a mean, crusty old whammy like himself, and she slapped that Doggett girl and gave the board an excuse to close the school out from under her, he went and shot himself.

Is Corey a believer, Val wonders? Loren never would have given a preacher the time of day, but Corey, maybe. Does she hope to be resurrected with her father?

Val's hopes for resurrection get a little snarled when she thinks about seeing her own father again. Are there recriminations in heaven?

Who knows why, thinks Annie. She had dreamed again last night. A dream like any other, without a beginning, getting more and more complicated, requiring more from her than she could accomplish, until she was trying so hard to find or count or gather or protect whatever she was supposed to be counting or gathering or protecting that she woke exhausted.

The old barn with its stalls for the workhorses and its haymow as vivid as though the first thing Doc Mackenzie hadn't done after he bought the place was to have it bulldozed and burned. Yes, who could have supposed that the old barn would go right on existing, the grain of its unplaned lumber, knotholes and splinters and the musty smell of ancient hay and tired horses contained in her memory and resurrected during her sleep, every nail and bucket. Harness hung on spikes, the leather rigid and cracking from the cold, hames and horse collars, and spider webs so dense she could have thrust her whole hand into them.

In her dream it had been winter, and snow had sifted through the cracks in the walls. She had come into the barn—reasons gone the way of dream logic, something to do with children, had children been hiding in the barn? But no, standing in one of the workhorse stalls in his frayed mackinaw cap and the tattered black silk scarf he always wound around his neck in cold weather, was her father with his face as white as frostbite, his nose running from the cold, his eyes running with tears, and he had fixed on her an expression of anguish and accusation that had brought her sitting up in her own bed, shaking.

"Oh!" she cried aloud, and woke herself completely. "I wish I hadn't dreamed that dream!"

Alone in her trailer bedroom, where the shadows did strange work at the foot of the bed, and the mirror over the dresser opened like a tunnel where faces appeared and disappeared as the moon raced behind clouds, lightening and then darkening the curtains, it occurred to Annie that it was a terrible thing to be dead. The decomposition of the flesh. Worse, the knowledge of that decomposition. Wasn't that what she had seen in her father's eyes?

"No," she had said aloud, and turned on the lamp. The foot of the bed was the foot of the bed. The mirror was a mirror.

No, she had told herself. Death is nothing. No thoughts, nothing. Sleep, the deep sleep they give you with anesthesia at the hospital, like the time she'd hemorrhaged after the birth of her second boy. Sleeping that deep sleep you don't want to wake from is the closest we can imagine to death, and that's also where to keep the past. Asleep.

The pallbearers bend to their task. Up the center aisle they bear the casket, and then—yes, thankful release—children accounted for, purses located under seats, hats retrieved from the backs of folding chairs, the doors of the chapel propped open on their little metal sticks. Time to move on. Annie touches Corey's arm.

Outside the mortuary, sunlight glares on pavement as James and Nolan and Bobby and Will Ballard and Annie's sons load the casket into the back of Saylor Lambert's black-varnished spring wagon. Old Whitey Phipps rides the wagon seat with his cheek full of his chaw and his hands full of the lines of Saylor's four matched black Hanoverian horses. Whitey is craning his neck to make sure the pallbearers get it right, get the casket loaded and secured and themselves seated, three on a side facing the casket, before he clucks to his team to clatter forward. Shod hooves ring on concrete to be echoed by the hooves of a second and younger team of four black Hanoverians drawing a second black wagon.

"This is for us," says Annie.

"Oh God," says Corey. She should never have let Annie have her way, she should have stopped her somehow. The procession is going to be a spectacle, a sideshow worse than ever she could have imagined.

Saylor takes her elbow and tries to help her up the high step to the wagon seat, although as decrepit as Saylor has become, Corey knows she should be helping him. "Now don't you worry none about that colt of Loren's," he tells her. "That little stud will be just fine until you have time to come and get him."

She wants to ask him what he's talking about, but the Sheriff's Posse has just shown up, and the riders are forming themselves into ranks of four abreast with a clatter of hooves and shouted directions. One of Annie's grandsons is trying to coax his saddle horse to jump down to the street from the back of his pickup truck. The big palomino snorts and rears, his eyes rolling white over the top bar of the stockrack.

"What do you think you're doing?" somebody yells. "Can't you afford a horse trailer?"

Toward the middle of the block, a city cop in sunglasses watches in the rearview mirror of his patrol car, waiting to lead the procession down Main Street hill and out to the cemetery.

"Looks like a rodeo parade," says Corey. "All we need is the high school band and a drum of Indians up from Crow Agency."

John Perrine, looking like an illustration out of a western-wear catalogue with a long white duster over his dark suit, is riding up and down on a powerful quarter horse. Evidently he's in charge of the Sheriff's Posse, because he's yelling commands.

"Whatever does he want with that long coat on a day like this?" Annie marvels.

Corey looks away, embarrassed for him. She'd have hoped he'd be more, what. Dignified, she guesses. If she'd thought about him, which she hasn't. Whatever is it that he or anybody else likes about dressing up and playing Western?

The Presbyterian minister hurries up to Annie and Corey's wagon. He hikes up his cassock, revealing new blue jeans and Reeboks, and takes the long step to sit beside the driver, an uneasy teenager with a hive of acne across his forehead and white knuckles on his bunched lines. Some young relation of Saylor's, Corey supposes.

Whitey turns from his high seat on the lead wagon, waves back at the procession, and slaps his lines across the backs of his wheel team. The big Hanoverians break into a slow, stately trot. Up ahead, the cop eases his patrol car out from the curb at five miles an hour, and they're off, trotting past the gas station on upper Main Street, the courthouse in its shade of trees, the library, the old land office, the *Democrat-Star* building, the Majestic Hotel, the bank.

Corey can't help but look back, and there's John Perrine in his Old West get-up, riding at the head of the Sheriff's Posse and touching the brim of his hat when he sees she's noticed him. The funeral procession is attracting as much attention from bystanders as any rodeo parade, and, as in any parade, some of the riders are having trouble with their horses, which roll their eyes at the strange street sights and sounds, fight their bits, drip foam and sidestep out of line. Somebody yip-yip-yips like a cowboy, showing off, and a woman in shorts and a halter top screams and snatches back a toddler to the sidewalk in front of the bookstore. The sun beats down. A funeral program flutters in a breath of breeze, dances briefly in the street, and end-over-ends between the hooves of the young team pulling Corey and Annie's wagon. The off lead horse shies violently, rears and bolts.

In the first seconds, as the harness mates are dragged for a startled stride or two, then flatten their ears and bolt with the lead horse, Corey sees details: dumb watching faces from both sides of the street, as though a runaway team is part of the sideshow; James Tendenning in the lead wagon, trying to get himself disentangled from the other pallbearers and yelling back at the horseback riders; Whitey Phipps looking back over his shoulder, astonished, and larruping his own team. Whitey doesn't stand a chance of keeping the lead, because the young horses have their bits in their teeth as they thunder past him and his wagonful of pallbearers and casket. Wind tears at the corners of Corey's eyes. Cars parked by the opposite curb loom up and are gone. Ahead, oh dear God, are traffic lights and pedestrians. A white Wagoneer has started across Main Street on a green light and just avoids collision with a screech of brakes and a terrified face in its window. Then it's behind them.

Corey gets a grip. Balances herself on her mother's awful shoes and squeezes between the driver and the minister. The boy's face is so pale that his acne stands out like a spattering of blood. He sees Corey, moans, and drops the lines.

"God damn it to hell," says Corey. She catches the lines before they can fall down into the traces, spreads her legs and braces herself.

The right lead mare appears to be holding firm, and Corey thinks if she had room to maneuver, she could lean on the right line and eventually wear down the panicked young gelding. Maneuvering on a town street is the difficulty. Parked cars, parking meters, plate glass windows—thrashing horses, broken forelegs, gushing arteries—trampled children, smashed wagon, broken necks—her other option is straight ahead and pray nobody gets in the way. She just hopes the minister has sense enough to hang on. She knows Annie does.

Her eyes stream and the sun blisters, but she can see astonishment washed with terror in the face of a young fellow in a droopy T-shirt and a backwards cap who was about to cross lower Main between the Ace Hardware and the Mint Bar when he sees the horses thundering down on him and leaps back with a yelp.

They are approaching the city limits, which is good. Or is it. No, an old man in a dirty straw hat, oblivious of what's coming up behind him, jounces along the road on a little John Deere tractor, the old poppin' Johnny model with a mower blade attached, mowing the high grass along the cemetery road. Corey judges her clearance and thinks she just might make it around him without upsetting in the ditch. She throws her weight on the left line and feels the lead horses respond enough to give her hope. One wheel running on gravel, the other spinning inches from the tractor with its deafening pop-pop-pop and smell of grease, the driver so close that Corey can see the green flecks of grass on his teeth when he turns and sees her and drops his jaw.

The wagon rights itself behind the horses and rockets on.

And now the road to the cemetery is straight and wide and empty, and Corey, her flowered skirt blowing and her teeth full of dust and her hair pulling out of its braid and streaming behind her, feels the tiring lead horses yielding to the drag of lines and bits. What the hell. Four fast horses and an open, hard-surfaced road, let 'em rip. Tire them out, serve them right. Yippee. Yahoo. All the neighbors and gawkers that wanted a sideshow, they might as well get their money's worth. She may not be much of an artist, and she may not have had sex in years, but she can, by God, drive a four-horse team, just the way Loren taught her.

"You wanted to run, now let's see you sonsabitches run!" she yells, and she lashes the wheel team with the ends of the lines and sees them gather themselves for a last hard-breathing effort. Through the wrought iron gates, thunder and racket, hell for leather around the deep turn in the shade of cottonwoods with spreading lawns and tombstones on either side, down the graveled avenue where a backhoe operator has dug Loren's grave and set up a canopy over it and is withdrawing with his equipment behind the caretaker's shed, but swivels his head in time to see, at the very edge of his fresh berm, the four horses and wagon slide to a stop.

Foamed and soaked with sweat, dripping under their harnesses, the horses shiver and lower their heads and gasp.

Corey looks back. Annie is gripping the sideboards, looking like she's seen a revelation.

The minister crawls out from under the seat, dragging the acned kid by the wrist. "That was quite a ride!" he remarks.

And here comes the Sheriff's Posse, thirty or so riders pounding along with their faces flushed and their horses champing at bits as they spill across manicured lawns to cast up divots from shod hooves, horses and riders everywhere, milling among tombstones, all talk-ing at once, yelling, marveling, and dividing down the middle to al-low Whitey Phipps to come galloping through with the pallbearers and the casket bouncing behind him.

Corey has to admit that she feels pretty good. Maybe a sideshow is her true element. She forks her hair out of her face with her fingers and sees, beyond the cemetery gates, cars honking in procession and blink-ing their lights. John Perrine tears up on his sorrel gelding, swings out of the saddle, and loops the sorrel's bridle reins over an ornamental spike in time to give Corey a hand down from the wagon and help her steady herself on her wobbling white shoes. His face is shining with what Corey knows, knows absolutely, in spite of anything that Andreas or Virgil or even Loren could say about old maids or bad daughters or bad artists or freaks or cowgirls, is pure admiration.

"That was wonderful!" cries John Perrine, and an answering cho-rus rises from the riders and from rolled-down windows of cars, ev-erybody's voices in an expression Corey is pretty sure isn't true—but what the hell—"Loren would have loved it!"

8

June passes and July begins a whole new story. The hot sun of late June had dried the foothills to the tinder point and stressed the wheat on the benchland into ripples of dwarfed stalks and ruined profits, and now all the ranchers are cursing the weather and praying for moisture and wondering why they ever wanted to live in such a goddamn country, anyway, while the new people phone or E-mail their distant friends about the beautiful region they live in, where the sky is not cloudy all day.

After Loren's funeral, Corey Henry spent the rest of June in what she's starting to realize was a whiskey stupor. Now she's trying to pull herself together. Driving into Fort Maginnis in the early morning of the first day of July, she hears the staccato of early firecrackers and swears to herself. Grass fires get started from fireworks every July, bringing the fire trucks screaming up one street and down another to find the flames, which sometimes leap beyond the city limits into hay meadows and underbrush and crackling dry pines. Damn town kids, as Loren would have said, either they have no idea of the damage they can do, or they don't care.

Fort Maginnis lies along a creek bottom, overlooked by what's left of the old brick fort on the hill that has been renovated into a country club and nine-hole golf course. It never was much of a fort, never had to defend against anything worse than wolvers or whiskey traders, and most of its buildings have been torn down and the bricks recycled into foundations and a warehouse or two in town. Corey drives along a sleepy street of narrow frame houses that once were officers' quarters and now peel their paint behind overgrown hedges and ripening grass. Dandelions grow through the cracks in these sidewalks, and bindweed crawls over curbs and spreads its pale morning blossoms, pink and lavender. Nothing more exciting than firecrackers has happened here in a long time.

The address on the business card John Perrine gave her turns out to be just off Second Street, in the old dressed-sandstone Ganz Building, which Corey remembers from long ago as the Northwestern Bank. The Ganz Building had come down in the world since its days as a bank, serving in recent years as somebody's front-end shop, with apartments upstairs. Recently, however, its stonework and fluted pillars have been cleaned and touched up with pink and gilt paint, and its name and completion date, Ganz 1902, freshly chiseled into the facade.

Corey finds a place to park the red truck in the shade of a crabapple tree and sits with the window rolled down, taking her time. Hand out the window, draws her own face with her finger, upside down in the dust on the truck's door, pokes for eyes, straight line for mouth. So warm for so early in the morning. She takes shallow breaths of unripe fruit and melting street tar and gasoline. Listens to steady traffic a few blocks away on Main, a stereo playing from somebody's porch, love oh careless love, more firecrackers in the distance, then the sizzle of an illegal bottle rocket. Across the street on the ground floor of the Ganz Building are the state liquor store and a real estate office and a shop called Treasures, Etc., offering expensive dresses and jewelry and local arts and crafts for sale. Corey has visited the liquor store often enough during the past weeks, but until today she hasn't noticed the discreet sign on polished oak that points upstairs to the law office of John Perrine.

Better do it.

The sun whitens the street, dazzles on the windshield of an empty grain truck changing gears to turn at the light on Main. No other traffic in sight. Corey squints, feels the heat of the pavement strike the soles of her boots. Pats her watch pocket to be sure of her keys. She can drive well enough, she's been driving around the ranch from an age when she could barely see over the dash, but she can't get used to walking away from the truck in town, where keys can't just be left dangling from the ignition, and one of these days she's afraid she's going to forget.

The sign on the door at the top of the stairs reads John Perrine, Attorney at Law. Should she knock? Walk in? Walk in, she decides. Pats her watch pocket again.

The door opens on a large room, clean and fresh-painted and full of light from high windows on two sides that offer a foreshortened view of the street, the cab of Corey's truck, the tip of the flagpole over the liquor store, and a pigeon strutting across the next roof as if he owns it.

The woman sitting at the computer senses Corey's presence and swivels around. She's a large woman, probably as tall as Corey and much heavier, with small eyes and a snub nose in a large expanse of face. She speaks in a curious, stiff-lipped diction.

"Got'na pointment?"

"John said he'd see me," Corey mumbles. She's all hands and boots and hat in front of this woman who wears silver eye shadow and an embroidered denim dress that Corey guesses is woven on purpose to wrinkle and have to be ironed.

The woman rolls her eyes, flips some pages of a desk calendar, picks up her phone and speaks into it.

"Arright, go on in," she says, waving to the door behind her, and turns back to her computer screen.

As Corey walks past the window, the pigeon on the roof takes fright at something, abandons dignity, and disappears in a frantic purple flurry. She feels like flying after the pigeon. But she opens the door as John Perrine leaps, well, lumbers is a better word for what an overweight man can manage from the padded chair in which he's been tilting back with his boots on his desk. He disentangles his legs and advances on Corey with an outstretched hand and such beaming enthusiasm that she takes a step backward.

"Corey! Is it all right if I call you Corey? How've you been?"

"Okay."

The other two times she met him, she'd either been on horseback or on the seat of Saylor Lambert's wagon, looking down at him. Now he's looking down at her with his warm eyes and his soft handshake, and he's standing so close that her nostrils sting from what she supposes is not perfume but men's cologne.

Take a look at them fancy boots! Loren jeers. *Take a look at the goddamn city cowboy with his clean fingernails!*

She's been talking to the dead for so long that she has to remind herself not to answer Loren out loud, but at least John Perrine doesn't seem to notice that she's flustered.

"Here, sit down. Can I get you a cup of coffee? Cookies? Ingrid's got some Danish wafers out there. They melt in your mouth. Takes about six to make a mouthful. Sugar? Cream?"

Corey feels as if she's been pushed into the buttery leather of the couch, which sinks under her. She crosses her arms for protection. "Just coffee. Just black. Really."

John hurries out. Corey has time for a hasty look around his office. The hum of air conditioning, the restored white plaster walls, the tall clean windows. The sumptuous couch, the matching leather chairs, a coffee table of some dark polished wood. Diplomas framed on the wall behind the desk and a brushstroke print of *Riders of the Open Range* in an expensive gold frame.

Corey stands up to be sure of it. Yes, the same cowboys riding out of the river bottom at dawn, shivering, with their hands cupped to light cigarettes in the cold pink light. How many times had Loren gazed at that painting, and what had it absorbed of him?

How many prints of *Riders of the Open Range* are there in the world? Has to be thousands. This one can't possibly hold anything of Loren. He'd be too watered down. She imagines the painted riders casting thousands of shadows of Loren and every other old rancher who ever wanted to believe in horses and a cold dawn.

John Perrine is back, carrying a tray with a carafe and two transparent china cups and saucers.

"Sure you don't want sugar? Cream? I've got the real thing."

She puts her hand over her cup. "No. No cream."

Don't dah-de-dah fuss over me!

And yet here's John Perrine in his yoked gabardine jacket and his Western string tie with a moss agate slide fastener, fussing over her like an old aunt and pouring coffee into a cup decorated with violets. He pours coffee for himself and doses it with sugar and cream from a little pitcher, sets his cup carefully on its saucer, settles himself in one of his leather chairs, leans forward, and meets her eyes with an earnestness that brings the blood to her face. To hide her distraction, she sips her coffee. It isn't bad. Too strong, of course.

"I've come about the estate," she says. "It—well—what do I have to do?"

She wishes he would stop looking at her, but when she drops her eyes, she's focusing on his crotch, the way his Levi's strain at their inside seams and fray where they cross. God damn it. She isn't up to this.

"Is there a will?"

"Not that I can find."

"Hmmm."

There have to be other lawyers. Maybe she can find one who's about ninety years old. Or a woman. They have women lawyers now.

"Do you think there was ever a will?" he asks. "Did he ever talk about a will? Do you remember him seeing an attorney for any reason?"

"He never said, one way or another. But then, he didn't talk about his private business."

No, by God! I never was one to spill my guts, and neither are you! Just remember that!

John remembers his coffee. Corey wrings her eyes from following his hand as he reaches for his cup. A big hand with dark hairs creeping down from the cuff of his sleeve. Fingernails perfectly clean, of course.

"What about other family?"

"Just me," she hastens.

"And your mother died when? And your grandmother?"

She tells him the dates, and he jots some notes on a yellow pad.

"Even if it's intestate," he says, "it shouldn't be a problem. Do you know how much that ranch is worth?"

She shakes her head.

"How many acres?"

"Twelve hundred eighty."

He nods. "Of course it's mountain pasture. Timber? Probably logged in the thirties. Any logging since then? No cropland, is there? Hay-fields? He hadn't borrowed against it, had he?"

"Not—" she hesitates, thinking of the check to Saylor Lambert. "Not that I know of."

"Banked at Seafirst, didn't he? We'll find out." He jots more notes.

Corey clears her throat, forces herself to speak. "It's just—well, I've got less than six hundred and fifty in my pocket. It's got to last me until, well, until. And I've got Tim McClanahan to pay. And you."

"Don't worry. We'll draw up your letters testamentary this afternoon. And we'll see what we can do about opening his checking account for you. Did he have a safe-deposit box? Insurance?"

"I don't think so."

"Livestock?"

"We've got a few head of yearling steers to sell in the fall. And the horses."

He lays down his pen. "You haven't heard anything from Hailey Doggett, have you?"

"Hailey? No. Why would I hear from Hailey?"

"He's apparently made some statements, that he thinks he might have grounds for a lawsuit having to do with the, um, incident at the school."

Sue a beggar and get a louse, sneers Loren.

"How much do people stand to collect on suits like that?" she asks.

"It isn't going to happen. Like I say, we'll have your letters testamentary done by tomorrow, if you can stop by—or I can bring them out, it's on my way home, no trouble at all."

He's talking all the time she's backing out of his office, promising, reassuring, bearing down with all his warmth. She's concentrating on her feet, not to fall over them. Not to lift her eyes and meet his gaze.

"Will you be listing the ranch, Corey?"

Putting it up for sale is what he means. It's too much, she's about to overflow. She tears her hand from his. "I—don't know. I haven't thought about it."

The big woman glances up from her computer screen, starts to say something, but Corey flees.

Back in the street, in the sun, she's blinded for a moment. Too much brilliance. Where did she park? Right across the street, that's where. When her vision clears, she's standing under the awning that shades the window of Treasures, Etc., and makes a mirror of it, and she sees her own dark reflection like a filter over a display of expensive junk: a beat-up cowboy boot holding an arrangement of cattails, a dark red silk dress on a faceless mannequin, silver jewelry spread out on black velvet, and a galvanized washtub that someone has painted with an all-over floral design. Behind the washtub hangs a crosscut saw, painted with what she recognizes as the outline of the Snowy Mountains. Her mountains. Bright green pines, bright blue oil-painted sky, bright white clouds and snow-tipped ridges.

Next door is the real estate office. Its window holds color photographs of ranch property. Corey shades her eyes from the sun's glare and reads the copy under a picture of rapid water overhung by willows. Mountain acreage bordering Nat'l Forest with pine trees and a trout stream. Very desirable area for hiking and horseback riding over miles of trails. Winter activities include excellent snowmobiling and cross-country skiing. Close to airport with jet capacities. Subdivison an option. $465,000.

A price tag like that is probably the source of Hailey Doggett's thoughts on lawsuits.

She lingers on the sidewalk, letting her mind drift from Hailey to John Perrine. Finally walks up a block and crosses over to Main. Has to do something, doesn't she, to get her knees back to normal. Another bull rider, does she have no sense at all?

Much of Main Street has changed, what with the discount stores taking over the old locally owned establishments. Also the city park board has made a valiant attempt to offset the drabness of summer dust and drought by planting saplings along the sidewalks in little iron cages and decorating the lampposts with baskets of petunias. But there's the Bon Ton, still in business and looking hardly different from when Corey was in high school.

Ranch kids like Corey, who had to catch a bus right after school, hadn't been among the chatterers and gigglers, the girls who thronged into the Bon Ton after school to buy cherry Cokes at the soda fountain at the front of the store, or to eat ice cream and show off their pretty clothes. But Corey had looked in once or twice, must have, otherwise how would she know what went on behind that screen door? Now she sets her shoulders and crosses Main on the green light and pulls open the door.

Cool air and the smell of fruit and sugar and cream. The little wire tables and chairs, the milkshake machine (has to be an antique by now, and the wonder is that nobody's painting flowers or mountain scenery on it), the bowls of lemons and cherries and bananas, the glassware upside down on the shelves in front of the mirror behind the counter. No customers at this time of morning, no high school girls enlarging their mouths with lipstick and flirting with themselves in the mirror, no sign even of a waiter or clerk.

A woman in a gray smock glances out from a cubbyhole and returns to her paperwork, so preoccupied that Corey hates to disturb her. She won't order a lemonade, after all. Walks past the counter and into the dustier and less well-lit space at the rear of the store. Little change here, either. Display tables hold plaques engraved with sweet messages, cookie jars in strange shapes and colors, plates and vases with silver rims and 50th Wedding Anniversary in silver lettering, souvenir spoons of Montana, souvenir mugs, souvenir plates, knickknacks, figurines, and tiny crystal animals, all a little grimed from years of being passed over.

Farther back are racks of greeting cards. Post cards. Stationery. Office supplies. A few shelves of hardback books in shopworn jackets. Joke postcards featuring giant trout and jackalopes. Art supplies.

She glances over her shoulder. It's all right just to browse, surely. Just to price what they've got.

Last night she set all her old brushes in turpentine, but she'd wondered if they would ever soften. Now she sees that the prices for new sable-hair brushes are alarming. Eight or nine dollars even for the smallest ones—and the tubes of oil paint—everything costs so much. Even Grumbacher seems murderously expensive. She counts on her fingers, thinking what she can get by with.

Oh, the lovely names of paints. Chrome yellow. Vermilion. Cobalt. Umber, raw and burnt. A tube of ebony black. One of the big tubes of zinc white. Canvas boards, maybe—she looks at the price of the three-by-fours and winces.

She drops the canvas like a guilty thing at movement from the front of the store, but it's only a couple of customers—no, not even customers, two passersby on the street in front of the Bon Ton having an argument that is muted by the window, like a silent film through the shadow cast by the awning. Corey watches for a moment before she

realizes that the man with the tight dark curls is Hailey Dogge t, yelling at one of his daughters.

As Corey watches, the daughter—Ariel—tries to run, but Hailey
catches her by the shoulder. He's shouting at her, his face a contor-
tion, all the more violent in the silence imposed by the plate glass. But
maybe he can be heard at the front of the store, because the smocked
woman comes out of her cubbyhole and around the soda fountain to
see what's going on. Hailey wrenches Ariel by her wrist and spins her
until her hand opens and lets go a sheaf of bills that spiral up like pigeon feathers in frantic flight, then flutters down. Hailey looks around,
realizes he's got an audience, and hauls off Ariel, leaving the window
empty of all but the street.

The woman glances back and sees Corey. "What was that all about,
do you suppose?"

Corey shrugs. "He's her father."

"I suppose it's all right, then."

In the end, Corey decides to forego the canvas and instead buys
three new brushes and all the paint she needs. She has to talk herself through it. It's all right. Do it. Get that tube of cadmium if you
want it. Use both hands, carry it all up front. Sue a beggar and get a
tube of oil paint.

Nobody is at the cash register when Corey carries up her paints,
but then the bell jingles and the smocked woman enters through the
door from the street. She carries the greenbacks over to the counter
and lays them down.

"They were twenties!" she says, counting. "I think I found them all.
Nine, ten, eleven—my gosh. Two hundred and twenty dollars and
they threw it on the street!"

"Maybe he can afford to throw money away."

"Do you think so? I hated to go out and gather them up, like a scavenger, but they were just lying out there on the curb. Anybody could have taken them. I hope he'll come back for them. Will you tell him if you see him?"

"Sure," says Corey. It's a safe answer. She won't be seeing Hailey if she can help it.

The woman nods.

"We've had these brushes for I don't know how long," she says. "I can give them to you at half price."

"Wait," says Corey. She adds in her head. At half price, she can get more brushes. She hastens to the back of the store, agonizes over her selection. Pointed or blunt-tipped? Large or small? Maybe one of the big expensive bristle brushes? She snatches the big bristle brush and two medium-sized ones before she can change her mind and brings them back to the cash register.

Even with the discount, the amount the woman rings up is over a hundred dollars. Corey takes out her roll and counts it out. A fifth of her summer money.

"Hell with it," she says out loud, and the woman looks at her strangely. "He could buy the goddamn colt. I can buy paint."

Back on the street, walking the few blocks to where she parked the pickup, she thinks about *Riders of the Open Range* and the faces of all the old ranchers and wanna-be cowboys who have contemplated it, until anyone would think that their longing would surely have worn the colors off the canvas, or at least off the posterboard of the thousands and thousands of prints, and she visualizes the colors melting in such heat of desire, the faces of the cowboys elongating into flaccid cheeks and necks and chins, into the faces of old men.

And then. The end of desire. The heads resting on satin pillows. Rouged. Hardened into congealed wax.

Annie sees that the flag is down on her mailbox, so she walks out along the verge just as Hailey Doggett roars up the county road in his expensive white outfit—SUVs, her sons call them—slams on his brakes, and spins gravel to make the sharp turn into his own property. Why is he always in such a hurry? From the glimpse she got, Annie thinks he had one of his girls with him, and she hopes nobody is sick. She fans Hailey's dust out of her face and shuts her mailbox and notices Doc Mackenzie walking down his road that used to be her road. Likely he's seen the mail carrier's truck and the flags down, same as she has.

As she watches him puff along like an old walrus wearing his mustache out ahead of his face, Annie asks herself just what she thinks of Doc. Guesses he's friendly enough, but she dislikes the idea of anybody with enough money to come along and plunk it down on the ranch that should have stayed in her family, not that any of her boys wanted it, but still.

In the unhurried buzz of tiny insects, Doc wipes the sweat off his face. "Hot enough for you?" he asks, as Annie has known he would.

"Sure was stuffy last night," she agrees. "Don't know what I'd do without the window unit in my bedroom."

"I can usually get enough of a draft at night if I open the upstairs windows on both ends of the house and shut them again in the morning."

"Yes," she says, "it always did stay a little cooler, there where you built at the top of the draw."

She watches him think it over. Wonders what it feels like to see pine hills and aspens instead of sagebrush when he gets up in the morning and looks out. "Guess it gets pretty hot in the summers, over where you come from," she ventures.

"By God, yes! I'll tell you it gets hot over east. I used to drive those little roads on ranch calls—calving time, lambing time—and either it was so bejezus cold you'd freeze your ass off, thirty-forty below, or else you could look off across the alkali and watch the sun sizzle the mirages, just like it was real water."

Annie doesn't like his language. It may be customary in eastern Montana for men to say words like *ass* in front of a woman, but Annie doubts it. Annie's never been as far east as Plentywood, where Doc used to live, she's been no farther east than Billings, where Nails was hospitalized toward the end. For Annie, Billings is a cacophony of traffic, two and even three frightening lanes of cars and trucks on some of the streets, blatting their horns and stinking out their exhaust even around the hospital with its blue Quiet signs, until Annie had felt the noise and confusion following her down the hospital corridors that she hopes she'll never set foot in again.

Don't think about what you can't help. At least Annie's back in the foothills, if she is alone, and she blesses the constant chuckle of creek current as the loudest sound there is. The familiar gravel road, the chokecherry bushes hung with heavy fruit, like miniature clusters of green grapes that one day will darken to purple and then to black, and it will be time for Annie to pick chokecherries for jelly, if there's anybody left in the world who likes chokecherry jelly. Doc, now, he looks like a man who would enjoy hot biscuits and chokecherry jelly.

Doc grins at her. He reminds Annie of an overgrown pup. Next thing he'll be wagging his tail at her. There he stands, all ruddy-faced and genial, with big circles of sweat darkening his shirt under his armpits and sprouting around the line of his belly that overhangs his belt. A jiggle of a belly. Annie looks away.

"I been wondering," says Doc. "You don't know the name of that young fellow that's been hanging out over there?"

"Where, at Doggett's? I haven't seen any young fellow."

"Great big tall fellow—powerful built—rides a Harley?"

"The fellow on the motorcycle," Annie remembers. A stranger to her. Thinks again how it must be for Doc, being a stranger. She doesn't know what force in the world would make her move away from home even if home were that blasted prairie country over in eastern Montana which she's never seen but supposes to resemble the landscape around Billings, rimrocks and shortgrass and scorched sagebrush with stunted jackpine the only cover for miles.

"Hey," says Doc, grinning hugely. "Want to see my belt buckle?"

To Annie's fascinated horror he lifts his belly off his belt buckle so she can see it. It's a big square brass-toned buckle with the outline of a seated girl with bunny ears that Annie's seen previously only on the mudflaps of trucks.

"Oh!" she gasps, shocked, and Doc drops his belly and laughs and laughs and laughs.

Rita Doggett also tries not to think about what she can't help, and apparently she can't help Ariel. Ariel won't talk to Rita, won't talk to Hailey, and treats Eugene as though he's contaminated with a substance only she perceives. This morning she screamed something vile at him, then screamed fuck yourself Daddy at Hailey when he told her to apologize. Flung herself out of the house in the direction of town, followed by Hailey, who dragged her home an hour or two later. Her loud sobbing gradually subsided into silence after Hailey locked her in her room.

She'd got a ride into town with that Staple kid, Hailey had said. When they caught on it was me following them, they stopped on Main Street, but they were heading for the bus depot.

Oh Hailey.

That kid shows up around here again, I'm taking a shot at him.

Hailey you can't mean that!

I do.

Think of something pleasant. Rita gathers magazines and a pillow and a rug, lets herself out of her bedroom through the sliding doors. Crosses the sun-heated flagstone terrace, steps over the eight-inch box hedge, and trudges with her bundle across the twenty yards of close-mown grass to a tiny trail leading down through the underbrush to a secret bank of white clover where benign willows droop their long yellow trailers and narrow leaves over the creek. Rita drops her bundle, spreads her rug and pillow where sun and shade move gently with the stir of air. She's safe here, sheltered by these soft leaves and lulled by the sound of the current. She'll read and nap, probably. She's been napping a lot.

Ariel is thirteen. Surely she'll grow out of her tantrums, and she and Rita will be each other's best friends. Rita will get through this summer, and in the fall she'll look for work, apply perhaps at the school where Val Tendenning works as a teachers' aide, put her degree to good use. Surely Eugene will be gone by then, and also Albert, the gofer, as Eugene calls him, and Hailey will have gotten his home-schooling bee out of his bonnet, so the girls can go to school in town. Rita drifts. Sees herself driving Ariel and Rose down out of the foothills on crisp mornings. All three of them singing rounds in the car. Parking back of the school, the girls tearing off to meet their friends, herself in professional suit and pumps heading for the school counselor's office. Her own office. Pretty curtains, comfortable chairs, snapshots of Hailey and the girls on her bulletin board.

For now she'll dream.

Rita startles awake. Gunfire. Yes. No, firecrackers. Another long string explodes, snap-snap-rattle bang. That awful Staple boy bought the firecrackers at the stand outside of town, and all day he and Amy and Rose have been setting them off along the creek. And why a boy that age would be spending all that time with children so much younger— horrified, remembering, Rita sits upright. *If I see him around here again, I'll take a shot at him*—but oh, surely not! Hailey had spoken in anger, understandably angry, he hadn't meant it. She had been angry herself.

Another burst of firecrackers followed by gunfire from farther away, like a parody. Rita's just going to have to get used to the racket. She's seen where the men have set up a row of empty wine bottles for targets, against the hillside behind the house, and she's watched them pulling on their shooting muffs to take turns with Hailey's rifle flopping on their stomachs to fire and then, as they become more accustomed to the action and the explosions, firing from a sitting and then a standing position. Eugene and Hailey are as bad as kids about it. They laugh and give each other grief about what bad shots they are. Those games guys play with guns that fire paint bullets? If it was us we'd have that hillside painted red.

Why, she had pleaded, why all this noise?

Have to know how to protect ourselves, don't we?

We're going to need more firepower, said Eugene, and started talking about on-line sources for weaponry.

Albert is the only one who is at all a good shot. Rita stifles the disloyal thought that, if it came to shooting Bobby Staple, Hailey would have to get Albert to do it for him.

Like an ungainly fledgling, Ariel hunkers on the edge of her windowsill with her toes curled for balance as she watches her mother out of sight. The willows along the creek trail shake briefly at her mother's passing and then are stilled, the lawn as empty as a baby's game: Whe-e-rre's Rita? A-l-lll gone!

Probably went to take a nap by the creek. The woman's been napping a lot, lately.

Ariel waits. The lawn waits. Nothing trembles in the midday heat, not a grass blade, not an aspen leaf. The grass is as green and even and perfectly groomed as broadloom. No deer takes nervous steps out of timber onto that grass, not with all the gunfire. Probably the deer are hiding in the brush until sundown, trying to sleep through the racket. Ariel has seen their empty, crushed nests, and now she imagines fitting herself into one of those warm imprints, wishes herself reborn with a spotted pelt and sharp little hooves. But first she must slide down from the windowsill and run across that exposed space, and meanwhile firecrackers explode along the creek while gunfire answers from the hillside. Ariel tries to count the shots. Are three men shooting at the target, or only two? No way of knowing. She's got to run for it. She's done it before, she can do it once more.

With her bundle slung over her shoulder, she jumps from the windowsill and lands on her feet with a slight dip of her knees to absorb the shock. The grass is just as slippery as she feared. It sticks to the soles of her feet, squishes and drags until she feels as though she's running in a dream, making no headway. Her shoulder blades itch with anticipation of a bullet, which is stupid, because of course they wouldn't shoot at her, they'd just catch her and drag her back. Her lungs burn, because Ariel is no sprinter. But she's a stayer, and she runs, runs, her bundle bumping on her back, until she falls gasping against her father's ornamental rail fence and rolls under it.

Hailey, as she's been teaching herself to think of him. *Hailey's* been talking about installing chain link, twelve feet high, all around the property. But he hasn't done it yet.

In the safety of the aspens she allows herself a minute to get back her breath and strength in her limp legs. *Wet spaghetti legs*, she excoriates herself, *you puss, you wuss,* although she knows it's fear that has drained her. What he'll do to her if he catches her this time—

There's going to be a couple of wood screws keeping that window closed, he had warned as he flung her through the door to her room, and he actually had started off to get screws and his drill. All that had saved her was Albert the Giant, showing up at that opportune time. Ariel couldn't make out the Giant's gruff mumble, but whatever he had to say must have distracted Hailey, because he'd gone off with the Giant and—fingers crossed—forgotten about wood screws and Ariel herself for the time being.

Now the warm light dapples down on her. She listens to the buzz of tiny insects in the overripe grass, she's lulled by the reassurance of time crawling along as it always has. She's still Ariel, in spite of what's been done to her. Closes her mind to what's been done to her. Gives herself one more minute to rest with her head on her bundle, which contains, besides the blanket, socks and an extra pair of underpants, her own pillow, a plastic bag of trail mix and candy bars stolen for her by Rose from her mother's stockpile, a paperback copy of *Just So Stories* stolen by Ariel herself from the shelves of the Mill Creek school, and a small green jade frog on a chain, which she'd dug out of a box marked for the Goodwill after Hailey's blitz through the house in Santa Monica.

Yard sale! Yard sale! That's all it's good for! Piss on it all! We'll have everything new!

Thinking back, Ariel realizes she must have forgotten some essential bit of information during those last days in Santa Monica when everything familiar seemed to explode into fragments. Try as she might, she can't resurrect the one fragment she needs.

Uncle Eugene. Hailey and Rita had whispered and worried over the girls' heads, but Ariel had known he might be going to prison.

She didn't care, he was just an old turtle who was forever crawling in and out of Hailey's study, peering into one of the computer screens and pecking away at the keyboard. It was easy enough in those days to stay out of his reach.

Then he did go to prison.

Will he testify, Rita worried.

He didn't talk to the grand jury, and he won't talk now.

But the money.

The money's ours.

Fragments that she can't connect. Overheard words. Indictment. Hailey, you're not, you won't be indicted? Hell no, not if we get out of here in time. We'll get rid of everything! Have everything new! Bits of Ariel's life scattered and lost. Her hand slides into her bundle, closes around the jade frog.

Well, she's always known she might have to fall back on Plan B, and this is Plan B. At the thought of Plan A, she blinks and swallows. She'd come so close! Then her father's grip on her wrist, his sharp twist, and Bobby Staple's lovely twenties sailing out of her grasp. The memory of that loss quickens her, and she sits up in the grass with buckbrush dragging at strands of her hair and opens her eyes on Albert the Giant.

Against the dazzle of sunspots, he looks like a young tree with his long legs planted apart and his arms folded and his stubbled head up there somewhere in the green dapple where gold shafts fall like destruction upon Ariel. Possibilities tumble through her head even as she berates herself, oh, why didn't she make sure all three men were taking target practice, why didn't she ask Rose to stand sentinel, and if worse comes to worst, should she offer her poor bod to the Giant?

No. Running is her best option. She'll leave her bundle if she has to. Can she, will she—in her mind she feels thorns tearing at her clothes, at her face and arms, as she scrambles along animal trails too tiny for the Giant to follow her—she'll evade his fingertips, run like the wind—surreptitiously she searches for such a trail through the haw-thorns and sees none.

Albert is watching her eyes, he's reading her mind.

But all he says is, "Hey, little girl!" and steps out of her way.

9

The prairie northwest of Fort Maginnis was homesteaded ninety years ago but retains few traces of that failed venture. An abandoned shack or two, weathering to gray splinters in the distance, and the ghost town of Yeager, well, almost a ghost town, nothing left of Yeager but a grain elevator on the horizon and what used to be the community hall, a long low building with white siding that looks pretty good from a distance. Corey can remember when there was a school at Yeager, and a general store. She can still see the foundations from the highway.

Most of the homesteaders dried out and moved away in the 1920s. Those few farmers who managed to hang on through the drought years and the depression grow wheat on thousands of acres and can count themselves wealthy, in land at least. They cash in on the tourists as best they can, leasing their fields for upland bird-hunting. There's not much evidence of new development out here in the sun and wind, though. Corey guesses that rich transplant people don't find these open stretches as scenic as the foothills.

The highway loops through the wheat country, circles the base of a flat-topped butte, and then drops into the irrigated bottom land along the Judith River. Corey had put the stockrack on the pickup this morning, and it rattles as she leaves the blacktop and turns on the gravel road at a careful thirty miles an hour with the river on her left and hayfields on her right. She has to decide between rolling up her window or leaving it down and breathing, along with the dust, the midsummer odors of sweet clover and irrigation water and freshly mowed second-crop hay. She leaves it down. Supposes her face will be grimy by the time she gets to Saylor Lambert's, but the hell with it.

Anyway, she feels surer of herself driving on gravel. Mirages dance and recede in the road ahead, while the greens and yellows and umbers in the borrow pits liquefy behind her in streams. On the bare bluffs across the river the sun catches sparkles, like diamonds, that she knows would turn out to be quartz deposits looking like shards of dirty glass if she were to climb after them. Painting them would be something else again. She can feel her new oil paints, dark in their sack on the seat beside her, stirring to be opened and used.

As the valley widens, she can see the railroad trestle between the old Eberle post office and the Yeager cut-off. The road takes her under the legs of the trestle with its smell of ancient black creosote, then up-river for another three miles before the shingled roof of Saylor's barn shows through the tops of the cottonwood trees where Willow Creek flows into the river.

Saylor Lambert is even older than Loren. He's lived forever down here on the river, raising grass hay and horses and running several hundred head of cattle. He's been a county commissioner, been on the fair board, respected and looked up to. The years are getting the better of him, though. Somewhere Corey has heard that Saylor has sold off most of his cattle. Kept his horses, of course.

She crosses Willow Creek on a rattling plank bridge and finds herself in Saylor's kingdom. The huge log barn with its pens and pole corrals, the horse trough made from a single hollowed log where water trickles and runs down to the creek. The cabin below the barn where Whitey Phipps probably still lives. Shop and tool shed and machine shed and garage, all kept as trim as a dude ranch, but with a sober purpose, self-contained and ordered. Time was when it was even more self-contained, when Saylor had kept his own store out here, for his hands.

Well back from the working operations is the filigreed white house on its acre of lawn. Although the house doesn't look all that well kept up. Shingles missing, the roof of the veranda sagging. A crumbling cement sidewalk leads through a double row of dead stems that once were Mrs. Lambert's peonies.

The only other time Corey has been down here was at a branding, with Loren. She'd thought it was going to be a party, and she'd dressed in her school clothes, blue blouse and flowered blue skirt. Loren had taken one look and sent her back upstairs to change into her Levi's and boots. What did she think a branding was, he had demanded. Work to do!

Mrs. Lambert had seen them pull up in the truck. She came across the lawn in her jersey dress and lace-up shoes, and Loren instantly removed his Stetson.

You've brought your daughter! Mrs. Lambert spoke in a back-east accent everybody made fun of. She had been a second and much younger wife, and she had brought the money to the marriage. She leaned in the window to smile at Corey, who realized that her Levi's had been dirty when she changed back into them and were going to get dirtier.

We'll just drive down to the corrals and find Saylor, Loren had said, and put the truck in gear.

This afternoon a figure moves behind a screen door leading out to a veranda, a youngish woman looking to see who has driven up. The daughter. Corey talked to her on the phone this morning. She remembers her name. Kim Walter. Kim had married a man by the name of Walter, who had a degree in engineering something-or-other, and Kim had moved out to California with him, but now she's back in Montana, and she's coming down the veranda steps. A fair-skinned woman in her thirties, wearing shorts. Corey remembers the talk when she was born, about how old Saylor was, the old bugger. Saylor spoiled Kim, Loren always said, and of course he'd had the money to spoil her with.

"I bet you're Corey," Kim calls. "I bet you came to get the colt."

"Is Saylor around?"

"He's down at the barns with the boys. Gosh! He'll be glad to see you. He feels so bad about your dad."

Corey nods and lets out the clutch.

Loren, your little girl don't have to hang around the corrals. We got plenty of help, Saylor had called long ago, tramping up from the icehouse with ampoules of vaccine.

She came to work, said Loren.

Ah, let her go back to the house.

Get your rope, Loren told Corey, and she slid down from the cab and got her rope out of the back and followed him to the branding corral, where a pitch fire burned hot and fragrant, and branding irons heated, and vaccine guns were laid out on a log, and calves stared out through the corral poles, wall-eyed and bewildered and splashed with sloppy green manure.

Now grass and pigweed grow in Saylor's branding corral, and the pens stand vacant, but the round horse corral looks well-kept. Perched on the top pole are two boys with slumped backs and backwards caps. Corey recognizes the older one as the acned driver she took the reins away from the day of the runaway. The California grandsons, watching as Saylor lunges a colt.

Forty years ago Saylor seemed old to Corey, and now she thinks he looks transparent, almost as though she can see through the bones of his legs to the bare corral dirt where the glare of the sun casts the sharp shadow of a stick man. He looks over his shoulder and sees her and lets the colt slow to a walk. The colt turns and points his ears at the stranger, and Saylor instantly doffs his Stetson to her, reminding her of Loren, of all the lost manners. There are those two lumps of boys, looking like their caps have grown on their heads, and here's Saylor with his thin white hair and the damp line of sweat across his forehead where his hat had been. His cane under his other arm.

His sunken hawk's face glistens, and he mops at his narrow chin with his shirtsleeve. "So you found your way down here at last!"

"I remembered the road, once I got on gravel."

"These are Kim's boys. Travis Walter. Scott Walter."

The boys glare down at her. They aren't out here in the dust and sun because they want to be.

Corey ducks through the corral poles to look at the colt. He's a long yearling, a rangy dark bay with a straight back. When she holds out her hand, he touches it with his nose, interested and unafraid.

"He's got decent legs under him," says Saylor. Saylor might have married money, but that doesn't mean he's going to waste his words or exaggerate.

Yes, the colt is a good colt. A seventy-five-hundred-dollar colt. He nuzzles her wrist, blows out rollers at her scent. It raises the hairs along her forearm. She feels the tingle. A stud colt, another damned male in the controlled arrogance in the arch of his neck, the closed penis sheath, the dark balls like precious stones between his legs. What the hell is she going to do with him.

Suddenly, the colt shies.

Saylor turns on his grandsons. "What the hell have I been telling you two? Don't you ever listen? You got no more notion how to behave around a good thoroughbred colt than a couple of stray dogs."

The boys are grinning secretly at each other.

"Get down off that fence! You look like a pair of damned dudes!"

"*Dudes!*" laughs the older boy, and the younger boy chimes in, giggling, "Grampaw's cool, *dude!*" They take their time climbing down, in no hurry to mind Saylor, and run skirting off toward the house.

"Raised in town. They don't know a goddamn thing," he mutters. He has suffused a rose-brick color.

"They probably know a lot we don't," Corey says, thinking of the kids she has taught in the last ten years, Doggetts and others.

"That's the truth. But what they know ain't worth a damn."

He puts his hat back on his head. "Kim brought her microwave with her. Couldn't get along without it. Those boys of hers wouldn't know how to rustle up a wood fire or boil themselves coffee. They don't think their grandfather ever worked for what he's got, and they don't know how to work, but the time's coming when they'll wish they did."

They are the most words she has ever heard him speak.

He's looking at his empty pens, his barn. "Do you want to know how long all this is going to last?"

"How long?"

"About as long as a man can by God hold a rifle before he gets shot down, is how long, because there's a day a-coming."

She has heard that Saylor has gotten a little strange in his opinions, doesn't know how to reply. Hates to ask straight out about a bill of sale for the colt, but doesn't want to keep Saylor standing out here in the bare corral, in the heat of the sun, flushed as he is. Finally she says, "Hope my dad took care of the paperwork," and adds, "hope his check cleared?"

"Loren Henry's check? Wouldn't have expected anything less from Loren Henry. Not that it mattered a helluva lot. Drop in the goddamn bucket."

He is glaring after his grandsons. "I was counting on those boys. And now Kim wants me to take her and them for a ride on that goddamn Freedom Train they got running now. You know about that? The train that fat attorney rides down and robs? That's an attorney for you, all right. Robbing trains when they're not robbing everybody else."

"I hear they'll give you a good dinner on the train," says Corey. "And a good show."

He spits into the corral dirt. "Show is all those boys know."

Corey brings her truck around and backs it up to Saylor's custom loading chute, green-painted metal. No peeled-log ramp for Saylor, and no stockrack on the back of a pickup, either. His expensive red-and-white goose-necked horse trailer is parked in the weeds below the corral. He watches her, slit-eyed and angry, as she ties her rope in a bowline knot to the colt's halter and leads him up the chute. The stockrack will hold him just fine. He's a beautiful colt. She will feed him for the rest of the summer, and then what.

"I hear you're thinking of selling," says Saylor.

"Thinking about it."

"There's other ways to go. And don't pay any attention to Doggett. If you want to go the other way, you come and talk to me about it."

On her way back down the river road, she sees Saylor's Hanoverians grazing under the cottonwoods, at least he's hung on to his Hanoverians. What else he might be planning, she doesn't want to think. He must be ninety, after all. His wild talk is probably the reason Kim has come home for the summer.

Whatever he meant about Hailey Doggett. Corey shakes her head. Maybe it's just her, but it does seem like Hailey's name turns up everywhere.

In the late afternoon she unloads the bay colt and turns him into Baldy's old pasture and watches him take a few hesitant steps into his new and solitary confinement. Babe suddenly notices him from her side of the pasture fence. Her head shoots up. She comes at a hard trot to the fence between them and sends a ringing nicker over it, and the colt nickers back.

"Yeah, fall in love with each other," Corey growls. She hopes Babe isn't coming into heat. That'll be the next thing she has to worry about.

She needs to put a block of salt out for the colt. But at least the grass in the stud pasture has had a chance to grow. Loren had gotten to the point where he didn't notice that Baldy often grazed it down until only the thistles stood and Corey had to toss him hay, night and morning. Now she wonders if Loren had sunk so deep into the past that even the grass stood still for him.

She wonders what the colt's name is. Saylor had said he'd given Loren the bill of sale and registration papers, and Loren apparently stuck them somewhere she hasn't yet looked.

The heat of the day has weighed on the gulch. The birds are staying in the shade, the deer hiding in high timber, while gnats rise like a fine mesh over the tall grass along the creek and the hawthorns sag under the dust on their leaves. Even the ridge pines have silenced themselves, for once. Over their ominous dark tips the sky burns a metallic blue, and Corey thinks the weather might be going to break. It's hot enough for hail.

At least the house is comfortable. She can thank these thick sandstone walls that will hold the cool air until well into August, when a few nights will stay hot, even here in the foothills, and it will be time to unroll quilts under the firs and sleep with their shadows between her and the stars. She sets down her sack of art supplies on the kitchen table along with her glass and plate, egg yolk stains and toast crumbs from breakfast that she hadn't washed before she left this morning.

Another long, long day. And what has she accomplished, but to follow in Loren's footsteps, trying to track down his dealings. Maybe she really is getting old.

Something about the kitchen doesn't feel right. Too quiet. And yet nothing has changed that she can see. Walls. Sink. The refrigerator and its hum. She looks into the front room to make sure Sonny has water in his bowl, and the old dog thumps his tail at her but otherwise doesn't move.

A chair pulled out from the table? A cupboard door left ajar? She can't remember just how she left things.

That girl walks around with her head in the clouds! Can't remember what she had for breakfast, now that they've sent her to Minneapolis to make an absent-minded professor out of her! An educated fool!

Since his funeral, it's been Loren's voice she mostly has been hearing, as though death has freed him to fire at her all the accusations he had not deigned to speak to her in life.

Some things you ought to know without being told! What that lawyer's got on his mind, for one. You think he doesn't have his eye on his fee? Did you ask him what his percentage is going to be for selling my ranch?

She pushes herself out of her chair, one hand to her back. It's too hot for coffee, too early to start on whiskey. She goes to the refrigerator and opens it, starts to reach for a beer. Sees the empty space where she'd put the six-pack.

In the cool of the evening she climbs the hill between the pasture fence and the house. The lower chicken house has fallen into a heap of logs that Loren talked of setting on fire one of these days, getting rid of the goddamn eyesore, but Corey can remember her grandmother keeping hens in the upper chicken house, which still stands more or less upright under its shingled roof. Its door has long ago parted from the doorframe, and its hinges have lost their screws, but the old boards have

sunk themselves in black soil and pigweed until they stand by themselves like sentries with nothing to guard but vacant laying nests and
fallen roosts. Corey bends double to peer around them and sees that
the floor has built up, over the years, from chicken dust and chicken
droppings, until it's within three feet of the roof.

If Annie Reisenaur is right, a family lived within these walls for
a few years. Loren and his mother and father. It hardly seems possible, but Corey notes that its boards still retain a trace of blue paint.
At one time a half-loft was built across one end of the room, where a
boy might have slept, and a square piece of tin once accommodated
a stovepipe.

No wonder her grandmother always thought the stone house was
a fine one.

What Corey's really hiked up here for is the old drill that Loren,
instead of selling in town for the price of scrap iron, had dragged out
here and left to rust. Grass and thistles have grown over its wheels
and tongue, bindweed flourishes over it, until its iron seat is all that
rides above a sea of waist-high verdure. The seat is what Corey wants.
Holding her arms above the stickers, she crushes herself a trail from
the chicken house to the drill, walks up the tongue, and goes to work
with her wrench on the bolts that hold the seat to its spring. The rust
scales off on her hands, reddening them to the wrists until, by the
time she's worked out the bolts, she looks like she's been butchering
something.

As she straightens, her eyes catch the movement at the edge of the
pasture, fifty yards away. Two does and their fawns, slipping out of
the pines for their evening grazing, watching her and lifting nervous
hooves at the clang of the iron wrench on iron as she frees the seat.

She and the does, neighbors all their lives, her world and theirs
as separate and silent as bubbles—except, of course, these aren't the
same does, they only look the same. They would be, let's see, how

many years in the generation of a whitetail deer—five, say—say she saw her first deer at age three—eleven generations. These does are the great-granddaughters to the eighth power of the first deer she ever saw, their lifespans intensified into a few summers and winters. Deer never die of old age. Starvation, maybe. Gunshots. She doesn't suppose the grass stands still, even for deer.

On impulse, carrying the drill seat, she follows a tiny trail, hardly a trail at all, just a gentle dividing of the grasses by rabbits, perhaps, which she with her clumsier feet is trampling wider. The does whistle and vanish, but the trail leads her higher on the hill, through third-growth trash pines and aspens that smother the pasture grass, toward the fence, where one huge old pine tree clings by its roots to the shale and holds up three strands of barbed wire in place of a post.

Corey props the drill seat against a sandstone ledge and ducks under the barbed wire. Nailed to the pine tree on the side away from the stone house are chunks of scrap lumber that she used for hand-holds and footholds when she was what, ten years old, maybe eleven. She remembers using her bare feet (her boots weren't much good for climbing), the rough bark, the sticky ooze and smell of turpentine, and how the pine needles had screened her from the upstairs windows of the house, which, from where she now stands, looks foreshortened and remote. Not a point of view she's familiar with any more, although at age ten she'd nailed those boards into the divide of limbs where she could crouch and spy on her grandmother feeding her chickens, yes, watch from one dimension into another and imagine how it must be for the deer. And yes, there's her board roost, still in place above her head.

Something's been gnawing on the bark. Porcupine, probably.

She looks back down at the house, and it seems like somebody else's house with just the tops of its upstairs windows and its roof showing above the firs. Above her, the old milk-cow trail follows the fence farther up the hill until it is crowded out of sight by a new growth of pine seedlings and a density of chokecherries bending with unripe clusters of fruit. Something white shows through the chokecherries.

Too white.

Corey follows the trail until the seedlings brush her waist with their needles, and the chokecherry twigs reach for her hair, and she feels gooseflesh rising. Something is holding her back, something doesn't want her following this trail any farther. Then, at the level of her knees, she sees the fresh knife gouges where a kind of tunnel recently has been carved through the chokecherries. Severed branches caught in the grass and barbed wire, berries shriveled and leaves already turning brittle from the heat. Corey bends double to see down the green tunnel. Gets down on her hands and knees. Pine needles and hard-baked dirt clods dig into her palms, but she crawls farther, heart pounding, as the tunnel leads into a pile of deadfall that has been hollowed, like a cave, where cracks and slants of daylight fall through the dead pine limbs upon someone's hidden bivouac. Blanket, pillow, flashlight. Candy wrappers and a white Styrofoam cooler.

The white cooler is what she had seen. She lifts a corner of the lid.

Beer in the cooler.

She's trespassing here—no she isn't—*yes she is!* Corey backs out of the cave on her hands and knees, knowing that branches are catching and tearing her shirt, ripping bloody lines on her face and arms, but she's too panicked to feel pain. Once out of the chokecherries, she stands, listens to her pulse. Sees the stone house below her, the fir trees and the fence. Babe and the new colt, ears pointing up the hill toward her, wondering what she's doing.

Somewhere she's dropped the drill seat.

Back at the house, in the dusk, she pulls down all the window shades on the south side of the house before she turns on any lights. The shades resist her, curling and cracking at their edges and showing signs of wanting to rattle back up and wrap around their rollers. With the windows finally covered, the rooms look unfamiliar, dark and closed-in. Still Corey prowls, upstairs and down, peering around the shades to watch the hillside for any flash of light from the watcher.

Well. She can't wait all night.

After a twenty-minute search she'd finally found her drill seat by stepping on it where she'd left it under the boulder, in the stubby wild roses along the fence. She had carried it back to the house and propped it on the kitchen table. Now she studies it by the harsh light of the bare ceiling bulb. The weathering on the drill seat, she supposes, is part of its salability, its *authenticity,* but the dirt and scabs of rust will never hold paint, so she has scoured them off with steel wool that left bright patches across the dull iron. She'll have to plan her design to cover the patches.

The drill seat looks like a saddle whose cantle spreads into a flanged edge to accommodate somebody's butt and whose pommel rises in a metal prow to separate the somebody's legs and, she guesses, slap his balls against—an uncalled-for flash, like a splice of ancient film, and why, when she's never seen them, Loren's balls hanging in slack old skin that still sprouts a few white hairs—she shudders.

A dozen round holes in the bottom of the iron seat would have aerated the driver's hind end through long hot days of drilling seed. The picture takes motion in her head, time reversed. The seat bolted back on the drill. The drill pulled across the harrowed field by six steaming horses. Lather rising on massive hindquarters as hooves dig into the soft ground. Sweat dripping from the driver's armpits and groin and oozing down the sides of his shirt and through his pants. Corey feels the scalding iron seat, the imprint of the holes, the slap of the rusty prow against her own crotch.

Of course women can't paint, said what's-his-name, the oils instructor. It was the same thing Andreas was forever telling her. Women can't paint because they don't have balls. Although sometimes, the instructor had added, kindly, women can create these little jeweled pieces—lots of detail—women are good at detail. Corey wonders if they're still telling that to girls in art school.

Her old pinched and tortured tubes of oil paint wait in their shoebox lid beside her new and unblemished tubes from the Bon Ton. Her old brushes, cleaned but stiffened, wait in their fruit jar. She shakes her new brushes out of the paper sack, sets them in the fruit jar with the old ones.

Paint what, is the question.

Daisies, maybe.

It would be easy to paint daisies. A sphincter of sharp white petals around each of the round holes. A scatter of sharp green leaves to hide where she's scoured the iron. Once the paint dries, she could make yellow pom-poms out of her grandmother's yellow yarn, fluff the pom-poms and stick them through the holes as centers for the daisies.

Somebody's going to want to buy an old drill seat painted with daisies to hang on the wall?

It seems like such a damn-fool thing for anybody to do, even in a world turned to damn-foolery, that she can't bring herself to reach for a brush or the tube of zinc white. Because she can just see it. The six horses straining to pull the drill through the soft earth and the driver—Loren?—riding high on his iron seat of painted white daisies with fluffy yellow centers.

The more she thinks about it, the more she has to laugh. Loren, scandalized at having to ride on a drill seat painted with daisies and fluffed with yellow yarn!

What, then.

She stares at the round holes, and the holes stare back at her, like eyes full of absence. Or full of light. Depending on which way they're looking. Because they can look both ways, inward and out.

Horses' eyes, full of light, between one dimension and another. Eyes strangely placed and contorted because of the pattern of the holes and the containment of the iron flange around the seat, but horses' heads and horses' eyes, yes, and why not. It isn't as though anybody's really going to buy the goddamn thing, that's more than she can believe, even in a world of fools, and so she reaches for the new tube of raw umber, and then the rose madder and the crimson lake and the vermilion, and squeezes dollops around the rim of one of her grandmother's dinner plates.

Darkness eventually falls on the other side of the cracked window shades, but she's too absorbed to notice.

Much later, stiff-necked and exhausted, she lays down her brushes and wanders out into the cool of the evening. Stars waver in the deepening blue, shadows overcome the chokecherries. Birds will be sleeping in those densities of leaves. The world is not what it is by day. Halfway down the road to the springhouse, Corey turns and looks back at the stone house in its phalanx of firs. In the dusk it looks to her like an illustration of a fortress in a fifth-grade history book, its windows as narrow and unrevealing as arrow slits. What could a watcher be watching for, what could a watcher hope to see?

In their pasture, Babe and the colt are dark fragrant shapes, sleeping on their feet. Ahead of her the barn looms, another last bastion with solid sandstone walls that hold the warmth of the late-dying day. Corey thinks of its haymow and mangers, thinks of taking dusty dark shelter where a watcher would never find her among the junk stored there, odd spurs and canning jars and stiffened leather harness hanging on pegs, but instead lets herself through the pole gate and finds her feet taking her down the county road. Where are you going, feet? Where did you come from, where you gonna go? What you gonna do there, Cotton-eye Joe?

She jumps, pure atavistic panic at sudden movement, a dark living thing scuttling across the road in front of her, humpety-humping for the safety of the underbrush. Listens to her heart beating, remembers the stories some of the children told at school of seeing cougar tracks or bear tracks in their backyards, the big wild predators coming back down from the mountains to reclaim their old territory. This was just a porcupine. That's all. More scared of her, probably, than she'd been scared by it.

The road lies open ahead of her, bleached white gravel in contrast to the shadows. Corey hesitates. What next? Ghosts? Souls on the move. There went a bat, swooping past the power lines over the old hayfield. What's the matter with her, letting her imagination run away with her? Her fingertips feel raw, her eyes sore with strain, all her nerve ends out on stalks. Was that gunfire?

It is gunfire. A large bore rifle booms from the other side of the gulch. Somebody on Hailey Doggett's property is firing off rounds— three, four, five, six, then a pause as the echo rings back and forth between the ridges. Somebody's reloading.

Then boom-keeracka, boom-keeracka, boom-keeracka, boom, boom, boom, six more rounds. Target practice? So late in the evening, so nearly dark?

She freezes. Holds her breath, hopes she's hidden in the shadows of the pines that lean over the fence corner. A man stands in the road, looking in her direction. Corey cannot see his face, but the lines of his body are tense with interrupted motion. He'd been crossing the road at a fast walk when something—was it Corey?—caught his attention.

Boom-keeracka, boom-keeracka, boom, boom, boom, boom. Another set of rounds fired at what must be a target, another ringing and fading of echoes, and still the man waits and watches. He's a big man, big shoulders, legs like trees. Holding something to his ear, listening. A cell phone?

Anger rises in her gorge. It's still Henry property, after all. She's got the right to walk this road, any time of day or night.

She's got the right, but he's got the might!

"Shut up," she tells Andreas, automatically, but in a whisper. Or was it Virgil taunting her. She must have looked away, must have taken her eyes off the stranger for a fraction of a second, because when she looks again, the road is empty.

She walks backward, keeping to the shadows and watching, until she comes to the pole gate and the familiar bulk of the stone barn. Scent of pine needles, scent of horses. Babe and the colt still warm and sleeping on their opposite sides of the pasture fence. Tells herself she goddamn well won't be afraid to walk between the barn and the house. Squares her shoulders and counts her steps. Past the root cellar, past the springhouse, up to the picket fence.

The firs hold the shelter of complete darkness. Corey feels her way finds herself in the kitchen, decides not to turn on a light. Pours a whiskey by touch, carries it to the window. Nothing to see but the night.

So who the hell was he. The stranger, maybe, that Annie has been worrying about. And doing what, damn him to hell.

Keeping surveillance from the hillside? Worse, been in her house, taken a look around, taken her beer?

In solid darkness, she finishes her whiskey.

10

The wild woods, even an abased, logged-over, homesteaded, sold and resold, overgrazed, damaged, and neglected wild woods like that which remains on the foothills surrounding the Henry Gulch, is a different place at night than it is during the day. Does the tree make a sound if it falls in the forest when no one is there to hear it, etc.? The horses, intermediaries between one world and another, sleep on their feet, startle awake at faraway sounds, drifting odors. The deer leave their beds and slip out to browse in the borderlands between overgrown fields and the still cultivated. Appropriately for night prowlers, deer do not perceive color but see the stone house and barn and corrals in the sharpened shadows and highlights of an old film. The porcupine that startled Corey, on the other hand, has dim eyesight and hardly any brain. It's an evolutionary slowpoke that rustles along inside its bristle of armor. What mind it's got is on its own business, which is food. Because a slap of its tail can embed a dozen or so quills in the muzzle of a curious bobcat or inexperienced coyote pup and send it off, whining, to fester and starve, the porcupine fears very little. The scratch of claws as it climbs its tree and crawls out into the smaller branches to chew bark is what wakens Ariel, wrapped in her blanket at the foot of the tree, and scares her nearly to death.

What is it? Her fingers stiffen, her jaw aches to keep her teeth from chattering. All she can see is the dark lump, heavy enough to sway the branch directly above, all she can hear is its soft snuffling. What is it doing? Is it about to jump on her? She's about to *freeze* to death, she never would have supposed it would get so cold outside at night. And oh God the thing is moving, it's doing something up there in the needles, maybe it'll be doing it all night. Oh god she can't do this. Can't sleep out in this horrible cold dark, can't sleep with these unnatural mumbling shapes and sounds all around her and above her. Can't live like this.

Maybe it's a *vampire*.

In his bedroom in the added-on ranch house in the midst of alfalfa fields on the bench between the foothills and the town, Nolan Staple lies awake. The light had lasted too long, a whitish light that lingered on the horizon after the hot blue darkened and the air bore down, making Nolan think about hail. He hopes to hell it won't hail. First he got rain on his alfalfa when he didn't want it, and then no rain on his wheat when he needed it, and now it's getting ready to hail on him. He tosses, kicks off the comforter, hopes he hasn't waked Barb, and finally gives up. Eases himself out of bed, pads down the hallway to rummage for Ibuprofen in the bathroom. Sees his face in the half-dark mirror and hardly recognizes himself. Hair standing on end, pale T-shirt skewed at his neck like the dumb farmer he's turned out to be. Swallows a handful of Ibuprofen and goes back to bed to lie on his back and watch the faint light in the window and worry.

As though she'd just noticed the sneaking that's been going on all spring, Barb had got into a tizzy because Bobby was out someplace with the pickup, *all night*, where could he be, Nolan was going to have to put a stop to his running around, blah, blah, blah. He'll put a stop to Bobby, all right. Wring the little bastard's neck if he has to. He'd put him to work summerfallowing, except he's afraid the kid would tear up the harrow and run the tractor off into the fence.

Nolan's been thinking about Loren Henry, on and off. One thing, Loren sure raised Corey to make a hand. What Loren's secret was, how he kept a kid on the straight and narrow, Nolan wishes he knew. He sure can't fault Loren for leaving the world like a man. Hard on Corey, finding him like that, and no note, but he can just hear Loren. *Don't have a thing to say.* Nolan just hopes he'd have the guts to do the same, if the world were to go to hell and the price of fuel and fertilizer kept going up and the price of wheat down—one kid almost ready for college and the other for high school, where's the money going to come from—before he can stop himself, his brain is racketing like a squirrel on a wheel—eighty dollars a ton for good alfalfa hay times the hundred tons of hay he managed to bale is eight thousand dollars, which by the time he pays the bills will have evaporated—he'll be in the hole—by Christ, it's to the point where he's as good as paying the government for the privilege of farming—Barb talking about going to work as a cashier at Safeway, minimum wage—oh hell no, he tells himself, forget it, get some sleep. You're not going to lose the place.

No. Won't happen. In spite of the rumors and the talk about how hard the banks are making it to get operating cash, the neighbors' loans that won't be renewed, the foreclosures. *Three and four gener- ations on the same ranch, working and building it up, and now all those years for nothing, because the bank's kicking them off*—but no, it won't happen to him.

He listens to Barb's easy breathing beside him in bed, takes comfort from the broad curve of her back, her scent of lotion. She's freckled and levelheaded and warm and willing and strong, and she came with a paid-for ranch with good benchland for growing wheat and alfalfa, to add to the skimpy mountain pasture he inherited. Barb's father had been miserly as hell and left them in good financial shape, with enough insurance money for her mother to move to Arizona. In decent years they'll come out a little ahead, surely they will, if they don't count depreciation on the machinery. Which doesn't mean he can afford to lose even a couple hundred—the money from a check he'd cashed—fresh twenties that he knew he had in his wallet when he left town and where the hell is Bobby, out again all night with the car, Barb able to sleep now she has Nolan to do the worrying—

Who is the girl? What is she after?

Hell! He explodes out of bed with his head feeling twice its normal size and goes to the window to look at dark lawn and dark gravel between the house and the machine shed. He'll wring that kid's neck for him when he gets his hands on him, he really will.

Rita lifts herself cautiously from the bed to read the numbers on the digital alarm. Two a.m. Twenty-six hours, and no telling how long Ariel had been gone out her window when Hailey went to unlock her door and let her out for dinner. If Ariel isn't back by daylight, she will call the county sheriff, she really will, because Ariel really can't be allowed to defy her dad, not for twenty-six hours, and what if she's tried something really silly, like hitch-hiking to—where—surely Ariel won't try to hitch-hike back to California, but she has no sense of personal danger, and why would she, she's been too well protected by Hailey.

Even as a newborn, Ariel was her dad's daughter, with Hailey's dark coloring and the fine features almost too pretty for a man but beautiful on the baby. Sometimes it was hard for Rita to believe that Ariel was hers, too. Ariel had liked Hailey best, averting her eyes from her mother, preferring to wave her fists and kick against the cheap carpeting of that first apartment that looked down on the tops of the yellowing palms around the parking lot. But now.

Reminding herself that Ariel is thirteen is not enough to console Rita.

The next time Rita reads the numbers on the alarm clock, it's four-forty, so she must have fallen asleep, after all. Her dream wakened her, a dream so vivid that she sits upright, eventually swings her legs over the side of the bed and goes to the window. She'd been so certain that Ariel was looking through the bedroom window, but sees nothing but faint gray light and empty lawn.

Behind her, Hailey rolls over in his sleep, dreaming his boy's dreams. Rita turns, watches the rise and fall of his chest as she once watched her sleeping babies to make sure they were still alive. How young he looks! Her heart twists for him, for all his troubles, and now Ariel.

The light grows, birdsong rises from the creek. Drawn by the promise of day—oh, she has no difficulties in sleeping during the day, it's the night that keeps her awake with its exaggerated shadows—Rita steals barefoot on the carpet, through the bedroom door and past the room where Rose breathes quietly in her sleep. Dimly the furniture in her living room takes substance. Such furniture as Rita's mother never dreamed of possessing. They've come so far, Rita and Hailey.

The sliding glass doors are a pale gray square. Rita feels her way, lets herself out, noting how much louder metal sliding on metal sounds in the absence of light. No, she corrects herself, that's silly. It seems louder in the absence of other sounds. Disproportionate, like her fears. She listens. When she crosses the deck, she hears the soft pat of her own bare feet. A hunting bird calls from down the creek, hoot-hoot, an owl, perhaps, making its last sweep.

As she leans on the deck rail, she sees the dim shapes moving along the underbrush at the edge of the lawn. The wary steps, the graceful necks and heads. Does and fawns. The doe in the lead senses Rita's presence, flares her ears and freezes with one delicate foreleg poised between one step and another. Rita holds her breath as one of the fawns nudges the doe, pushes ahead of her and catches a shadow in its mouth, no, not a shadow, but leaves. Rita can see the branch shake, dark on dark. She can make out the mottling of white spots on the fawn's coat.

Then—no alien sound or movement, no alarm that Rita can apprehend—and the deer vanish. The empty lawn stretches below her in the strengthening light.

Corey wakes on the broken-backed couch in the front room, her clothes on, her boots toppled where she pulled them off at midnight and collapsed a few feet from where she finally set the painted drill seat in the north window. She'd raised the shade to see the effect, but it had been too dark. Now she sees she'd forgotten to pull the shade back down, and the firs brush the window, the light fills it. She's been dreaming something, yes she has.

What the hell time is it. She sits up groggily, looks around. Full daylight, yes, although the drawn shades on the other side of the house make the room seem dim. The odor of fresh oil paint and turpentine is stronger than the old-dog smell.

No tail-thump. She rises, goes to kneel beside him.

"Oh, Sonny."

Well. It had been going to happen. All that tug-of-war between her and Val had prolonged the old dog's life for what, a few weeks. A month at the most. Made him suffer through another month. Would have been better if she and Val had let him die.

Poor old dog, he'd been alive when she'd finally stuck her brushes in turpentine and turned off the light in the kitchen. She can see where he'd managed to lap a little water, then voided his bowels and died by himself. She feels her gorge rising, feels like howling over the din of voices. *Had to happen, better that way, wouldn't want him to suffer, don't be wasting tears over a dead dog—*

No! It isn't better! None of it is better! It's bad, it's the *shits*, in the language of the children she's taught during these recent obscene years. It's the shits, it's all the shits, and if she had tears in her, if she had a voice, she would howl and scream and cry tears in rivers. But no, she's as bad as old Saylor, dry and silent.

First thing is to get Sonny out of the front room. She can just hear her grandmother—*a dog in the house, let alone a dead dog!*—which helps her to cowboy up, and she gathers the four corners of Sonny's blanket and tries to lift him. He's heavier than she had expected. She'd carried him in the house by herself a month ago, although she understood it had taken Val and Rita Doggett between them, each with an end of the blanket, to carry him out. But now her back is killing her from her night on the couch, and his awkward shape, rigid neck and rigid legs, bumps against her knees. By the time she's got him as far as the kitchen, her arms ache and she has to set him down.

"Damn it, Sonny," she says out loud, to show herself her voice is all right. "And you were nothing but skin and bones."

Now. Another heave. Do it.

Something's stuck in her hair, a burr from yesterday's crawl through the brush, but she can't pull it out now, her hands are coated with dog hair from the blanket. She wipes them on the thighs of her Levi's and heaves and blunders forward with the dog. The narrow door into the lean-to is coming up, and how the hell is she going to get him through it and past the washing machine? For a moment, tilting him, she thinks he's going to spill out of the blanket.

One more door.

In the early sunlight she sets him down and sneezes from the dog hair that floats off her clothes. She probably smells as bad as the dog did.

Now what. She thinks about a shovel, thinks about the weeks of dry weather that have baked the ground to the texture of sandstone and how long it will take to scratch out the shallowest of graves.

Anyway, nobody buries dead animals. They leave them for the coyotes and magpies to clean up. She remembers Loren backing the tractor around, climbing stiffly down from the seat and walking back to hitch the chain around old Baldy's leg. He'd climbed back on the tractor and headed for the coulee that began in the wild gooseberries back of the chicken houses and widened into a glut of aspens. The chain tightened and Baldy slid by one leg behind the tractor. At the time she'd been annoyed with Loren for not dragging him farther, out of sight and out of smelling distance from the house. But Loren was Loren. He'd taken Baldy, a horse he'd owned for twenty-five years, as far as the aspens and unhooked him and came back into the house to shake a cigarette out of his pack and pour himself a cup of coffee.

That particular stink is almost gone now, and Corey thinks Sonny can't make it any worse. She gathers up the four corners of the blanket and lurches down the plank walk with her load, remembers that she hadn't stopped to pull her boots on, she's barefoot, and then she looks up and sees, at the pole gate beyond the barn, a black pickup truck in idle and John Perrine in his gabardine suit and black Stetson, just letting himself through the gate.

She watches him drive through the gate and get out to close it again, drive up to the house and park and get out with a folder under his arm. Stopping by with her papers on his way to work, just as he said he would. He's at the picket fence before his eyes find the strange load in the blanket at Corey's feet.

She answers the question in his face. "Dog died."

His mouth drops open. "I'm sorry," she hears him say, and then, who would have supposed he could move so fast, he's beside her, his arms around her, holding her. *Hugging* her. She feels his muscles under his coat sleeves and his surprisingly solid belly, and oh hell, she's going to bawl. Does. Bawl. And bawls. So she's not dry of tears, after all.

Eventually she stops and he lets her go. "When?" he asks.

"This morning. Just found him. He was okay when I fed him last night." Corey wipes her face with her hands, gathers up the corners of the blanket, starts for the gate, and nearly falls off the plank walk. Wonders what the hell has happened to her balance.

"Corey!" He's taking the dead weight away from her, never-minding the dog hair on his expensive suit. "You don't have to do it all by yourself. Where's your shovel?"

She must be explaining about the rock-hard ground, about laying Sonny beside Baldy, because John is nodding.

"Down the coulee? I'll carry him. You go get your shoes on."

He waits for her, and when she comes back outside with her boots on, he hoists the blanket and its load, making it look easy. Follows where she opens gates for him. The new colt raises his head from grazing and watches as they cross his pasture on their way to the coulee.

"Nice colt," says John, and she nods.

"Have you decided what you're going to do with that bunch of mares? They'll eat you out of house and home, you know. Sorry, wrong time, I don't mean to bother you now."

They've come to the edge of the coulee. Corey winces, then scolds herself. At least Baldy is past the putrid stage, and maybe his stiffened hide over a tent of bones is a sight that won't hurt John Perrine to see. Remind him what everything comes to. He seems such an innocent to her in so many ways.

All he says is, "Are you sure you don't want me to get the shovel?"

He looks at her face, then half-walks, half-slides down through the gooseberries with his burden and arranges it on the bay hide and bones that's all that's left of Baldy. Fusses with the blanket, smoothing it. As though it matters. *Don't cry over dead animals! You can't cry over every little thing!*

Now he's climbing back, trampling grass and gooseberries and breathing hard from the exertion. He takes off his ridiculous black Stetson and wipes perspiration off his face.

"Are you okay?"

She nods. Knows there's more she should say. "Thank you," she adds.

"I stopped by to go over those letters with you, but maybe there'll be a better time."

"No. It's all right. It'll be cool in the house."

The sun burns down as she and John walk back across the pasture. Even the grass looks dead. Only the thistles lift their wicked spikes, thriving. Corey can see where the new colt has picked his way around them, grazing, and reminds herself that she's going to have to toss him some hay.

In the relief of the dim kitchen, she stops at the sink and runs cold water over her hands, soaks the dishrag to wipe her face. Turns and sees John Perrine removing his hat, exotic as an overgrown gray orchid in his suit and what had been an immaculate shirt and a silk tie before he started lifting dead dogs. A real tie, not a bulldogger tie, he must be going to be in court today. His eyes travel around the clutter of newspapers and unwashed dishes, paints all over the table, shades pulled to the sills, cobwebs on the ceiling. Corey swats at a gray line of silk that descends over the sink and sees herself, burrs in her hair, clothes creased from being slept in, dog hair all over her.

She's got no manners, either. It's been too long since she's lived like a civilized person.

"You want some coffee?" she asks, thinking to start the pot. "Or—" she was about to offer him a beer, then remembers. The beer moved itself up the hill back of the house. Whoever helped it move itself. Tells herself it's too early in the day for a beer, anyway.

John doesn't answer at once, and she looks to see what's got his attention.

Her drill seat. At midnight last night, she'd known only that she wouldn't put another brushstroke, and she'd propped it on the window sill, stuck her brushes in turpentine, filled Sonny's water bowl, and collapsed on the couch. Thought she'd take another look at it in the morning and decide—decide what, she didn't know.

Now she sees the heads of the red horses with their eyes filled with light from the window, and how they resist the flange that encircles them, decorated though it is with extravagant gold filigrees and pendants, wild swirls, pulses. She had layered the paint thicker than she should have, remembering how to make the gold jewels glow, daubing highlights on highlights instead of waiting for the first layer to dry, and now her new tubes of rose madder and vermilion and crimson lake are spread, a crumpled mess, across the table. She'd used way more of her zinc white than she'd thought she would, too. She hates seeing the tubes looking so depleted.

John Perrine seems at a loss for words. "I never saw anything like that before," he says at last. He walks to one side of the window, then the other, to look at the red horses from different angles. Finally he sits down at the kitchen table and opens his folder, but he keeps turning to look again at the horses.

Finally he collects himself and takes out some papers. Looks from the papers to Corey. She supposes he's going to explain what she has to do to list the ranch for sale, and she braces herself. She'll do what she has to do. Same as Annie did, same as a lot of people have had to do. Or at least maybe he'll tell her how she can withdraw the five hundred or so in Loren's checking account. She realized last night how much more paint she's going to have to buy.

But no. He's got something else on his mind. His eyes, warm and earnest, search hers.

"I've been meaning to ask you, Corey. Would you consider being a train robber? Doesn't pay a whole lot, but—a few dollars—a hundred dollars a rehearsal, same for performances, once we get rolling— you'd have to furnish yourself, of course—old-time clothes, the target date's 1882—bring your own horse—rifle—"

He's babbling, she thinks. He's babbling.

"She didn't say no," John Perrine reports to James and Val Tendenning, when he drops by that evening to discuss train robbery rehearsal.

"How does she seem?" asks Val.

"She's thin. I don't like to think of her living up there, all alone. You've seen what the house is like. She doesn't even have a shower. Heats her water on the stove. And now she's trying to run that ranch by herself. I've advised her to list it."

Glances are exchanged. Val and James know what they think of that plan, and Val flares up—"It's not the ranch work! Corey can do the work. She's always done it. Like we all do!"

To her surprise, John leans forward in his chair, his face reddening. Fists on his thighs, clenched under the table. "And where is it written that she's got to work herself to death?"

Val stares, opens her mouth to argue, changes her mind. First time I ever saw John Perrine riled, she will tell James, later on. You don't think he's interested in her, do you? She must be ten years older than him. And James will shrug, oh, wouldn't think so. He's got that big girlfriend, what's her name, Ingrid.

"I hope she'll rob trains," says James, now. "It's a good idea. Anything that would get her out, talking to people. Keeping all to herself like that, no wonder she's half-crazy."

"When was she in art school?"

"Oh, years ago." Val starts to tell John how her dad and Nails Reisenaur and Des Ballard and some others got together and incorporated the school privately, to keep it open, and then passed their hats for enough money to send Corey Henry off to Minneapolis to learn how to teach it, but she went to art school instead, until the money ran out, so she had to come home and take correspondence courses to earn her teaching certificate. But John's heard it before.

"If she sells the ranch, it'll be so she can paint. Have you seen her artwork?"

"That old Charlie Russell?" says Val, surprised.

"I don't know about Charlie Russell. I mean those red and gold horses. They're—wild. Like they could have crashed through that window. I couldn't sit with my back turned to them."

"Are they any good?" says James.

"I don't know enough about art to judge. But it's what she's doing. All she's doing. I wouldn't say she's crazy."

"Painting *red horses*?"

"Well."

Corey tells herself it won't hurt her to clean house. It may take her mind off Sonny and John Perrine, and at least it'll be work worth doing. After a search she finds the broom stuck back of the washing machine, and she starts on the front room, sweeping up the last of Sonny, dust curls and dog hair. She ought to get the disinfectant out from under the sink, run some water in a bucket, and mop the linoleum. After the floor, the walls. But what to do with the walls. The old plaster is falling off the laths, the wallpaper is water-stained and pulling loose from the plaster. Where to start. She stops and leans on the broom, weary with the weight of the house.

When she finished painting the red horses, she had felt—what. Emptied. No. Replete. Satiated. But the tension is back now, jerking at her muscles the way it drove her tired feet on last night's fool's errand in the dark. She's being goaded to paint again, she knows that, but she also knows what she's got to do first. Housecleaning is just a way of putting it off. Maybe painting is also a way—no, no, she stifles that thought, which feels like one of her grandmother's. *The devil makes work for idle hands. No rest for the wicked. Sooner started, sooner done.*

Sooner started on this task, sooner done. She props the broom against the wall. Finds her glasses and makes herself open the drawers of Loren's desk and lift out all the papers she'd crammed away on the morning of his funeral.

The answer will be in the paperwork, John Perrine had said. Look for insurance policies, he'd said. Even if you don't think he had any insurance. Look for investment statements. Tax statements. It'll be there, somewhere.

Maybe, but not in Loren's desk. Corey sits cross-legged on the floor, reading every slip and scrap of paper, stuff she's already examined twice or three times, the envelope of deposit slips, receipts and lists, none very recent, some very old, and leafing through them all over again isn't going to change them.

Finally, with her back aching and her eyes itching, she forces herself up off the floor, bundles the stacks back, and slams the drawers shut. For two cents she'd have a bonfire and burn the lot, except that it's too dry in the foothills to start a bonfire. She'd have the whole gulch aflame.

Meddling in what's mine! It would serve you right if you set the ranch on fire and lost it all.

"Don't worry, I'm not starting any damned fires," she tells Loren. But she pauses at the north window and sees that the sky above the ridge pines is baked blue. The morning is wasting away. God! She'll seize on any excuse to get out of the house. Slaps her hat on her head and goes out to do such chores as she has. The yearling calves to be checked, Babe's water trough to be checked, Babe and the new colt given a handful of oats apiece, the new colt made over. He'll forget what he knows about human touch if he's left alone for too long, and it would be a shame to let his gentleness go to waste.

Corey stands for a while in the shade of the pines with him, rubbing his ears and his neck and telling him what a fine fellow he is. A sweet matting of dead needles is underfoot, and also the colt's biscuit-shaped droppings, over which the small insects rise and hum. The colt stamps his hoof and switches his tail and nudges Corey with his head to get her attention. He likes having his neck rubbed, likes being rubbed around his tail—"Sure you do," she growls at him. "You're a man, aren't you."

At least it's quiet, no gunfire. Hailey Doggett must have won his war last night and slept in this morning. What a night Annie must have had, living just across the creek from all that smoke and noise! Annie will have plenty to say about it.

So what do you think, Loren? Was that watcher watching me, or was he watching Hailey? You're all the time telling me how much I don't know. Why can't you tell me something useful for once?

But Loren doesn't have a thing to say on that topic.

The colt butts her, asking for more strokes. Corey wonders if there's a chance of finding his registration papers, wherever Loren stashed them, and finding out his name. Calling him by it. Or if there's any point in it. Any point in starting to lunge him, getting him used to a saddle. Baldy had never been saddle-broken, hardly even halter-broken. Spent his whole life in this one pasture.

Highly unlikely this colt will do the same.

She knows of one other place she can search for Loren's secrets.

11

Corey pauses irresolute in the upstairs hall, listening to flies buzz. The
door to Loren's room stands ajar as it always has, taking advantage of
the cross-ventilation from the opposite window during the cool of the
night. When Corey was in her teens, she hated the sounds that came
through his doorway, and she had lain awake listening to the creak of
his bedsprings and the jingle of fluids when he got up to use his chamber pot. Her grandmother had slept on beside Corey, snoring and undisturbed. Corey supposed her grandmother had gotten used to Loren's sounds. She had gotten used to them, herself.

But to walk into his room.

To put it off, she decides to start with the boxes stacked in the hall.
Cardboard boxes that probably were retrieved from the old Olympian
Grocery, years ago, boxes that once held products she doubts are man-
ufactured any more. Oxydol soap, Dutch Cleanser, Tang salad dress-
ing. Flaps tucked in, crisscross, to contain their bulging contents.
What do they hold? Has she ever known?

She lifts down a box and sets it at the head of the stairs. A stale scent rises with the flaps when she runs her hand under them. Her grandmother's clothes! Her black coat, her black lace-up shoes with the Cuban heels. A squashed black straw hat with a gray ribbon around it. Flowered housedresses. Aprons.

She wonders whose hands folded and stored these clothes. She has no memory of it, but surely it wouldn't have been Loren. Annie Reisenaur, more likely.

Her grandmother, wearing one of these faded aprons over a dress, even when she was building fence or helping with threshing. Standing solid in her lace-up shoes, shouting at—who—Virgil! Be careful with that goddamn pitchfork, don't you let it stick in that threshing machine. We can't afford to stop for no funerals just because you've killed yourself. Oh, now, Granny, said Virgil, taking her jibe as a joke. But he'd deserved it. And he knew it.

Corey tears herself out of the past. Lifts down another box, another and another, finding clothing that gets older and more friable as she works her way down. Long serge skirts, blouses with ruffled bosoms and strange sleeves, hugely puffed from shoulder to elbow, but tight and buttoned at the wrists. *Shirtwaists*, she supposes they are. Whose, she has no way of knowing. The fine fabric splits and shreds when she touches it.

Other boxes hold children's clothing. Her clothing. A six year old's blue jeans, worn to velvet, patched and re-patched over the knees.

Had they thrown nothing away?

She's only postponing the moment.

When she finally brings herself to the threshold, she cannot remember ever walking through this door. Up here, under the eaves of the old house, the air feels thick, the linoleum sticky underfoot with accumulated grime. Windows spotted, flies lying dead in drifts on the sills. All she recognizes is his silver-mounted prize saddle on its sawhorse.

Don't need to be cleaned. Do what else you got to do.

Corey reaches over the flies and opens the window so she can breathe. Turning, she sees that Loren had left his bed unmade from the last time he'd climbed out of it, the pillow folded in half, the sheets half-dragged off, the blanket kicked down to the end of the mattress. Normally he had given her his sheets, along with his shirts and socks and underwear, once a week or so to be washed and ironed, then given back to him to carry upstairs with him and put back on his bed. But she can't remember whether she'd washed for him the week before his death.

The curtain that hangs over his clothes has been pinned back, and Corey startles at the sight—who?—but then she remembers that it must have been Annie, weeks ago, looking for his good Pendleton suit and his white dress shirt to bury him in. And yes, the Pendleton suit is gone, and nothing behind the curtain but a few pearl-snap shirts on wire hangers. His extra Levi's and underwear will be in the drawers of the oak dresser. The chiffonier, *shiff-on-eer*, as her grandmother called it. Buying time, Corey ponders the word, *shiff-on-eer*, *shiff-on-eer*. Curious word. Where had her grandmother acquired it. Repeats it to herself, *shiff-on-eer*, *shiff-on-eer*, until it loses its meaning.

A scattering of junk on top of the chiffonier. More wire hangers. A handful of small change. A tin of black boot polish. His wallet with nothing in it but three dollar bills, his driver's license, and his proof of insurance on the red pickup. His jackknife and the comb he had carried in his shirt pocket. How have they gotten there. Annie again.

She starts with the top drawer of the chiffonier, which sticks and then screeches when she forces it. Inside the drawer, more dead flies and a stack of red bandanna handkerchiefs, ironed by herself. Ironed white handkerchiefs in another stack. He'd never been known to use Kleenex. She lifts the handkerchiefs. What else. A broken—what, a watchband, maybe. A mayonnaise jar full of nails. Loose screws, a pair of pliers, a broken pencil, rubber bands, old keys, a drift of unopened mail. She gathers up the envelopes with some hope, sees that they contain promotions for credit cards, offers of magazine subscriptions, record clubs, advertisements. She should have brought a plastic garbage sack upstairs with her.

No, wait, what's this.

Manila envelope with its flap folded inside. She rips it, getting it open. Yes, the bill of sale. Received from, sum of, etc. And the colt's registration papers, which of course Loren would have wanted if he'd had ideas of starting up his stud again. She unfolds the papers, follows a family tree with more branches than most humans can trace, probably all the way back to the Godolphin Arabian, yes. Let's see. Back to the beginning, here. This colt's name. Good grief. Good God. Who hung that on him?

Judith River's Tragic Dancer.

Well.

She stuffs the papers and bill of sale back in the manila envelope, sticks the envelope in her hip pocket, sweeps the avalanche of unopened mail on the floor, and tries the next drawer of the chiffonier, which is full of the long-handled underwear Loren had worn, winter and summer. She has to flatten it back down with her hand to get the drawer shut again.

The third drawer holds his three or four pairs of extra Levi's, carefully ironed by her. Socks, washed and rolled by her and put away by Loren.

He'd probably been too stiff to want to bend down to the lower drawers, because nothing is in the fourth drawer but a pamphlet advertising Roundup weed killer, and nothing at all is in the bottom drawer.

Where, then?

Dark green roller shades on the windows, rolled all the way to the top. Wallpaper with a pattern so faded that it's difficult to make out. The plaster's coming loose in here, too. The iron bedstead, the curtain over the closet, the chiffonier. Windowsills stacked with back issues of *Western Horseman* and *Farm and Ranch Journal. Smithsonian. National Geographic.* What he'd liked to read. Probably he'd brought home old copies free from the library in town.

She lifts a magazine, shakes its pages, gets nothing but dust. Should she sort through them all?

She turns for a last look at his room. Then bends down. Under his bed, his chamber pot, brimming. She wrinkles her nose against the odor. At least he'd never asked her to empty his pot for him. But what's the pot sitting on but stacks of manila envelopes, dozens of them, carefully arranged under the pot like a stack of bricks.

The mares and colts in the butte pasture are fat on grass and somnolent, hardly bothering to move out of the shade when she rides past them. The pump in the butte pasture is working fine when she lets Babe drink from the tank, although the water looks warm, with a green tinge of scum. Corey watches the scum separate and float as Babe drinks her fill and lifts her head and shakes droplets from her bridle chains. Babe's belly gurgles as the water goes down. Her hide ripples and gleams. The water, the grass, the hawthorn leaves, the aspens, saturated with the last gold light filtering all the way down to their roots, glowing as though the sun won't set in a few minutes and take the gold with it. Corey herself is glowing. She mistrusts the feeling, doesn't expect it to last any longer than the sunset will, but the hell with that, the hell with gloom. She's laughing inwardly, she's drunk without whiskey, which she's sworn off, at least for today. She's thinking she may be headed for a fall, but to hell with that, also. She's by God going to enjoy herself. For a little while. This afternoon, anyway.

She catches a whiff of something putrid, a skunk trailing its odor as it passes invisibly in its wild dimension. To the west the sky has gone dark blue, verging on purple in the lurid colors of sunset. Surely this weather has to break. Even in the foothills, the thermometer has been over ninety degrees all week.

So. She'd better get a move on. Through the resin-scented pines, through the hidden gate, to the edge of John's clearing where the cottonwood shoots nod and bow in the growing shadows around the old log house.

John has been making good progress on the house. Even in the twilight Corey notes that the logs have been oiled, the frames around the windows freshly painted, the old roof replaced with a tin one, dark green. She approves of the tin roof, especially up here in the timber, where wooden shingles are such a fire hazard. Imagines using Loren's money to put a new roof on the stone house.

And why stop there! She could have the cracks in the stones cemented! She could have the house fumigated to kill the flies and bedbugs. Maybe get a new furnace that doesn't burn coal. Hell, as long as she's going to daydream, she may as well add a hot water heater, a plumbed bathroom, and an upstairs studio, flooded with light from the north window, in the bedroom that was Loren's. That last idea is so daring that she can hardly imagine more. But yes! Herself at an easel, with an expensive canvas, with tubes of oil paints spread around her in profusion.

Babe snorts and jerks at the bridle reins.

The clearing is quiet, the grass still. The windows look vacant, but John's black pickup is parked by the log shop, so he must be home. The newish blue Volvo sedan is probably Ingrid's, which gives Corey pause. She hadn't calculated on Ingrid. She shifts herself in the saddle, her weight on one leg, letting the other leg swing out of the stirrup, watching a shape like a torn piece of black paper flit through the half-light between the grassheads and the horizon, an early bat hunting insects. Well, no reason to sit out here with the bats, she tells herself, and she nudges Babe out of the cover of pines just as a door bangs and Ingrid charges out of the house, shouting back over her shoulder.

Corey's hands on her reins are in automatic check, but she's too late, Ingrid has spotted her. Ingrid's mouth drops briefly in her large face, stops, leans against the car, and waits.

Corey waits also, wondering what Ingrid will say, Ingrid with her arms crossed and her face thrust forward, obviously mad as hell. The bat wings and dips like a shadow of a shadow that vanishes over the eaves of the shed. Then she sees that John is standing in the doorway, looking out through the screen

"The older you get," says Ingrid, into the air beyond Corey, "the less you'll put up with."

The less you'll puwup with.

Corey nods, carefully.

"This is not what you think," says Ingrid.

Corey waits.

"He's such a baby. Am I his mother?"

The only answer to that question that Corey can think of is *no*, and so she says it, "No," and the word ignites something in Ingrid, because she wrenches open the door of her car and slams herself into it, then catches her skirt in the door so she has to open and slam it again. The Volvo's headlights come on. It wheels in a tight reverse arc, then spins up fresh gravel as it burns out of the yard. In the twilight, the odor of the dust it raises on the county road is sharper than the cloud itself.

"You picked a good time," says John through the screen door.

"Is it a bad time?" says Corey. She has dismounted, has tied Babe's reins to the fence, is unbuckling her saddlebags.

"No, no."

"I could come back."

"Hell, no, this is a fine time."

He turns on the light in the kitchen and holds the screen door for her. Corey, ducking under his arm with her saddlebags, sees that he's been busy inside the house, or else Ingrid has, because the windows are clean and the walls freshly painted, and the floor looks like it's been sanded down and sealed.

"Polyurethane," says John, when he notices her looking at the floor.

"Are you planning to live out here all year round?"

Because if he is, he's going to need chains to get to town during the worst of the winter, even with his four-wheel-drive truck. He won't know what snow is until he's lived for a winter in these foothills.

"That's what some of the discussion was about."

Corey hesitates. His face is heavily shadowed with stubble, he obviously hasn't shaved since morning, but he's still dressed in his, well, office clothes. She can't think of gabardine pants and a white shirt and tie as working clothes, exactly. So he hasn't had a chance to change clothes yet, and he's had a fight with his girlfriend, and here's Corey Henry, busting in on him. She hitches her saddlebags over her shoulder, and says, "I better get going. She'll be coming back, won't she?"

"Oh, sit down. You'll drink a beer with me, won't you? What are you carrying there?"

His eyes had lit up at the sight of her saddlebags like a kid hoping for treasure, so Corey sits and watches him bustle to his new refrigerator and take out two cans of beer. What is he after in the freezer side? He wouldn't put ice cubes in beer, would he? He keeps his *glasses* in there?

He sets one of the frosty glasses in front of her, pops open a beer, and pours carefully, not to raise too big a head. Pours his own beer and sits opposite her, rumpled and five-o'clock-shadowed and expectant.

After all his preparation, she hates to tell him that she doesn't care much for beer, she only bought that six-pack the other day because it cost less than whiskey and because she wanted to see whether it would taste any better to her than it did when she used to drink beer in the barn with Virgil. She glances around the well-lit room, wishing she knew whose space she's filling. Mizzy's kitchen, John Perrine's kitchen, maybe Ingrid's kitchen. Somebody has given the old Monarch wood range a good cleaning. John or Ingrid?

She tastes John Perrine's beer, politely, and opens her saddlebags.

She's been looking forward to the expression on his face, and she's not disappointed. As she stacks manila envelopes on the table in front of her, and then starts counting out the hundred-dollar bills from the first envelope, his mouth drops. It isn't until she's emptied the first envelope—ten hundred-dollar bills—that he finds words.

"Hold on! How much have you got there?"

"Thirty thousand and a little more. It must have been closer to forty thousand before he bought the colt."

"Holy shit!"

He reaches across the table, gathers the stack of envelopes, weighs them in his hands, and counts them. Thirty of them, as Corey knows. He lays down the envelopes and picks up one of the bills, turns it over and looks at the other side, as though he expects to find an explanation encoded there.

"Where'd you find all this?"

"In his bedroom." It's all the detail she's prepared to give.

"Hmm." He hands back the bill and drinks the head off his beer.

"Do you think it's—?" She can't finish her question.

"Yours now? Yes. But where do you think he came by a stash like this? Insurance policies, possibly? On your grandmother? Or your mother? I know you said you didn't think so."

"I don't believe Loren ever took out any insurance he didn't have to, like on the truck. And a policy this big, if he'd taken it out on my mother before she died—" she pauses, silenced by the idea of Loren sleeping over so much money for all those years. *Peeing* over it.

She takes another sip of beer. It isn't half bad, once she's gotten past the initial bitterness. And it wouldn't be so much the size of the premiums, she wants to tell John. It was Loren. She remembers the fit he'd kicked when car insurance became mandatory. What the hell did the government think it was doing, making a damn-fool rule like that? Why, a man ought to be able to take his own chances!

What if you hit somebody and killed them, she'd asked him.

Ain't going to hit and kill nobody!

"What are you going to do with it?" says John. "I mean, where are you going to put it? Have you got a safe-deposit box?"

He pushes back the cuff of his sleeve, looks at his watch. "It's too late to get it into the bank tonight, anyway. You could lock it in the trunk of your car until morning—no, you drive that pickup, no trunk. So put those saddlebags back of the pickup seat and lock the pickup, and first thing in the morning, drive into town and rent yourself a safe-deposit box."

She nods, she hadn't thought that far ahead.

"The next thing is to figure out where it came from. Have you found his canceled checks? His deposit slips?"

"Not yet."

"Well, damn. Keep looking."

He finishes his beer and set the glass down and leans back in his chair, looking dreamy, himself. "I wish I'd known him. I wish I'd had a chance to visit with him. About his army service—"

"He never talked about New Guinea."

"—or about his rodeo days. The way people describe him, spurring out of the chute on a saddle bronc—"

He's embarrassing Corey almost as much as though she were the one that he's praising. Her grandmother speaks up: *Praise to the face is open disgrace!*

"Loren was a good hand," Corey says.

She hears what she has said and wonders what the words mean to John Perrine, who didn't grow up with the old strictures, the rationing of words, the careful understatements. There he sits, innocent as a boy in spite of his five-o'clock shadow and the hairs at the neck of his shirt, with his clean fingernails and his clean clothes in his clean, renovated kitchen. She remembers Ingrid's parting words.

"What did you like about rodeo?" she asks, curious.

His face lights up.

"I loved every day I was on the circuit. For somebody like me, raised the way I was, it's hard for me to see the way I am now and then remember back. The day I rode my first bull out of a chute was the first I really knew I was alive. It was the first time I ever felt I was living in the moment and not for the future. The first real thing I'd ever done."

His eyes beg understanding.

"My dad had a seat on the New York stock exchange," he says.

She thinks he's reaching for one of the manila envelopes, but no, he's reaching for her. His fingertips touch hers. In the gentle light from his new overhead fixture she sees his big meaty hand, so well kept, and hers, with its scars. She cannot raise her eyes. Then a gust of wind hits the house. It whooshes across John's new tin roof, rumbles off through the tops of the pines. Weather blowing in. Maybe rain. The windows in the kitchen are sheer black oblongs now, reflecting the bright room and the man and the woman at the table. A big man in a loosened tie and a white dress shirt, sleeves rolled to his forearms, leaning across the table toward a woman with her hair falling out of her braid and her hawk's eyes softening out of focus.

She hears Babe outside, whinnying and tossing her bridle chains. She should have started for home sooner.

"You don't want to ride out in that," says John. "You could stay here tonight."

Their eyes do meet, and suddenly it's too much, too warm, they both have to look away. Corey's so embarrassed that she can't see straight. What if he could read her thoughts. She shakes her head, pushes her chair back, mumbles something, God knows what, she doesn't know, got livestock to feed, something like that. He's on his feet, also, helping her to pretend that the moment never happened.

He follows her out to the gate, holds her saddlebags for her while she buckles them behind her saddle. The wind tears at his hair and mustache and whips his thin white shirt taut against his arms and chest. The shirt glows almost to neon in the weird light. "Are you sure you want to ride out in this?" he shouts. "It looks to me like it could rain like hell."

"I'll be all right."

Rebound, she thinks. Rebound is the word for it. He's on the rebound from Ingrid, that's all it was about.

Toe in the stirrup, one hand on the horn and the other on Babe's neck with the reins, and she's in the saddle. "Thanks," she yells belatedly, over her shoulder, and kicks Babe into a lope as the wind chases the wild grass through the dark.

The pines writhe overhead and roar as Corey rides for home. The charged air excites Babe, she's full of energy from not being ridden enough, and she flattens her ears at the thunderclaps and runs. Underbrush thrashes, pine boughs slap, and then they're out of the timber, over the last hill, and tearing along the two-track road through the old hay meadows. Lightning divides the sky with a single many-branched bolt that leaves a glowing imprint on Corey's eyes. Maybe she should have stopped, found lower ground, at least removed the chains from Babe's bridle reins. But the electricity invigorates her and she lets the wind water her eyes and claim her hair. At the last gate she swings off Babe, opens it, shuts it again, and is astride almost before Babe can more than break her pace. They've reached the barn when the next roll of thunder explodes overhead and lets loose a smatter of rain.

Babe's hooves echo on the floorboards when Corey leads her into the barn. She jerks at the bridle reins, picking up her feet nervously and showing the whites of her eyes at the drum of rain on the shingles. But she's had her run, and she's wet and breathing heavily and willing to stand while Corey unsaddles her, hangs up the saddle, and gives her a handful of oats to nuzzle off the floor.

Corey's listening for sounds of hail in the rain. She knows she cut it close.

What the hell, she can't get any wetter. She'll turn Babe loose in the barn for the night—the colt will have sheltered under his shed—and make a run for the house.

Rain sweeps down in sheets. Corey holds her hat and runs, and yes, she can get wetter, her boots squelch water and her braid bats back and forth against her shoulders like a sodden rope as she runs past the springhouse and through new standing puddles where the rain drives down. Up the incline, through the gate in the picket fence, into the lean-to, where she leans on the washing machine and breathes hard. So far no hail in the rain. In fact, damn it, it's letting up. It's been just another summer electrical storm, mostly noise.

"Son of a bitch," says Corey aloud, and takes off her hat and pours a brim-full of rainwater out the door. Gives herself another minute to catch her breath, then pulls off her boots and sets them on the old woodbox to dry. Pads into the kitchen in wet stocking feet, stops at the sink to take off her shirt, wring it out, and hang it on a nail back of the door. Turns on the overhead light. Turns on the burner under the coffee pot to warm up what's left.

Her paints draw her. She's started another animal portrait, this time on the back of her grandmother's breadboard, and this time in greens, since she's used up most of her reds. The green faces of deer gaze back at her from the breadboard where it's propped on the kitchen table, green faces that don't not quite emerge from the green blades of grass and green leaves, don't quite disappear. She wonders if she should have tried for more contrast. Decides not. But the eyes of the deer worry her. She's been working for the same effect that the holes in the iron drill seat created for the horses' eyes, has tried painting tunnels for the deer's eyes so that they look inward as well as outward. Isn't satisfied. Now she thinks she'll just try a few strokes while her coffee heats. She squeezes a dollop of zinc white on the edge of her dinner-plate palette, selects a fine brush.

Stops.

No gunfire tonight from down the gulch. Hailey must have gotten rained out of whatever he was doing. And yet, and yet. She listens to the silence after the rain, the silence of the night composing itself around the stone walls. Hears the absence of thunder, the abating of wind. The hair on her arms and neck rise, she feels the primitive pulse of panic. She's wearing nothing but a pair of wet Levi's and a white cotton brassiere, she's armed with nothing more lethal than a paintbrush, and she's alone in the house.

No. She's not. Not alone.

Corey lays down her brush, carefully. Takes three silent strides across the kitchen in her stocking feet. Jerks open the door to the stairs.

The child who crouches back against the coats hanging from hooks above her head is set and fearful. Her eyes show their whites.

Corey catches her by the wrist. "Come out of there, Ariel. What do you think you're doing?"

She drags Ariel into the kitchen and sees her eyes shift like a colt about to make a break for it, so she's ready when Ariel wrenches away in the direction of the door. Corey holds her with both arms. It's like embracing a terrified colt, all soft bones and writhing flesh and voice.

"No! Don't! Don't!" screams Ariel.

But she stops kicking, and Corey lets her go. Ariel backs off. Her jeans and shirt are sodden, and her hair hangs over her shoulders in wet ringlets.

"You've been in here before," says Corey. "This time you came in to get out of the rain."

Ariel murmurs something inaudible, a ploy Corey remembers from when she taught her in school. Speak up! I can't hear you, she'd have to ask Ariel, repeatedly, until Ariel would yell at the top of her lungs, I said I don't know the answer! And I don't care what it is!

"You've been hanging out in the brush. You came in here and stole my beer."

A lip trembles. "I needed to go to your bathroom."

"All I've got is the outhouse. You can use that."

"Ick."

Ariel may have been living rough in the brush, lately, but she looks to Corey as though she's gained weight since June, when school let out. Her breasts and hips are rounded on the child's slight frame, and her face also seems plumper. Not a healthy plumpness. Swollen, maybe, with those dark eyes sunken like sloes, sliding up to watch Corey and gauge her chances.

"I've got some peanut butter," says Corey. "I think I still do. I'll make you a peanut-butter sandwich and find you something dry to wear, and then you're can tell me what you're doing here."

Ariel says nothing, but nothing isn't no. Corey rummages in the cupboard and finds the peanut butter and a jar of jelly, gets out the rest of her loaf of bread and spreads a sandwich while Ariel watches. When Corey sets the plate in front of her on the table, Ariel falls on it. Shoves a good half a sandwich in her mouth at once.

"Want a glass of water? I'm out of milk."

Ariel nods, she can't speak for peanut butter.

Corey goes upstairs and puts on a dry shirt, gets out one of Loren's clean ironed shirts from his closet, and brings it back downstairs. Wonders what she would have done if it had been the giant stranger in the stairwell instead of Ariel. Half-wonders if Ariel will bolt, but no. When Corey comes back downstairs she's wolfing down the last of her sandwich.

"Put this on," said Corey. The shirt is threadbare but warm from hanging upstairs, under the eaves. "Do you want some more to eat?"

A nod.

Corey fixes her another sandwich, sets it in front of her, and Ariel crams it down.

"So why aren't you eating peanut butter sandwiches at home?"

A mumbled answer, mouth full of peanut butter.

"I can't tell what you're saying."

"I said, I fucking can't go home!"

Old bitch, Ariel had called her. You old bull-dyke, cunt, fucking bitch. And all the old sores and tribulations had erupted out of their long dormancy, Corey's rage had overflowed, and the red print of her hand had risen on Ariel's face.

"You've been sleeping out there in the brush? How many nights?"

"I don't know. Two, I guess."

"Why?"

"Because I want to."

"That's bullshit," says Corey, surprising herself. *That's man's talk.*

The last bite of sandwich, almost to Ariel's mouth, stalls. Ariel looks up at Corey, meeting her eyes for the first time. Corey thinks again that Ariel's eyes look sunken and unhealthy.

"Because I don't want to have sex."

"You don't—want to have sex. What are you talking about? You're thirteen."

"I knew you wouldn't believe me."

It's not disbelief that Corey feels, but the sense that the story has twisted ahead of her, in a direction she doesn't want to follow. Her green deer are watching her, to see what she will do.

"Who is it you don't want to have sex with?"

Mute obstinacy on Ariel's face is all she gets.

Ariel, more modest than Corey would have expected of a child who once pulled up her T-shirt in school and silenced the boy in the seat behind her by thrusting her young breasts at him, ducks through the arch into the front room to change into Loren's shirt. Ariel's wet clothes fly out in a sodden bundle, and Corey wrings them over the sink and lays them in the oven to dry, as Mizzy Ballard once had done for her. Turns them in the oven when they steam and wonders what Mizzy would have done about Ariel. What Loren would have done. Ariel had been a truthful pupil, Corey has to admit. Ariel would always brazen her way out of a corner before she'd lie her way out.

Yes! I copied my math answers! I already knew how to do those problems, they were too boring to do again. So what are you going to do about it?

So what's she refusing to admit now?

Ariel comes out, barefoot, in Loren's shirt. It droops over her shoulders and hangs to her knees, but she's rolled the sleeves and combed her hair with her fingers, and she's gotten back some of her swagger. She sees Corey's painting of the deer and stops, arrested.

"What's the matter with their eyes?"

Corey is surprised. She would have expected her to object to the green paint. "What do you mean?"

"They're watching me watch them."

Corey shakes her head, goes to the window and cups her hands to see through her reflection. Droplets are still falling through the fir branches, but the rain has stopped. To the northwest, ragged night clouds are blowing past the stars. As she surmised, it's been a fizzle of a storm, thunder and lightning but not enough real moisture to relieve the July drought. And Babe's still in the barn, ought to be turned out, thrown a little hay—and the saddlebags. She'd forgotten all about the saddlebags.

Oh well, hell. Even with prowling strangers, the damned money is no riskier in the barn than it had been under Loren's bed.

"How come your house is so dirty?"

Oh yes. She'd started to clean house. Now she remembers the cobwebs, the clutter. The fresh mud starting to dry on the kitchen floor. The overflowing ashtray on the table—

"It's disgusting," says Ariel. "I didn't know you smoked."

"I don't," says Corey. It's Loren's ashtray, and it's the first she's realized that she has never emptied it, not in nearly six weeks.

"I could clean your house for you," says Ariel. Her eyes slide sideways at Corey.

"You know how to clean house, do you?"

"No."

"Thought not."

"What are you doing?" cries Ariel in alarm, as Corey reaches for the wall phone.

"Calling your mother to come and get you."

"No! Don't! Don't! Don't! Don't!"

Corey stops with her hand on the phone at the sight of a transformed Ariel, the thirteen-year-old world-weary sophisticate turned into a bawling child who jumps up and down in the middle of the kitchen with her fists clenched and face red, mouth open wide enough to see the back of her throat, crying projectile tears. Inchoate sounds—"No, don't call my mom, don't, don't—"

"What?" says Corey, aghast.

"Let me stay tonight, just tonight, just one night, I promise—"

"Ariel—" what would Mizzy do, what would Gran do, what would Loren do—"I can't just keep somebody else's kid without telling them where she is. I'll call your mom and say you're staying here tonight and tomorrow we can—"

She stops at the sight of Ariel, more puddle than child, howling on the kitchen floor. Snot running from her nose, bubbling on her upper lip. Corey goes to do what, scrape her up off the floor, she guesses, because she doesn't know a damn thing about raising kids, she's always dealt with them after they're old enough to sit at their desks and more or less behave themselves. This tantrum, if it's a tantrum, is beyond anything she's seen.

"Okay, okay, you can stay tonight, I'll think of what to do in the morning."

She reaches for Ariel, and Ariel stiffens. Pounds her fists on the linoleum, throws back her head until the cords of her neck are ready to snap. Raises her eyes to the ceiling light bulb.

"Uncle Eugene!" screams Ariel. "Uncle Eugene! Uncle Eugene! Uncle Eugene!"

A last late spatter of rain blows across the window, hurried by the wind. Corey listens to the roar of the ridge pines, heaving out there in the dark and flinging their boughs after the departing storm, as she sits on the kitchen floor with her arms full of Ariel.

"We'll think of something in the morning," is all she can think to say. Whatever the hell it might be.

12

By daybreak Corey's up and dressed, pacing and sipping coffee and occasionally looking in on Ariel, for whom she'd made up a bed last night on the horrible old couch. Ariel, being young and soft-boned as a puppy, sleeps on its broken springs with her face flushed and her eyes crusted shut, as though she'll never wake.

God! What to make of her tale, which sways like cobwebs from the ceiling, gathers obscurity in the corners of the cracked old windows, until the very room dims with its unlikelihood in the dawning of this new day. Charlie Russell's two sightlines have never seemed so profound. But what can Corey do, except drink her coffee and drive to town and deposit Loren's goddamned money in the bank and hope none of Ariel's story is true?

Finally, although she knows the bank lobby won't open until ten, she can stand it no longer. She writes a note, props it against the toaster with the rest of the loaf of bread. Probably Ariel will have vanished again by the time she gets home, and that'll be the end of that.

That story of Annie's, about the time Loren backed her father up against the side of the barn and threatened to beat him bloody with the spoke out of a wagon wheel. Maybe Corey ought to go after somebody with a wagon spoke. But how to know?

Meanwhile the early sunlight catches droplets from last night's brief rain and strings its glittering beads along the fir boughs and hawthorn leaves and the heads of grasses, as though the world is still a fresh, clean place. Corey gets a baptismal shower that spills off the dent in the roof when she opens the door of the pickup. She climbs in, turns on the wipers to clear the windshield, and watches rainwater drip off the brim of her hat. Nothing is as it seems. She's elated for reasons she won't let on to herself. In spite of Ariel, she feels as though she's sitting an inch above the seat, her hands steering an air wheel just above the solid one, her thoughts bubbling over like the water in the creek, which looks muddy and brings her back to something more like normal. Maybe they'd got enough rain last night to green up the grass, at that. Maybe the grass in the butte pasture will last the mares and colts until fall, and then it will turn brown, a source of hidden protein under the snow crust for the horses to paw and uncover for winter feed.

Wherever the horses will be, this winter.

What she ought to do with Loren's money. Feed it to his horses. They'd eat it all, she knows.

Damn right, you ought to be using it to feed my horses!

At the barn she jerks the brake on the pickup, leaves it running, and rolls open the heavy door to the mow. Sees nothing but hollow darkness until her eyes clear. Her heart pounds once when she thinks her saddlebags aren't still buckled to her saddle, but it's all right, it's only a trick of the shadows, there they hang in the dim light, in the warm scent of hay and dust and ancient leather, harnesses and hames and horse collars and spiderwebs. She kicks aside the old Surge milking machine—something else she could paint on—unbuckles the saddlebags, takes out the manila envelopes and counts them.

Stealing from me, Loren accuses.

Yeah, you'd have kept your goddamn money under your bed for the rest of time. And you couldn't even be bothered to leave me a note. What if I hadn't found it? The house could have caught fire and burned down. Or what if I died and somebody bought the place, moved in, and hit the jackpot.

Letting that little liar spend the night with you. Who knows what she's up to. Probably looking to see what else she can steal.

What's left to steal? Your new little stud? Ariel wouldn't know how to catch him.

She stows the saddlebags back of the seat in the pickup. Opens the pole gate. Drives through, gets out and shuts it again. How many back-and-forth steps in her life, opening and shutting gates behind herself. Some people would have put in a cattle guard, saved themselves a lot of trouble.

You're letting yourself in for a whole hell of a lot more trouble than opening and shutting gates. You should have sent her back to her dad. He'll give her what she needs, which is a damn good licking.

"You're a fine one to talk," she tells Loren. "You're the one who stood up for Annie Reisenaur. How's Ariel different from Annie?"

That silences him for a few minutes. Corey can feel him thinking it over while she drives the familiar road to town. The embankment where pines hang over the gravel, their roots exposed where the highway crew got a little too close with their grader. The deep bend where snow often drifts the road shut in the winter, so that residents of the gulch must either shovel their way out or stay home. The narrow curve where it's easy to let a wheel drop off the edge, a hundred dizzy feet above the creek. There's the fancy wrought-iron gate to what used to be the Reisenaur place, sun glinting off the glass on the retired veterinarian's A-frame, and there's the turn-off to Annie's trailer in its dusty lot. On the other side of the road, Hailey Doggett's driveway disappears into the willows. We like our privacy, Rose Doggett had explained to her, when they first started coming to the Mill Creek school. From the road, Corey can get just a glimpse of the spreading lawn and the glass and timbered house, all as quiet as though the gunfire isn't likely to resume at twilight.

Annie's a neighbor. Known her all my life, and her old man, too. What do you know about them Doggetts that ain't bad?

That's just it, Loren.

Surely no parent would—well, of course there are perverts in the world, Corey knows that. She attended that continuing-ed workshop, for example, when the Mill Creek school got the computers, and listened to all that discussion about the perils of the Internet, which Corey visualizes as an endless, shapeless wasteland echoing with the din of all the voices in the world, all talking at once in a chaos like her own mind, which apparently contains every word, fragment, conversation she's ever heard or imagined, warring and bumping into each other and competing for the narrative. Maybe the Internet's where Ariel got her story.

He waits until they go to bed, and then he comes in my room.

Can't you call out?

He'd say it was my fault. My dad believes everything he says. My dad would take his belt to me again.

What about your mother? Corey had asked, disbelieving what her ears were telling her she'd heard.

Her! What would she say, *oh Hailey, no-ooo?*

Even as Corey had sat on the kitchen floor with Ariel in her arms, under the bare glare of the electric light, to the sound of the wind exploring the eaves and the windows rattling as though in indignation at such a tale, she'd had to bite her lip to keep from grinning, Ariel so perfectly mimicked Rita's bleat.

No, by light of day, it's got to be a high-drama story made up by Ariel. Young girls are not being raped in their own beds by their uncles. Corey's mind balks. Nothing of the kind is happening here in the foothills, not here in this protected bastion where the mountains hold the world at bay, and where roads are still graveled and the creeks run with clear, cold water, and where, if Corey keeps her eyes off the housing developments, nothing seems changed from her own childhood.

There, for example, is the same little cottonwood grove by the culvert, fed by springs from the coulee, where Barb Staple's father used to get off the school bus. A freckled, skinny kid with a lunch pail.

Lunch pails! Ariel sneered, fifty years later. We have to carry lunch pails to this school? In Santa Monica, we were catered by McDonald's!

Oh, Corey remembers Barb Staple's father well. And what was he going home to but chores, ranch work, like all kids in those days. He'd grown up to be a working fool. Worked himself into an early heart attack.

God! Her mind feels saturated. She doesn't want to think about the old unforgiving work ethic, or about the new leisure and affluence, where kids like Ariel Doggett can scatter small change and not bother to stop and pick it up and their fathers can do the same with twenty-dollar bills. What she had wanted to think about, had planned to indulge herself remembering in the night, is a moment in a lighted room when a man reached his hand toward her, a moment that won't happen again, and yet buoys her, lights her vision, levitates her, until she hardly feels the bumps in the county road.

What a pretty dream!

You keep out of my dreams, Andreas.

All the misery in the world, and you can still dream like a teenager?

Never said that. I just—

Damn right, chips in Loren. *It's your fault. If you'd behaved yourself, hadn't got yourself fired, hadn't mixed it up with that little son of a bitch, Hailey Doggett, in the first place—*

"Shut up!" she yells, and in frustration at their ganging up on her, she pounds at the steering wheel and hits the horn by mistake, and the truck lets out a blast that startles one of Nolan Staple's fat heifers, grazing along the fence, into jerking her head up with a mouthful of grass sticking out both sides of her face.

Andreas changes the subject. *What did the old women mean when they said a man was ornery?*

Overheard voices. *Old Reisenaur was ornery,* said Gran. *She lost it, was the blessing,* said Mizzy. Corey, the eavesdropping child, imagined a baby lost in the grass and went to look for it. Perhaps it would be like a fawn, curled so still that she could hardly see the rise and fall of its breath under its spotted pelt. She knew never to touch a fawn. The doe wouldn't come back for it if she smelled the human contamination. But she would have lifted the baby out of the grass, if she could have found it, the shivering baby, and wrapped it in warm cloth and brought it home.

In Fort Maginnis Corey turns down Main Street at the traffic light and parks in front of the bank. Thinks she might walk up to the Majestic for a cup of coffee, but what to do with the saddlebags. Guesses she could carry them with her, but how odd she would look, not to speak of how odd she'd feel sitting on a counter stool in the Majestic with thirty-odd thousand draped over her knee. In the end she props one bootheel on the dashboard of the pickup and pulls her hat over her eyes to wait the hour and a half for the bank to open. Feels good to close her eyes. She guesses her short night is catching up with her. Surely she can let it all drift for a while. Forget about the brat, at least. Forget about the thirteen year old's histrionics.

She leaps awake, arms and legs thrashing in the confines of the cab, what the hell was that! A shotgun blast right next to her is what it sounded like. She shoves back her hat so she can see what's going on, and it was a shotgun blast, because through the windshield she sees the shotgun man with a bandanna tied over the lower part of his face and headed for the bank with two or three bandanna-disguised henchmen, all armed to the teeth with knives and revolvers and what looks to Corey like a single-shot buffalo gun. Somebody's liable to get hurt, because they're firing their revolvers in all directions, and sure enough, a sparse crowd seems to have gathered to watch what's going on, a few local business people Corey recognizes, a smattering of tourists in colorful clothing, quite a few children.

Corey belatedly realizes what's happening as a shadow materializes behind the plate-glass doors of the bank, a young woman in a red blazer and navy skirt who opens the doors with a key and, looking resigned, passes out what looks like an old-time strongbox, weathered wood with brass fittings, to the shotgun man. She instantly closes and locks the doors again. The shotgun man turns and holds the strongbox aloft while his henchmen cheer and clench and wave what fists aren't encumbered with revolvers. Arrright! The shotgun man is wearing a long black frock coat over blue jeans and knee-high fringed boots. One of the henchmen wears leather chaps, although he can't bend his knees under them when he walks, and another sports a bobcat-skin vest that must be excruciatingly hot in the morning sun, and still another is apparently supposed to be an Indian with a bow and arrow.

And now there's gunfire from back of the crowd. Heads turn. It's the posse, of course, armed with enough black-powder pistols and rifles to re-fight the Plains Wars. Corey recognizes the younger Tendenning boy, Steve, as the head of the posse, and he gives her a sheepish glance and a grin when he sees her. Like the bank robbers, the boys in the posse (a couple of them are girls) are all dressed up in fringed leather and beadwork and Stetson hats that, from their antique styling, could have belonged to their grandfathers. One kid's even wearing spurs. Corey has to wonder how they think ordinary townspeople used to dress. Probably think they wore their spurs to bed.

The firefight spreads across the street and interrupts traffic. Bullet wounds appear to be plentiful, especially shoulder wounds, which allow the re-enactors to grab themselves, stagger, and go on firing. Gradually the bad guys take more and more shoulder wounds, until they're forced to their knees. The Indian goes down, clutching his throat and kicking in his death agony. (Good God, it's the older Tendenning boy, Park.) The air reeks of black powder. Down goes another henchman, and another, and now the shotgun man in the black frock coat is the only bad guy left standing. With the strongbox under his arm, he snarls hideous defiance at the posse. But it's no use, they have him cornered and outnumbered. Bam! Bam! Bam! Bam! Fighting to his last breath, he writhes and rises to fire one last shot before he dies in a heap.

A smattering of applause. The members of the posse congratulate each other, shaking hands all around, even those hands attached to arms and shoulders that have taken bullets. Steve Tendenning, wearing his sheriff's star, wrests the strongbox from the dead shotgun man and, on his way to the bank to return it, delivers a passing kick to his older brother's dead body, which doubles up and yelps.

It's the third of July, after all. Every third of July in Fort Maginnis there's a reenactment of the day in the 1890s when a local individual known as Dick-Dog tried to rob the bank and was shot and killed in the attempt. The performance will be repeated several times during the day. Indeed, Dick-Dog's picking himself up now, shaking out the skirts of his frock coat and rubbing his elbows.

The crowd has scattered. Corey is thinking it's too bad John Perrine wasn't here, it was his kind of show, when she catches sight of him at the other end of the block, helping to move the sawhorses that had blocked off traffic during the reenactment.

Her first impulse is to duck down under the dash so he can't see her. But he's busy and unaware, and she can't help watching him as he helps lift a stack of sawhorses into the back of a city truck, then brushes dust off his suit pants. His not knowing she's watching is an unearned pleasure that she'll pay for the next time she faces him, and yet she can't tear her eyes away, she absorbs the way his muscles strain his coat sleeves, his easy way of shaking hands with one of the city workers. Well-liked, well-known in town, isn't he, and then the way he walks, used to wearing cowboy boots, at least he's got the walk, in spite of all the insults Loren keeps coming up with. And then he's gone, presumably back to his office, and the sun is still shining on the street, and traffic is resuming.

Corey climbs out of the pickup with her saddlebags, slings them over her shoulder. Pats her watch pocket to be sure she's got her keys. Where the young woman in the red blazer had been, she now sees herself reflected back darkly in the plate-glass door to the bank. Boots and hat and saddlebags. God. She herself looks like something out of an old gunslinger movie. She looks like she ought to be playing shoot-'em-up with the kids in the street. Maybe she ought to get her hair cut.

A safe-deposit box, she explains to the bank officer, another young woman in a red blazer and navy skirt, identical to those of the tellers and clerks.

"How big a box?"

She shows Corey the measurements. Corey decides the regular size will do. She signs the forms, pays a year's rent on the box in cash from the roll in her pocket, and follows the bank officer back into the echoing vault, where her new key and the officer's key together open a steel box that slides out like a drawer from a wall of similar drawers. The bank officer retreats, discreetly, while Corey unpacks her saddlebags and stuffs manila envelopes into the steel drawer. Wonders how Loren's money feels, after all these years to be locked in the dark inside stainless-steel walls.

Where does money come from, where does it go—*what you gonna to do there, Cotton-eye Joe?*

"Ready?" asks the bank officer.

"Guess so."

Together they fit their keys and lock the box.

"Looks like you had some excitement out there in the street," says Corey on the way out of the vault.

The bank officer laughs. "The exciting part was getting permission from management for us to participate. Firearms that near the bank, even loaded with blanks? Did you see how fast I unlocked that door and locked it again?"

Outside the bank, Corey debates what to do next. Enough rain must have fallen in town last night to leave the street clean in the morning sun, although a mat of twigs and leaves clog the gratings, and the petunias in the hanging baskets look draggled. Well, what the hell. She pats her watch pocket again to make sure of her keys. There's the Bon Ton on her side of the street. She may as well pick up a few more tubes of paint before she has to go home and decide what to do about Ariel.

An alternative version of Ariel's story has occurred to her, a version involving Bobby Staple.

It's her story, sneers Loren, *and she can tell it any way she wants to.*

"Yeah, well, you just let me take care of it."

Ariel wakes, sneezing. Watches a gray cloud rise like dust motes in the stream of sunlight pouring over the couch. Is it alive—*lice?* No, *hair.* Some kind of animal hair, she guesses. She sits up with effort from the sag she's been sleeping in, something jabbing her every time she moves, a broken spring on this couch. Oh, oh, she's got to pee. Where is she, and why does she feel so awful?

Why did she have to wake up, when sleep felt so much safer? Maybe she could scrunch down again in the warm spot, back under this heavy *whatever,* this quilt made of old blue jeans sewed together, and let her dream find her. Because she'd been dreaming—except she can't quite recall—dreaming of home, perhaps, because she can still hear the withdrawing roar of freeway traffic reminding her that the world is still the world, humming with live people going about their oblivious business. And oh shit she's going to cry again, she can feel the tears, the desperation in her throat, because she never realized how much she misses the hum of traffic, misses traffic the way she misses *tacos*—how long has it been since she has bitten into a taco, savored the crunch of lettuce and the beef and cheese as soft as baby food, felt the satisfying hot orange juice spill over her mouth and run down her chin?—because if they sell tacos in shitty old Fort Maginnis, she's never found them, not proper tacos from a proper chain.

Because where she's ended up is on horrible old Corey-borey's horrible couch. She remembers now.

Ariel lets the quilt slide to the floor and looks around in the unforgiving sunlight. Dust, dog hair. A piano with its keys off-kilter and its ivories missing. A wooden rocking chair with a seat that sags as badly as the couch. Drifts of dead flies on the window ledges where the strange green deer gaze back at her with faces like hers, and a smell she can't identify, fetid, awful, reminding her how badly she needs to pee.

She won't go into that outhouse again, she'll squat outside instead. Wipe with leaves, she's done it before. But when she stands, she feels light-headed, so she sits down on the couch again, wondering why she's so empty.

What she'd told Corey.

Ariel runs over her story in her mind as though it's a video she's watching for the second time. Horrified at herself. What had she been thinking. She hadn't been thinking, that was what, because if she had, she'd have realized that Corey, being an adult, would be bound to tell *somebody*. And then what. Ariel fast-forwards, sees the *authorities* coming, dragging her home. Her mother's horrified face. Eugene? Couldn't have been. O-ooh, Hailey, what possessed Ariel to tell such an awful lie about Eugene. Oh, she couldn't have. That Henry woman must have made it up. Yes, that's it. It wasn't Ariel's story at all. You see, officer, we're filing a lawsuit against the Henry woman, she actually slapped, slapped this child right here, which in itself makes it so improbable that Ariel would have run to her with such a story, you have to agree. Thanks for bringing her home, officer, we've been so worried. And then her father stepping in, yes, thanks, officer, we'll handle it from here.

Telling the story to Corey last night, Ariel had cried. Ariel, who never cries. It shames her to remember.

Ariel tries her legs again, finds herself steadier. Stumbles through the kitchen, bumps against junk, blinks her way into the bright sunlight of the yard. No, she *can't* go into the awful outhouse, not after seeing it by flashlight last night, with its wavering shadows like spiders and its corners clotted with webs as thick as her wrist. And its *smell*. No. She locates a sheltered spot underneath the firs, pulls down her pants and squats and lets loose.

Oh, the relief. Oh, surely she can do what she needs to do, surely she can find the means to stay alive a little longer.

She finds a handful of grass, looks up as she wipes herself, and sees horses watching her. A big horse and a little horse, ears pricked curiously at what she's doing.

"No!" cries Ariel. "Go away," and their ears flicker at her voice, but the dumb things don't budge, and suddenly it's too much for Ariel, earth and sky and grass and trees and huge living brutes she can't predict. She grabs her pants and—what choice, after all, does she have?—runs, runs for the timber.

Feeling guilty, Corey has skimmed off a few hundreds from Loren's stash before consigning it to the steel safe-deposit box. Guiltier still—there's Ariel, after all, she should be going straight home, doing something about her—she heads for the Bon Ton where, at the sound of the door chime, the woman in the smock leans around her office door, recognizes her and gives her a distracted wave as she goes back to whatever she's doing. Corey threads her way past the dusty gifts and souvenirs. Pauses at a display of evaporated milk cans, labeled *Jackalope Milk*, with a picture of a jackalope instead of a cow. What next. A new line of picture postcards catches her eye. Glossy black-and-white photographs, a man on horseback with two dogs behind him on his saddle. *Montana double date*. Another of a man shoveling manure while two horses watch from their corral. *Practicing for Montana politics*, it reads.

She wonders who buys such things. Who the joke is on. The jackalope joke was on dudes, that they would believe such a thing really existed, a cross between a jackrabbit and an antelope. But nowadays a dude isn't a greenhorn, a dude is *cool*, and she has a feeling that the joke has been turned upside down.

Back among the art supplies, she picks out the tubes of oils she can't do without, another large zinc white and a replenishment of her reds. A canvas, why not. She can see that the bill will come to at least another forty dollars. What the hell. Maybe she should have skimmed off more.

"Money, money, money," sighs the woman in the smock as she counts out Corey's change in pennies and dimes from the cash drawer.

"Do you own the Bon Ton?"

"Inherited it. I couldn't bear to close it." She glances down the empty counter, laughs. "We aren't always this empty. Really. We—well, my partner has a paying job, which keeps us afloat. But we're hoping for more tourist trade."

"I suppose the kids all want to drive up the hill to McDonald's." says Corey, and the other woman makes a rueful face and nods.

"Have you got kids?"

"Got a thirteen-year-old girl at home," Corey hears herself say.

"Oh, dear. So you know what it's like. Mine are fifteen and seventeen. *Bored*."

Corey nods. Wonders what possessed her. Wishes she could ask the other woman's advice.

"It's so hard. Even in a small town like this—the *drugs*—with a thirteen year old, I'm sure you know. Or can imagine. I'm Lucy Valach, by the way."

"Corey Henry." And there's a whole lot she'd rather not imagine.

She walks back to the pickup, tosses in her art supplies. Waits for a couple of cars and a Winnebago and a motorcycle to pass before she pulls out on Main. The Winnebago's got Minnesota license plates, but its passengers won't be giving Lucy Valach any business. When the light changes, it goes lumbering up Main Street hill on its way out of town. The big fellow on the Harley turns east, he's not a Bon Ton customer either, with his red bandanna tied over his head and his cell phone clapped to his ear. Corey watches him until he hangs a right on the Mill Creek road, wondering how he can balance and talk at the same time, let alone hear over the roar of those pipes.

She drives a block and parks in the Safeway lot. Sits in the cab for a minute, trying to remember what the Doggett girls used to carry in their lunch pails. But the sun's already strong, burning down on the windshield, and so Corey gets out and finds herself a shopping cart and pushes it through the automatic doors into the sudden freeze of air conditioning.

White bread and butter and milk. What else do kids like. Hamburger, she supposes, and buns. Frozen french fries. Ketchup. Ice cream. She's been thinking of turning off the refrigerator to save on the electric bill. Now here she is, buying groceries for a girl who probably will have vanished by the time she gets home.

In the check-out line, the women behind her are discussing the proposal for the new hospital in Fort Maginnis. What it'll cost the taxpayers.

"They got a web site that you can go to."

"Can you print it out?"

"Yeah, just go to hospital-dot-com and it will be real small, but click on it and it'll get bigger."

Don't even know what they're talking about, says Loren. *Glad I'm dead. Sure wouldn't have wanted to die in such a hospital as you'd have to click on.*

"Yeah, well," Corey says, aloud.

227

The woman ahead of her in line turns at the sound of her voice. "Hello, Corey!"

It's Val Tendenning, tanned and sturdy in T-shirt and Levi's and with a cart full of groceries. Pretty Val, her face so familiar, so much a part of what Murray County has always been. Val hasn't changed, Val isn't chattering about clicking on any dot-com. Well, yes, actually Val has changed, she's thirty years older than she was when she graduated from eighth grade at the Mill Creek school. Time has gouged its tracks around the famous blue eyes and silvered the hair that everybody was so proud of when Val was voted the county dairy princess back in, when, 1975 it must have been. A quarter of a century gone!

"I'm glad to see you buying groceries," says Val. "You look to me like you've lost weight this summer."

Corey glances down at herself. Same old, as far as she can see. Song lyrics, *she's knock-kneed and old, with a long lower jaw, you can see with one eye she's a reg'lar outlaw.* Val's no outlaw, she's a princess, and she's led her life right. Stayed home and took care of her dad after her sister took off, never complained but got prettier and married James, who everybody liked, even if he was a bookworm, and then he and Val had the boys, and now here she is.

"I hear you're coming to robbery rehearsal."

"What? Oh, yeah. Yeah, I guess." Corey takes a chance and asks, "What do you hear from Rita Doggett?"

Val looks blank. "Haven't seen her all summer. Not since your dad's funeral."

"Are the Doggett girls going to school in town this fall?"

"They still plan to homeschool them, last I heard."

Val is signing the check she has just written to pay for her groceries, and Corey looks at what Val's been buying, white bread and cereal and bananas poking out of the tops of bulging plastic bags.

"I did look at that one kind of cereal like you got," Corey says, "with those little colored bits, but it sure was expensive."

Val's eyes fly from the check she's just signed to the box of cereal—"Yes, but the boys like it."

Oh hell, she's made Val feel bad. Val thinks she's criticizing her. She realizes now that she'd sounded just like Loren. Probably sounded just like Val's father, too. *Don't be bringing home no five-dollar box of that pig swill! It ain't even as good as pig swill! Nothing in it but sugar and hot air, hell, the goddamn pigs would starve to death on it! Might just as well pour milk on the box it came in and eat that!*

"What else do kids like?" she asks, trying to do better, but all she gets is another strange look from Val. Has she been living alone so long that she sounds as strange as the hospital-dot-com women? Or maybe everybody but her sounds like the hospital-dot-com women, maybe everybody in Murray County has learned to speak a new language while her mind has wandered elsewhere, in conversations with the dead.

"Mine like chili," says Val, carefully. "They like spaghetti, stuff like that. Frozen pizza. Stuff my dad wouldn't have touched."

"Loren neither," admits Corey. "Mashed potatoes and gravy was what he liked. Roast beef. Or roast venison. Canned corn was the only vegetable he liked."

They stand briefly together in the glare of fluorescent lights, thinking their thoughts about old beef-and-venison fathers, until the cashier coughs and Val jumps and pays for her groceries. Wheels her cart toward the automatic doors. Pauses.

"Corey, you want one of Mugsy's puppies? We saved one."

"Dunno. Let me think about it. Might be moving to Billings."

Corey sets her groceries on the conveyor and watches the cashier ring them up, digs into one pocket for her roll of bills and into another pocket for the exact change.

What if she'd asked Val straight out if she'd heard anything about a runaway Doggett girl.

What if she'd asked her what she knows from sources as mysterious as the stars, hospital-dot-coms and cable-news channels beamed by satellites into the foothills, word of mouth and ill wind and shifting rumor about a world that contains Dick-Dog and jackalope milk and Uncle Eugene. Asked her to explain what Corey can't understand, how the old order has changed, and how one good custom can corrupt the world?

Asked her straight out whether her kids are having sex yet, or when they started. What they said about it and what she did about it.

Driving home, she glances across the alfalfa fields at the Staple place, tidy gravel and machine sheds and the roof of the house just showing over the cutbank. Bobby had been a good enough kid when she had him in school. Bashful when he was in the lower grades, a little mouthy as he got older. Hard to imagine him—well, no, not so hard to imagine, not with Bobby's lengthening young body, his gold-flecked glance—no, nothing ridiculous about the young in one another's arms.

Corey wouldn't have supposed Ariel Doggett would be smitten by a decent ranch kid like Bobby Staple. Maybe it was more a case of Bobby's being the nearest male in the neighborhood who was anywhere near Ariel's age, which certainly is easier to believe than to believe in an uncle who sneak into her room while her parents slept—or parents who could not be aware—or worse, parents who would pretend not to be aware—no.

No. No, even Corey can think of a more convincing version, having to do with Hailey's happening on Bobby and Ariel—a verisimilitude of pine needles under the naked children, the shafts of sunlight falling upon them—Hailey's blood-infused face—for Hailey would have been furious. From then on, some of Ariel's story could have been as she told it. Dragged home by the wrist, locked in her bedroom, escaping by night from the window, making up her details as she ran.

That's how it must have been.

Home again, Corey drives up to the picket fence and climbs out, and she's lifting her groceries out of the back of the pickup to carry them into the kitchen before she notices that the door off the porch is standing wide open. She stops, listening to the trickle of the creek, the faint chatter of wind through the battered hawthorns, the background roar of ridge pines, and the more immediate noise of magpies, quarreling somewhere in the pasture. Babe and the colt drowse from their opposite sides of the fence, occasionally stamping or swishing a black tail at nothing worse than flies. Nobody is alarmed but her.

A robin wings down from the firs. Corey watches as he studies the deep grass and hops a little farther with his head on one side. Thinks he owns the place, she supposes. The magpies probably think they own it.

Well. She squares her shoulders. Marches up the boardwalk. Feels the emptiness of the house along with the cool of the thick stone walls and the dimness. Sets down her groceries and sees the note she left for Ariel. Reads the added line at the bottom in stilted pencil.

I lied about all of it. Don't call anybody, because I lied.

That's the end of that, then. Good thing she didn't go off half-cocked.

All she needs to do now is forget about it.

13

For several days Corey keeps telling herself how thankful she is that she didn't make a bigger fool of herself. She's so glad she saw through Ariel's story that when she sees a white SUV pulling up to the pole gate, her first reaction startles her. *Hailey?* Come to confront her for spreading awful stories about him, or at least for thinking them? But no, it's not Hailey's SUV, it's got a bubble light on its roof, and the figure that gets out to open the gate is in uniform.

Sheriff, then. Corey watches the SUV pass the barn and ease toward the house, taking plenty of time on the gravel. When it crosses the plank bridge by the springhouse, she leaves the window and goes through the lean-to to the door.

Getting out and walking up to the picket fence is the deputy girl from the night of Loren's death. Corey recognizes her by her plump cheeks and anxious eyes under the brim of her cap.

"Corey Henry?"

"That's me."

She proffers a clipboard with a sheaf of papers. "Need you to sign here."

"What is this?"

"Hey, they don't tell me that. I just deliver. And I'm the only one that knew where you live."

The deputy girl interrupts herself, and Corey realizes she's part of a memory that's all too vivid for the girl, a rush of wind and moon clouds, a crazy old woman and a dead father. Probably told the other deputies how spooky it had been, how she'd kept talking, talking, using words to fill in the black hole until the coroner finally got there, and now here she is again, talking to Corey crosspatch.

But Corey's not what's on the girl's mind, after all, because she's flinching at the rattle of gunfire from down the gulch. "What's that?"

"Just the neighbors. Target practicing. I guess."

"Sounds like a war."

Corey has been listening to gunfire for so long that she's stopped hearing it. And maybe the deputy girl remembers her from a month ago, or maybe she doesn't, but Corey's not the same woman she was a month ago. The realization elates her, she's not stuck in some goddamn time warp after all.

Loren's growl rises under the throes of the ridge pines that are beginning to heave themselves and roar in the afternoon air currents. *Just because you bought paints and paint brushes, don't get to thinking you know something!*

She takes the papers she's been served. Turns to read the cover page as the deputy girl climbs back into her outfit and drives away.

In the District Court of the Second Judicial District of the State of Montana, Murray County. *Hailey Doggett v. Corey Henry.*

So it was Hailey Doggett, after all. So he really is suing her.

So another trip to town.

You just have to keep that road hot, complains her grandmother. *Town! What's in town that's so all-fired important?*

"Can't help it!"

Don't talk like that to your grandmother! shouts Loren, as if it hadn't been his own trips to town that used to annoy the old woman.

Corey parks across from the liquor store on a strew of brittle cotton-wood leaves last night's wind brought down and the city crew hasn't gotten around to sweeping up. A whine of wind with the feel of fall brings down another straggle of leaves as she crosses the street. Summer will be gone, winter coming on, song lyrics she half-remembers. The space behind the Western goods store with the reserved sign for J. Perrine is empty, bare glaring pavement and a blank wall of patched stone where his black truck usually is parked. Doesn't mean anything, she tells herself. He could have parked on the street in back of his building.

She knows where she's going, this time. She remembers the board stairs that echo under her boots, the rough masonry between the bricks that catches at her sleeves. This time she's ready, after the dim corridor, for the door that opens on a flood of light through the tall windows, the white space of the law office with its lofty ceilings and plaster garlands, even ready for Ingrid swiveling around on her chair behind her computer.

"He's not here," says Ingrid in her stiff-lipped way.

The window behind Ingrid holds clear, cloud-floating blue and just a glimpse of dusty rooftop. If she stands on her toes, Corey can see the tarnished knob on the top of the flagpole over the liquor store and a bit of the sun-faded color that is the flag, hanging limp, but no pigeon today, no purple swirl of feathers.

"Went to do something about his train-robbery business," Ingrid adds. Wenna do somin boutis tren-rorry bidnes. She studies Corey, as though for signs of the same irresponsibility.

"Yeah, well, I need to talk to him. About these papers I got served with."

They both look at the thick, stapled packet she's carrying.

Ingrid reads carefully for the first page or two, flips through the remaining pages, and lays the packet down on her desk. "Little shit," she remarks.

"So what do I have to do?"

Corey is startled to hear her voice wobble, it's the hint of sympathy from Ingrid that's done it, and Ingrid, who has started to swivel back to her computer screen, pauses. Something almost like an expression crosses her face, and Corey wonders, in a stray thread of thought, whether Ingrid's stiffness, her curious diction, is pathological. A partial paralysis, perhaps from a stroke.

"You don't have to do anything," says Ingrid. Yudn hafta donthin. "What's the date on it? You've got thirty days. John'll get his act together in thirty days and answer the little bastard."

At the common sense of it, Corey realizes she's been on the edge of panic. Expecting what. To lose the ranch, to hand over the safe-deposit stash to Hailey, to have to pack her duds and slink out of Murray County without money enough even to get as far as Billings?

"Nothing here to keep me awake at night?"

"Well, you can't ignore it. I'll tell John."

Corey nods. She's picturing John and seeing Ingrid, who almost certainly has horsed with him. Not that *horsing* is a word easily associated with Ingrid, who, with her large pitted face and thick body looks like somebody who could slap down John and his train robbers, not to speak of Dick-Dog and his whole gang, all without messing a strand of her shining coronet braids or creasing the purple dress she's wearing this afternoon, in a fabric with a nub and a sheen. Silk, Corey guesses. Probably cost what, a hundred dollars or more.

"Guess it's just the idea of Hailey," she says.

Ingrid nods—"He's a weird little shit. I betcha he beats that wife of his."

Rita Doggett, colorless as a moth in her neat denim skirt and jacket. Corey remembers the slump of Rita's shoulders, the indirection of her eyes. Voices thunder from the back of her head, Loren, and even Andreas, even Virgil, for once united, for once on her side. *Any son of a bitch that would lay a hand on a woman!*

"Easy to think the worst of Hailey Doggett, I guess."

"Tell you what," says Ingrid, "I'll have John stop by your place on his way home. No, it won't inconvenience him. He's been dying to."

Words fill Corey's head, buzz and zip and bump into each other. Words she could speak to Ingrid. Reluctantly she turns toward the door. And then Ingrid's phone rings.

Ingrid picks it up—"Lawoffica John Perrine—" listens for a moment—"he's nottsere atternoment—what do you mean, you don't where your kid is?"

Corey pauses with her hand on the doorknob. Silence behind her. She looks down at the scuffs of her boots on the dense carpet and thinks that a little boot polish wouldn't hurt. She thinks she knows where Loren kept his.

"You don't know where your kid is, you call the sheriff, is what you do," says Ingrid.

A pause.

"She hung up on me," Ingrid says. Shung upon me.

Back from town, Corey opens the gate in the picket fence and nearly jumps out of her skin as a cloud of dust puffs out the door toward her. Behind the dust is a broom wielded by Ariel Doggett.

"Jesus!" says Corey. "You startled me. Where have you been?"

Ariel leans on the broom, watching to see what Corey will do. The broom is as tall as Ariel. Corey pushes past her and threads her way through the goddamn obstacle course, washing machine and wood range and boxes and stacks of books. At the sink she stops. "Good God. What happened?"

Ariel follows her, still sulky. "I cleaned house for you."

"Where are my paints? What did you do with my paints?"

All the clutter on the kitchen table has vanished. Paints, brushes, breadboard painting of green deer, newspapers, dirty cups, Loren's ashtray. The table itself shines from a scrubbing and polishing, even its poor old scarred oak surface, even the brass claws on its legs. The place smells of disinfectant and lemon oil. Even the old linoleum has been swept and scrubbed, although no scrubbing could improve its rusty patches.

"Where the hell are my paints? What did you do with them?"

She realizes she's shouting when Ariel's chin quivers.

"They're in there." And oh hell, the kid is crying, mouth squared like a six year old, tears brimming over the sloe eyes and cutting tracks down the dirt on her face.

Quit your bawling! roars Loren. *Quit your bellyaching! If you don't quit your bawling, I'll give you something to bawl about!*

"You shut up," Corey tells him, and he growls off to the edges of her mind while she strides to the archway into the front room and stops again.

Ariel has dragged out a card table that Corey had forgotten they owned, and she's set it up where the broken-backed couch used to be. The breadboard with the green deer is carefully propped on the card table. The deer gaze back at Corey. In front of them, arranged in a neat row, are her tubes of oils. Her brushes in their jar on the windowsill. The couch, Corey notices, now sags its broken springs in Sonny's old corner.

"I thought you'd like it," weeps Ariel. "It's a north light, like you said was best."

The floors in here also have been swept and scrubbed. The windowsills cleared of Loren's books and stacks of magazines and the dead flies. The windows, for God's sake. Even the windows sparkle, and when have those windows ever been washed? How many layers of ochre from Loren's cigarettes has the kid scoured off? In this new clarity, this fresh view of fir branches and sunshine, Corey has to wonder how she's been seeing out of those windows up to now.

"What did you do with the stuff in the windowsills?" she asks, and she thinks her voice must sound halfway normal, because Ariel snivels and wipes her nose with her hand.

"I s-stacked all that shit out there on that old stove. I didn't have time to get to the utility room."

"No. I can see that."

She wonders where the kid found the cleaning supplies. Must have been stuff her grandmother had stored, maybe under the sink. Corey wouldn't have guessed that there was a bottle of lemon oil in the house.

"Well, hell," she says. "Just don't touch my paints again."

She looks again at the blotchy little face. The kid really is filthy, she notices, and not just from housecleaning. The sloe eyes ringed with grime, the dark curls matted and flattened, their gloss gone.

"You did a good job," she adds, gruffly. "So now. Are you hungry?"

And Ariel nods.

It takes Corey ten minutes to find the frying pan, which Ariel has scoured and hung on a nail in the cubbyhole under the stairs. She gets out a package of hamburger and flattens patties and fries them while Ariel digs through the pantry.

"No cheese? No pickles?"

"What would it take to satisfy you? Drink your milk."

"I don't like milk."

"Drink it anyway. It's good for your bones."

Ariel drinks, makes a face. "That's what my dad says."

Corey glances at her. "What did your mother say?"

"Her. I told you, all she does is sleep. You're not going to try to call her, are you? Because my dad always answers the phone."

"Haven't decided what I'm going to do."

"Anyway, I'm just *visiting* you. You don't call people's parents because they *visit* you, do you?

How would you know, jeers Virgil. *What do you know about kids? You're not even a real woman.*

"You can just crawl back in your hole," Corey tells him, and Ariel gives her a funny look. God. How often is she answering the voices out loud? And why couldn't she be hearing her grandmother's voice, or her mother's? At least they might have some worthwhile advice for her.

"Don't tell me you've been sleeping at home. Or have you got a new story for me?"

Ariel can't answer. She's gobbling down her hamburger, leaning over her plate with both elbows on the table and chewing with her mouth open, which would have earned Corey a dirty look and then a reprimand from Loren, and then Loren's stone cold treatment if she hadn't straightened up and eaten like a civilized girl. But Ariel, mid-bite, glances at the window, swallows and shoves away from the table.

"Who's that?"

"It's just Annie Reisenaur," says Corey, looking, but Ariel has vanished into the stairwell like a coyote pup into its hole.

Annie's taking her time getting out from behind the wheel of her old Subaru, one foot and then the other, then her knotted torso and finally her dandelion fluff of white hair, shining in the sun. She plods around the car and opens the passenger door, reaches into the seat. Looks like she's got a cake on a plate, a kettle of something, and what is probably a loaf of bread wrapped in a clean dishtowel. Corey hurries out to help her, takes the kettle and the cake.

"One of the boys brought me some venison burger, and I made myself a big pot of venison chili. Rather than eat chili all week, all by myself, I thought I'd just bring you some."

"You think I'm starving to death, Annie?"

Annie stops on the steps to catch her breath. Little beads of perspiration are popping out along the seams of her face. "Hoo-ee! Sure is getting hot. The only bad thing about my trailer house is how hot it gets. These old stone walls sure feel good."

She stops in the kitchen door and stares. "Well, my land! You sure cleaned house! You even scoured that old linoleum. I think your dad laid it right after the war, when we first could buy linoleum again."

Then she looks at Ariel's plate, on the table in plain view, nothing on it but crumbs and a smear of hamburger grease.

"Well," she says. "I'm glad to see you're cooking for yourself."

Corey guesses that Ariel took her hamburger with her when she ran. Probably she's sitting on the stairs, chewing and listening. She lifts the lid off Annie's kettle—"How much did you make? Gallons? Were you thinking we were going to have a blizzard this July and wouldn't be able to get to town? Or were you thinking we were going to have to hold off a siege?"

"You're too thin, Corey. Now if I could just lose a pound or two." Annie looks around, sniffs. "Smells like you've been painting. Sprucing the place up?"

"Yeah, well—"

"What on earth's that?"

Corey glances involuntarily at the stairwell—Ariel?—but no, Annie has wandered through the archway, admiring the clean floors and clean windows and expecting, Corey realizes, to find a fresh coat of latex paint on the walls. Instead, Annie has come face-to-face with the red horses. She looks away from the horses only to be confronted by the green deer. Stares at them for a minute.

"Colorful," says Annie, finally. "I guess."

She stumps back in the kitchen and sits at the table with her back to the archway, but she keeps looking over her shoulder at the paintings. Finally she moves to another chair.

Corey puts the coffee pot back on the stove, turns on the burner to warm up what's left from morning. She finds Annie a cup—clean! Corey wouldn't have thought that a girl raised with a dishwasher would know how to heat water and wash dishes, but Ariel has even bleached out the old coffee stains.

"Not that some days I don't think we might be under siege," says Annie, "what with all that racket from across the creek. Seems like they cut loose, bangety-bang bang, about the time my soaps come on, and sometimes they're still bangety-bang banging into the night. I bet you can hear them clear up here."

Annie sips, makes a face.

"I can make fresh," Corey offers.

"No, no. I've been drinking coffee with Doc Mackenzie, is all. The way he makes it, he grinds up whole beans in a little grinder, and then he pours boiling water in a glass jug and uses a kind of a plunger on it. He makes awful good coffee. He makes it too strong for me, is the only thing. I always have to add a little more water to mine."

"Loren used to build a little fire and boil coffee if we were riding all day. It always tasted good. Out in the open air, of course."

"Doc doesn't exactly boil it." Annie's eyes travel the kitchen, return to Corey's paintings. The eyes of the deer stare back, full of blinding clean light from the windows. Corey feels as though she's seeing Annie through their eyes, seeing a change in Annie that she can't quite put a finger on.

"Annie, did your kids ever tell you they hated you?"

"What?" Annie looks surprised. "No. No, but I suppose they must have thought it, sometimes. That's kids for you."

Part of the change in Annie is her freshly washed hair, Corey thinks but mostly that she's left off her baggy, elastic-waisted pants, and she's put on a loose smocked dress patterned in swirls of raspberry and pink, and she smells of raspberries. The colors make her seem, well, not younger, because her face is brown and seamed as always, her hands knotted and twisted, but what? And does the difference make it harder or easier for Corey to ask the questions she wants to ask Annie?

"Nails would never have stood for them giving me lip, though. And of course my kids were ranch kids, Corey, same as me and you, and they always had work to do. Keep the kids' noses to the grindstone, my father always said. That's what keeps their noses out of trouble."

"Do you still hear him say it?"

"Well, in a way. In my mind, clear as a bell. Corey, you might have thought hateful thoughts about Loren when you were young, but you never meant anything by them. I just wish you'd come down and visit more often. You sit up here at the high end of the gulch with nothing to do but—" Annie glances involuntarily back at the portraits of the deer propped in the window—"nothing to do but think about Loren and what he was like. It isn't good for you."

"Annie, why didn't he want you to marry Nails?"

Annie spreads her hands on the table and studies them as though she can't believe they are hers. Wrinkled and brown-blotched, joints distorted. Corey wonders what ripped the white scar that worms along Annie's thumb, what split the nail on her index finger so it grows in two thickened halves. Wonders about all she's never asked.

"All that old misery," says Annie. "What's the good of dredging it up?"

"If it would help somebody else?"

"My father kept his fences up," says Annie. "He always paid his bills. Same as Loren did. You don't want to be living in the past, Corey."

"Hailey Doggett—"

"You don't need to be worrying about him, either. It's like I tell Doc. As long as them Doggetts keep to their side of the creek, we got no call to be watching and worrying what they're firing guns at."

"I'm not talking about firing guns." Corey has her eye on the stairwell. But so what if Ariel is listening? "The son of a bitch is suing me."

She watches Annie mouth the word, *suing,* as though she doesn't know what it means.

"Suing you," Annie repeats, finally. She starts to say something else, changes her mind, shakes her head. "I sure never thought he'd do a thing like that. Over slapping that little girl, I suppose. That's awful. That's just awful, Corey. But he can't get away with it, can he? After the way she behaved to you? Can he go to a court of law and make you pay him to let his girls cuss at you?"

"Don't know the answer to that."

"Oh, my goodness."

Annie ponders the stale coffee in her cup as though she expects some revelation to rise out of the scum. "I'm so sorry, Corey. I sure never thought anybody would be suing you in a court of law. Do you want me to say something to Doc Mackenzie? I could find out what Doc thinks you ought to do."

"No," says Corey, watching the stairwell. (And if she raises her voice slightly, so the listener on the stairs can hear, who can blame her?) "No. I've hired myself an attorney already, and he's a cracking good one."

In the early evening Corey looks up from her solitary bowl of reheated venison chili (first thing she'd done after Annie left was look for Ariel, but had found the stairwell empty, the whole upstairs empty, even the curtained closets, even the dust-rolled undersides of beds, but no, Ariel had done another of her flits; Corey can't quite believe Ariel climbed out a window and dropped all the way to the fir needles but how else?) and watches John Perrine's black truck pull up to the picket fence and John Perrine himself climb out, suited and Stetsoned and briefcased.

The sight of the briefcase makes Corey feel a little sick, and she pushes the bowl of chili away, but John, exotic as a dark-blooming flower in the familiar kitchen, sniffs so appreciatively as he sets down the goddamned briefcase that she has to offer him a bowl.

"Don't mind at all if I do!"

Before she can stop him, he's seating himself in Loren's chair, overflowing the worn oak that used to accommodate Loren's flat cowboy rear end and spare cowboy thighs. Rubbing his hands over the steaming bowl she sets in front of him—"Hardly had time for lunch today, wasn't looking forward to cooking for myself."

Corey thinks she may as well slice him some of Annie's bread to go with his chili, and he nods with his mouth full—"You wouldn't have a glass of milk?"

At first she doesn't think she does, then she remembers the gallon she bought for Ariel. A milk-drinking man! She sits at the corner of the table and watches him enjoy his meal. "So what about these papers Hailey's filed? Is he serious?" she can't help asking as soon as he pushes back from the table.

"A lawsuit always has to be taken seriously. Still—" he's made no move to open his briefcase. "What kind of physical damage are we talking about here? What exactly happened?"

"Well—" Corey pauses. What had happened. The answer, she's realizing, is more complicated than she would have supposed a month ago. The slap, of course, that's an undeniable fact, as are the hurtful, hateful words made worse by the child's mouth they spilled from. But the words, of course, were not a beginning, but a culmination.

"She'd never been easy to teach, but—"

"She. Ariel Doggett?"

"Yeah. Ariel. Don't know if you've ever seen her. She was twelve when she started at Mill Creek. A lot of twelve year olds are, well. Gawky. Awkward. Growing too fast, don't know what to do with themselves. But not Ariel. She was—she is—well, she's a beautiful little girl, and also she's (recent sobs and snotty nose come to mind, but no need to describe that to John) *knowing*. Used to be, at least."

"Twelve going on thirty?"

"Something like that."

Corey is seeing the light from the north windows of the Mill Creek school, so often the clean, reflected light from fresh snow. She's watching Corey Henry watching the silent fall of flakes on the cold side of those windows, the bent heads of concentrating children at their desks in the warm schoolroom. Corey Henry wishing she was on the cold side, Corey Henry with her craw full of half-realized resentments, her temper always on the verge of cracking like a whip over somebody's poor head.

"Ariel always hated the school, or said she did, said it was the sticks and the rest of the kids were hicks. They were in awe of her, and I guess

I was, too. She was so poised. It wasn't just that she was looking down on me, but I deserved looking down on. What I started to tell you," she hurries over John's interruption, "is how it got worse."

"Worse in what way?"

"She'd always been a handful, but also she was curious, and she could be very generous with the other kids. I almost liked her, even. I remember one time she brought her manicure kit to school—I thought it probably was her mother's, it was so expensive-looking, until I saw the colors—and she painted everybody's fingernails with stars and swirls and little designs. She even painted the two little first-grade boys, and they were so proud, holding up their green fingernails." Corey has to laugh. "She even painted mine. Green with glitter. I thought Loren was going to have a stroke when he saw me."

Painted up like a goddamned buckle bunny! Worse! You look like a buckle bunny from outer space! And how you're going to get that stuff off of your fingernails—

"But then she turned thirteen, and all of a sudden it was like she hated the world and everybody in it. She was driving me crazy—"

Ariel looking up when her head was supposed to be bent, ripping a page out of her social studies book, crumpling it and hitting Corey in the shoulder with it as she turned from the window. Ariel erupting from her seat when she'd been told not to, passing the teacher's desk on her way to the bathroom and knocking over a cup of coffee with a sideways slam of her hand.

"It was one thing after another. Rudeness, ridicule, destructiveness—of course her dad would always pay for the ruined books and so forth."

Corey had felt at the time that Ariel was punishing her for her slow wit, for her lack of knowledge of the world—what was the word Ariel had used—for being a *clod*—and yet, when she looks back, she wonders why she assumed that Ariel's behavior had to do with her, at all.

"Maybe I was too hard on her. Maybe I wasn't paying enough attention. I ran the school the way I always had. Kept the kids sitting in their seats, raising their hands if they wanted something. All of a sudden I couldn't do that any more. I talked to Hailey several times, and I tried to talk to Rita. They gave me to understand it was my fault, I didn't understand Ariel, I was too old-fashioned, she wasn't used to being thwarted, whatever that meant. But Ariel was a kid, and I was a grown-up, and I should have seen that something was wrong."

John has been listening, leaning forward out of Loren's chair with his arms folded, as intent as though he's never heard such a story before. Corey sneaks a look at him. Knows if she makes eye contact with him, she'll say something stupid, it's been that kind of day.

"So one way we might go is that you'd be willing to offer Ariel and her parents an apology? You were under stress, you acted hastily, you regret it—"

Loren boils over: *No, by God! No apologies! No bull-riding, so-called attorney is going to sit in my chair, fat as a goddamned ox, and he might as well be an ox, the way he rolls those big brown eyes at you, and try to say it wasn't that foul-mouthed little trollop's own fault that she got what was coming to her! Who the hell is telling this story?*

I am, Loren.

"I could do that," she says, "if you think it'd help."

"It might."

Corey ends up pouring a whiskey for John and one for herself, sits at the kitchen table with him and spreads out the scrapbooks her grandmother kept for Loren. At least it takes her mind off the Doggetts, she tells herself, and anyway John's been longing to see the scrapbooks ever since he's known about them.

He turns page after crumbling page, reading all the newspaper clippings and poring over the pictures.

"Looks like he rode more what they called center fire, in those days, than I'd have expected a Montana boy to ride. Single cinch, pretty much centered under the saddle? And the way he sat back in the saddle, with his stirrups forward?"

"Just the way I ride."

"So I've noticed. And he was a dally man, wasn't he?"

"Always. He never liked to tie a rope. Taught me the same way. Said more cowboys got their necks broken with a tied rope than dally men ever pinched a finger."

John studies a snapshot of Loren riding a stocky gray horse sometime in the 1940s, just after he got out of the service. "That center fire rig was good for riding the rough stock. A lot of the bronc busters and rodeo riders used it. Maybe that's where he got started."

"Could be."

"What I wouldn't give to have known those old boys."

He thinks you're part of the glory, Loren warns.

You can't paint lies, says Andreas, *and glory is a waste of oils.*

Corey shrugs—"Yeah, well. It wasn't all great. Poor old Will Ballard—you met him, he grew up on the place you're living on—he wanted to go away to school and be a teacher. When his dad died, he came home, but he couldn't make the ranch pay. Had to sell. Some people still make fun of him, calling him an educated fool and telling him what a good absent-minded professor he'd make."

"You taught."

"Yeah. It was okay for a girl to teach, as long as she—"

"As long as she what?"

Corey wishes she hadn't started down this trail. "I don't know," she says, embarrassed. "They never spelled it out. As long as the girl didn't get ideas about herself. Didn't get to thinking she was somebody."

John closes the scrapbook carefully, reverentially.

It's not you that the fat attorney is interested in, Loren warns. *It's the glory.*

It's not that Corey hasn't tried to tell John Perrine what the old life was really like. Told, hearing Loren's voice in her head:

These hot-blood colts we got now, they got to be handled different. Not like we did before the war, when we was working with four-and five-year-olds that never felt a rope until we run 'em into a corral and front-footed them. We'd hog-tie 'em, sack 'em out, throw on a saddle and let 'em buck. We figured eight, ten saddlings to take the rough off 'em—

Oh, Corey remembers. She has tried to describe it for John. The sun streaming down on the round corral. A gasping horse, hog-tied. Trying to raise its head, letting it fall back into fine dirt and pulverized manure. The smell of fear and settling dust. The dog before Sonny, no, many dogs before Sonny, watching through the corral poles in hopes of bloody flesh, a tidbit from a gelding, and risking a cussing-out from Loren. Loren sitting on the hog-tied horse's flank, legs crossed, smoking a cigarette. Face obscured by his hat, sweat beading on his neck, sweat soaking the vee between the shoulders of his blue chambray work shirt, washed and faded to near-white and rolled at the sleeves where his forearms had burned dark brown.

Corey the child, watching through the corral poles with the dog.

Corey the older child, retrieving her father's hat when it sailed off during a first saddling, trying it on and feeling the damp of its sweatband as its darkness settled past her ears and hid her eyes until she tipped her head back.

Corey the teenager, working in the corral with Loren.

A hard life," John had agreed. But his eyes were soft and distant, and she feared he had not heard the story she had told.

What are you going to do about Ariel? How long has she been hanging around?

Corey shakes her head. She isn't even sure which voice she's hearing—Andreas's, Ingrid's, maybe even John's. But if Ariel is a runaway, why isn't everybody talking about a runaway girl? Articles in the paper about her, posters on telephone poles, whatever folks do when a thirteen-year-old kid runs away?

Bobby Staple lifts the baggie of weed out of his shirt pocket, breaks open the cigarette for its tobacco, and rolls the split. Strikes a match and, careful Montana boy, pinches out the flame and rolls the blackened head between his fingers before he drops it into the pine needles. He passes the split to Ariel, and she takes it like an old friend and draws deeply. Closes her eyes, lets the sweet smoke fill her. Never, never, never would she have dreamed a time would come when she'd be so starved for it. How long—she starts to count on her fingers—not since the night of her parents' party, when the Lambert boys gave her a toke and felt her up.

She exhales and passes it back to Bobby. "I hate it when you split it," she says. "It's better to smoke the sweet weed and smoke the cigarette after."

"Hey, I ain't got that much."

Bobby takes a nip, but his heart isn't in it. His eyes wander back down the trail where the little girls, Rose and Amy, squat between the old fence and the big pine tree, keeping watch.

"How come your folks aren't raising more ruckus?"

"Give me another hit," she says, and draws deeply.

"Why aren't they?"

His persistence makes her exhale before she wants to. Serious golden-eyed Bobby with his head and shoulders cross-hatched by the shade, leaning toward her in the scented warmth. Shoulders that break her heart. She glares at him, lip trembling.

"Want me to talk to m'dad?"

"No!"

Has your uncle got some *power* over your dad, Bobby has asked, and Ariel guesses he has. Something he and her dad both know, the fragment she can't recover. Indictment, a word. Money, more than a word. First her family had enough money, not exactly rich, but enough. Suddenly they had tons of money, enough money to move to Montana and buy everything new. Now? Something's happened to the money, she doesn't know what. But if Bobby talks to his dad, the next thing will be the cops, and Ariel can just see herself being dragged home and made to explain herself. Either she's lying or she's not lying, and the cops will want to know which, and of course her mom and dad will say she's lying. But what if the cops get to sniffing around. If they hike up the hill to where her dad and Uncle Eugene have parked the camper—the stockpiles—Ariel shrivels at the thought, won't let herself imagine the absolute end of the world and how it will have been all her fault.

On the other hand, she can't live up here in the brush forever. Winter will arrive—she imagines herself shrouded in snow, slowly freezing to death.—she has to do something, she can't think what.

Also. How many days is she late. She tries counting on her fingers again, but she's lost track of time, can't remember how long ago she slept on Corey's couch or how many nights she's huddled on the pad of newspapers in the brush tunnel, tightening her blanket around her and trying to sleep and worrying about wild animals in spite of Bobby's reassurances. No bears, he keeps telling her. No wolves. Well, maybe coyotes, but they won't bother you.

Something rustles on a pine branch over her head, a shadow shaping itself into a ruff of tiny arrows. The nightmare thing! The vampire thing, in broad daylight! An animal with a little snout and dark pig eyes that glare down at her. "What is it?" she screams.

Bobby looks up—"It's just a porcupine. Hey, it's harmless, as long as you don't—"

But Ariel is sobbing, and to show her that it really can't hurt her, that it really is harmless, he finds a dead branch that's long enough to poke and jab until the porcupine loses its grip and drops scrabbling into the pine needles, trying in its slow way to find its footing and hide itself in the underbrush. But Bobby's ahead of it, and while Ariel watches through her fingers, horrified, he hits it a good crack on its one vulnerable place, its snout. The porcupine goes limp. A tiny seep of dark blood mats its coarse hair. Bobby whacks it again.

"What are you doing? What are you doing?"

"I'm killin' it. Isn't that what you wanted me to do?" he says, baffled, as Ariel flings herself at him, hysterical, pounding at him with her fists, crying, shrieking, until the two little girls come running up the trail to see what's happening.

"No! No! No! No! No! No! No! No! No!" she screams, and nothing Bobby can say, none of his flustered explanations that it's no big deal, that killing porcupines keeps quills out of the calves' noses, that he's always done it, that his dad does it, that everybody does it, and if she could just once see a dog or a calf that's had to have quills pulled until its nose looks like raw hamburger, not even that image calms her. In the end he has to put his arms around her and hold her while she sobs and sobs until she can sob no more and pulls away from him, trembling, to sink on her knees on her bed of newspapers in her pitiful last refuge, her pine bower.

14

"You again," says Corey, annoyed that she's got to stop staring at her blank canvas and look at Ariel, bedraggled and defiant in the arch-way between the kitchen and front room. "Have you been home or not?"

"Sure."

"Sure you've been home, or sure you've been hanging out? You look like you've been hanging out. You've got beggar's lice in your hair."

"*Lice?*"

"Burrs. *Plant* burrs. Don't worry, they're not alive."

Ariel doesn't bother to give that an answer. She flounces out of sight, but Corey hears the refrigerator door being opened.

"Hey!" she calls. "You drop in, you disappear, you drop in again— oh hell, I suppose I've got to—" grumbling to herself, she lays down her brush and pushes back a strand of hair with her wrist, then sees the streak of paint on her wrist and supposes she's got paint on her face and in her hair, too.

"Don't be so picky. You ought to be damned thankful for anything I've got that you can eat. If you're hungry, open yourself a can of soup and heat it up."

She shows Ariel the cubbyhole under the stairs where she keeps stores. So she can see what she's doing, she screws in the lightbulb that's never had a switch, one more of Loren's halfway electrical installations that ought to be fixed, and watches as the kid burrows into the tiny space. Notes the mud caked on the seat of Ariel's jeans, the grime worn in over days, and now fresh cobwebs in her hair when she emerges with a can of pork and beans, one of Loren's old favorites.

As haughtily as though she's wearing silks instead of filthy jeans and a filthy T-shirt, Ariel finds the can opener and a saucepan, starts her beans and stands over them, stirring. Corey has to laugh, and yet her eyes keep going out of focus, seeing Ariel as a set of planes and shadows, nothing easy. She wonders how women stand to raise kids.

"I have permission to stay the night with you," says Ariel without looking up from her bean-stirring.

"Yeah?"

She waits. Sure enough, Ariel can't keep from sneaking a glance, assessing her chances.

"One good turn deserves another," says Corey. "How about if you pose for me?"

"Do what?"

"Eat your beans. Then I'll show you."

Corey has been trying to decide what she wants to do with her new canvas. Its clean blank surface has repelled her and drawn her back. What is it trying to tell her? She has watched it sideways, as if she can see through the coarse weave. Wondering where she dared lay a brushstroke. Knowing in her bones that her quandary has to do with the questions that wake her up at night.

Now she arranges Ariel on the deep windowsill. Ariel (beggar's lice picked, tiny burr by clinging burr detached from strands of silky black hair—ow! ow!—bathed and shampooed in the galvanized tub—I'm supposed to get into this? In the kitchen? Don't watch me!—clothed in moldy-smelling jeans and shirt worn by Corey at age ten or so and dug out of one of the boxes upstairs) sits willingly enough, although she keeps pulling up her knees and dropping her chin. Corey has to keep looking around Ariel's knees to catch the girl's expression, so finally she incorporates the knees into the painting, transforming them into the rough trunks of pines, with Ariel's face looking slant-wise through pine needles and the shadows of aspens that tint her skin in shades of green, as though she is growing into the trees, or the trees growing into her.

Gradually, as Corey paints, the faces of deer emerge from the pools of green behind Ariel's face, and their eyes meet the eyes of the viewer and deplore the down-cast eyes of the child.

What do you think you're doing, Corey? If you treat the kid well enough, do you think that maybe Hailey Doggett will let you live?

The hell with Hailey. And if he won't go to hell, at least he can stay out of her thoughts. After a while, he does. She paints with concentration, aware and irritated when Ariel gets tired of posing and pouts, otherwise as obsessive as though her life depends on layering the colors. Painting, she's in stasis. Time stops, the grass stands still. Surroundings recede, sounds are muffled as though over a long distance, until, exhausted, she has to lay down her brushes. Roll her shoulders, flex her aching back, look at the clock in disbelief. Three hours!

Ariel bounces off the couch and comes around the table to see how far Corey's gotten.

"Ick."

"What do you mean, ick?"

"I don't know. Why do you have to make me look as if I'm turning into a tree? I hate trees."

"So why've you been living under one?"

"Haven't."

"Sure."

Ariel stamps off. Stops, looks out the kitchen window. "Somebody's driving up to the gate. Is it your attorney?"

"No. Well—maybe."

"Where's Rita Doggett?" Barb Staple asks Val when she runs into her in town. "Have you seen her?"

"No, have you?"

They ask around. Anybody seen Rita Doggett? What's become of her?

"She's doing fine," says Annie. "Corey heard that Rita sleeps a lot, but what else has she got to do?"

Who told Corey?

Get rid of those Staple kids, Hailey has told Rita. They don't need to be hanging around. But supposing she tries to send Amy home, how is Rita to dismiss a child she so seldom sees, or sees only at a distance, flitting in and out of the willows? She can't call Barb, can't think what she could say to her without sounding as if it's Hailey's fault. Maybe she could ask Rose to send Amy home, but between Rita's naps and Rose's regular bedtime and rising, they are simultaneously awake only for a few overlapping hours. Rose has become a shadow. Probably she's playing along the creek with Amy Staple, keeping her knobby little body out of everyone's way.

Rita hasn't seen Bobby Staple since she can't remember when.

In some ways Eugene's extended visit has reminded her of their college days when he and Hailey hung out in Hailey's dorm room, peering into Hailey's computer screen until three or four in the morning, the two of them so absorbed that they forgot to eat until they looked up, faces greenish from the glow of the screen, and saw her with a six-pack and a box of pizza from the all-night restaurant.

Eugene was always the big brother. He was the planner, he knew which trades to make, when to click and where. In other ways, it was Hailey, even though he was so much younger, who was the big brother to Eugene. Smoothing over Eugene's social blunders—oh, Eugene really was a dweeb—even trying to set him up with one or two of Rita's friends. There were no problems between Hailey and Eugene. Their parents were out of the picture, the mother dead of cancer long before Rita met either brother, the father drifted off somewhere in a fourth or fifth marriage. No roots. But Hailey and Eugene were brothers, and they knew how to conjure money, and they trusted each other. It was just when they got rich on magic money that the really terrible things started to happen. Hailey had tried to explain to Rita what was coming down and why, but Hailey had been abrupt and fearful, and Rita had been terrified for him. Bad enough that Eugene was going to prison, but not Hailey, please not Hailey, she had prayed. When Hailey came home that last day and said he had closed out the accounts and they could find their dream home where the troubles couldn't follow, Rita hadn't spared Eugene a thought.

Now Eugene's as good as living with them, and nothing has changed, except that Eugene's got no hair at all, and he's tetchy in new ways, and he and Hailey hang out in Hailey's den, entertaining each other with their end-of-the-world fantasies and occasionally calling for her to bring them ale in glasses frosted from being kept in the freezer compartment of the refrigerator. Or else they're up in Eugene's camper where he's parked it in the trees. Or else they drape themselves in the deck chairs on the patio and while away their afternoons until it's time to go to the firing range. Sometimes Hailey and Eugene talk about the cost of electricity versus the expense of setting up a wind-powered system for absolute self-sufficiency, and sometimes they send Albert—Albert, how Rita loathes him, with his huge frame and his pale eyes that search everywhere, missing nothing—they send Albert on mysterious errands while Hailey jumps in the SUV and roars off to fetch the Lambert grandsons, who are being taught to fire pistols. And sometimes all three men shut the door of Hailey's den behind themselves like boys who shut the girls out of their clubhouse and discuss heavier topics.

Where's Ariel?

Ariel, even more shadowy than her sister. Invisible as the air she's named for, at least to her mother. Where's Ariel, she asks Hailey, and Hailey glances around. Why? She was here just a minute ago. Didn't you see her? You saw her, didn't you, Gene?

Who, Ariel? Oh yeah, sure, she was right here. Just a minute ago.

Punishing her mother, that's what Ariel's doing. Rita shrivels when she remembers her secret phone call to John Perrine's office. How could she have been so overwrought? Thank heaven Hailey doesn't know. Thank heaven John Perrine never returned her call.

Maybe Hailey's sent Ariel to spy on you, Corey.

What's he got her looking for?

Same thing you've been looking for. But by God, I knew what I was doing when I hid that money. No goddamn tax records! No bank records! Nothing for the government to sink its teeth into, and nothing for that little devil of a Hailey Doggett to get his hands on, either.

Has she gone upstairs on her own? Have you caught her looking through your desk?

No, but—

Because with Ariel, who can tell? Ariel walks as silently as a cat on her bare feet. She'll appear from nowhere at Corey's elbow, she'll laugh when Corey nearly jumps out of her skin, and then she'll barrage her with questions. How long have you lived here? Why do you want to live somewhere else? Why?

Corey has to admit that she'd eventually start to care about a stray cat, wouldn't she—well, maybe not a cat, she revises, to head off an explosion from Loren, who hates cats—but she doesn't want to think that Ariel's laughing face has only to do with flattery. Not that she's fool enough to believe that Ariel cares about her. Her! Old Corey Cowgirl, with her dry breasts and her desiccated womb? What could Corey nourish a child with? Jackalope milk?

Ariel sulks, swinging her legs—"I'm tired! Do you know how long you made me *sit* there? When are you coming home?"

"I've never been to a train-robbery rehearsal before. Dunno how late this one will run."

"Oh, sure! Staying out late with *him!*"

Corey can't tell if Ariel is teasing her or jealous of her. If it's teasing, it's not the kind she grew up with. Kidding, ribbing, joshing. Men kidded each other for their own reasons, but children were teased to tell them who they were and who they weren't. Put them in their right place!

What's the matter, you been patting yourself on the back so long that your elbow won't unbend? Who do you think you are? Maybe you think you're better than the rest of us. Well, you aren't. Oh! Look at her! She's mad now! We got her mad, now!

"Is that him?"

God yes, it's John Perrine, walking over from the barn. He's left his truck and horse trailer at the pole gate, ready to load Babe beside his big gelding and drive out to Eberle for rehearsal. Cursing to herself, Corey sets her brushes in turpentine and caps her paints. One damned interruption after another. The shadowy deer gaze back at her from their screen of grass and leaves, the half-painted Ariel averts her eyes to hide the truth: Face it, Corey, you're looking forward to this little excursion of John's.

The flesh-and-blood Ariel sticks out her lip—"What is there for me to eat tonight? More soup? Do you know how sick I am of soup?"

"You got better at home? Go home and eat there."

Corey won't stop to argue longer. She grabs her jacket off a nail in the lean-to in case the air turns chilly after dark and heads for the barn to catch Babe and help John load her.

Oh, she's tried to tell John about the harsh old life.

You know you live on the old Ballard place? Do you know anything about Des Ballard?

Corey well remembers the wiry little cowboy from an older time. His shoulders thickened by age, his shock of white hair sticking out from under his hat, exactly as he was in life. Some blip in her brain has resurrected him, every last detail, the way he walked on his bow legs, the grizzle of stubble on his face, the tattered black silk scarf he always wore around his neck.

Loren never told how he learned to ride, John. He wouldn't have learned from his folks. All that talk about being born in the saddle, fourth-generation cowboy, that was just talk for the newspapers, well, and for himself, I guess. His folks were homesteaders from North Dakota that lost their farm in the drought and moved over here to Montana to work for the Clevelands. The Clevelands thought horses were to hitch to plows.

Loren harrumphs, interrupts. *You don't know that.*

I think Des Ballard taught him to ride. I think that's why he rode center fire.

Des had been an Irishman, the brogue still caught in his voice after all those years. He'd got in some kind of trouble in Ireland when he was a boy, bad trouble—Corey doesn't know how she knows these details, she admits to John. From listening to her grandmother and Mizzy, she supposes. Anyway, Des had to get out of Ireland in a hurry, and he managed to stow away on a ship to New York. From there he got to Texas somehow. Got on with one of the cattle outfits and rode up to Montana with one of the last big trail herds. He'd met Mizzy when she was fifteen, and she had lied about her age to marry him.

A story with the feel of the often-told, told often enough to take on its own truth about a time when the world seemed new. Re-telling it to John, Corey realizes she too is enlivening the dull here and now. How much fiction, how much truth realized years afterward? The flooded rivers across the trail from Texas, the hailstorms, the cattle stampedes, the ten minutes of terror and courage in a month or a year of dust and boredom, all grown to epics in an old man's mind.

Poor Will Ballard. Des's son. He never made a hand. Folks ridiculed him something awful. So maybe Des took an interest in an apt neighbor boy. Got to talking to young Loren. Des rode center fire, Des was a dally man, two more reasons to think he taught Loren what he knew—

Corey couldn't have been more than ten, and Loren was yelling at her for letting that brockle-faced steer run over her when she was supposed to be guarding the gate. They had been branding steers up at Ballard's, and Corey had been riding old Daisy. Daisy was afraid of the steer, with his wicked little horns that somehow had avoided the dehorn saw the spring before, and she sidestepped and let him dodge around her, even when Corey screamed at her and dug in her spurs.

203

Then, after about the sixth time the steer charged past Corey and Daisy, up rode the ruddy little cowboy with the shock of white hair. Here, kid, said Des. I'll give that son-of-a-bitchin little steer a reason to remember what a man on horseback is for. You just run him past me one time. Des had been building his loop as he spoke. He gave his hat a tug and nodded at Corey, and she spurred Daisy after the steer and headed him back toward the gate. As the steer dodged, Des's loop snaked out and over those mean little horns, and Corey saw the blur Des's hand made as he took his dallies and set himself hard in the saddle. She saw the steer hit the end of the lariat, which sang as Des's little sorrel gelding sat back on his haunches to take the shock. The steer sailed through thin air, landed flat in corral dirt, and never moved again.

Jesus Christ, Des, you broke his neck, said Loren, riding up.

Ornery little son of a bitch. We're out of fresh beef. He'll make good butchering.

John Perrine had seemed to ponder the story. Shook his head. Got up to carry his coffee cup back to the sink. John, always careful about such gestures, always careful not to overstay his welcome, but certainly in the habit of taking the long way home to stop and visit with Corey.

Now John drives toward the reddening sun, never over fifty miles an hour even on the blacktop, although the horse trailer tows easily, with none of the shaking and stamping that Corey would have felt from two horses in a stockrack behind her pickup. The cab of his truck is clean, and it smells new. There had been a moment when they first got in that she was embarrassed, wondering what he was waiting for, not letting out the clutch, then realized that he was expecting her to fasten her seat belt. She had drawn it down and snapped it, trying to remember when she'd ridden in a vehicle new enough to have seat belts. The old red pickup had never had seat belts.

But finally they're on their way. The air conditioning in John's truck blows a steady draft of cool air into her face until she figures out how to adjust the vents.

John glances at her. "I could turn it off?"

"It's okay," she says. She's feeling overloaded. Too goddamned much going on. How can she concentrate on any of it? Air conditioning. Ariel. Ingrid, how does she fit in? Scolds herself. Yes, you, Corey Henry. You'll end up listening to his bull-riding stories and his rough-riding stories until you get sick of his stories.

"Don't know how many will show up tonight," he says. "James and his boys are coming. And some of the guys from the sheriff's posse."

He has explained the plan. They'll park their trucks and horse trailers out of sight behind the rimrocks that overlook the ruins of the old Milwaukee depot at Eberle. They'll saddle their horses and get their gear together. When they hear the whistle from the train, they'll know it is on the trestle and slowing down. That's their signal to ride full speed down the hill, whooping and firing blanks from their rifles and pistols. Once the train stops, they'll dismount and enter the passenger cars, robbing the tourists of phony money passed out in advance. For the tourists, the train robbery will be part of their fun. Part of the price of their tickets.

But John's mind is stuck on another track. "Have you found Loren's bank statements yet?"

"No. We've—" well, yes, Ariel has helped, but she doesn't want to tell John about Ariel. "I've looked everywhere I can think of."

"That thirty thousand would be enough to see you through for a few years."

"On the ranch."

"That's what you want to do? Stay on the ranch?"

"You're the one that told me to list it. And now there's Hailey. Maybe it'll be his ranch. He can turn it into his wildlife refuge or his beauty-forever ranch."

"When I talked about listing it, I didn't think you'd have the money to operate it. I hated to think of you working your heart out for nothing."

Corey looks out the window, at the long fields of green wheat just starting to turn gold. The old bootlegging road from Canada is out there somewhere, but ploughed and planted over since prohibition days. The late sun is making the wheat look riper than it really is, but summer is half over and those old boys out there will be harvesting before they know it. The custom cutters will soon be rumbling up the highways in convoys, working their way north from their early start in Texas and through the Midwest to finish up their season in chilly Montana and then Alberta and Saskatchewan. They'll harvest the whole continent with their big combines, working three and four to a field, cutting wheat in circles at a slow three or four miles an hour in circles like futuristic metal dinosaurs. Separating the wheat from the chaff internally, disgorging straw into fresh stubble.

Custom cutting isn't something she knows a lot about. These big farming operations are beyond anything Loren ever dreamed of. But the only way that folks make money farming nowadays, if they do make money, is large scale. Sure isn't done on a piddling little thousand or so acres in the foothills. Maybe Hailey Doggett's got the right idea. Tear out the fences, let the deer and the skunks and the porcupines take over.

Beauty, according to Ariel, is what her dad wants. He wants to restore the foothills and prairie to their natural condition so the grass will grow over the roads and the streams will run free. The world will be the way it used to be, the way it's supposed to be, and there will be no more ugliness.

Ariel's heard it so many times she can repeat it, but she can't explain it.

He wants to set up some kind of conservancy? Corey asked her.

What's a conservancy?

Like a public trust? Where people could come and camp and hike? Commune with nature, like that?

But Ariel had looked blank.

"Been thinking about art school," she tells John.

"I see."

He takes his eyes off the road for a moment, reaches over and touches her hand, but thankfully has to look back at the road because he's towing the horse trailer, after all, and Corey, with no way to withdraw because she's strapped in the goddamn seatbelt, curses herself for an old maid, spinster, cowgirl, foolish yokel, *clod*, Ariel's word, who can't tell what his gaze held. Pity? Or Loren is right, and what John sees is glory.

In the distance, along a ridge in the sagebrush above the wheat, a little band of pronghorns run, then pause and look back, curious, the setting sun gleaming on the white bands on their chests. For a moment she's drawn with them, dissolving into their dimension of no past and no future.

John downshifts, makes his careful wide turn on gravel with the horse trailer easing along behind the truck. Paying attention to what he's doing, hands competent on wheel and gear. Old ranchers' hands got to be bent like claws by the time they were John's age, with ingrown grime and fingernails as hard as horns popping out of their beds, but John takes better care of his nails than Corey does hers. She wonders again about Ingrid. Where she fits in.

They drive a few miles between irrigated hay meadows along the river, then take another turn on a dirt road that leads up through the sagebrush to the rimrocks. This road runs along the top of a palisade of sandstone boulders that overlook the river. These are the Judith River breaks, *breaks*, because the boulders are eroded by wind, cracked by sparse jackpine, and riven with coulees that deer and cattle can follow down to water. The road is now reduced to parallel tracks through grass and sagebrush, and Corey looks for the handle to roll the window down, finds the automatic button instead, pushes it and breathes air that is suddenly cooler. The sun is sinking now. Through the breaks in the rimrocks she sees the railroad trestle and the distant curve of the river and, farther away among the cottonwoods, the roof of Saylor Lambert's barn.

Fifty yards ahead are several trucks and trailers parked in flattened grass. Horses being unloaded. Corey recognizes James Tendenning's outfit, and one of his blond-headed boys, Steve, saddling a little pinto mare. There's James himself, walking around the stockrack with a bridle and a feed bucket. John pulls up beside James, in the scent of sage and warm grass and horse droppings.

"Minneapolis?" says John.

"What?"

"Would you go back to Minneapolis to go to art school?"

"Oh. No. I don't know if I'd want to try that again. State university in Billings, maybe. They've got a good art program."

She opens the door on her side, takes the high step down to solid ground. Leaves John to see to the trailer. While he lowers the ramp for Babe and his gelding, she follows an old cattle trail to where she can look through a crack in the rimrocks at what used to be the town of Eberle, far down the slope.

It's been a long time since she's been to Eberle. Loren could have told stories about the old days, when Eberle was a railhead and they used to gather cattle in the now-ruined corrals to ship to Chicago. Loren and Des had ridden for Saylor Lambert, helping him and his cowboys chase pairs of cows and calves out of the river breaks. Saylor's cattle, other ranchers' cattle, ranchers long gone now, too old or too tired of fighting high feed bills and low cattle prices to stay in the business, and now there's only Saylor.

Didn't want to live to see it, Loren reminds her.

From the rimrocks she can see the old pens and loading chutes, built of blackened railroad ties soaked in creosote to last forever. To the north, along the railroad tracks, the freight platform and the old depot are beaten by weather and bereft of paint. A heavier growth of weeds on the sidehill where something used to stand, maybe the stationmaster's house, probably hauled away on skids. An oblong of crumbling concrete farther down the tracks is probably the foundation of the hotel where the bootleggers used to unload at night, if the old stories can be believed. All smaller than it ought to be, the reality shrunken from what Corey remembers.

The hill, though, looks pretty damned steep to go charging down on horseback. Maybe she should have ridden up to the butte pasture and caught Perry to ride, instead of little green Babe.

Why are you doing something so stupid? had been Ariel's question. She wasn't impressed when Corey explained John's plans to promote tourism and get cash flowing into the county.

He's got a crush on you, Corey!

She should have told Ariel that the guys were looking forward to their train robbery like kids to a party. Corey has never seen James Tendenning and the posse guys so loose and laughing. Of course they've probably got beer in their coolers and been into it already.

"Corey!" It's Val Tendenning with a camera slung around her neck. "How's your new colt? Are you going to break him to ride?"

"Thinking about it."

They both turn as laughter bursts up from the parked trucks, a tailgate clanking down, and an exuberant yip-yip-yip. "I can just hear what my dad would say about all this," says Val.

"You ever wonder what he and Loren did for fun?"

"To hear him tell it, neither of them ever had any fun. They'd have gone to hell if they had."

Corey leads Babe a few steps, tightens her cinch. Slides the bridle on Babe in place of the halter, hangs the halter and rope on the back of John's trailer.

"A pity about Saylor," says Val.

"What do you mean?"

"James says the bank's foreclosing on him."

Corey turns, looks at Val.

"He says he'll die in his boots before he lets the bank have the place. That's why his daughter came back from California. To talk sense into him."

John rides up on his sorrel gelding—"Everybody ready?"

Corey swings astride Babe, joins the line of a dozen riders poised on the opposite ridge against the setting sun, while Val steps back to take their picture. Corey hopes she looks Western enough for Val's camera. She hasn't changed from her ordinary clothes, Levi's and boots, except to put on one of Loren's pearl-snap shirts, and she's stuck a cock-pheasant's tail feather in her hatband. For weaponry, she's got Loren's unloaded 30/30 rifle in a saddle scabbard. John had offered her blanks to fire in it, but she'd thought she'd let everybody else make the noise, this time anyway, and they're making plenty.

Babe's starting to prance, and Corey has to growl at her. Next in line is Park Tendenning in the Indian costume he wore as a henchman the day Dick-Dog got shot down in Fort Maginnis. "Hi, Corey," says Park. "I like your feather."

Guns are raised for the sake of the camera, shots fired down at the end of the line, lots more yip-yip-yips and yells to make everybody feel like cowboys. Val waves, to show that she's got her picture, and here's John again, spurring his gelding down the line—"What's going to happen when we do it for real, we'll hear the train whistle from the trestle, and we'll have about a minute before we ride. They'll have the train stopped, broadside, so the folks can get a look at us when we burst over the crest. We'll have the sunset behind us, and we'll look terrific. Okay, everybody ready—let's go!"

The next minute, all Corey knows is that she and the dozen others are pounding down the slope toward the ruins of the depot, and she thinks she can hear Val cheering over the thunder of hoofbeats. No time to think about pitfalls, badger holes or rocks or sagebrush on the precipitous descent, no thoughts of fallen horses or broken necks, no, it's a suicide race, it's full speed ahead with air roaring in her ears, air streaming in her eyes and grit in her teeth, and she hardly feels the jar of the saddle in the downhill plunge. A rider passes her, it's the older Tendenning boy, Park, grinning and oblivious, with his hat hanging on by its strings. He looks just like his grandfather. Bullshit, thinks Corey, that the old cowboys never had any fun. They just didn't want the kids to know about it. She's hearing very little gunfire, everybody is saving on blanks, although James Tendenning does let loose a blast from his double-barreled shotgun, which spews fire into the twilight, but the boys are making up for the noise with their cowboy hoots and yells. On they thunder, hell for leather, damn the consequences, and next thing they're pulling up at the old depot, no clear idea how they got there, on horses beside themselves with excitement, stamping and foaming at their bits and rearing and ready to race.

Corey reins Babe in sharply. Just what Loren didn't want for his horses, letting them get a taste of racing. But hell, she's as bad as Babe, wide awake and quivering, ready to go again. Doesn't know when she's felt so fine.

Everybody's laughing and talking at once and trying to calm down their horses.

John rides up, grimed between his mustache and his hat, his teeth startlingly white when he smiles. "It's going to work," he says.

They do look like desperadoes. Filthy and exuberant, panting like a pack of coyotes.

"And now we gotta ride all the way back up the hill with our loot?"

"Right!"

They're off again, this time uphill. With Babe's speed under her, Corey can stay well in the lead and out of the dust. She can just hear Loren. Running horses uphill! It almost seems a pity that he and Val's dad aren't here to carp, they'd have so much to carp about.

At the top, back at the trucks and trailers, laughter and dust being slapped off chaps and hats and fringed vests, spurs ringing and beer broken out of coolers. Familiar faces in a context so extraordinary that it takes a minute to recognize them. Buck Harris and his boys from south Willow Creek. One of Annie's grandsons, Chuck Reisenaur from over east of Yeager. Chuck's wearing a patch over one eye, and he's blacked out his front teeth. He's making his horse rear, showing off. Somebody's shaken up a can of beer and spurts foam on horses' flanks and horses' faces. Somebody thrusts a can of Coors at Corey, and she takes a long swallow and feels the dust loosen in her throat.

More beer gets shaken up and squirted, and now a bottle rocket soars over the rims. Pinwheels and fizzing color as the last light drains away and the moon rises over the rimrocks. A string of firecrackers goes off under a trailer, and horses jerk back on their halter ropes— "Cut it out, you goddamn kids!" somebody bellows, but nobody really cares. Out in the shadows and the coulees, the coyotes are probably thinking they're sure being out-howled tonight.

"That was great," says John. "That was terrific."

He's laughing. Corey can't keep from laughing, herself. Anybody would think they'd actually robbed a train and gotten away with it.

"You look like you've been riding drag for a month," she tells John, and he throws a big arm around her, hugs her, knocks her hat off her head and nuzzles her, gives her a big smacking kiss on the cheek. Everybody cheers.

Midnight in the silvered shadow of the stone barn, getting out to open the pole gate so John can drive through. John helping Corey to unload Babe, rub Babe down and grain her and turn her into the pasture. A ringing whinny from the stud colt, coming at a hard trot to greet Babe. Soft nickering over the fence that separates them. Probably they thought they'd never see each other again.

"I can walk from here," says Corey, but John doesn't even bother to answer. He opens the door of the cab, shuts it after she's climbed in. She sees his shadow in the headlights, larger than life, as he walks around to the driver's side and gets in and drives down the incline past the fragrant shadows of the two nuzzling horses, past the springhouse and the creek and up the rise of the road to the picket fence and the guardian firs.

Neither of them moves. A filtered light shines in a downstairs window.

"So you want to come in for a drink or something?"

"Thought you'd never ask."

They grope their way through the lean-to in the dark, through the goddamn obstacle course where something tips over and lands on the floor, maybe *Western Horseman* magazines and *National Geographics* that Ariel stacked there. Let them lie where they fall. There's enough light in the kitchen to find the bottle of Jim Beam, find glasses, speak the necessary words. Want ice, no, maybe a splash of water. Not enough light at the far end of the kitchen to see the faucet, but she feels for it and hears water running and guesses how much is a splash. And now what she's about to do, handing a glass of whiskey to John Perrine, her fingers brushing his, its accidental, they're both awkward, he's holding his glass to hers, and she understands he wants to clink their glasses together. Does. He drinks, and she thinks she must have, she can taste whiskey. He's setting his glass down. What she's done with her glass, she doesn't know. She sees his eyes in focus, then out of focus, and when he kisses her, *well yes* is all she thinks.

The next instant she's drawing back, her lips burning as though they've been branded, and where's Ariel, Ariel listening from the stairwell or from the front room—the now-you-see-her, now-you-don't child—no, in all probability she's done another flit. *He's got a crush on you, Corey!* But Corey is old, old, her lips thinned, her skin dry, what can she possibly look but a fool?

John is holding her hand. "Don't," he says. "Don't pull away, Corey."

The softness of his mouth, the ridiculous brush of his mustache. They're on the stairwell, at least Ariel isn't on the stairwell, probably she's gone, let's hope she's gone, and then Corey and John are in Corey's room, and the taking off of clothes, which has always seemed to her such an awkwardness, is no awkwardness at all, and his skin is so soft, and his hands where they ought to be, and so are hers, and she's thinking about the shape of his head in her hands, the heavy bones of him, heavier than either of the men she's done it with, so long since she's done it that, for all she knows, her hole's grown shut.

From then on, it may be as much a suicide race as any they've ridden tonight, but they're riding it together, and their finish line is as far away as morning.

Next she knows, it's still dark but there's air on her bare skin, and no sheet. A horse was neighing in her dream, no, not a dream. The horse neighs. She rouses on her elbow—"What?"

John is moving around her bedroom, finding his pants. "Forgot," he says, "that damned gelding. He's been tied in the trailer all this time."

The gelding neighs again, peremptory, he's had enough of being forgotten. Corey can't help but laugh. Her eyes have adjusted to the point where she can see John's pale shoulders and the roll of flab above his dark Levi's as he bends to pull on his boots. He laughs, too, but reluctantly—"See you," he says, and kisses her with a soft brush of mustache, and he's gone.

"See you," she manages, yawning, and finds the warm sag in the mattress where he had lain. Curls herself into it. Locates the sheet and drags it up.

So you did it. Horsing with your fat attorney. I knew you would.

Shut up, Loren.

15

In the creeping pace of her dream, Annie follows a path, familiar as the soles of her feet, that winds through the cattails where the deer have been coming down to drink from the creek. The deer have left their deep tracks in mud that has dried hard, and also their droppings, like scattered handfuls of dull black berries. Dull dark serviceberries bend their boughs and reflect in the water like mirror images of the droppings. Annie picks a few berries, puts them in her mouth, but cannot taste. Where have the children gone?

Annie calls a name—what name?—hears silence. And yet she is sure she had heard their voices, seen their shadows. Her feet find the little path down to the creek, her arms remember the cool touch of willow leaves on bare skin. In the absurd logic of dreams she knows she has been here and done these things before.

The branches part, and there in the pool under the opposite bank, two shadows wade in water to their knees. Bits of gold fall and float over the current, golden willow leaves. What are the children doing,

in their water-bubble of present tense? Counting a handful of dripping pebbles, following a dragonfly's looping arc? The little girls are
telling secrets, that's what they're doing! They're laughing! But their
faces are as blurred and distant as though they are enclosed in one of
the droplets of water, water nymphets in their shower of gold.

One of the little girls is hers. Annie calls to her, wades into the current after her, but the willow branches catch at her skirt and pull her
hair, and the children recede into their reflections.

Someone taps her on the shoulder, and she turns, but it is only
Doc Mackenzie.

I've lost her, she says.

Doc speaks, but she cannot hear him. His face melts into the green-
wood.

Moonlight invades Annie's bedroom, and the headlights of a vehicle
slowing on the gravel to make the turn into the Doggetts' sequestered
driveway. But instead of making the turn, the vehicle sits idling until
Annie forgets her dream and gets up and pulls her curtains shut. Not
that the curtains are heavy enough to do any good, being the shoddy
stuff that came with her trailer house, with loose threads and uneven
hems. The next time she's in Fort Maginnis she ought to buy some
decent fabric and make herself some better curtains, or at least sew
linings into these.

She watches the shadows cast across her bed by the glow of the headlights and wonders when she ever worried about curtains, because
she had never closed her curtains in her life, never until she moved
into this tin trailer house with all its windows and all the night traffic back and forth on the county road, more night traffic than this
road has ever known. And now what in the world is this unknown
fellow doing, sitting by himself in the middle of the night with his
engine idling?

Doc is certain that what they've got on their hands is a nest of surviv-alists. All the truck traffic on their road by night means the Doggetts are hauling in supplies so they can hole up and hold off the federal government. He's seen it before, he explains to Annie. Doesn't she re-member those old boys over in eastern Montana, on what they called their Freedom Township? When the bank tried to foreclose on their ranch, they built themselves a watchtower out there in the sagebrush, and when the sheriff drove out to see what was going on, they fired warning shots over his head. The next thing, a bunch of out-of-state loonies moved in with the Freedom Township boys and told them the government was illegal and taxes were illegal and writing bad checks was the same as spending cash. Why, they even brought along a woman who'd tried to marry her little girls off to some old polygamist down in Utah, and when the state stepped in to take custody, she went on the run with the other loonies.

So there they were, said Doc, with their watchtowers and their as-sault rifles and their food and water and those little girls. What was the sheriff supposed to do? Go in with grenade launchers and maybe hurt those little girls?

That's awful, said Annie.

But where the Freedom Township boys made their mistake was that they offended their neighbors, explained Doc. There were ranchers they owed money to. There were ranchers who'd taken out loans to buy that foreclosed ground, and they wanted to get in and cut their wheat and sell it and make their payments without getting shot at. You bet-cha. Their own neighbors got fed up and called in the FBI.

Just because Hailey Doggett is suing Corey doesn't mean he's likely to go shooting at the FBI, said Annie. Or just because he moved in from somewhere else. You're from somewhere else, Doc.

I am not, said Doc, aggrieved. I'm from Plentywood.

Where's Plentywood, if it ain't somewhere else?

Annie has been able to shake her head and tell herself to mind her own business, even laugh at the behavior of newcomers in the gulch, for instance the way they build their big houses and then leave them to stand empty most of the time. The Doggetts are a puzzle, though. At least they live in their house, although it looks closed. All those heavy curtains kept drawn, the kind of curtains Annie herself ought to buy to keep out all the night traffic. But to keep curtains drawn in the daytime? How can they live like that? Don't they have any work to do? What do they do with themselves, what does poor little Rita do with herself all day?

Suddenly Annie's window goes dark, pulling her out of her thoughts. The fellow in the truck must have turned off his headlights! Now what? Annie listens. She's wondering if she really hears the faint idling motor, or if she imagines it, when the truck revs and makes the turn into the Doggetts' driveway.

What in the world.

Hailey tried buddying up to me, Doc had said. All his talk about beauty. Back to nature and that. What it got down to was my bank account. He wanted to buy himself some semi-automatic rifles with my money is what I think.

Rose, the princess warrior, has been watching the fleeting patterns of night clouds through her open window. The glowing red numerals on her digital alarm clock make no sound as one minute slides into another. One-Zero-Three a.m. Another minute, then another minute, as the house around her settles into silence. The princess warrior waits ten more minutes, to be on the safe side, before she rises from her bed. A human watcher might see a tough little bowlegged ten year old in a nightgown without perceiving that she's a strong and shining fighter who can throw flames from her fingertips and repel adversaries with darts from her eyes.

The princess warrior prefers, of course, to be silent. She pads barefoot across her carpet to her bureau, slides open the top drawer. By touch she finds the plastic bag that holds trail mix and her report, and then she's out the window with it.

Cool air from the creek stirs the hem of her nightgown and sends goose bumps up her legs as she flits across the lawn. Once she rolls under the fence and finds her way into the chokecherries, she's as good as invisible. Somebody is parked on the county road with motor running and headlights on, maybe maker-outers from town, *big kids*, but the princess warrior isn't worried. She can't be seen down in the creek bed. She keeps the creek on her left by the sound of the current's light laughter and the smell of water, feels through the soles of her summer-hardened feet the familiar deer trail that she and Amy Staple have explored a hundred times with no thought of previous children whose feet have also known that trail.

An owl silently swoops off its branch, a dark spread of wings and a disturbance of air, but the princess warrior knows an owl is just an owl, and she's not afraid of it. When the trail opens into a clearing, she makes out the dark bulk of the Henry barn. The warm-grass smell of horses, their soft snorts. She's cut across the pasture often enough that the mare and the little stallion know her, and the outline of their pricked ears follow her, unalarmed.

A barb catches at her nightgown as she follows the fence, rakes her leg and makes her whimper, but she reaches the foot of the big pine and stuffs the plastic bag into the waiting hand that reaches out for it.

Now to get back without being seen.

She slides easily under the fence this time, looks in all directions before she chances the expanse of lawn in the moonlight. As she darts out, a watcher who caught a glimpse of her might think he's seeing a small transparent ghost in blowing white, but there's no watcher, as far as the princess warrior knows. She's reached the terrace and is about to follow the curve of the retaining wall around to her own bedroom window when she hears the truck crossing the bridge over the creek, the same truck but with its headlights off.

What's going on? Is it the feds?

Rose shrinks back into the shadow of the retaining wall to watch and find out. After all the talk of feds she's eavesdropped on, she's curious to see one. She waits for a long minute as the dark truck waits, until it seems to her that she can hear music, distinct lyrics to a sad song she doesn't know, somebody lamenting his last sunset and his last holdup, but she does recognize the country station out of Fort Maginnis, which disappoints her, because she doesn't think feds would sit in people's driveways listening to the Fort Maginnis country station. Still Rose waits, until suddenly the truck revs to life without turning on its lights, reverses in a spatter of gravel, and roars off.

From his sleeping bag under Eugene Doggett's camper, Albert the Giant watches the headlights of the truck that sits idling on the county road. His first reaction had been the same as Rose's, if more graphic: teenagers from town looking for a private place to screw. Was it worth his while to check them out? Probably not. But he is wide awake now, which is how he happened to spot the little white blowing ghost on her way across the lawn to the creek.

Albert has to smile. Of all who know Rose, Albert probably comes closest to guessing the existence of the princess warrior. Not that he could call her by that name. What he surmises is a kindred spirit. What he recalls are hidden trails of his own and intermittent warfare with gangs of boys from the oil patch in Gillette, Wyoming. Albert, who once was what Loren Henry would have called a *damned town kid* who caused damage to people and property in proportion to his size, is pretty sure he knows the purpose of Rose's middle-of-the-night flits. It's his business, after all, to know everything that happens around him.

The longer he watches the beam of headlights cutting its white shaft, the more questions it raises. Maker-outers, as Rose would call them, tend to find themselves a side road or a level patch of grass, preferably screened by underbrush, where they can grope each other without drawing attention to themselves by leaving their headlights on, and maker-outers would cut their engines for the same reason unless it was winter and they needed the heater, which they wouldn't on a warm late July night like this. Therefore Albert sits up in the shadow of the camper and pulls on his pants. If there's an off chance these are the folks he's been waiting for, he'll take a look.

As he's lacing his boots, he sees the small white shape of Rose emerging from the creek bottom. Back from her errand. He watches as she slips under the rail and scurries across the lawn. Doesn't smile this time. What is going to become of this tough little girl?

We need to get a line on what Eugene Doggett's doing for money, Albert had been told. That's where you come in. Oh, Doggett has made threats. Getting even with the feds, etc. But it's probably just prison talk. You're not there for heroics, you're there to uncover the money trail. Another thing you can keep an eye out for is the hold he's got over his brother. We never could get him to rat out Hailey. But we know Hailey took what money was in their joint account, and we know he's living large. See whether old Eugene isn't having second thoughts about protecting his little brother.

What Eugene and Hailey are up to, Albert has mixed feelings. Their talk, yes, and Albert's bored out of his gourd with it. *Hole up and hold 'em off with rifles. Try to get Saylor Lambert in with us. Here, add this to our lists of supplies. Order a generator. Bury underground tanks for fuel.*

They've managed to store enough ammunition to take out Fort Maginnis, that's the most worrying part. And yet, was there ever a more inept survivalist than Eugene Doggett? Unless it's Hailey? Or that slinking pair of Lambert kids that Albert is supposed to be teaching to shoot? Albert would be inclined to write off the lot as men and boys playing shoot-'em-up games in the woods, if they weren't playing with live ammunition.

Then there's the kitchen in the camper. Are Eugene and Hailey any better at chemistry than they are at riflery?

Albert's biggest worry is the little girls. If he didn't have a pretty good idea where Ariel has disappeared to, he'd unbury his cell phone and make his call, and the hell with waiting for the connection to show up.

Now Albert gives Rose time to disappear into the shadows around the terrace. He's thinking whether to circle up through the timber on the ridge and work his way down to where he can get a look at the plates on the truck without making a target of himself, when the headlights are cut and the driver guns his engine. Roars across the bridge, past the screen of Hailey's trees, roars up the long driveway with a spatter of gravel under his tires, stops under the dark and curtained windows of the house. Sits there, engine running, but no lights.

What the shit, thinks Albert.

Although he can't make out the numbers, he's pretty sure the truck wears Montana plates. He's considering his options when, from the open window of the truck, he hears the same fragment of music that, if he only knew, Rose hears at this precise moment in her lair under the terrace. I think I have seen my last sunset, I think I have robbed my last train. Less acquainted than Rose with the Fort Maginnis country station, Albert shakes his head. What the fuck.

And then the truck revs to life without turning on its lights and—as the princess warrior witnesses from her parallel world—reverses in a rattle of gravel and roars back the way it came.

Annie's trick for putting herself back to sleep is to follow one of her berrying trails in her mind. On her back in her bed in the wavering darkness, she leaves her body for the grove where the best serviceberries are ripening, fat and luscious and staining her thumbs purple as she fills her pail. Hailey Doggett owns this land along the creek, but Annie's not trespassing. These are her serviceberries, which she will bake into pies with lard and flour crusts just as her mother baked serviceberry pies. If she pauses with her pail half-filled in the flickering shade of leaves, where the creek current talks to itself as it always has, she'll get a glimpse of the fine house with its deserted terrace and its immaculate, watered stretch of lawn broken as if by mole-digging where Hailey has begun to install chain link fencing. For Annie, Hailey's house is an aberration, a transparency superimposed upon the old hay meadow where—in her mind as fresh as yesterday—her father labors with mowing machine and sickle bar behind his team of old workhorses.

Surely if she goes and looks—Annie's foot jerks under the sheet—she'll find her father's water bottle in the fence corner where the grass shades it and keeps it cool. When she lifts the bottle, the broken leaves and grass fragments will stick to her fingers, and when she tilts it back, the water will gurgle and taste of mint from the little spring back of their house, and Annie herself will be ten years old and barefoot in the sweet smell of fresh hay, and she'll grin at her father as he makes his turn at the end of the meadow and heads toward her with his face blackened with dust and his hands full of lines and his horses jingling with harness rings while the grass waves and falls in front of his sickle bar.

She'll run to meet him, stubble sharp on her bare feet and ankles, she'll hold up her arms to be lifted into his lap, she'll have nothing to fear from the touch of his big work-calloused hands, because he's Pa, and she's only ten years old, and fear will come much later.

Faugh! She's gone far enough.

Corey's almost asleep in her bed in the stone house. Not quite dreaming. Driving home with John from Eberle. The warmth of the dark cab, the bulk of John, the shift of his body and the muscles of his thighs when he brakes for the turn onto the paved highway. She's aware of layers of sensations, she feels an urgency for peeling them back, experiencing them separately. The reflection of dashlights in the dark windshield, for example, superimposed on the black obscurity of the horizon, the long unknowable coulees and crevices, the distance of stars.

"Saylor Lambert," John had said at one point. "He's in pretty deep. And he's mad as hell."

What Saylor had said to Corey. That there was a day coming. At the time she'd thought he was, well, what. Worked up. Lathered over what couldn't be helped, the way Loren used to get lathered. *By God, the way this country's gone downhill, I'm sorry I lived to see it! What a man ought to do is crease some of those sonsabitches with a thirty-ought-six, and then maybe the bastards would by God realize they've got us with our backs to the wall!*

Corey had more or less stopped paying attention to Loren's tirades. What else could she have done? She'd felt unsettled by Saylor's grim forecast, but there again, what was she to have done? Truth was, she hadn't taken Saylor any more seriously than she had the train robbery rehearsal, or the death of Dick-Dog, for that matter.

She had said that to John, and he, absorbed in deep thoughts, had nodded without answering. In the silence she had watched the night landscape slip by, telling herself to treasure up and remember details that would never come round again.

Now, sticky-thighed and replete in deep darkness, she smiles and pulls the other pillow to herself—but suddenly Corey's sitting up in her bed, because there's light in her west window where light ought not to be. What the hell.

Lightheaded with her swift transition from half-dreaming to wide awake, she wraps the end of her sheet around her and takes the three strides from creaking bedsprings to uncurtained window.

Light of stars. Silence of firs. Empty road. Shadow of the root cellar in its bank, ragged shadow of the chokecherry grove, the more substantial shadow that is the springhouse. At the other end of the road, the staunch bulk of the barn and somebody's headlights at the pole gate.

Has John come back?

The longer she watches, the more certain she is that it's not John. John wouldn't be sitting on the other side of the gate with his headlights on. By now he would have opened the gate and closed it behind him and would be pulling up to the picket fence.

Who, then?

A tumult of voices, living and dead, offering up their fears. Mysterious watchers! Strangers from elsewhere! The feds! The survivalists!

Without warning Corey is overwhelmed with the complexities of the universe. Stars winking in their unknown millions, night clouds drifting in unrepeatable patterns. She's never understood the concept of endlessness. What rules of what games can account for so much? Countless shadows, countless leaves, countless live things with their minds on their private errands that wind and meander and crisscross and occasionally bump into each other with bewilderment on all sides. Somewhere the deer have left their beds to browse in their slice of the night. Somewhere the bats swoop out of their crevices, chasing night-borne insects that must feel a miniaturized dread. Somewhere a woman stands at a window and listens to the voices of the dead, while the fir trees just stand where they're planted. Somebody else sits in a darkened truck with his headlights on, thinking who knows what thoughts.

Corey shakes herself out of her fantastic vision, thinking how foolish it would seem if it weren't the middle of the night. And as though at that exact moment the unknown driver of the truck has shaken himself out of his thoughts, the headlights are reversed, their shaft briefly cutting a tunnel back down the county road. Taillights wink, vanish.

In the silence of firs Corey remembers what she should not have forgotten.

Ariel. Where the hell is Ariel.

Where are the children? The hidden trails hold the impressions of small bare feet, the current bubbles with laughter. Surely the children are just out of sight. The pools along the creek reflect the tips of willows, shadows of movement. The children must be wading upstream, unless that's a water bug's skittering wake.

Where's Ariel, Rita wonders, as she opens her eyes and turns in bed. Winces as her cheek touches fine cotton and not the crosshatching of grass and clover that carpets her favorite shaded spot. Then, as her bedroom resumes its shape, she realizes she's been dreaming. The pale face in the mirrored closet doors is her own, the knot under the dark silk quilt is her husband. Hailey, sleeping as he always does, with his knees drawn up and one hand clutching Rita's hip as his security blanket.

If she's careful, she can slide out from under his arm without waking him.

Rita scoots to the edge of the bed, finds the floor with her feet Lets the draft from the air conditioning cool the damp patches left by Hailey. Meets the eyes of the ghost in the mirror.

I don't know what you see in him, Rita.

Mom! He's handsome, he's bright, he's generous, and I love him.

He's the neediest man I ever met.

He needs me, Mom.

And how he had loved the girls when they were babies! Ariel in particular. She had been such an enchanting baby. How Hailey's face had softened when he held her! How he coaxed smiles from her! Oh Ariel! The baby fat, the creases at her wrists and thighs, the mercurial changes of expression—what was the baby thinking? She was eight or so before she and her father crossed swords.

Eugene, on the other hand. Rita would have said he disliked the girls.

How can you stand him, her mother had demanded. Living with you!

Mom! He's a lovable old dweeb, that's all.

The lovable old dweeb, emerging from the green flow of his computer screen to glare at the little girl who had tripped over his power cord—the apartment was so cramped, they were always getting in each others' ways—but the glint behind Eugene's glasses when he looked at Ariel? Rita might almost have called it hatred. But then the money started rolling in, and they were able to move into a bigger place. Eugene was still living with them, but at least they weren't on top of each other.

Then had come the troubles, troubles too enormous and frightening to spare thoughts for Ariel.

Rita is thinking about sliding back into bed, trying to fall asleep, when the heavy draperies glow faintly from headlights.

Bobby Staple, is her first thought.

Her next thought is for Hailey, and she looks anxiously to see whether he has wakened. But no, he sleeps as profoundly as though he has never been disturbed by worries, emitting the faintest of snores from beneath the down pillow he has pulled over his head.

It must be Bobby. Of course! He's bringing Ariel home. Ariel will be found sleeping in her own bed in the morning. Relieved, Rita slips under the sheet, finds her pillow. Feels Hailey's hand moving in his sleep, finding her hip.

Nolan Staple has been driving the county road, bracing his poor aching back against the bumps in the gravel and searching the shadows as best he can in his headlights. Where, where is Bobby. Not in his bed, Barb had cried, and you've got to find him. He's sneaked off to see that little Doggett bitch, that's where he's always sneaking off to. And no, you can't call the Doggetts. I've tried. I don't even get their voice mail.

Ariel Doggett? She's what, twelve?

Thirteen.

Like one out-of-focus photograph flipping over another, the girl-friend he'd been imagining, the one with the chewing gum and the kid of her own, had been replaced by the face of the child he'd seen only once or twice, the child who always seemed to be pouting. Lovely cloud of dark hair, lovely pale skin. But thirteen! Jesus! Bobby!

So what do you want me to do?

Go over there and bring him home!

It's the middle of the night. Everybody will be in bed, asleep, and I'm not—oh hell! I can see where I'm not getting back to sleep. Damn but my back hurts, oh Christ but it hurts. No, leave me alone, I don't want your heat pad, it doesn't help. All that's going to help is getting some rest, but no, I'll take the truck, take a look around for him. Anything for peace.

What Nolan hasn't told Barb. How his wallet weighs as heavily as though what is lost has gained in gravity. The two hundred and twenty dollars in new bills, the money he was counting on. Counting on money. Does Hailey Doggett count his? Oh, he's a dot-com millionaire, everybody said when Hailey bought the Reisenaur meadow and poured the footings for that house. Everybody guessed he made a killing, everybody guessed he got out of the dot-coms just in time. He better have, because Nolan saw some of the construction and heard the guys talking about the real marble and the real crystal and the imported Italian fixtures they were installing, a cool million and a half sunk into that one house is what they had claimed.

When Nolan has driven as far as the fork in the Henry Gulch, he pulls over by the row of mailboxes under the shadows of the pines where dry needles crunch under his tires. Leans back, rubs the ache at his beltline, oh holy hell he hurts, worse than ever he remembers hurting in his high-school linebacker days. He'd be black and blue after a game, wincing all the way to his toenails in the locker room, but at least in those days he had a body that rebounded, ready to run the four miles home after football practice the next week, because his old man had no notion of spoiling kids, chauffeuring them everywhere or handing them the keys to drive themselves.

Running had been a pleasure in those days, even for a big a kid like Nolan. Frozen gravel and sometimes snowpack under his feet and below-zero air searing his lungs, because high-school football season in Montana could be damned cold. Nolan thinks that if for only an hour he could have his sixteen-year-old body back, he'd run that goddamn Bobby into the ground.

Handling heavy equipment is what's killing him. The only help for his back would be to quit farming. Nolan groans. The radio in the truck is playing some kind of boom-dy-boom-boom music, if music is the right word for it, which he has not been listening to but which now reminds him that Bobby must have been the last one to drive the truck. God damn the kid. Nolan punches the Seek button until he hits the Fort Maginnis country station, and that's better.

On the other side of the road from the mailboxes is a pale space in the willows that used to be the gate to old man Reisenaur's hay road. Moonlight blanches the fresh gravel of Hailey Doggett's discreet driveway, which Barb expects him to follow across the bridge over the creek and around the oval to that humungous house and pound on the door, like a dumb farmer, and wake everybody up in the middle of the night demanding to know where Bobby is.

Bobby won't be there, God only knows where Bobby will be, the only certain thing is that Bobby will be where Nolan won't find him.

So he sits in the cab of the truck for a while—at least Barb will think he's been gone long enough—watching the moon turn silver and balance on the silhouettes of pines on the ridge to the west. The moon reminds him of Ariel Doggett, the time or two he's seen her. Ariel with her round face, like a dangerous baby, and what Nolan now knows is her odor, borne on Bobby, and he feels ashamed, being aroused by a thirteen year old.

Damn, he thinks, it's quiet out here, as quiet as though he's a hundred miles from town. Something runs past his headlights, a flutter of white that startles him, and feeling like a fool ten times over, he presses the lock button. Suddenly he's grateful for the lighted digital window of the radio and the soft harmony of guitars like a thread between him and the world.

Nolan has his own theory about Hailey Doggett's so-called dotcom millions. In Nolan's experience, money is not generated by tapping computer keys, but by marketing a product, and he's been curious enough about Hailey's product to get on Barb's laptop and see what he can learn. Amazing, the amount of information a man can turn up on the Internet! How to identify a clandestine methamphetamine lab. Lists of ingredients! Everything from pain medication to flashlight batteries! Rat poison! Telltale white residue in the bottoms of pots and pans, and a lot more signs that Nolan has forgotten. What stays with him is how much money such an operation can turn over, and also how "clandestine" describes the secretive Doggetts with their closed curtains and strange nighttime traffic. On impulse Nolan puts his truck in gear, then on second thought turns off his headlights, waits for his eyes to adjust, and eases out of the pines.

Dark bulk of the million-five house, pale expanse of lawn. Silence.

Nolan hesitates while the truck idles and the oblivious radio plays on. What does he think he's doing, what does he expect he'll see from the cab of his truck, white residue in the bottom of a pan?—and then his eye is caught by a slight movement on the terrace, a shadow slipping into the shadow of the house. Somebody watching him watching.

He hits the accelerator, spins on gravel in his haste to reverse. Crosses the creek before he remembers to turn his headlights on. Forces himself to slow, reverse again, and drive as far as Corey Henry's pole gate.

Nothing to be seen here, either. No Bobby. Nolan may as well go home, tell Barb whatever, rest his aching back and catch what sleep he can. At a sedate thirty miles an hour he drives back down the gulch

toward his own turn-off with no idea in the world how much speculation he's stirred.

"Areyul."

"*What?* Oh, it's you. You scared me."

"I'm sorry," he whispers. He can't do anything right in the eyes of
this girl, but he keeps trying. What else can he do.

"The porcupine," she remembers, and for a moment he thinks she's
going to scream, scream until the hills echo and everybody in the
gulch wakes up.

"Don't," he pleads. Her face is lost in the pine boughs, but the glow
of her eyes tells him that she remembers the danger, and he takes a
chance and slides into her bed of pine needles and newspapers beneath
the roughened bark. Dares to puts his arms around her, and feels her
tremble, but she doesn't resist. How he's longed to hold her! All the
times she's been on her knees before him, and oh God the memory
of her mouth and tongue electrifies him, he's rigid with lust even as
he remembers how she always avoided his touch. Kissed his mouth
only, he knows, when she wanted something from him.

"Wouldn'ta kilt it if I knew how upset you'd be." And oh the fragil-
ity of her bird bones, the pulse of her heart against his chest. He realizes he could hurt her if he wanted to. He could crush her in his arms,
and this new knowledge excites and appalls him.

"It's dead!"

"Everbody up here kills porcupines."

"Dead! It didn't have to be dead! Dead is always!"

She is crying silently against his shoulder, and he holds her as long as
he dares. "Got to get home before my dad does," and he kisses strands
of her hair in the dark without, he hopes, her knowing.

Still, he's worried. "Yer not goin to stay out here all night,
Areyul?"

"Maybe," she says.

"Mebbe you should tell Miss Henry."

"I can't!"

Her voice has risen, frightening him again, but she takes a deep breath and leans back against the trunk of the pine.

"Maybe I will," she says. "Maybe."

16

July slides into August, and the grassheads whisper of the end of the season, the hawthorn leaves curl into themselves, and reddening buck-brush stains the edges of the coulees. Summer will soon be done for, and the newcomers on Mill Creek look forward to another great up-land bird-hunting season, followed by a great skiing season while the old-timers say yeah, that's the seasons in Montana for you, nine months winter and three months damn late fall.

At night the firs pry at the windows of the stone house, trying to claim it as the uneven heap of rocks that it is, and the wind saws away at the eaves. Some mornings the bedrooms and the kitchen are un-comfortably cold, and the windows are clouded with condensation. In spite of Ariel's disgusted sweeping, dead flies continue to collect on the windowsills, because it's that time of year. Usually by midday the sun has burned away the chill, but one of these days Corey will have to figure out how to fire up Loren's old coal-burning furnace.

She puts it off, though. Turns on the electric oven for a while in the mornings, leaves the oven door open for her and Ariel to huddle around, if Ariel happens to have spent the night in the house.

"What are you filling out?" Ariel asks.

"An application." Corey's got the pad on her knee, thinking over her answers. Whether or not she actually puts the goddamn thing in the mail is another decision she can put off a little longer.

"Application for what?"

"Montana State University. Billings campus."

They're sitting together at the kitchen table. Ariel props her chin on her crossed arms and watches. She has developed an irritating habit of getting too close to Corey, getting right up against her elbow, like a cat.

"Why do you want to go to college?"

"Why not? They got what they call financial aid now. Never had it when I was college age. If your dad wins his lawsuit and takes the ranch, I can always get financial aid."

"Sue a beggar and get a louse," Ariel quotes her.

"Who am I, the louse?"

"If you go off to college, what's going to happen to me?"

Corey lays down her ballpoint. "What I said. You have to use that test kit I bought for you. And then come to a doctor with me, to find out for sure. And then you make up your mind. Either you talk or I call children's protective."

Knows what they'll ask. *Do you believe her story?*

Which of Ariel's stories?

"Or else you have to go home. And stay home. None of this bobbing in here, bothering me when I'm trying to work. I mean it this time, Ariel."

"You don't believe me! You've never—"

"Ariel, will you just shut up and let me finish this?"

And Ariel the drama queen pushes back her chair so hard against Corey's arm that her ballpoint skitters off the form she's checking in an uncertain wavery line that oh hell, how's she going to fix that, and what will it say to the admission folks about the old maid country clod who wants into their art program. Meanwhile Ariel the drama queen is stomping out of the kitchen with her small rear end twitching righteously under her borrowed blue jeans, nobody believes me, nobody *ever* believes me, what do I have to *do* before *anybody* will *believe* me, how many times has Corey heard it.

"Okay, don't come back!"

Corey with her back turned hears the door slammed.

Silence.

Gossip along Mill Creek has been flowing like water, although Corey knows she misses out on most of it. She supposes the neighbors are keeping tabs on the number of times the attorney's black truck turns up the Henry Gulch instead of heading straight home along the paved road. Also she supposes there's speculation as the lawsuit against her drags on: will Hailey Doggett end up with the Henry ranch? Does anybody want to see Hailey Doggett get his hands on the place? Surely not. Not even the two or three really rich householders who barely know who Hailey is, let alone Corey. They're getting ready to close up for the summer and jet back to wherever they came from, California or wherever, and their viewpoints are known only in wisps and drifts picked up by Doc Mackenzie, who keeps a foot in both worlds and passes what he knows to Annie Reisenaur. *Hailey's probably all right,* is what they're saying. *Just a little squirrelly. We'd probably invite him and Rita if we gave a big party when we got back to Montana for the bird hunting, if that brother of his wasn't such a creep.*

Corey's routine this summer has been to paint until the light is gone and then walk down to the pasture to feed Babe and the colt. Afterward in the long twilight, she will walk back to the house, pull off her boots, wash her hands at the sink, and pour herself a whiskey with a handful of ice cubes and a splash of water. Drink in one hand and a kitchen chair in the other, she'll return to the porch, sit on the kitchen chair she's dragged out, prop her legs on a nail keg and sip her toddy while she listens to the ridge pines rage at their fixed roots and watches the outline of barn and corrals fade into silhouette against the last of the glow. Wonders what's next. What she'll do. Back in June it sometimes took two or three, even four toddies before her conscience eased and the voices faded out of her head and into the complaint noise of the pines, just part of the confusion of the cosmos, and she could stagger back through the lean-to, set her empty glass in the sink, and weave up the stairs to bed. Now she's down to one stiff toddy, most nights, but even one toddy horrifies Ariel.

You're getting *drunk* every night. Why do you think you have to drink all that whiskey? Don't you know it's a *crutch?*

Corey tries to explain the imperative of the painting, how she can't free herself from it, can't stop thinking about it even when the brushes aren't in her hand. How the painting clamors for her, louder than any of the voices, even Loren's voice, and more inexorable, and how she's drawn, without choice and without resistance. Are her paintings any good? Ariel certainly doesn't think so, Loren would have been outraged, and even John has his doubts. And yet the question means less and less to Corey. Are her paintings any good, is *she* any good? Who wants to know? An admissions committee at Montana State University? Whatever those folks decide, she'll paint as long as she can afford the tubes of oils.

What do you mean, you can't? insists Ariel. My mother says alco-
holics try to drown their pain instead of doing something.

Yeah? Like what? Like starting up this whatever, conservancy, you
keep talking about, and turning back the clock?

No way! shouts Ariel. It's one thing for her to trash her parents,
but she hates hearing criticism from Corey. They're not turning back
any clock! They just want to put everything back the way it was. Trees.
Water.

Sounds like turning the clock back to me. Anyway, what should I
be doing, besides what I'm doing?

You could pick up after yourself, says Ariel.

John breaks Corey's routine, spending more and more time drinking
coffee with her in the mornings before he goes to work and whiskey
ditches with her when he returns at night. Then he spends the night.
He interrupts her painting, and yet she can't stay irritated with him.
There's so much of John, his good nature, his warmth. Fat is what he
is, she has to admit. Having him naked in her bed is like sleeping with
a beached seal, but she loves his muchness, and his transparency,
even the way he heaves over on his back and snores, then swears he
never snores. With John, what she sees on the surface is what's there,
with no overlay.

"Gotta get a better mattress on this bed," he complains.

What about Ingrid? Corey had worked up her nerve and asked
about Ingrid, once, but John had only looked unhappy and looked
away. Not what everybody thinks, is all he would say.

Corey also was uneasy when John began to take over the cooking,
but after the high sodium and flavor enhancers of Ariel's menus, she's
relieved to be eating real food again. At night he grills steaks brought
from Fort Maginnis, sometimes adding a little mustard and lemon

juice to the drippings, which would have driven Loren to apoplexy—
ruining the taste of good beef!—or he marinates a pork loin in ingredients with names strange to Corey, five-spice and sesame oil and hoi-
sin sauce. He bakes potatoes or he boils rice in a saucepan, measuring
how much water by half the first joint of his index finger, fluffing the
rice with a fork when it's done. No wonder he's fat.

Although he does like salads, and he brings grocery sacks of ready-
washed spinach leaves, bunches of green onions, bunches of fresh
parsley that he never gets used up before leaves and stems blacken
and turn liquid inside the plastic bags. He doesn't care, he just buys
more. But he won't have a thing to do with supermarket tomatoes. He
promises he'll get a garden in next summer and grow real tomatoes
and Corey will see the difference, although Corey believes he's overes-
timating the growing season for ripening tomatoes in the foothills. In
the mornings he ties a dish towel over his suit pants and makes pan-
cakes, stirring up the batter with eggs and flour and milk and frying
them in Corey's grandmother's cast-iron skillet, which he rescued just
before she started to paint faces on the bottom of it.

Buy some more canvases, he told her, and leave us enough pots
and pans to cook with.

John has finally gotten access to Loren's checking account for Corey,
which has added another five hundred dollars to her summer funds,
but because she promptly splurged a hundred of it on more paints and
another canvas from her friend Lucy Valach at the Bon Ton, she's beginning to worry again. She's got to have paint and canvas and whiskey, and also the expensive items that Ariel has privately added to her
grocery list, frozen enchiladas and frozen pizzas and Dove bars.

There's the mystery money in the safe-deposit box, but she feels
almost superstitious about it. Won't touch any more of it unless she
has to.

Yesterday.

It's just a test, Corey had told her. Bought it for you in Safeway. To find whether or not. She unwrapped the little package and set the kit on the kitchen table and tried to explain to Ariel. You pee on the stick, and you have to watch and see whether it forms a little purple line.

Looked at Ariel to see whether she was getting across to her or not. What to say to that tight little face.

When was your last period?

It was before school was out.

So you've missed two? *Three?*

I hate that outhouse. What if I drop your little test down the hole?"

Then I'll be out the $14.95 I paid for it, and I'll have to take you to a doctor.

Somebody will have to do that anyway. What she will have to do is call Ariel's parents—oh yes she's tried, but the phone rings and rings, rings and rings and rings without even the Doggetts' voice mail picking up. Call children's protective in Fort Maginnis—but Ariel will vanish at the first suggestion, swear she's going home, swears she's talking to her mom and dad, oh yes, everything is just fine—and then a few days later she resurfaces, starved and dirty, swearing her story is true.

Next breath she's swearing it's a lie.

Or else she's flinging herself on the broken-backed couch, poor Ariel who has nothing to do. No TV, how can you stand it without TV? She nags Corey to buy a microwave oven, which she says costs less than a hundred dollars at the discount store, and what's a hundred dollars?

You're so thin! she accuses Corey. You look like a *scarecrow.*

She's beginning to sound almost as bad as Annie Reisenaur.

At least now the house is quiet this morning. At least she's got it to herself now. She's seen the last of Ariel, she really has, because by God she meant every word she said to her. She did, by God.

With the pasture grass so short and brittle, Corey has been pitching hay every morning and evening to Babe on her side of the fence and the little stallion on his. This evening she's leaning on her pitchfork, thinking deep thoughts and watching the horses nuzzle up the wisps and spears of good timothy, when she catches movement from the corner of her eye. Just beyond the barn, on the edge of the timber.

It could have been a deer, but something tells her it wasn't, so she doesn't react. She heaves another good forkful to each of the horses, looks to see that they've got water in their tank, and walks back into the barn through the big sliding doors at road-level. But instead of hanging the pitchfork on its nail and leaving through the big doors, she pulls some of the junk out of the way and climbs down a ladder through the trapdoor to the old cow barn, where ancient wooden stanchions still hang awry in dusty light and the floor under her feet has long been buried under equally ancient layers of pulverized, odorless manure. Carrying the pitchfork, she slips out the small door the cows used to file through.

Here she's at creek level, where willows and a glut of brush overhang a current diminished and nearly silenced by dry weather. Her grandmother used to pick wild gooseberries along here, and sometimes wild raspberries, rare as garnets. The trails are overgrown now, with the cows long gone and only the deer to keep them trodden, but Corey knows the way. She follows the water, protecting her face with her forearm as thorns catch at her shirt. When she comes to the fence, she ducks between strands of barbed wire. Freeing her hair, she climbs cautiously out of the creek bottom and into the aspens.

Sees the two boys with their backs to her.

The aspen leaves dapple like camouflage over droopy T-shirts and droopier cut-offs with crotches that hang almost to their knees. She can't tell what they're doing, but their secretive shoulders say nothing good. Then suddenly they seem to sense her and whip around to face her.

The two of them, almost as alike as twins with their wide blue eyes and narrow chins and a sharp body odor that reminds Corey of an aluminum cooking pot her grandmother gave up on and threw away. After their first startle, they don't seem at all concerned that they're where they shouldn't be, in fact, they're starting to grin at her. Grinning like they know a goddamn thing about the world. She recognizes the taller one as the fool who dropped the lines and let the horses run. And now he's daring her to think she's got any right to her own pasture, not when he chooses to do whatever he's doing here. As he takes a step toward her, her rage rises.

"What are you up to?"

"What's it to you?" he grins.

"I live here, that's what."

Loren fumes, demands to be heard: *Pimply little bastards that think they're so smart, I'd rap the handle of that pitchfork across their heads, I would! And what's that written on the big one's shirt? Chronic what? Chronic fatigue?*

The taller kid's T-shirt does read CHRONIC in big washed-out letters. Corey wants to laugh, but she's in an uncertain standoff, even if she is carrying a pitchfork. But damned if she's going to walk away, not from her own goddamned cow pasture, practically her own backyard. So she fixes on the taller kid and narrows her eyes, the way she's stared down eighth-grade boys over the years, not quite meeting his gaze but focusing instead on the bridge of his nose. It's a stare she can hold forever, and meanwhile on the periphery of her vision she can scan for contraband, rubber bands and cigarettes and .22 shells, all the things that eighth-grade boys carry, or whatever it was these boys were hiding from her in their first furtive seconds.

Sees nothing except a bit of white half-hidden in the hillside grass, the crumpled end of an envelope, maybe. She could walk back to the house and call their grandfather, but she wonders how much authority over them Saylor still has.

A new voice. "What's goin on here?"

He's well over six and a half feet tall, in blue jeans and a washed-out navy T-shirt stretched over broad shoulders and a long line of spine as he pushes branches out of his way, a tree emerging from trees.

"What's goin on?" he repeats.

The boys have been silenced. Corey watches their eyes slide down, careful not even to look at each other.

She raises her chin. "Trespassing," she says.

"Nice ground you got here."

"Yeah, and you're on it."

He must be the giant young fellow Annie and Doc have been worrying about.

"You're Miss Henry, right? Is that your tree fort up there?"

"Built it when I was a kid."

From the creases around his eyes, Corey judges he's a little older than he first appeared, maybe closer to thirty than twenty. Laundered T-shirt, clean hands with scrubbed, tended nails. Too clean for the woods. But it's the size of him that's so ominous.

She realizes she's tipping her head back to look him in his white-lashed eyes. Shifts her gaze to the bridge of his nose. "Didn't hear your name," she says.

"Albert," he says. Adds, at her glare, "Albert Anderson. I guess you'd just as soon the boys didn't hang out on your property."

"Just as soon."

"Travis—Scott—let's go, let's get."

Corey steps out of the trail to let them pass. The two boys slouch off as sullen as chastened hounds, taking their strange, sharp odor with them, but Anderson, if that's really his name, smiles a flash of perfect white teeth at her. Dentistry like that, and he's what he pretends to be?

"Keep hearing things about you, Miss Henry."

"Yeah?"

"Hey, I heard good things."

He waits, as though for an answer. Corey has a strange feeling that he is speaking in a code he expects her to understand. But what?

"Yeah, well," she says, finally, and stabs the pitchfork tines through the leaf mold and into parched earth with more force than she intended.

For just a moment his eyes search her face, and she has time to remember what those eyes and coarse white eyelashes remind her of, a wall-eyed Belgian studhorse Loren had for awhile, and then Anderson seems to give up and says, "Hope to be talking to you again," and turns and dodges pine stubs and low-hanging branches on his way down the creekbed.

She hopes that's that.

But then the bit of white catches her eye, that old envelope or something stuck where it shouldn't be in the grass under the tree fort, and she climbs up to retrieve it, thinking to find a piece of trash blown by the wind. But it turns out to be a piece of lined paper torn from a spiral notebook, bits of chaff still hanging from the torn edge, and covered with careful cursive writing in blue ballpoint, like a school book report.

"Report," Corey reads, "by the Worrier."

Holding the sheet of paper, Corey looks down the trail along the creek. Sunlight on aspen leaves, pine needles recovering their silence, grass as unrevealing as though it has never been trampled. Her pitchfork, standing on its tines where she left it. They're gone; she's alone as far as she can tell. Still, she folds the paper and tucks it into her shirt pocket. She'll wait until she's back at the house before she reads it and finds out what's worrying the Worrier.

Loren had had to get rid of that young Belgian studhorse. He was too wild even to be halter-broken, and he had fought against the ropes and the snubbing post until it was clear he would die of thirst before he would submit, while his eyes, white-rimmed and shaded by coarse white eyelashes, looked inward or perhaps beyond the world of torment, it was hard to know which.

> *"Report by the Worrier"*
>
> *They were talking and I had a real good place to listen and they didn't know I was inside the stack of tires. And they were standing right there in the storage shed and Uncle Eugene said you know where she is dont you and Dad said what makes you think that and Uncle Eugene said I know you is what makes me think it and I want her back. And Dad said are you crazy and Uncle Eugene said what if she talks and Dad said what is she going to say she dosent know anything about this goddamned kitchen of yours and Uncle Eugene said thats not what I meant and Dad said well then what and Uncle Eugene said Hailey you know I would never hurt one of the girls and it sounded like he was crying. And Dad said Im sorry Eugene and Uncle Eugene said what about Rita and Dad said Im worried about Rita. And they dident say anything for a while and then Dad said I never thought anything like this and then they walked off and I couldent hear anymore.*

Night has darkened the windows and invited the wind to try to get indoors. Corey has put her paints aside, although the crick in her neck and the cramp in her painting hand feel good to her. Alone in the house for once, assuring herself that alone also feels good, she sips her toddy and ponders the Worrier's document by the bare light of the bulb in the kitchen ceiling. No clue here to prove or disprove Ariel's various stories, and yet the paper curls at its edges, seems to want to levitate. What story does it tell, what part of how many stories? How many versions of stories waft up and down the Henry Gulch? *Who is Hailey, what is he,* an echo of verse from one of her grandmother's books or possibly from a schoolbook, the fragment lodged in the ragbag of Corey's mind and no more significant in itself than a rag.

Loren stirs himself: *What goddamn nonsense! Only one way of telling a story, and that's the right way. Rags and be damned.*

Maybe, Loren.

She can name the Worrier, of course.

Thinks she might as well have another toddy.

Bolt upright in bed, electrified out of sleep by howls from somewhere, where? John's not beside her—why not—Ingrid?—meanwhile, ululating howl upon howl, and her hair's standing on end, has she been dreaming she was dead? She's alive, she's awake, she sees by the faint bloom in the window that dawn is just breaking, and yet the howls rise from under the earth, as far as she can tell. Finally awake enough to know that what she's hearing is real, whether human or animal, she leaps out of bed and looks down from her window to see the fir branches just taking shape out of darkness, the picket fence turning white as the light grows. Moving silhouettes in the pasture beyond the fence, Babe and the colt with the jitters, their ears pricked toward the ridge.

It is real. What in the hell is it. She falls over herself running downstairs and out the door, still in her nightgown, bare feet wincing on planks that still hold some of the night's damp. Through the gate behind the outhouse, past the collapsed chicken houses—

"God! You!"

Ariel erupts, screaming, out of the underbrush and throws herself upon Corey.

"Calm down! Calm down! Tell me what's happening!"

But Ariel is beyond being soothed, she's a wild thing in Corey's arms, struggling in unreason to escape from her own skin, and all the time shrieking with what's left of her vocal cords. Nothing is emerging that Corey can make out as words, but she's realizing, as Ariel's throat gives out, that not all the screams are Ariel's. Farther up the hill, someone—something!—screams on the same animal pitch as the child's, while another, an inhuman lightning bolt of a sound, soars and screeches in an interwoven dissonance, like the music of hell.

"What? What?"

Ariel can't speak, but she manages to point. Corey drops her and runs uphill, hardly feeling what's under her feet, pinecones and pine needles and sharp-edged ruts from whenever it rained last. Reaches her tree fort, stops, gasping. The barbed wires of the old cow pasture fence have taken on a life of their own, shrieking and jerking.

"Oh hell," she says.

The sound of her voice halts the struggle of the young deer that, moving down at daybreak to browse at the timber's edge, had tried to leap over the barbed wires, miscalculated, and caught itself by its hocks. Ariel, sleeping rough, must have been startled awake. The deer hangs, petrified beyond pain by the human presence, but when Corey takes a step closer, it resumes its futile wrenching that only buries the barbs deeper into its flesh.

Corey backs away. Backs into Ariel, who has pulled enough of herself together to follow.

"What are you going to do?"

"I'm going to go back to the house and get some clothes on, and then I'm going to look and see whether there are any shells for Loren's rifle."

"You're going to *kill* it?"

Corey stares at the swollen, defiant little face, wondering if she heard right.

"Look at it," she says. "You've got eyes. Do you want to watch it hang there and suffer?"

Ariel is jumping up and down, tears flowing, fists clenched in her passion. "No-o-o! You can't kill it, you can't kill it, you can *save* it—"

"Ariel! Will you quit screaming and listen? We can't save that deer for one thing it's crippled itself on that wire, and for another thing it would tear itself to pieces before it would let us near—"

But Ariel will not be reasoned with, Ariel will not be consoled, Ariel slaps at Corey, which sends the deer into another hopeless spasm of struggle—"Save it, save it, why won't you save it, you could save it if you wanted to, why won't you save it, why won't you save it—"

"Because I can't save it!"

Corey tries to put her hands over her ears, but Ariel is grabbing at her wrists, kicking at her—"Why won't you try? I came to get you because I thought you'd *try—try—*"

The words chase each other around Corey's head. Why won't she try. Because she knows it can't be done. The deer's going to die. Why won't you try, the deer's going to die. Because that's not how it's done, that's because why. You can't cry, you can't try, not over every little thing, you can't try, the deer's going to die.

Maybe the alcohol from last night's second stiff toddy is still in her bloodstream. Maybe she's legally drunk, maybe that's it.

"Ariel," she says, and says her name again. "Ariel. Okay. Ariel. I'll try. But you're going to see. All right? You're going to see."

And Ariel lets go of Corey's wrists, lifts her tear-blotched, blubbered, hopeful face.

Can the deer really be saved? On the way back to the house to get dressed and find a pair of wire cutters, Corey muses on the possibility. Supposing she were to phone Doc Mackenzie, ask him to drive up the gulch with a tranquilizer, because it would take a tranquilizer before the deer would endure human touch. She imagines herself and Doc cutting wires, carefully working barbs out of hair and torn flesh and tendons without doing more damage than the deer already has done in its frantic fight to free itself. And then suturing, she supposes. And then what. The tranquilizing drug wears off, the deer scrambles to its feet—hind legs useless, dragging—the other deer flee at the smell, knowing it will attract coyotes and roaming ranch dogs. It can't possibly survive.

So she pulls on her boots and Levis and a shirt, digs out a couple pairs of heavy gloves, and wonders what Loren did with the wire cutters, last time he used them. Probably shoved them in the glove box of the red truck. Goes to look. Yes.

As she hikes back up the trail in full early sunlight, she can see Ariel, a small figure in a red T-shirt and matted dark hair, waiting patiently in the buckbrush as she was told. (You can sit up here and keep it company if you want to, but don't you go near! I don't care how sorry you are for it. It's got hooves as sharp as knives, and when it gets to thrashing around, it could slash you to the bone.)

"That deer is going to jerk against those wires as soon as we come near. Put the gloves on and be careful, or you'll end up with a rusty barb stuck in your hand."

She waits for Ariel to sniff the gloves and say ick, but Ariel doesn't, she pulls them on and waits for instructions.

"Your job is to try to hold the wire steady. I'm going to get as close as I can to cut it, otherwise—"

Otherwise the deer is going to tear itself loose, trailing lengths of barbed wire from its wounds, snarling on haws and pine stubs, embedding itself deeper.

Corey closes her eyes, opens them. The deer lies, panting, its tongue stuck with pine needles and its hindquarters absurdly elevated on the fence. She notices that it's a little buck, probably one of last year's fawns. Its eyes are so glazed with disbelief and trauma that she would think it was dead if it weren't for its rapid breathing. Corey's voices are hard at it, clamoring, criticizing—*all this trouble for a goddamned deer that's likely going to be shot in a month or two—why don't you just put the goddamned critter out of its misery—you think it's the first deer that ever hung itself up on a fence and starved to death*—the voices will take charge if she'll let them, but she won't, she'll concentrate on the barbed wire that, as she steadies it in her gloved left hand, cutters in her right hand, awakens and sings and shrieks and jerks against its staples up and down the line. Her idea is to cut the top wire as close as she can to where it's embedded in the deer's near leg, hope it's old and brittle enough that it won't snap back across her face or Ariel's face—*this is a goddamn stupid thing to be doing,* rages Loren, *because somebody's going to get their eye put out, that's what's going to happen!*— then circle uphill to the deer's other side and cut again.

That's as far as her plan goes. She's telling herself she'll worry about the two lower wires when she gets to them, she's close enough to the deer's haunch that her gloved knuckles brush against its bloody fur, close enough to imagine its thrill of revulsion at human contact even through the fight its putting up, even through the unholy singing of the wire, and then she's got the blades of the clippers around the wire, bobbing with the wire as it thrashes up and down, bearing down on the clippers, twisting on the wire until it snaps.

As she anticipated, the wire lashes backward, carrying her with it. Corey hears Ariel's yelp as Corey staggers to keep her footing and the deer rolls downhill, its own body weight tearing one leg free, tearing the other free, forelegs in frantic scramble, dragging its hindquarters in a slimed trail.

"It can't walk!" screams Ariel. "Corey, it can't walk!"

"No. It can't."

"What are we going to do?"

Corey shakes her head. She can't think of a word to say. She's sick to her stomach, she wishes she'd never taken a hand in the whole sick, sorry, predictable attempt. The early morning sunlight bores down on pine boughs and dust, broken wire, mashed grass. The deer has dragged itself into the hawthorns. After such a ruckus, the silence seems profound.

Ariel slips her hand into Corey's. "Is it going to die?"

"Yes."

"Will it starve?"

"No, because—well."

"Because you're going to shoot it?"

Yeah. What she should have done in the first place, only now she has to hike back down to the house, get down Loren's 30/30, find the shells for it, hike back and find the deer. Tells herself it probably hasn't dragged itself far.

"I held the wire just like you told me to do."

"Yes. You did. You did just fine."

"I didn't want it to die."

"No. Neither did I."

They're walking downhill now, toward the foreshortened stone house as the sun climbs into the day, whatever it holds.

17

After her experience in downhill racing during the great train-robbery rehearsal, Corey decides she needs more horsepower under her than little Babe. Early in the morning in the butte pasture she dismounts into brittle grass and shakes her bucket of oats until, gradually, a few curious colts emerge, slow and dappled with leaves and sunlight. They've grown long-legged over the summer, they need to be halter-broken and handled until they're used to human hands. By somebody's hands, such as Corey's. Such short lives as the colts have. Such a sad future. But such a short life as Corey has. Such ambitions, so little time.

The colts reach velvety noses for the bucket of oats she passes around, and the mares follow, taking their time, but long-legged buckskin Perry smells trouble and stays at the back of the bunch, sidestepping and snorting like a wild one while she talks to the mares and gives old Paint an extra handful of oats.

And no, that damned Perry is not going to let her sneak up on him. Finally Corey climbs back on Babe and shakes down her lariat. Hazes the bunch out into open grass where she'll have a chance of spreading a decent loop. Gauges her distance.

Perry watches her, turning his tail toward her and flattening his ears. She knows he won't give her more than one try. She's never been a great roper, and she's out of practice. Cursing Perry under her breath, Corey builds herself a small, tight loop, gives it three hard whistling swings over her head, and lets sail.

"Gotcha, you smart old son of a bitch!"

As the loop falls over his head, she takes her quick dallies, just in case he gets it in his head to fight the rope. But Perry's too savvy to fight. He knows all about ropes, he knows when he's caught. He allows himself to be led behind Babe on a trot, back down the track toward the ranch buildings, while the bunch of horses watch for a while and then go back to their afternoon's snoozing in the shade. Mares switching at flies with their eyes half-closed, colts sleeping on their sides, oblivious of passing time.

John hoped to stage his first for-real train robbery on the Fourth of July, but he's had to postpone over and over because of all the conflicts, fireworks at the fairgrounds and the Kiwanis barbeque and a rodeo and now a Calcutta, whatever the hell that is, at the golf course at the Elks Club. So the real thing has been put off and put off, but finally scheduled for good and certain.

God! They all must have been crazy, that night! Still, even with everything else that's on her mind—the end of summer, Ariel—she still has to remember and laugh. Down that hill, yipping and yelling—she guesses she's as bad as the guys for cowboy games.

And then afterward. Her and John. She has to smile.

Smile even though it reminds her. Ariel's story. Corey shakes her head to blank out the images, and Babe shies at such unpredictable behavior and jerks at Perry's lead rope.

She's a little liar.

Loren, you sound like a cracked record.

The wisdom used to be that kids never lied about abuse, John had told her, when she brought up the subject. But now I hear all the time about convictions on kids' testimony that are being overturned.

Back at the barn, Corey unsaddles Babe and throws the saddle on Perry, thinking to find out he remembers his manners before she tries riding him off cliffs and such. Perry snorts and humps his back, putting on a show of wild and making the cantle stick straight up, but he knows what's coming, he's resigned to it, and after Corey's led him around in a circle, he stands for her to mount.

Long stretch to the stirrup, after little Babe. Perry stands a good seventeen hands at the withers. He's been well-broken by Loren, even if he likes to pretend that he's wild, and at a touch of the rein and sour he pivots and then canters in figure eights with tiny dust-puffs rising and falling under his hooves.

He's a handsome devil, a true line-back buckskin that's not often seen in modern horses but throws back, Loren always said, to the old Spanish strain and before that to the prehistoric line. He does look like he's got a touch of the zebra in him, with a black line down his back, and faint black stripes shading from his four black legs across his sleek, buff flanks, and a heavy black mane and tail that Corey needs to brush out before she rides him tonight.

And get him shod.

A loud neigh from the little grove of pines in the lower pasture. The new colt comes at a hard trot up to the fence to see the strange horse. Muscles quivering, eyes ablaze. He throws up his head and lets out another challenging neigh. He knows he's the intact male. Perry's just a gelding. Perry knows it, too. Corey feels him cringe under her. Thinks about strange male power and then looks where Perry and the little stallion and even Babe, tied by the bridle reins to the corral fence with an outline of sweat on her back from where her saddle was, are pointing three pairs of ears toward Ariel, who trudges toward the barn in the bright afternoon sunlight.

For the past three days Ariel has been staying indoors, drifting around the downstairs rooms, arguing with Corey about food or whiskey-drinking, and hiding from John Perrine. There's been no more talk about her going home. Sometimes she trudges out behind the firs with a roll of toilet paper and a shovel (she refuses to use the outhouse). She poses for Corey to paint her portrait, and she does housework, and she plays with her little green frog that she keeps in her pocket. Sometimes she reads articles in Loren's old issues of *Western Horseman* or *Smithsonian*, or else she tries to coax a tune out of the old piano, which Corey can't remember anyone ever playing.

It's not in tune!

Well, no, don't suppose it is.

My dad has perfect pitch.

Now here comes Ariel, venturing out in broad daylight. She looks as pale as though she's been raised in a cellar, and yet she walks with an infantile determination, chin down and hands fisted. She crosses the plank bridge over the creek without a glance for the laughing current and plods up the short rise toward the corrals, hitching at her jeans.

Babe swishes her tail, and Perry snorts and flicks a black-tipped ear, trying to make up his mind whether Ariel is worth his while to spook at, but the bold little stallion trots to the fence to see what she's all about.

Ariel pauses, interrupted from her self-absorption. She studies the colt, and the colt studies her. Two young things. The sun glistens on his bay hide, on her cloud of black curls.

"What's his name?" Ariel asks, at last.

"Judith River's Tragic Dancer."

"What?"

Corey can't blame her for that reaction. Even since she brought the colt home, she's been trying to think up a name she can call him by. Dandy. Swell Fella. Hailey. That last name makes her laugh, the way it fits the colt, with his complacent good looks, though she can't say that to Ariel.

"Tragic Dancer's just his name on his papers. What would you call him?"

"Beauty, maybe," says Ariel, thoughtfully. She holds out her little nail-bitten hand (bitten nails! shouldn't Corey have known from those nails with their worn-off flakes of green nail polish that Ariel hasn't been home in weeks) and the colt stretches his head over the fence and sniffs her, backs off, lifts his tail and drops a pile.

"Ick! Horse turds! Can I ride him?"

"He's not broke to ride."

"He likes me. I bet I could ride him."

"No, you can't."

"Yes, I can! He likes me!"

"Can't you ever take no for an answer? Anyway, he's too young. It'll be another summer before he's ready to bear the weight of a rider on his back. You wouldn't want to make him sway-backed."

Corey's thinking, though. Whether she might put Ariel's interest to some purpose. She sees herself and Ariel in the horse corral with the little stallion. A lariat looped around his hindquarters to get him to move, to follow the tug of the halter rope—well why not, he'd love the attention—and Ariel doing the tugging, learning how to handle a colt.

Ariel's watching her.

"I peed on the stick. I got a purple line."

The next minute, a rumble on the gravel. Somebody's driving up to the pole gate, and Ariel's diving through the barn doors, out of sight. The little stallion tosses his head and blows rollers after her, astonished.

It's John, of course. He's had his truck washed and waxed, and it gleams wetly, reflecting a foreshortened John as he climbs out to open the gate. He's looking for Corey, his face lights at the sight of her. Corey's glad to see him. She leads Perry across the corral with his bridle reins draped over her shoulder and thinks that she might had been gladder to see him if he hadn't picked just now.

John admires Perry, walks around him to get a good look at his hindquarters, then climbs back in his truck and eases along beside her as she rides up to the house.

"He looks fast."

"He's fast, all right."

In the cool of the lean-to, after the glare of sunlight, John is a bear-like silhouette. When he puts his arm around her, he is heavy and warm, Corey can't help herself, she likes how she fits against him, her hip into the swell of his belly. In the back of her mind she can hear the chorus of snickers—Andreas, Virgil—*look at her, look at the old maid!*—but still she allows herself the moment, even the ridiculous bump of her hatbrim against his shoulder until he lifts the hat off her head and hangs it on the nail over the washing machine. Oh, the foolishness of it, the softness of his hands that for all his horsemanship don't do real work, the softness of his mouth.

John knows where to find the coffee cups by now, knows to feel the pot to gauge its heat before he pours for himself and her. Ambles into the front room, carrying his coffee with him as though he has all the time in the world—and he probably does, what with Ingrid holding down his office for him, fielding phone calls for him, filing his briefs for him. Corey doesn't have time to think about Ingrid, however, because John stops short.

She goes to see what he's staring at. Her second portrait of Ariel, left in plain view.

She was never satisfied with the first portrait she tried of Ariel, it seemed too slick, and she hated to go to the expense of ruining another big canvas, but then she happened to think of her grandmother's washboard, stowed back of the washing machine in the out-kitchen for what, probably fifty years or more. So she dug it out and rinsed the spider webs off it and tramped through the long grass to set it by the picket fence to dry, then carried it back into the front room and propped it up.

The washboard has turned out to be an interesting surface. Old green me, Ariel said, sticking out her tongue when she saw herself, but the corrugated metal gives her face a rippling quality, not quite as distorted as a funhouse mirror, but with the same impression of qualities that shift and change before they can be recognized.

Corey watches John as he studies it. The bewildered not-quite-cowboy in the funhouse. Her growing gallery surrounds him. The various surfaces she's found to paint on. Hubcaps, pan lids. Distorted fox faces peering down at him. Magpies watching him from her grandmother's dinnerware. Where the magpies' eyes should be, Corey has allowed the floral design on the platters and plates to show through, creating an eerie impression of transparency that she kind of likes.

You like the *Riders of the Open Range* better? she had asked John, the first time he looked at her paintings and shook his head over her foxes and owls.

At least there, I know what I'm looking at. One thing about all these red and green animals, though, they do tend to hold your attention. I keep looking at them and wondering what they're seeing. I wish I knew something about art. For all I know, they're damned good.

"The Doggett kid," he says now.

She tries to read his expression.

"Her mother has called twice. We can't get much out of her. Ingrid told her to call the sheriff, report the girl missing. We don't think she did."

John and Corey study the washboard Ariel. The rippled surface gazes back at them.

"How long has she been living with you?"

"Off and on? Sometimes I don't see her for days. Also, I've had a feeling they know where she is. They've been keeping an eye on the place."

Silence. Sunlight falls through the deep windows, blinks in the eyes of the horses and foxes and scavengers and deer.

"Most of the summer," she admits. "Off and on."

"Last place in the world I'd expect her to be," he says after a while. "What—I mean, why?"

Why.

"It's pretty bad," she says at last.

John waits, and she understands that she hasn't said enough, and she wishes she could read his face, but his back is to the window now, and the flood of sunlight blinds her, and she takes a breath deep enough to steady her voice. Launches into it. Ariel's whole goddamn story. Hailey Doggett and Uncle Eugene. She tells everything but the home preg-test kit, and that's because she doesn't get that far, John steps away from the window and his face stops her, it's not just the sun-spots darkening his face.

Her voices are reassembling, rebutting. Loren, Andreas, Vergil. *You damn fool, you stupid old maid. You believe the little liar? Such a story as she's told! And you, you ought to be ashamed of repeating it!*

"And you believe her?"

Corey steadies herself. Looks at her paintings for courage. Fox eyes, deer eyes, scavenger eyes, the eyes of Ariel on her wavy washboard.

"Yes. I believe her."

"Then we've got to call the county prosecutor."

Easier said than done, as Corey could have foretold. First question, where's Ariel, last seen running into the barn to hide from John. Has she gone to ground under the tree fort again, even after last night's scare? Gone home? Or—some instinct sends Corey silent-footed to the stairwell—has Ariel somehow sneaked indoors, to eavesdrop?

"There you are. I thought so."

She drags out Ariel by the wrist, then leans against the kitchen sink to watch the head-to-head between the attorney and the little girl. Knows which one she'd put her money on.

Ariel slumps, watches through her eyelashes as John squares himself away in Loren's chair.

"You can't just pretend that nothing happened to you, Ariel. Sex with a child is a felony. And I'm an officer of the court, I can't—"

"They'd go to jail?"

"For a long time."

"I lied."

"Now wait a minute. Did it happen or not?"

"Didn't."

John keeps trying for some time, but nothing, as Corey could have told him, will budge Ariel from whichever story she's picked to spin.

Corey can't help herself, though, she has to give poor John what help she can. "What about your purple line? Who gave you your purple line?"

"I didn't have a purple line. I lied."

Up on the main fork of Mill Creek, everybody's busy getting ready for the train robbery. James Tendenning, in his leather farrier's apron, has fired up his forge on the gravel turnaround by the kennels. He'll replace the off front shoe that Steve's little pinto mare keeps throwing, hoping a hot-shoeing will hold her for a while, and then he'll slap cold shoes all the way around on Perry for Corey, because it's going to be tough on horses, running up and down that suicide hill of John Perrine's. Meanwhile in the cabin Val has set up her sewing machine on the kitchen table and plugged it into an extension cord from the socket behind the stove so she can tackle the stack of ripped shirts and torn jeans from the train robbery rehearsal.

"Any more of these boys pretending to be shot out of the saddle and dragged, and you can start doing their laundry and mending," Val has told John Perrine, and she's half-serious, she's got enough of the old folks in her to be fed up with games.

But who can stay angry with John? Val leans over her seam and buzzes along with a zigzag stitch and tries to imagine Loren Henry's reaction to John Perrine. Loren might have given John some credit for decency and good will, even if he made fun of his manners and his way of making a living. John's hero worship, the way he hangs on every word about the old glory days—surely the old man would have swelled up and started on his stories. But what Loren would have said about John's romance, if romance is the word, with Corey?

I worry about her, living alone in that house. She might as well be living in another century, John had told Val at the beginning of the summer.

Val runs her pressure foot off her seam and has to back up and start over. Looks at the heavy white thread on its wobbly course, thinks she'd better keep her mind on what she's doing or else stop sewing. Her own father had been bad enough about his daughters. Val's sister ran off and got married young and divorced young, lives in Seattle now and won't set foot on the east side of the mountains. Val herself, when James Tendenning started hanging around, wondered from one day to the next if the old man would explode. But eventually he got fond of James and started to depend on him.

Why she's worried, she doesn't know. Well, yes, she does know. John Perrine's unmistakably clean and polished black truck on the Henry Gulch road, morning after morning on his way to his office in Fort Maginnis, and everybody in the neighborhood noticing, even Arnie Reisenaur remarking to Val in an undertone that she saw that attorney driving down the gulch again this morning, and she sure hopes Corey isn't getting taken advantage of. Val and James have talked it over in dark of night. Not like Corey's under the age of consent, says James. Yes, but I can't stand to think of her getting hurt. And what about Ingrid. Dunno about Ingrid, says James.

Val finishes reinforcing the knees of one pair of blue jeans with the backs of another old pair that's worn past the point of mending. Folds the jeans and goes to the window. From here she can watch James shoeing that big line-back buckskin gelding of Loren's. The pups in the kennel also are watching, some of the pups up on their hind legs with their faces pressed against the chicken wire to see better. Val has to laugh. Eight pups with no idea until now there was anything in the world half so interesting as horseshoeing.

The gelding isn't as entertained. He's flattened his ears as his big body twists at an unnatural angle with one hind foot being held up by James. Val can see James's rear end and the flaps of his farrier apron and, now that she's not running the sewing machine, hear the click-clink of his hammer on horseshoe nails.

Corey holds Perry by his halter rope. Her hat shades her eyes and the straight line of her mouth. She's as thin as a teenager. From this distance, she could be a teenager, except for her sharp angles and her containment, which is a kind of grace. Does Corey know she has it? Has she always had it, and has Val simply known her too well to see it? Or is it new, and has it been cast by the warmth of John Perrine?

James lets Perry's foot drop. He straightens his back and turns off the switch on the electric forge as Corey leads the gelding for his first few steps on his new iron shoes, into the shade of the big pine where light and dark dapple his hide and obscure Corey as though she's stepped into camouflage. After all, she's still Corey Henry. Grouchy maybe, but that's not new. Val doesn't want to see Corey get hurt, but she also hopes for one constant. Let Corey stay the same as ever.

The pups hurl themselves against their chicken wire, yapping into the middle distance. Val looks up and sees her boys leaping down the shale hill from the sheep pasture. She watches Steve run out on a half-buried sandstone boulder and teeter on the brink, while Park waits. Steve, so like the pictures of his grandfather at that age, with his grin and his dark eyebrows and his light hair caught in sunlight. He's waving his arms as though he's about to dive off the boulder and swim through thin air, and Val puts out an involuntary hand to stop him and comes up against window glass, but of course he's not going to jump. He's showing off for Park, who is angry. Val can see his mouth move, although she cannot hear his words.

She wonders if it's really any harder for the girls to grow up in cowboy country than it is for the boys. Here's Park, ready to graduate from high school next year, and then what. All he wants to do is ranch, and here's this poor mountain property that can't support one family, let alone two. If Val and James want to hang on to their ranch, they have to work to support it, not the other way around.

And so will Park, if he wants to stay. He can go to work for the railroad. Lay ties. Rob tourist trains in his spare time.

Park bursts into the kitchen—"Mom! Steve's taken my bow and arrows!"

"Did not," says Steve.

Park is as petulant as a little boy. "I wanted to ride as an Indian again!"

Have you seen Rita? Val and Annie have asked each other.

Corey was asking about Rita when I saw her in town, said Val.

I never see hide nor hair of Rita, said Annie. Dr. Mackenzie, the fellow that bought my place? He's a veterinarian, you know, or used to be. Sold his practice in Plentywood and came here to retire. He's a real nice fellow. Wife died of cancer, two-three years ago. He stops by and drinks coffee with me. Always asks me if I need anything from town, and you know what else he did? He dug up all that strip of sod along the fence in front, and then he brought a sack of peat moss and spaded it in, and now I've got a place to transplant my irises next spring. Doc says they bloomed real pretty last spring, up there where Ma and me always grew them.

Doc saw what happened over east, when the Freemen holed up from the law. Says he's never liked the looks of that Doggett setup. He's seen them with a flatbed truck, hauling crates and crates of stuff. And all that target practice! Doc thinks Hailey and that bald-headed buddy of his are likelier to shoot themselves in the foot as not. It's that big young fellow he's concerned about.

And lately they've been running a backhoe next to the property line. The noise and dust they raise! I get so sick of it.

Corey has to admit one thing. After a spring and summer astride green, rough-gaited Babe, she's finding Perry a pleasure to ride ever as he gets used to his new shoes. Perry pivots at a touch of a rein for her to reach the chain and open and close the gate—

Where are you going, Ariel demanded.

Just down to the mailboxes to mail my application.

He's not going to call the prosecutor, is he.

Guess not.

Are you mad at me? You're mad at me, aren't you. You don't believe me.

From the windows around the room, Corey's deer and ravens and foxes had looked back at her, hollow-eyed and speechless that the old woman had the idea she could paint, when she couldn't even tell whether a child was lying or not. Andreas was right. Washboards and the seats of drills and a waste of good oil paint. The fact is, they'll be laughing at her at Montana State as soon as they read her application. Old Corey Cowgirl, when will she ever learn.

Maybe she could get a thousand dollars, or more, for Perry, if she trucked him over to western Montana where the pleasure-riders are thicker and richer. Maybe she could use the money to get the rest of Loren's horses through a few more months. Maybe it doesn't matter, maybe they'll be Hailey's horses.

She doesn't know why she's worrying about horses. She's still got time before her money runs out and her first court hearing is scheduled. Thirty days is forever, compared with tomorrow, which is how long she's got to worry about Ariel. Ariel. If she's missed three periods. If she swears up and down she hasn't.

Can I even take her to a doctor, she'd asked John.

Let children's protective services do it, said John. If she's—how old? Thirteen? God!—and pregnant, they'll put her in temporary foster care, no matter how she says she got that way, and they'll set up a meeting with the Doggetts.

What I don't understand, he said, is how you let her hang around all summer.

Now Corey ponders. Not that she's going to try it on Ariel, but the old women had a recipe, turpentine and sugar. Wonders how she knows about it, because the old women would never have discussed such a thing in front of a young unmarried woman. Annie would know the proportions.

She's riding through the shade of pines and into patches of sunlight where the road curves, and Perry, soft from his summer on grass, is sweating by the time they reach the mailboxes on the side of the road opposite Annie's place. Annie's car is parked under the trees. Annie is probably in her trailer, watching her soaps and pretending nothing bad has ever happened to her.

Corey leans from the saddle to open the mailbox, a far stretch down from tall Perry. Finds three offers for credit cards and a renewal notice for *Western Horseman*. Sticks them in her shirt pocket. She's carried her application this far, she may as well mail it. May as well give the folks at Montana State their laugh. She sticks the thick envelope in the box and raises the red flag as birdsong rises from the cattails along the creek. Blackbirds, oblivious of her. She wonders whether she might really do it. Move to Billings. Take Ariel with her. Forget about Hailey, forget about John Perrine, forget about children's protective services and temporary foster care. Just let them try to find her.

Ariel kneels on the kitchen windowsill, trying to see through the glare of sun on the road to the barn. The creek has shrunk to a trickle, and the dust of late summer weighs down the hawthorn leaves. Halfway to the barn, the door to the old root cellar hangs off its hinges. Ariel long ago had investigated the root cellar as a potential hideout, but found only a barricade of collapsed rafters and dirt trickling down into boxes of jars full of spider webs—eew, why would anybody want to keep jars of spider webs? She'll never understand these people.

Now the dark entrance of the root cellar stares at her from behind its crooked door, mysterious as ever. A hundred yards on, the stone barn looms over the pole gate and the road to anywhere. Ariel watches as, from the shadow of the barn, Corey leads out the big tan-colored horse. Ariel wants to scream a warning. *Be careful, keep away from that huge beast!* But oblivious of its hooves and the big yellow teeth it shows when it wrinkles its nose and yawns, the indomitable Corey mounts the beast and touches it with reins and spur to dance it around the opening and closing of the pole gate. Next minute, Corey's out of sight, and the barn, the root cellar, and what's left of the creek have settled into themselves.

The rooms of the stone house are waiting for Ariel. She won't have much time. She slips off the windowsill and sidles through the archway into the front room, wondering why she's being careful to be quiet. Only the painted faces of deer and foxes and strange birds and her own painted face are watching what she does.

It takes Corey twenty minutes to ride down to the mailboxes, twenty minutes to ride back. Ariel's timed her.

For a moment Ariel hesitates—where to start? The rolltop desk is crammed, overflowing with papers, some so soft and faded and ancient that they can't possibly be interesting. She tosses aside bundles tied with string, bundles held together by rubber bands so old that they break when she tries to pull them off. What is she looking for, what does she think she'll find? Broken-backed notebooks, coverless address books, empty envelopes with one side addressed to Loren Henry and the other side jotted with illegible lists and rows of numbers? Still she pulls open drawers, lifts out stacks and bundles, not knowing that Corey has sorted through the same stacks and bundles. Money is what she hopes to find, the mystery money of the half-heard talk between Corey and the attorney—not her fault for listening, is it? Not like she's going to *steal* anything.

Where does money come from, where does money go? Her dad—*Hailey*—used to generate money out of the same computer that down-loaded pictures of girls with guns up their snatches and guys with their whangs stapled to their abdomens with safety pins until Hailey caught Ariel looking at them. However, like the goose that stopped lay-ing golden eggs—as Ariel knew from her eavesdropping—the com-puter eventually stopped shaking out money.

O-ooh, Hailey, cried her mother.

Money has to come from somewhere, doesn't it? Isn't that what I keep telling you?

With one eye on the clock she is halfway through her allotted time when her prying fingers find what Corey should never have missed. Between the keyholes of the rolltop is a secret drawer, which slides open when Ariel happens upon the catch. Jammed into this drawer is an oversized envelope. Ariel lifts out the envelope.

It is unsealed, its flap merely tucked inside to contain its contents. Ariel's hands tremble with the bulk of it. She's found something that matters, she can sense it, but is it money? Her thoughts swoop. *Yes!* Santa Monica! And yet she can't quite bring herself to unfold the flap, she feels the way she did when she was finally old enough to see her stocking on Christmas morning and know that nothing in it was go-ing to be better than the moment before she opened it.

Money has to come from somewhere!

Something like a film clip unreels through Ariel's head.

Eugene! Get out of our lives! We don't need you! cries her father as Ar-iel puts the money, lots of it, into his hands.

O-ooh Hailey, bleats her mother, *what has Ariel done?*

She's saved us, that's what she's done. She's twice the woman you've ever been.

But there's no money in the envelope. Instead, it's stuffed with what looks like bank deposit slips. Ariel spills out the slips, upends the envelope and runs her hand around inside to feel for anything she's missed, but finds nothing but paper dust. She sneezes, puts her hands to her face and sneezes again while dust motes float in a shaft of sunlight and sift down on her.

Notices, on the flap of the envelope, a line of writing in fresh, sharp pencil.

If you've found this, it's yours.

Ariel drops the envelope into the mess she's made of the desk. She's known all along that anything she found would be Corey's, but she can't help running a new bit of film clip: *Oh Ariel, you wonderful girl, you've found—what?—bibbity bobbety boo—just what I've been looking for, and I'm going to take you with me to Billings where your uncle and your dad will never find you.*

Her hands are filthy. Ariel licks her fingers like a cat and wipes them on her blue jeans, which bite uncomfortably into her waist and remind her of her purple line. She begins to cry.

Annie Reisenaur has foregone her soaps to watch the neighborhood spectacle with Doc Mackenzie. From folding chairs on the little platform in front of her trailer house that Annie calls her front step and her sons call a deck, she and Doc are well positioned to view the mailboxes, the fork in the county road, and the turnoff to the Doggett place without being seen themselves behind their sheltering screen of pines.

Some might think iced tea a more appropriate drink in this weather, but Annie and Doc both grew up in Montana, and they take it as an article of faith that coffee, hot coffee, cools the skin more effectively than any cold drink, and so they sip coffee all day long. Shade from the pine trees falls comfortably overhead, with a faint flicker of needles and a warm scent of resin, the world rolling through summer just as it ought, while in front of Annie's trailer the county road looks bleached white and glaring under the dry heat.

"Would you look there! There goes Hailey again! Why do you suppose he's always in such an all-fired hurry?"

Doc overflows his folding chair and barely has room to stretch his legs, but has made himself comfortable enough to nap. He rouses himself and squints down the road in time to see the rise and fall of settling dust.

"Don't know," he says. Looks into his coffee mug, which he's set on the deck rail. "I suppose that pot's empty? No, no. Don't make any fresh for me."

"It's no trouble," says Annie. She carries Doc's coffee mug back into the frigid blast of the window air conditioner, where the soap people on television are carrying on about love and betrayal. Annie pours coffee from the thermos she's taken to keeping filled for Doc. Sets the mug in the microwave and zaps it for a few seconds to make sure it's hot enough. Wipes a minute coffee stain off her counter with the dishrag. Her kitchen is hardly big enough to turn around twice in, but it's got every convenience, and how she would have enjoyed that microwave, that electric mixer, in the days when Nails was alive and her kids were little and she was doing real cooking. She wonders if Doc would eat a slice of her serviceberry pie, which she's got to get rid of before it spoils. Wonders if he ought to, as fat as he is.

Oh Brandon, sighs a soap person.

"You're spoiling me," says Doc, when she brings his coffee and his pie.

"Don't eat it, then."

"Oh, beings as you went to the trouble."

Doc forks himself a good bite and savors it as a drop of purple juice finds its way out the corner of his mouth to hang in his mustache. Annie has to smile. What kind of care his wife took of him, she can't guess, although she knows the big redwood A-frame on what used to be Annie's own foundations was supposed to be Doc's and his wife's dream home. She has seen the woman's picture, a yellow face shrunken like an alien's under a big puff of blonde wig, but that picture was taken during the chemo, and Annie, who nursed Nails through his chemo, suspects that any waiting-on, especially during the last year or two, was more Doc's waiting on his wife than the other way around.

Oh, Brandon. Such misery as there is in the world. Annie wonders about Rita Doggett, who tried to play pinochle but never remembered to count trump. Insubstantial, Rita always seemed to Annie, like a reflection of a woman seen through a sheet of glass in her neatly pressed denim skirts and blazers that always looked as though the price tags had just been torn off. Annie wonders how much truth there is in the neighborhood speculation. In the old days, a woman wouldn't have told anyone that her husband was—Annie shies away from the very word, substitutes *ornery*—but the other women would have known. What do Barb and Val know, what do they guess? Does Rita suffer? Does she sleep away her days in her dream house? (And where do these rumors come from, who can possibly know when or whether Rita Doggett sleeps?)

Doc rears up out of his chair at the sudden roar from across the creek—"There they go again. Sounds like a backhoe. God damn them to hell! Morning, noon and night! Bet anything they're burying gasoline tanks. That's what they do. They stockpile so they'll have plenty of supplies when the end comes."

"Can't be Hailey on the backhoe. We saw him leave."

Their eyes meet.

"Could be anything," Doc admits. "Could be, he's having his cesspool dug up. Maybe the little shit fell in it."

He laughs so hard at his own wit that Annie feels like kicking his chair out from under him.

Perry snorts and spooks as Corey sees the white sports utility vehicle roaring down the county road toward her. Here she is, letting her mind wander, and here's Hailey Doggett. He brakes at the sight of her, spins gravel, gets his Blazer stopped with its hood almost under Perry's nose.

Fumes of exhaust dissipate in pure air. Perry backs up and blows rollers, and Hailey lowers his automatic window and sticks his head out.

"Miss Henry! Long time no see!"

Not long enough, she thinks, but she nods, briefly.

"This great late summer weather we're having. And after all we'd heard about the cold. Is this typical for Montana in the summer, or what?"

How to answer him. That the dryness of grass and timber has everybody worried. That snow could fall next week, or not until after Thanksgiving. But what does Hailey care about the weather, when he ought to be asking about his daughter. How's Ariel getting along? Oh, she's getting along just fine, Hailey, I've been thinking of driving her over to Coeur d'Alene, Idaho, to get an abortion. Corey studies the tight little face with the upturned nose and mouth and thinks she sees a change. The curly dark hair and sloe eyes, so much like Ariel's—but the pallor and the pimples, what has Hailey been doing to himself?

How many times she has seen Hailey Doggett's face in her sleep? Hailey, putting on the charm in front of the school board. Putting on the charm for her, the first time or two he drove up to the school to complain. Then turning ugly. The threats, the explosion of words, the words that almost could have been Loren's, coming out of Hailey Doggett's mouth.

You may think you're somebody, but. You've got the idea that you know something, but. You're going to find out who you've tangled with this time.

old girl, and you're going to wish you'd listened to me, back when I was still telling you nicely.

And she had what. Cringed. Flinched at his hand, slapping down on her desk. His face so close to hers. His nostrils flaring, his eyes flaming at her, red-veined.

Now he leans on an elbow out the window, smiling up at her with a hand carelessly on his steering wheel. He knows what she's remembering, he's pleasured by the hurt he's done her.

Except that a lot of water has flowed down the creek since then, and now she's astride tall Perry, which means that she's looking down at Hailey as he looks up at her, and from this perspective she can actually see down into his nostrils, which gives his face the look of a pig's snout, and somehow she must have jabbed Perry with a spur, because Perry snorts, rears, and comes down with his chest right up against the door of the Blazer.

"You never know," Corey says, "about the weather, anyway."

The outside mirror is cutting into her calf. She has to lean down from the saddle to see Hailey. Hailey pulls in his elbow.

"I just stopped to get my mail," he says.

"Oh," says Corey. "Sorry. You want to get out?"

She draws back on her reins and Perry obediently backs a pace or two, but he doesn't understand the tension, he's fighting the bit and dripping foam. Hailey does get out of his Blazer, but cautiously. He's never seen Corey on horseback before, and he wants no part of Perry. He keeps a hand on the hood as he walks around it to get to his mailbox.

You know what I'd do to that little devil?

No, Loren, what?

I'd by God build me a nice tight loop, and I'd dab it around his neck and set myself real good. I'd take my dallies and drag him up and down

that gravel road until I either had that son of a bitch broke to lead or broke
his neck, one!

Corey's lariat still hangs on her saddle, where she coiled and strapped it after she caught Perry this afternoon. Her left hand finds the rope, her right hand lives a life of its own. Longs to shake out a loop, knows just how it would feel. The whistle of the three quick swings over her head, the lariat snaking out, settling over Hailey's neat little dome— yes, just now, as he turns his back to look in his mailbox. Perry has been used as a calf-roping horse, and he'll be backing away, backing away from the pressure on the other end of the rope, keeping his head turned toward the calf, in case the calf—Hailey!—takes it into his head to make a run behind him and tangle him in the rope. But Hailey won't be running, Hailey will be on his butt in the gravel with his hands ploughing furrows on both sides as he tries to stop himself, or else trying to loosen the noose around his neck with his fingers, always supposing his neck isn't broken in the instant Corey takes her dallies and sets herself and Perry, back on Perry's haunches.

Serve the son of a bitch right. What he let happen to that little girl.

Hailey takes his handful of mail out of the box. Turns. Corey watches his sloe eyes slide sideways, just the way Ariel's eyes slide sideways. Watches the beads of sweat. Hailey's calculating how much space he's got between Perry and the hood of his car, how far he's got to walk to get to the driver's side. For a minute she thinks he's going to chicken out, get in the passenger door instead and slide over the seat. But Hailey's not chicken, whatever else he is. He doesn't look at her, but he does walk his walk with his buttocks clenched in a comical way inside his Calvin Kleins, as though he hopes to repel bullets. He climbs in his car, slams the door. Glares at her, and for just an instant she thinks she's pushed him too far, that he's going to rev up his Blazer and charge at her.

Yeah, you do that, Hailey. You think about coming after me. Perry and I'll be up that bank and into the pines before you can get in gear. But you do that anyway, Hailey, and then I can tell my attorney how you climbed in your nice new white Blazer and chased an old lady on horseback.

Hailey doesn't. He puts the Blazer in reverse and backs slowly, deliberately around. Turns down his own driveway. Slowly, making sure she sees how slowly he's driving.

I'd a killed the son of a bitch. I would have.

"He's not worth going to jail for."

Another thought occurs to her. "What he let happen to that little girl? Is that what you said? So you think it really happened?

Didn't say that.

"Did."

Didn't.

She'll never get the last word with Loren, she ought to know by now. She touches spur to Perry and heads up the gulch astride his long ground-eating trot.

Sitting elbow-to-elbow in the shade on Annie's deck, Annie and Doc have witnessed it all.

"Why! I thought she was going to break his scrawny little neck for him," says Annie.

"Pity she didn't."

Annie considers Doc. Wonders how much he says is what he means and how much is just talk. She's sure not going to share her deck with somebody that goes around breaking the neighbors' necks.

But Doc's not going to break anybody's neck. He's living in the real world, same as her, where people don't break other people's necks. She's sure of that.

18

Rita has cried herself dry and slept and wakened to feel as though she's being jerked on strings. The backhoe is roaring away at the hillside above the house. Are they digging out the whole side of the mountains? Is the sun shining, does the world still turn? Do blackbirds sway on the cattails along the creek, and do Amy Staple and Rose still play in the shallows, under the trailing willows, up to their ankles in brown water, where the minnows dart around the distortions of their white feet? Rita automatically feels the bedside table for her glasses and then remembers they are gone.

She had agreed with Hailey that they would stop the clock and live without further destruction, out of reach of the so-called civilized world. Civilized police state, as Hailey called it, where children were threatened by drugs and violence while the cops focused on bringing down good men like Eugene. Hailey's silly conversations with Albert and Eugene, the silly plans they've been making, like toys playing computer games based on an alternative reality, have been indulgences, middle-aged entertainment that she's hardly listened to, because who could take seriously their imagined world of futuristic knighthood in flower?

And yet the sting on her face. Was it a slap? A shove? It was the end of her glasses.

Rita swings her legs over the side of the bed. The weight of her head almost overbalances her, and she holds it in both hands while she tries to make her mind work. Then gropes until she finds the phone.

Dials. When Ingrid answers, Rita says what she must.

She holds the phone in her hand until dial tone returns and she remembers to hang up. The four walls of her bedroom wait for her to come to her senses, to remember the silk panels that she picked out of the luxury catalogue. If only she could see them without her glasses. She tries to remember the sheets and pillowcases, the counterpane. Surely a room with a real counterpane is safe from the tremors of the world, surely nothing bad ever has happened in a room with a counterpane, and yet here is Rita, about to tip the world on its axis and set off explosions within explosions within explosions, like fireworks showering their expanding colors over the heads of those that merely watch and gasp. Oh, of course she won't leave this room, of course she won't set off explosions. She'll curl up and let the world stay as it is, and sleep and sleep and sleep.

But she staggers away from the bed, wondering whether her knees will fold under her. All that holds her up are Ingrid's words. She gathers her pillow, her rug. This time, under her rug, she'll carry—what. Tries to decide. Her magazine. Her silver hairbrush. Her *toothbrush*. Taking any one thing with her suddenly seems a violation of the whole. At the last minute she grabs a little crystal flagon with a silver top, meant to hold perfume. It's empty, she's never bothered to decant perfume from the perfume bottle into the flagon, but she thinks one of the girls, maybe Ariel, gave it to her last Christmas, and she tucks it into a fold in the rug.

She starts for the door and gasps, but it's only her own reflection in the full-length mirror, which appears to be walking toward her because she's walking toward the hunchback in the denim skirt and the black cotton turtleneck that makes her face look pale and disembodied, a face that floats along by itself with its sticky eyes and its flattened hair. She peers closer. Surely it's the face of a sick woman, a woman who belongs in bed. Not a woman to be taken seriously, not a woman who is about to ruin everything.

The backhoe has gone silent. Although her ears roar with the enormity of taking one step away from her bedroom, then another, she can hear the men on the patio, hear their lowered tones if not their words. She imagines them leaning forward in their deck chairs in the seriousness of their conversation to dip their crackers in salsa, point out their morning's work, plan what they're going to gouge out next for their ammunition depot, as they call it. She can't pick out Hailey's voice from the others. Maybe he has risen from his chair, maybe he's already edging down the carpeted hallway to catch her in the act. But Hailey's not there, she remembers. It was Hailey who brought the Lambert grandsons over for target practice and patrol duty this morning, and now he's gone to take them home. It must be Eugene and Albert who are talking on the patio.

The closed doors of bedrooms pass by her, the living room opens ahead of her in an assault of floor-to-ceiling windows. How has she ever lived in such a glare of light? The sound of the glass patio door on its metal runner is harsh when she slides it open, but the men are blurs and they hardly look up. They're used to her and her rug. She's a nonentity, as far as they're concerned.

You used to have a mind, Rita, her mother said the last time she talked to her. You have a decent degree. You used to be concerned about the lives your girls would lead.

You used to be concerned about our lives, said Hailey. His words, one by one, beads on a string that jerk her back.

Where's Ariel?

In the here and now, pausing before she takes the final irrevocable step into the sunlight, Rita hears Eugene's remark—"He can't handle the white bitch. You can get him to do anything for her."

For just a breath she thinks that Eugene is talking about her, but of course he's not, he's talking about Hailey.

"We'll have to ration him," Eugene says, and Rita fades off across the vacant lawn.

She trudges across empty lawn under direct sunlight that makes her squint and wish for her dark glasses (prescription! she could see through them!) but her dark glasses are in her handbag, back at the house. Her handbag, perhaps she should go back for it, because the willows hiding the creek are a blur at the edge of her sight. She's exposed to open sky and the shadows of clouds, as blind as some small live thing under the shadow of a plummeting hunting bird, faint with the certainty that, any minute now, one of the men will notice her and call her back.

Or Hailey. Hailey could come back at any time. She's lost track of how long he's been gone.

And yet, even at her creeping pace, she reaches the end of the lawn. Her feet find the little path down into the shelter of willows where children's voices paddle in the shallows.

"Ariel?"

Sudden silence. Rita pushes through willow leaves and finds herself on an unsheltered bank. The sun is hot, the water a glare. In the pool under the opposite bank, two shadows wade up to their knees. Bits of gold fall and float over their reflections. A flutter on Rita's shoulder is close enough for her to see a gold willow leaf, while the shadowy girls stare at her, as distant as though they are enclosed in one of the droplets of water, water nymphets in their shower of gold.

Rose comes wading toward her mother. Her dress is tucked up in her underpants to keep her hem out of the creek. That's been a recent change, Hailey's insistence on dresses for Rose. But who could wish to harm such scabby-kneed nymphets, little snot-noses with front teeth too big for their mouths?

Show some spine, said Ingrid. If you don't get yourself and your child out of there, it will be your fault.

"Come along," says Rita. "We're going, now."

The girls hesitate. An exchange of glances between them, Amy's pale blue eyes flickering across Rose's hazel eyes as subtly as sun dancing through the leaves. What are they thinking, what they are planning? For a moment Rita thinks that Rose will refuse to come with her—but no, Rose hitches at her dress and climbs out of the creek with Amy following her.

"You just going to walk up their road and gawk?" says Doc.

Annie doesn't lower herself to reply. She hangs her apron on the deck rail, makes her way down the steps, and trudges down her road as far as the curve that meets the county road, keeping a wary eye in case Hailey comes roaring back and she has to jump for the weeds. Pine needles and pine cones underfoot and a few ripe grassheads in the shade, everything dry as tinder. At first she thinks that Doc has taken himself home in a huff, but then she hears his footsteps behind her, shuffling and heavy as an old bear, and she smiles to herself.

Annie takes a quick look up and down the road, where the sun shines as vacantly as though Hailey Doggett hadn't raised a plume of dust not five minutes ago. Makes up her mind, ducks her head, and trots out into the open. She reminds herself of a fool gopher deciding to dart across the road just in time to get run over. But there's no traffic, only the persistent rumble of the backhoe from somewhere in the timber. Annie sinks into the deep grass of the verge and leans down to pick the burrs off her stockings. From here she can look down on Mill Creek, brown bubbling current in the shade of willows, the one stretch of water where she can hop across on boulders and ancient deadfall without getting her feet wet.

Feeling as though she's shed a skin between her wrinkled old self and the self that played along this creek in childhood, Annie skips along the boulders to a tiny bank that smells of mud and white clover. From the thrashing of branches behind her, Annie assumes that Doc's still with her, though he can't have an idea in the world where her dandelion-fluff head is leading him. The brush looks impenetrable, but Annie knows from experience of a tiny uphill trail that leads through Hailey Doggett's property.

She locates herself by the noise from the backhoe, drops to her knees in a crush of rosehips, and peers through the screen of leaves at a sight of raw earth, fresh yellow splinters, and oozing stumps. The backhoe looms over her like a behemoth, and her heart lurches—has she come too close?—but no, it's gouging its way in the other direction, heaving sandstone boulders and wilting, uprooted hawthorns out of its trench.

Doc crowds through the brush with his pant legs dark and wet to the knees. He squats down behind her with squelching shoes. Annie has to smile. Evidently he had bad luck crossing the creek.

But what are these men doing? From the destruction, it would look to Annie as though they're logging off some timber. Her own father

344

and later on Nails cut what timber they could sell to make ends meet, which was the reason for many of the old deadfalls throughout the foothills, and of course she realizes it's Hailey's property which he can do with as he likes. But the little bald man with the chainsaw doesn't seem to have any method to what he's doing. Annie watches as he gazes around, spots a standing aspen, and tramps through devastated underbrush to attack it with the saw, which screams and bounces. Next is a thin pine that tears away from its stump and falls, leaving a splinter pointing at open sky.

"Afraid of his saw," mutters Doc. "The way he's handling it, he's got a reason to be afraid of it. If he tries to fell anything bigger than those spindles, he'll bring it down on top of himself."

"I wish he would."

"Want to see him squashed flat, do you?"

Annie shakes her head. It's not that she has a thing in the world against him, it's the strangeness, the overturning of earth and the broken tree roots, the gouging and mangling for no reason. And now she notices, beyond the trench dug by the backhoe, the new construction. A fence of fresh, bright lumber and a platform on high legs that reminds Annie of an old-fashioned farm windmill except for the absence of blades. Or maybe it's a watchtower, maybe it's part of a boy's fort, the kind of play fort her boys might have built if they'd had the money and the time off from honest chores. Behind her, Doc is muttering, but Annie watches the backhoe as it roars and gobbles like a living thing under the operation of its shirtless rider, the huge young man with the shaven head and bronzed shoulders running with sweat that gleams in the heat of the sun.

"That's a rifle tower," hisses Doc.

"I got to get out of here before it makes me sick," Annie whispers. Maybe it's only the gasoline fumes and reek of turpentine that's making her feel softheaded. She pushes past Doc, stumbles down the trail.

Branches catch at her skirt and pull her hair, and she swats at them. None of her business what they're digging up or burying.

Doc, breathing heavily, catches up with her at the creek. "I know I've seen that young fellow somewhere before. I think he's one of them that hung out with the Freemen."

"I think I've lost a shoe," says Annie. No, there it is. On her foot, but darkened and strangely pliant where she must have stepped in creek mud without realizing it. All the things she's lost in her life without fully realizing it. And now here's Doc, looking anxiously at her, when from the dark red color of his face and the sweat that's rolling down it, she's the one who should be anxious about him.

Well. She pulls herself stiffly off her knees, straightens her dress and feels for twigs in her hair.

"I lost a baby, years ago," she tells Doc. "Buried it there by the creek."

"Is that so," says Doc.

Doc starts to lumber to his feet, and Annie reaches down and gives him a hand. Practicality, the buttress of her life, takes over. She's glad to see that his breathing has leveled out, that the ominous red flush is beginning to fade. Wonders how much more of her life story she was about to tell him, wonders if he'll ask, decides he probably won't. She picks her footing down to the creek, careful not to slip into the mud again, lifts away a branch and sees, knee-deep in the current like an apparition of the one so mercifully lost, the startled child.

"Amy Staple!" she gasps, recognizing her. "What are you doing here?"

"Playing."

Corey keeps watching for John Perrine and his truck and goose-necked horse trailer at the pole gate, but he doesn't show. Finally, concerned about the lengthening afternoon and the hour's drive out to Eberle, talking to herself about the need to be on time for the robbery, this time the real thing, and the train won't sit and wait to be robbed, will it, she backs the old red truck up against the corral fence where she's stacked the sections of the stockrack. Wonders what's keeping John, wonders if he's angry about Ariel, wonders. Gets out of the truck and starts hoisting the sections into place around the box of the truck, fitting the two-by-fours into their slots and tightening the bolts. The work spurs her temper, makes her want to slam things around. Just like a man. Just when he gets her used to the luxury of a horse trailer. And now this heavy goddamned tailgate. She lifts up the gate, balances it on her knee, gets her breath for the final heave. Slides it down into its groove.

"Jesus fucking H. Christ!" she snarls, as Loren would have snarled if he'd thought Corey was out of earshot.

"What's the matter?" says Ariel, squatting by the mow door and watching.

"Pinched my thumb."

Her thumbnail has swollen to a deep purplish red that will soon turn black. She supposes she'll lose the nail. Another goddamn scar on her poor old hands, and it's all John Perrine's fault. She glances up the road beyond the pole gate, but the gravel stretches around the bend, sunlit and empty. Hawthorn leaves curling from the dry weather, the grass gone yellow. Summer's almost gone. A fragment of some song from her Minneapolis days, somebody playing a guitar. Winter's comin on, I feel like I gotta travel on.

"I could come with you tonight," says Ariel. "I could stay in the truck."

Corey sucks her thumb, glances at Ariel in her droopy shirt and jeans. Underfoot as always. It's not so apparent out here in the open air, but body odor has grown around Ariel, a sour odor, and not that the kid's not washing herself, either. At first Ariel was horrified when Corey showed her how to heat buckets of water on the kitchen stove and pour them into the galvanized tub on the kitchen floor, and, after her bath, to bail water into the sink until she'd emptied the tub enough for her to lift and pour out the rest. Grumbling about life in the dark ages, Ariel had heated water for herself and gradually gotten into a twice-a-week bathing routine.

Corey takes her thumb out of her mouth and looks down the road again, but sees no dust rising, no familiar black truck with a trailer swinging behind it, no John driving too fast to make up for being late.

"Some reason why you don't want to stay home alone?" she asks Ariel.

Ariel shrugs—"Just don't want to—" but adds, "at least, if I had a saddle, I could ride Babe."

The thought of Ariel riding down that suicide slope is enough to make Corey's gut clench. It's bad enough to see the Tendenning boys out there, whooping and yelling and risking their necks, even when she knows Steve and Park have been in the saddle since babyhood, under the eye of their mother. Ariel's never ridden a horse, never even touched a horse except to pet the little stallion, Beauty, as Ariel calls him, or Hailey Dancer, as Corey's trying not to call him.

"You want to ride, you can ride Perry up and down the road a time or two, where I can keep an eye on you," Corey offers.

Ariel shakes her head. Her eyes slide down.

"What?"

"Nothing."

Corey shrugs. Boosts her saddle into the back of the truck, climbs up after it, flings it over the side of the stockrack, and straps the cinch to hold it there during the drive out to Eberle.

348

"How come you never use the pretty saddle?"

The pretty saddle. Corey's a blank. She looks from the top of the stockrack down at Ariel, who has slumped down in the dirt by the front tire, knees under her chin, arms around her knees. She might be seven years old, not thirteen.

Something's wrong, something's going on.

Pretty saddle.

"You mean the J. Hamley saddle? Loren's prize *Pendleton* saddle?"

Ariel looks up, startled out of her pout by the edge in Corey's voice.

"You've been upstairs in Loren's room? Snooping around? Oh, hell, I didn't mean to yell. Don't bawl about it. What's the matter?"

Corey climbs down from the stockrack, feeling creaky. Walks around the truck and squats in the wispy dust beside Ariel, who has buried her face on her knees. God damn it to hell. God damn John Perrine, too, who obviously is disgusted and done with her. Yeah, she may as well curse John as long as she's cursing the universe, because he's the reason she's feeling as empty as the road beyond the pole gate. Damn him. Damn Loren.

For that matter, why not ride Loren's Pendleton saddle tonight? Not that it's an authentic 1882 tree, far from it, but with all that silver encrustation, she'll shine like a rodeo star by the light of the moon.

"Hey, now," she says. Lays a hand on Ariel's shoulder. Her old battered, used-up hand. Whatever comfort on earth it can give a child. Lifts a strand of Ariel's hair and tucks it back. "Can't you tell me what's the matter?"

Ariel makes a small sound, a mew. Then she's casting herself at Corey, and Corey's sitting with her back against a truck tire and holding Ariel in her arms. Rocking her. Growling softly to her, as she would to a foal. Never thought she'd be choosing Ariel over John Perrine, but she guesses that's what she's done.

"I don't want any of this to happen!" sobs Ariel. "I don't want a purple line. I don't want to have to go to Coeur d'Alene. I want everything to go back the way it was! I want my mom and dad!"

"This way," says Rita.

"No!" says the princess warrior. The princess warrior feels as though she could float across the water, she's so full of herself. To save her sister *and* her mother! Even in her dreams, she could never have achieved so much. But now she must be practical: "We've got to go around by the bridge."

"Why?"

"Because you've got shoes on. Or maybe. Maybe you can hop across our secret place."

Muddy to her shins, Rose climbs out of the creek and trots ahead of Rita along an obscure trail. Rita follows her little girl. Rose hasn't been weakened by puberty, and her bare feet have toughened from running all summer without shoes, and she doesn't wince at clods and thistles gone brittle and treacherous from the drought.

"Here's the place we found. Nobody knows about it," Rose assures her mother, and leads her along one of Annie Reisenaur's paths at the edge of cattails, where deer have been coming down to the water to drink and left their deep tracks in mud that has dried hard. Dark clusters of berries hang heavily, and Rose picks a berry in passing and pops it into her mouth. Rita winces. How does Rose know it's not poison?

"They can't see us from the house," Rose promises.

Rita has lost her bearings. Somewhere, upstream or downstream, will be the bridge and the row of mailboxes. Somewhere is Annie Reisenaur's mobile home under the pine trees on the other side of the county road. She realizes that she could have walked down her driveway, over the bridge, and across the road to visit Annie Reisenaur at any time. She could walk to Annie's now if she could get her bearings. But right now there's the sound of a car on the road, getting closer.

Annie and Doc watch as a newish blue Volvo whips around the curve, slows, and stops. The driver leans across the seat and opens the door on the passenger side as a woman with dripping legs emerges from the chokecherries. The woman climbs into the Volvo, followed by a barelegged child who gets in the back seat. The driver wheels around in the middle of the road, makes a three-point turn, and speeds off in the direction of Fort Maginnis.

A moment later the little Staple girl pokes her head out of the leaves and looks up and down the road. She sets off walking up the road toward the Henry place.

"John couldn't make it," says Ingrid, in her curious stiff-lipped way. "He sent me to pick you up. Are you getting in, or not?"

One last thing Bobby can do for Ariel. He fits a stolen arrow to the stolen bow and lights the rag tied to the tip of the arrow. The sudden flare frightens him, he's ranch boy enough to know what fire will do to tinder-dry woods, but he's gone too far to stop; he draws back his bow and points his arrow and sends it arcing across the creek.

Nolan Staple straightens from the utility-room sink, where he's been dowsing his head and scrubbing the field grime off his face with his hands. The filthy bar of soap squirms in its dish as, dripping streams of muddy water, Nolan reaches for the towel. Stops, listens. Takes one long silent stride past Barb's washer and dryer piled with folded laundry, intercepts Bobby at the screen door.

"Where the hell have you been?"

Bobby leans back against his father's grip on his upper arm, but he knows he can't pull away, he's no match for Nolan's work-hardened muscle. He looks at Nolan's big red fingers digging into his smooth white skin and says nothing.

"Out all night, running the countryside, God knows where. I try to put you on a tractor, I set you to summerfallowing, and what do I find? Tractor shut down—you've run off somewhere—what my old man would done to me, if I'd pulled any shit like that—"

Bobby doesn't answer. Although he doesn't struggle, he's braced his legs and leans back with his eyes gone dreamy, making Nolan think of a calf that's been tethered all afternoon to a post, braced stubbornly against its halter rope with its eyes rolled back in its head, as if it thinks it can't uproot the post, but maybe it can outwait it. The comparison infuriates Nolan. He shakes Bobby, trying to get a reaction, but Bobby, while not quite going limp, also doesn't resist. Out of the corner of his eye, Nolan registers another absence. Amy. Where the hell is Amy?

"Where've you been? Where do you think you're going?"

No answer.

"Well, get it out of your head that you're going to sneak off somewhere tonight and worry your mother out of her mind, not if I have to chain you to the goddamn bedpost. Actually—"

Actually, that's not a bad idea, and Nolan's just outraged enough to carry it out. Walking off from the tractor this afternoon! That a ranch kid would walk away from work in the field! A log chain and a padlock, that's what will keep the shitting kid home!

Bobby must read his resolve, because for the first time he looks alarmed.

"Dad! You can't do that! Because—"

"Because why?"

Over Ariel's convulsing shoulder, Corey catches the movement, quick as a coyote, on the road beyond the pole gate. Corey's reaction comes not from her slow brain but from her bones. Just as Loren might have reacted. Her hatbrim concealing her eyes, her attention apparently fixed elsewhere, only her peripheral vision containing the sandstone outcropping, reddened by late sunlight, that hangs over the empty road.

The child's head pokes out, pulls in again, but not so fast that Corey doesn't recognize her.

"Amy Staple, what do you think you're doing? You get right down here."

Amy may be the princess warrior's lieutenant, but she's too much the well brought-up ranch kid not to hear her teacher's authority and heed it. She climbs down from the rocks as surely as though she's been roped and led at the end of Corey's lariat. Skinny-legged Amy with dust sticking to her damp legs in patches, a soldier in the army of children who have been playing their war games up and down the Henry Gulch all summer.

"What's going on?"

Amy tells her.

Rita sits by the window in John Perrine's office. Through the glasses Ingrid bought her off a rack at the pharmacy she can make out the pigeons fluttering above the opposite roof. Something's got their attention. One of the pigeons alights, struts. Examines whatever it is with one eye, tilts his iridescent head to examine it with the other eye. Suddenly pecks at it with a savage jackhammer motion of his neck that tosses the dead feathered thing—a dead pigeon! its own kind!—and gives it a brief illusion of life. There's a violent flurry as other pigeons descend, peck and fight for their share, flutter aloft.

Rita shudders. She feels eviscerated, with a preserved outer shell that continues to go through its motions long after any purpose remains. She'd throw herself to the pigeons if it weren't for Rose. Rose glances up, averts her eyes when she feels her mother's gaze. Goes back to whatever she's coloring. A feral child with her hair in strings. Who could have raised such a child, what dumb fumbling mother could have given birth to such a child. The creek mud had dried on Rose's legs by the time Ingrid got her and Rita to town, but still she had left the imprint of her bare feet across John Perrine's carpet. Oh honey watch where you're stepping, look at the tracks you're leaving, Rita had sobbed, as Ingrid ushered them in.

John had stood up from behind his desk. Oh hell, don't worry about leaving tracks, Rosie. Don't worry about the carpet, it'll clean. I've been on the phone with the prosecutor, he added, and we're waiting to hear from the judge. But the prosecutor's going to want to ask you some questions. About Hailey and Saylor Lambert.

The name sounded vaguely familiar to Rita. She had wanted to throw herself into John's arms. But then the phone had rung again, and John had snatched it up. Perrine, he said.

He listened briefly. Be right there, he said, and then to Rita, right here in my office will be the best place for you and Rosie. I'll be back when I can get back. He glanced at his watch. Of all afternoons. Ingrid will see to anything you need.

What's happening, Rita had pleaded. But there had been no time, John was dashing off, and she had waited and waited. When he did return, it was with a small dark man he introduced as Frank LeTellier, the prosecutor, and Ingrid had taken Rose out while the prosecutor began asking Rita questions. What had been their plan when they moved to Fort Maginnis. Who were they in touch with. Saylor Lambert? No, she kept insisting, she knew nothing about a Saylor Lambert, didn't think she had ever met him. Or had she. Eugene Doggett, yes of course she knew Eugene.

How long had she known Eugene?

Years and years.

Did she know he was wanted for parole violation in California? Had he been in on their plans from the beginning?

There was no plan! They talked, yes, but it was silly talk! The fantasies of little boys who built tree forts and fought imaginary wars. She hadn't paid enough attention to their ramblings to be able to repeat any of it.

Ariel's been missing how long?

Rita, said John. You're going to have to tell what you know. Testify. Otherwise you'll be charged.

The prosecutor's words hurled themselves at her, struck blows like stones. Accessory to child abuse. Rape. Children in foster care. No, not just Ariel. Rose, too. And not later. Right now. We can have Rose in temporary care in half an hour, said the prosecutor.

Rita, we don't want that to happen, said John.

We can get another warrant, said the prosecutor. We can jail you, right alongside the men.

Rita, we don't want that to happen.

Bludgeoned, battered from both sides, she had doubled over with her face in her lap and her arms wrapped around her head. Sobbed, sobbed. Said she'd do whatever. Whatever they told her to do. She'd say whatever she had to say, just please, please.

A signed statement?

Her brain was bloated from crying. She couldn't speak, so she nodded. If that's what she had to do. And to the questions that followed, it was easier to nod, to whisper yes, and yes, until eventually, blessedly, they left her in peace. They brought Rose back, with her new crayons and plenty of office stationery to color on, and then they went away, and Rita had been stunned to raise her eyes to the windows and see ordinary daylight, an ordinary afternoon in Fort Maginnis, with the dusty tops of cottonwood trees and pigeons fluttering over the opposite rooftop.

Now, gradually, she has pieced back a version of the day. What she had done, what she had said. What they said Hailey and Eugene had done to Ariel. What they had told her she had to say.

When the door opens behind Rita, she lifts her head, hoping that it's John, but it's Ingrid.

"John called," says Ingrid through her stiff lips. "I'm to check you into a motel for the night and order you some takeout. What kind of take-out food do you like, Rosie? We've got Chinese and we've got pizza in Fort Maginnis."

Ordinarily Rose hates being called Rosie, but she gathers up her crayons and slides off John's office chair, ready to go.

"I don't want to stay here by myself! I want to go with you!"

"Okay, okay. We'll drop off Amy on the way—your mom's home, isn't she, Amy, last thing I need is another loose kid on my hands— no, wait, get in the pickup and we'll drive over to the house and get the other saddle. Yeah, the pretty one. By God, I'm riding the pretty one."

All Corey can concentrate on is what's next. If she thinks about the periphery, about anything but what lies straight ahead, her brain will frazzle off in fragments. She's got a train to rob. Once the train is robbed, she can think what next. For now, she's got to drive carefully from the barn to the house, Perry throwing his weight in the pickup bed. Perry hates being hauled. Corey's got to ease up the slope and stop and park. Set the brake. Last thing she needs is the pickup rolling off into the coulee with Perry in it.

"You girls wait, all I have to do is carry down the saddle—"

But no, of course they're sliding across the seat of the cab and following her, Amy thinking her deep thoughts and tear-blotched Ariel with her shuffling catch-up step that Corey knows by heart. They traipse behind her into the cool of the kitchen.

"—I just need to bring down the saddle—what the hell's this, Ariel, you've been into my desk again?"

"Just wanted to see what was there," whimpers Ariel.

Odd papers out of the desk, receipts and old bills and clippings spread out on the kitchen table—"Damn it, what a mess! Why can't you leave my stuff alone—" a thought worms its way to the surface of the squirming maelstrom—"You were looking for papers to give your dad."

"No! No! I was looking for papers for you! To save you so he couldn't sue you!"

Or it might well have been Ariel herself, infinitely curious, burrowing into what doesn't concern her and spreading the evidence in plain sight. If Corey knows nothing else by now, she knows Ariel will tell the story that best serves her for the moment. Ariel is backed up against the refrigerator, half-bent at the waist and bawling while Amy watches. The tears Ariel has shed this afternoon would by God relieve the drought in the foothills. What to do with her. Helpless to know what else to do, Corey picks up a handful of the deposit slips to put them back in the envelope Loren had kept them in, slips starting all the way back in 1962 when she started teaching at the Mill Creek school and Loren deposited her warrants, and ending—when?

Whenever it was that Loren got fed up with automated banking and started cashing her warrants and slapping down twenties to pay for groceries and such. For the first time Corey reads the faded blue numbers on the slips. Cash back. Cash back. Cash back. A hundred a month cash back through the sixties—she riffles ahead—increasing to a hundred and fifty through the seventies.

"Yeah, you got rid of the bank statements, but you kept the deposit slips," Corey accuses the thinning air. Nobody answers. Amy stares, even Ariel stops howling at the tone of her voice. Corey's dizzy, her head's not right, she's trying and failing to multiply, but even having trouble remembering how much is twelve times twelve, it's sinking in to Corey how cash back, cash back, cash back every month, a little more cash back every year for forty years would multiply out to thirty thousand dollars of mystery money, and then some.

So. Any of you. Andreas. What do I do now?

You're asking me?

Why not? You're the one who knows it all.

In her mind's eye he's still wearing his black cape and his black sombrero, as youthful as the last time she saw him, and yet his face, if she could see it clearly, would surely be as time-scarred as her own. She senses the way he mulls over her words, knows he's wondering whether the cowgirl can comprehend irony, and so she clarifies:

You were right, I didn't know a damned thing. Still don't. Not about how people behave. Do they do what they do in books, or not? I'm asking.

You're thinking about your fat attorney?

Yeah. Him and, well. Loren. Hailey Doggett. Rita Doggett. All these kids.

His silhouette wavers like an afterimage at the back of her retinas, fades and then sharpens as he thinks about her question, taking her seriously for once; and she thinks that if she could see his face, she would see that it has softened toward her. Or is it only that she has softened toward herself?

Does this mean you're done playing the hermitess of the hills?

I guess.

You're going to do what you have to do, about your little girl?

Guess so.

Does he nod, or is she watching floaters in her eyes?

You can handle it, he says. *It's your money.*

Thanks, Andreas.

I don't suppose you'll be listening to me from now on.

Silence.

Any of the rest of you got anything to say?

Silence.

Annie and Doc can find nothing much to say, either, but reluctant to depart to their separate beds, they sit side by side on Annie's little deck in the gathering twilight. After the excitement of Corey's confrontation with Hailey at the mailboxes, and the escape of Rita, they watched Corey speed past with the little girls in the front seat with her and Loren's big line-backed buckskin rearing in the back to see over the stockrack, and an hour later they watched the attorney tear up the road in his big black truck, dangerously fast considering he was pulling a horse trailer. A few minutes later he tore back down the road again, horse trailer weaving behind him. What that was all about, neither Doc nor Annie could guess.

But now the action seems to be over, and the view from Annie's deck has settled back into the ordinary. The county road is vacant, the gravel undisturbed except for reddening rays from the inexorably setting sun. Annie supposes she should be feeling relief from the heat of the day, but she doesn't; she feels stale, the way she sometimes feels after an afternoon of television, absorbed in her programs until finally they're over and she's back in the humdrum flatness of her life. Not unhappiness, she insists to herself, but a flat life these past few years when she's had little real work to do. And now she can't settle down within her own skin.

There's plenty she could say if she just knew what. She glances sideways at Doc.

"I read a book last winter," says Doc, "that said your average survivalist is a thirty-nine-year-old male, married, with two years of college and two-point-two children."

"Sounds like anybody," says Annie. She picks vaguely at her fluff of hair, pulls out a twig and broken leaf that must have stuck to her while she was crossing the creek. Something's drawing her back to the creek that she'd like to isolate and examine, a particular pain, like a tooth missing.

"That's the whole idea, that you can't pick 'em out from the rest of the population. Thing is, though, they get to daydreaming, and they get to thinking what fine fellows they'd be, courageous and self-reliant and so forth, if the world would just come to an end and give 'em a chance to show what they're made of—"

"Crazy," she murmurs.

"Bored, is all."

"The one I lost," says Annie, finding words, "it was going to be a little girl. I never felt like it was such a mercy."

Silence, except for the creak of Doc's folding chair as he lays his book down. "Sometimes they're just not seeded right," he says, so gently that Annie's eyes fill and she's afraid she's going to disgrace herself.

"No," she says after a moment, "she wasn't seeded right."

The wind has picked up as the sky darkens and yard lights wink over the new houses on the other side of the creek. The ridge pines moan aloud and fling their branches as though they are trying to pull themselves out by the roots. Annie can smell the charged air. Her bottom feels as though it has grown into her chair, and her feet have gone to sleep. She twitches them, irritably, and endures the rash of tingles up to her knees.

Doc squints at the horizon. "Looks like we could get some rain."

"We could sure use some rain," she agrees.

"Guess I ought to walk home before it lets loose."

The moment lengthens.

"Well," says Doc. He finds his book and the flashlight he likes to carry to find his way home with, and heaves himself out of his chair. "Guess I—"

But he pauses as a single headlight infiltrates the shadowy undergrowth, edging the leaves with a surreal color and letting them fall back into darkness as the motorcyclist purrs down to the bridge, crosses it, and turns down the county road toward Fort Maginnis. Annie gets just a glimpse of the rider, a giant silhouette hunched over his handlebars. For a minute or two she sees brief flashes of the headlight, as though sliced by the dark pines that overhang the road. Then nothing. The purr fades into distance.

"Well," Doc repeats. He stands and stretches, and a whiff of his male odor bears a fleeting memory to Annie of Nails, so heartbreakingly clean in his hospital bed toward the end. She almost pushes herself up from her chair, almost asks to hold a man's unwashed hand again, but before she can think of uttering such a foolish request, before she can assure herself she'll do no such thing, the sky explodes.

19

John Perrine's morning had begun as usual, in court with a string of clients who hoped to be found not guilty of DUIs and reckless driving charges, drug charges and shoplifting and, in one case, attempted bank robbery, which at least kept John from worrying about his own upcoming train robbery. He got back to his office to learn that a client of his, a nineteen-year-old fugitive from a charge of battery in the course of burglary, had just been arrested in Las Vegas. For half an hour John sat and listened to the kid's tearful mother, who had bailed him out of jail after his first arrest and now, on top of everything else, faced losing her car, which she'd pledged to the bail bondsman. He tried to call Corey Henry, no answer, and then he called Frank LeTellier, knowing in his heart that at this late date a plea bargain for the nineteen-year-old fugitive was unlikely, but going through the motions anyway.

The dumb son of a bitch, had been LeTellier's assessment. Don't these kids ever *think?* And his mother, what's she thinking about? If thing into the truck. Hitched up the trailer. Loaded his startled sorrel gelding and hit the road again, raising dust. Even as late as he was running, he had turned up the Henry Gulch to Corey's place. Stopped at the pole gate and honked, hoping she'd be leading Babe around the barn, saddled and ready to go. But no. Cursing, he got out of the truck and opened the gate and drove over to the house. All was still, nobody home, not even Ariel, especially not Ariel, although Babe lifted her head and pricked her ears from where she and the stud colt had been drowsing and switching flies on their opposite sides of the fence.

Ariel. He hoped Ingrid had some ideas.

By that time the sun had set.

As Corey had grumbled to herself earlier, John grumbled under his breath that that train wasn't going to wait to be robbed. He tromped on the gas, recklessly backed his truck and trailer. Drove through the pole gate, leaped out to shut it, leaped in again, and drove as fast as he dared down the gulch. Closer to town he saw the red wink of a motorcycle's taillights ahead of him, some daredevil taking the curves on the gravel faster than John was. At that moment he heard a distant rumble and an explosion, and saw, in his rearview mirror, faraway fountains of light and shards and shooting comets. What the hell was that, he thought, and kept driving.

Now, having driven out to Eberle with his horse and trailer swaying behind him, John turns on the dirt track and sees from the dust and activity on the slope behind the sandstone rims that everyone else is here and unloading horses and saddling up. He's relieved, he should have known that James Tendenning would take charge and get the show on the road for him. He parks and unloads his sorrel, starts to saddle him, and then, across a long stretch of blowing grass, sees Corey's old red truck with the stockrack. So there she is. She hadn't waited for him. Why would she.

In the cab, a head raises briefly above the dash, disappears again.
Ariel. Corey's brought her along.

Corey has parked her truck with the tailgate against the high side
of the road. As John watches, she jumps down and goes around to
unload her horse, the big buckskin she brought down from the hills
yesterday. The buckskin is unhappy about being hauled. He rears to
see over the top of the stockrack and crashes down, and John cannot hear but imagines Corey's growl, the sound she makes to soothe
horses. The buckskin balks, then gathers himself and leaps out of the
truck like he's clearing the Grand Canyon. Lands in the gold-tipped
grass on all fours.

A damned good horse, John notes automatically, a long-legged horse
with a deep chest for endurance. Of course it would be a good horse,
it was one of Loren Henry's. And then Corey jumps backward off the
tailgate, a long-legged woman in Levi's and beat-up boots, and John's
heart wrenches.

Are you crazy, said Ingrid. She's eleven years older than you are. What
do you think you're doing? Boinking the spirit of the old West?

Do I criticize Lucy?

John changes clothes, shoves his wallet in his shirt pocket so he won't
have to sit on it, leads out his sorrel and hoists himself into the saddle, feeling heavier than ever. If he bought Corey a new pair of boots
as a present, would she accept them? A gust of wind, unexpectedly
chill, rushes across the sere grass and sends it rippling toward the last
sunlight, works a long white strand out of Corey's braid and streams
it past her face, and Corey catches it and tucks it back without stopping what she's doing, toting her saddle to throw it on her tall gelding
with an unexpected blaze of silver. John realizes she's riding Loren's
trophy saddle, and he shivers, a long intense shiver that runs down
his shoulders and back and arms and chest and ribs.

"God damn, I knew I should have worn a coat," he says out loud.

A kid riding past overhears him and gives him a strange look, measuring the thirty years between them. Won't ever get that old, the look says. Won't ever go around talking to myself, out loud. Won't ever happen. John recognizes him, the younger Tendenning boy, Steve, riding one of his dad's half-Arabs and wearing a neckerchief and a hat pulled low to disguise his young face.

Steve's probably what, fifteen, and as easy in his saddle as though he could sleep in it. Slender as a blade of grass. Makes John feel like a walrus on horseback, by comparison. John winces. If he can just live in this moment, forget the rest of this day. He spurs his sorrel and rides up the dirt track, counting riders. Eleven, twelve, counting himself. Everybody's here. He sees James Tendenning bent over a saddle, lengthening the stirrups. His boys probably grow longer legs between one time they sit a saddle and the next. Somebody, John can't tell who, leans against the door of his truck and uses the side mirror while he blackens his face. Corey rides past him on her blaze of silver, doesn't look at him.

The air smells of grass and horses. Somebody laughs. Somebody sings a fragment—oh, away up high in the Sierras peaks, where the yellow jack pine grows tall—and who should they meet but the devil himself, a-prancing down the road. The sun is sinking. For a moment all is gilded, deep-rutted dirt tracks and cattle pass and barbed-wire fence behind the rimrocks, the windshields of trucks and the fluttering shirtsleeves of riders on the move, Stetson hats and spurs and horses tossing heads with a jingle of bridle chain, shining bays and blacks and browns and ruddy sorrels, and John has time to remember that this is all he has ever wanted. The cowboy way. The next moment the sun tips out of sight and the air feels bleak. John feels his shiver again and wonders if it's something he's eaten.

"What do you think, James?" he calls down the slope, as much to hear the sound of his voice as anything, and James looks up from cinching his saddle and calls back, "I think it's about that time."

Twelve riders fall into line, John in the lead, Corey flashing somewhere in between, and James bringing up the rear, along the ridge where clouds blaze red and orange and torch the grass with an illusion of flame. A world on fire. Nothing now to listen to between one breath and another. Nothing but the dying wind and the muffled rhythm, like heartbeats, of shod hooves on grass. The flap of a lone crow's wings, beating it for cover into the obscurity of cottonwoods in the darkening river bottom. In the distance, the outline of the railroad trestle, sharp against the orange sky.

Twelve riders in silhouette on the crest of the hill. Waiting for the breaking point, the distant rumble, hardly perceptible, that will gradually swell into the roar of the approaching locomotive and the clack of cars on tracks. Everybody's tense now, even the Tendenning boys. The horses know from rehearsal what is about to happen, and they're ready and eager, frothing and champing. Chuck Reisenaur's mare fights her bit, breaks out of line, rears and paws.

"You okay, Chuck?"

"Sure."

Time stretches.

Then the three short whistle blasts from the locomotive, as arranged, and John yells, "Now!"

In that first instant he remembers how Val Tendenning had described them at rehearsal, twelve armed horsemen on the brink of the hill, riding abreast in all their regalia, their chaps and boots and beaded vests and double holsters and blazing guns. Horses plunging down the hill toward the slowing train, manes and tails whipping. Black riders out of the sunset, heart-stopping. Time for the chill at the bone and the snapping of pictures. But for John Perrine after the first instant, it's sheer downhill in a rising cloud of twilight dust with time cranked to its top notch and nothing to think about but the right-now, riding and plunging and sliding down shale, through bunchgrass and sagebrush, reins in one hand, his Colt .44 in the other. In the excitement of the charge he almost but not quite feels himself again, a part of all he's planned, a part of all he wants to be, and why isn't it better. He fires a blank into the air and feels his horse gather himself into a new burst of speed. It's dark enough now to see sparks from the gunshots. John hears James Tendenning fire his shotgun into the evening air with a concussion that sounds like a cannon and smells like brimstone, and he glances back in time to see the impressive spurt of flame and thinks he understands why, in the days of yore, the Wild Bunch rode after trains.

The train has come to a complete stop, the locomotive with its redwhite-and-blue bunting pulled just past the curve, to line the three passenger cars broadside with the old wagon road for a perfect view as, yipping and firing blanks, the riders thunder down upon them. John hears another teeth-rattling explosion from the other barrel of James's shotgun, and he fires his own gun again as dust swirls. The noise is enough for a war.

The windows of the passenger cars are lighted squares filled with cameras and faces with their mouths gaping at the charge of riders and the fire show. John pulls his sorrel into a rearing halt, flings himself out of the saddle, and feels the jar of sod under his boots. Damn, he's not as limber as he once was. Corey is also off her horse, he recognizes her by her fluid movements and by her flat-brimmed hat. James Tendenning has dismounted, others are dismounting and tossing their reins to Steve, whose assigned job is to hold all the horses. John catches a glimpse of Steve's smudged face just as he sneezes from all the dust.

The others are splitting off, three to a car as rehearsed. John grabs the hand bars of the last car when he comes to it and heaves himself up and through the door and into the warmth and the light and, briefly, the smell of roast beef from the dining car, and tobacco smoke and whiskey, until that odor is smothered by dust and horse sweat carried by himself and Corey and James, behind him in the narrow aisle with the shotgun and the strongbox, and he thinks that the roast beef and whiskey and horse smell, at least, is what it would have been in 1882. Although the restorers have done a good job with the interior of the cars, refitting the original light fixtures for electricity, oiling and polishing the walnut paneling, and installing heavy maroon velvet draperies and upholstery. The train robbers in their grime and period clothing and antique weaponry fit in better than the paying passengers in their brightly colored T-shirts and golf shirts and shorts or pressed slacks.

How the paying passengers will react, nobody in rehearsal had wanted to speculate. Their $75 cover charge includes, besides the thirty-mile ride on an old-time railroad train, a gourmet dinner, well, a pretty good dinner of prime rib in the dining car, plus entertainment—old-time fiddlers, guitar-playing and singing, and a train robbery. Will they think it's entertaining to be robbed of the seven-dollar bills that have been distributed to them as they board the train? James has said he thinks the period gear that John has so carefully researched to fit his target date, 1882, is interesting enough in itself. But no, no, argued everyone else. It's true we gotta make sure nobody's wristwatch shows, but it's the horses and the stampede off the hill and the blazing guns that'll get to them. Nobody's gonna care what year your saddle was made in.

Now they've come to the point of no return, and the smallish white-haired man in the first seat looks as pleased as if he's waited all his life to see train robbers. "Don't take my money, Mr. Robber!" he pleads, eyes twinkling. "You can take Dorothy, here, instead."

"Oh, Paul," says his wife, looking away.

John takes the little man's seven-dollar bills and hands them back to Corey to stuff into the strongbox. Barely brushes her hand by accident, really by accident. Takes seven-dollar bills away from the man in the next seat, who looks bored.

Next is a family group, identifiable by the tension that encircles them like an electrical current so furious that at first they appear only as types: the elderly rancher sitting by the youngish woman who must be his daughter, and, behind them in the next row, the two teenaged boys wearing headsets and sharing pretzels out of a backpack and who, from their resentful expressions and their feet on the backs of the velvet seats, are forced participants. Then their faces focus for John, and he realizes he is looking at Saylor Lambert, and that the boys must be his grandsons.

Saylor Lambert, who this afternoon was served with his eviction notice, who threatened the deputy sheriff with a rifle, who had the whole law enforcement of Murray County in a furor while they tried to decide what to do next, and who, this evening, has brought his family to ride on the Freedom Train. Typical old rancher, he's paid his good money for tickets, and come hell or high water he's not going to let those tickets go to waste.

Saylor leans around John with a tight, economical nod of his head and says, "Corey. James. Good evening."

Will they answer? John listens, but no, he's drilled them well. They'll stay in character. He takes Saylor's seven-dollar bills, which the old man has been holding by a pinched corner, as though they're distasteful, hands them back in a sheaf to Corey, and asks himself whether the grandsons would have been handed any of the funny money and if so, whether they have squirreled it away in that backpack. John takes one more step down the narrow aisle—"I'll take that," he says, reaching for the backpack, thinking to shake it out in the boys' laps, find any seven-dollar bills, make a show of taking it—when the younger boy, the one with the greenish curls, meets John's gaze, or maybe he does, it's hard to tell, his mouth is expressionless under a pair of those oval glasses with lenses the size of coins and just as opaque. John is thinking what bad luck the old man has had in those grandsons, just compare them to the Tendenning kids, for instance, when the boy jerks his backpack out of John's hands, gropes inside, pulls out a pistol, points it at John, and fires.

The Sunset Motel at the lower end of Main Street is stucco below and clapboard above, painted a rusty pink and shaded by cottonwoods. The neon Vacancy sign in the office window is lit but barely shows, even in late daylight. Ingrid goes in and comes out with a key on a plastic tag, stamped with the number 14. Fits it into the door of Number 14, which at least is on the corner farthest away from such traffic as there is on lower Main.

The door opens on the smell of dust and knotty pine paneling reminding Rita of her grandmother's basement recreation room in Terre Haute, Indiana, so long ago. The room has a kitchenette with a working stove and refrigerator, which, as Ingrid points out, will be useful if Rita ends up staying for a few days. Maple furniture, couch and chair upholstered in a soiled fabric that surely hasn't been manufactured in years. A TV on a metal stand. Through a doorway, a bedroom darkened by a plastic curtain over the small window.

Rita pauses in the doorway. There's an inevitability about the room, as though it has been waiting for her. Waiting for her to end up here. But when has she ever checked into a motel like this, how has she known that such a place existed? Stains on the carpet, dust on the blinds, where Ingrid stands, making out a list. Toothbrushes, hairbrush and comb, nightgowns.

Rose tugs at her mother's hand—"I want to go swimming."

And Rita sees that the Sunset Motel has a swimming pool with a woven wire fence separating it from the street. A small pool, bright turquoise blue water surrounded by a crumbling cement walkway and a few white plastic deck chairs. And poor Rose, who has had nothing this summer, a summer that was supposed to be one of swimming lessons and hiking and riding lessons, even. Somehow the lessons have been elided over, between her fatigue and Hailey's—what? Had he really, no, surely he had never said that the girls couldn't have swimming lessons. She can't bear to think that poor Hailey, unaware that he has been betrayed, is even now enjoying a late-afternoon drink with his harmless friends and spinning his harmless yarns.

"You've no swimming suit," she tells Rose.

"I'll pick her up one," says Ingrid.

And so—although Rita had had the idea of collapsing on the bed in the darkened room with the tiny window, chenille spread, three heart-shaped toss pillows—she ends up sitting with Ingrid over pizza and iced tea at one of the wobbly poolside tables while Rose changes into the new swimsuit that Ingrid dashed over and bought for her at Bonanza.

"The room's not so hot, but John's paying for it," Ingrid points out. "Also, if anybody comes looking for you, they aren't likely to look here. You're registered in my name."

That's something, Rita supposes. She wants never to be found, never to be exposed. Hailey hadn't hit her. Hadn't broken her glasses. It's all about what Rita has done. What she has done. What she has done.

From the door of the peasant hovel, the pool is a sheen of late sunlight. The princess warrior, nude except for the trifling scrap of spandex, runs across the crumbling pavement of an older civilization. Poised for a moment at the edge of the water, she raises her arms in the reddening light. Springs on her perfect legs and dives into the future.

Ker-splasheroo!

"Have you known John long?"

"Twenty years."

Rita looks a question, so Ingrid goes on—"Denver's where he set up his first law office. I was working for *High Country News* at the time—no? Never heard of it? The *News* didn't pay much, so when John advertised for a secretary—" she takes a bite of pizza—"yeah, so we worked out of the Denver office, and Denver got worse and worse. Drugs, crime, pollution—"

"Like California. Those are the reasons we left."

Ingrid glances at her. "Anyway, John hated Denver. And I never could get him involved in community action, like that. He'd make the contributions, it wasn't that. John's got money, you know. Even if he likes to act like he doesn't. Not that he's not generous. I'll never say that. He paid for me to get my lip repaired. But finally he said he couldn't hack Denver any longer, and he'd heard of this practice up in Montana that he could buy. Small town, clean air. And I thought, what the hell. We were used to each other by that time."

What with Ingrid's curious speech impediment, Rita isn't certain that she's understood all that she's said. And how had John and Ingrid been so much different from her and Hailey? Were you sleeping together, she is dying to ask. Are you sleeping together. Of course you are.

"It turned out all right for me," says Ingrid. "John always knew I swung both ways. And I met Lucy here."

The sun strikes brilliance across the pool, making Rita squint. She sees Rose holding her nose, then a swirl of water where Rose has been. A few seconds pass. No Rose. Rita sees herself jumping in after Rose, sees herself rescuing her child, comforting her sneezing drowned-rat child in her arms. But then Rose surfaces, gasping. She pushes fine wet strings of blonde hair out of her face and submerses herself again.

"Hailey always wanted beauty," Rita says.

Ingrid examines the hem of her dress, the embroidered linen dress that she had been wearing in the office and hadn't changed and is spotted now with water splashed by Rose. Ingrid shakes out her skirt and leans back in her plastic deck chair with her feet wide apart. She's not looking at Rita. "Beauty?" she asks, waiting.

"When they were in college, he and Eugene used to talk about self-sufficiency. How, if our country were ever invaded, they could go to the mountains with their rifles and live on game. They said there were canyons where no one would ever find them, and they could rebuild a little free world. It was just talk," Rita explains, "and of course we weren't invaded, so we never went to the mountains. But Hailey and Eugene enjoyed thinking about it so much. The talk, the planning. Like you said, like little boys."

"Yeah?"

"So then—after they made so much money, well, not *that* much money, not *billions* or anything, but they did do really well—and after Eugene went to prison—we had enough to buy the land and build our house. Hailey said it would be our little free world. He thought we'd have neighbors who still had backbone. It would be like going back in time."

"Yeah?"

"That way, if something terrible happened—the destruction of the infrastructure—we'd be all right, we'd be self-reliant, we'd have the supplies and the skills to see us through. The problem was, the money got spent."

Rita can see Hailey in her mind's eye. How he was. Flushed, alive, happy. Eugene's money had seemed like gold at the foot of the rainbow, stuff to throw up in the air and sparkle, and Hailey and Rita had been suffused, exalted, with the luck of it, until at some point *he can't use it where he's at, so of course he won't care* turned into *we owe him so much*. And yet when Rita looks back, Eugene and Hailey had seemed so vulnerable in their happiness that she had wanted to cross her fingers for them. Now they will be like disappointed children, their dreams shattered. Poor unwitting Hailey, unaware that she has betrayed him, betrayed him by all the horrible things she's told John and the prosecutor. She can't remember half of what she's told, and all of it blown out of proportion. At the thought of Hailey's innocent face, the bewilderment he's about to experience, the pity of it, she's on the verge of tears.

"They're like children," she tries to explain to Ingrid. "You can understand that, can't you?"

"What about the children?"

Ariel. That was what she was trying to remember. It isn't just poor Hailey, after all. It's Ariel.

"Where's Ariel?" she sobs. "If it hadn't been for the dirt, I'd have Ariel."

"Dirt?"

"The—" Rita's brain cells feel empty, she can't remember the words. "The crank," she finally comes up with. "The white bitch."

"That's what they call it?"

Frank LeTellier's day, like John Perrine's, has been one damned thing after another, and he's stayed late in his office, trying to catch up on the paperwork. Hearing the sounds of the county courthouse shutting down around him, doors being locked, good-byes called. Footsteps in the halls, then no footsteps in the halls. LeTellier works on, thankful for the peace and quiet. When a shadow looms up at the frosted glass, knocks, knocks again, he thinks it's probably the janitor. Except that the janitor would have her key.

Knock, knock.

Knock, knock. Knock, knock.

"What?" yells LeTellier. He finishes what he's reading, signs it, gets up from his desk, shuffles papers into his briefcase, ready to go home.

Knock, knock. Knock, knock.

He hurls open the door. Finds himself looking up at the all-state center from the Murray County High School Basketball Team, class of '73, who's got an iron grip on the arm of a scared kid who's taller than he is.

"Nolan!"

"Hello, Frank," says Nolan Staple. "I got my boy, here, with me. He's got some things to tell you."

The impact of the bullet knocks John across the aisle and almost into the laps of two women sitting opposite. Somebody screams, somebody laughs, they must be thinking it's all part of the show. He can't breathe. He's dying, and what a rotten fucking deal, after all that he's lived through, breaking away from family expectations, first the hippie years and then the rodeo years, the bucking bulls and the crashing into chutes, the spinning and exploding and himself flying through thin air to land hard on arena dirt, but never a serious scratch, never even a plaster injury until now, now, in a fool stunt, in a pretend train robbery with himself dressed up like a character out of a dime novel. Val had warned them, Corey had said it. Grown men playing cowboys.

"Don't anybody move."

John opens his eyes. It's Corey, delivering her line like a trouper and covering the passengers with James's shotgun.

"Jesus," he whispers. He looks down and sees, through his fingers, the scorch marks on his shirt, the powder burn the size of a dinner plate, the blackened hole and the ooze of blood.

"Can you get up?" says James in his own voice, low.

"Yes—think so. Must have—" he stops for lack of breath. Strange thing is that it still doesn't hurt.

Saylor Lambert is glaring past him with an expression that could twist crowbars and actually does flatten his grandsons back in their seats. "How the hell did you little sons of bitches get your hands on my revolver? Where'd you find it, Travis?"

"Don't talk to them that way!" cries his daughter.

"Tell me, you cock-sucking little bastard—"

"Dad!"

"Take it easy, Saylor," says James. "We need to get John out of here."

Necks are craning now, passengers starting to wonder if the shooting has really been part of the act. Old Saylor takes a quick, decisive look around, puts his hat on his head, and shuts his mouth in a tight line.

"Do you think you can walk?"

"Think so."

With James's arm around him, John finds his feet and turns to apologize to the two women he's nearly squashed. "Sorry, can't rob you this time," he gasps, and sees the relish shining on their faces. They probably would have enjoyed it all the more if he'd died on their laps.

He and James squeeze down the aisle while Corey covers them with the empty shotgun—"We train robbers take care of our wounded," James remarks over his shoulder, and gets a round of applause.

Cool air laves John's face at the door of the passenger car. After the bright lighting of the interior, the night is pitch black, but gradually he makes out a ragged horizon of river cottonwoods, and then the silhouettes of horses milling around Steve Tendenning. Dim figures are running back along the tracks to grab their bridle reins from Steve and mount their horses, and meanwhile he is being lowered to the ground.

"I feel like Emmett Dalton when he went back into the crossfire for his brother," James jokes. "I wonder if Bob Dalton was as heavy as you are."

Corey jumps down beside them, landing easily with a crunch of gravel under her boots. Illumination from the passenger windows falls across her face, and John sees her eyes go to the front of his shirt.

"Is everybody crazy?" she says.

Steve leads up their horses. John recognizes his sorrel gelding by his size. Struggles to sit up.

"What do you think you're doing?" says Corey. "Hold on. Let's have a look. Somebody must have a light."

She looks around for help, but the train is moving. The engineer up ahead in the locomotive must be oblivious of any rupture in the program. In the deafening blast of the whistle and the clack of wheels Corey turns back to John. Unbuttons his shirt by the light of struck matches and somebody's cigarette lighter. Takes her fingers away, sticky.

"I can't tell a damned thing. What's this?"

"My wallet," John manages. He's feeling the pain now, it's flooding over him. He closes his eyes, opens them and sees that all the train robbers are aware now that something's gone wrong, and he's the center of a circle of cowboy hats in dark silhouette. Above the cowboy hats are stars.

"Feels like the time the Brahma bull kicked me. Worse," he tries to joke, and hears Corey's horse-soothing growl. The pain intensifies, and he reaches out, finds her sticky hand and hangs on.

"—we need to get one of the trucks down here," James is telling somebody. "Used to be a track that dropped down from the breaks and ended up by the old shipping yards. Think you can find it? I can." And James is swinging into the saddle and disappearing in a thunder of hoofbeats.

The train whistle blows again, this time as far away as the trestle, headed back to Fort Maginnis. John struggles to sit up. "Corey," he gasps. "Call ahead."

"Take it easy. We'll call ahead. We'll have an ambulance meet us."

"No! The sheriff! Call the sheriff! Tell the dispatcher—the Freedom Train's due in Fort Maginnis in thirty minutes—"

He can sense more than see the realization settling around the circle of train robbers.

"Holy shit," says Chuck Reisenaur, catching on.

A burst of excited talk—get John to town, that's the main thing—hell no, didn't you hear what he said, we got a shooter headed to town with a trainload of passengers—where's the nearest phone, is Whitey Phipps still living out here—get Whitey, he's a good man—until finally Chuck remembers that he's got his cell phone with him. Everybody watches as Chuck pulls out his phone and walks along the railroad tracks until he's far enough from the barricade of the breaks to get reception.

By now the moon has risen over the ruins of Eberle. It casts its ghostly silver glow over the remains of the depot, the exposed foundations, the dark stockyards and loading chutes, the empty railroad tracks leading into darkness, past and present. Silver-coated grass and sagebrush waver and shift their shapes like disturbed ghosts as Chuck punches numbers into his device, the numbers that need no wires nor visible connections but rise into the very air. In a few minutes they can hear him shouting into the wind.

20

Corey drives west. Missoula lies behind her in its cleft of the great gray mountains that were burned over by the forest fires of the late 1980s and again in the 1990s and still bear the scars. In her rearview mirror Corey can see the whitewashed "M" on the face of Mount Sentinel looking out over the campus of the University of Montana and the high plains beyond Missoula and, still farther, the blue peaks of the Bitterroot Range between Montana and Idaho. Double gray lanes of interstate highway roll behind Corey, double lanes of interstate roll forward at ever-higher altitude toward Coeur d'Alene, Idaho, where Corey has never been.

Corey is driving Ingrid's Volvo (hate to think of you going that far in that old red truck, John had said) with Ariel napping in the seat beside her, toward an appointment made for them by Ingrid, who knows how to do everything. Sixteen-wheel trucks roar ahead of her, behind her, casting their sharp shadows, glinting their pronged mirrors, endlessly toward the horizon, always toward the horizon.

The voices that follow Corey are those of the living, not the dead.

Don't go, says John Perrine.

Well, I got horses to feed, she says. Your horses, too.

You'll be here when I come out of surgery?

Yes.

Don't worry too much about him, says Ingrid, looking up from her magazine. Ingrid's so tired that her eyes have shrunken to raisins in her large face. The big baby. Always has to have somebody taking care of him.

John tries to joke. The two of you ganging up on me.

She'd left the hospital and driven home, where she'd found James Tendenning unloading Perry as well as John's big sorrel gelding at the corral.

Thought I might as well haul John's horse here, said James, and save you having to riding up to his place twice a day and feed and water him. Big honker, isn't he. Has to be, the size of John. But that's a quarter horse for you. Loren's probably turning over in his grave, to think he's got a quarter horse in his home pasture.

Loren never liked quarter horses, Corey agrees.

I thought John was a goner.

Yes.

Can't believe you and I just waltzed him out of there, like it was all part of the act. Seemed like the thing to do at the time, but afterward I thought, did we all get to thinking we were the real-enchilada banditos, or what?

Our boys *knew* about it, put in Val. They'd heard Saylor's grandsons talking about it. They didn't believe them. I don't think they believed them.

In the dust of the departing Tendennings, Corey ran down to the springhouse and took a hurried cold bath in the tank, as Loren would

have done. She shook out her clothes and put them back on and drove
back to town, where she found Ingrid waiting.

He's out of surgery now.

Is he okay?

They say he will be. He's worried about the little girls.

So am I.

Rita's mother is flying out, said Ingrid, and I've been talking to the
judge. We think we can get Rosie released to Rita's mother and Ariel released to you. Which is what Ariel seems to want. If you'll do it.

What's going to happen to Rita?

Don't know. Maybe nothing, if she'll testify. She's got a long road
ahead of her, though, before she gets her girls back.

In her motel room Rita rocked herself but couldn't sleep, believed she
would never sleep again. What had she done, what had she done.

What I hate, said the prosecutor, is what's going to happen to Saylor
Lambert. I know he was a friend of your dad's. And my dad worked
for him for years, did you know that? Saylor's problem, he couldn't
keep up with the times. He couldn't figure out how to keep making
a living on the ranch. Then he thought he could work with that pair
of loonies and not get soiled, himself. We're going to try to keep him
out of prison. Release him to his daughter, if he'll go. He'll lose the
ranch, though.

That'll kill him, said Corey, if prison doesn't.

Oh, it's tough, said the prosecutor. It's tough as hell. But you know,
those old men like Saylor and your dad, they get to thinking that the
world's always been the way they want to believe it is, or was, or should
have been. But it was tough as hell for the Blackfeet and the Crow.
And it was tough on my folks, Corey. They lived through that revolt

in Canada and moved down here for peace and quiet, and then they got thrown off their homesteads because they weren't all white.

Doesn't make it any easier for Saylor.

No.

What a night that was, marveled Annie Reisenaur. Doc Mackenzie, he called nine-one-one, and then he got out my garden hose and hosed down my place, thinking the foothills were liable to catch fire, and then we walked up to his place and got out *his* hose, and afterward we just turned out the lights and watched through his windows. Fire trucks! Sheriff's cars! Highway patrol! And lights! They set up their own floodlights. We could hear them on the bullhorn, yelling at the Doggetts to come out. Doc, he said we were just lucky there were no bullets flying. Doc's a real nice fellow. He's going to seed me a lawn in the spring.

Knew all along what they were cooking over there, said Doc. They say those labs are just as likely as not to explode, so maybe it was an accident. Or maybe that young fellow touched their ammunition dump. I know I've seen that fellow before. I think he was over east at the time those Freemen made their stand. My theory is, he was working undercover for ATF. He was just stringing the Doggetts along until he got the evidence.

He was looking for the money, sneered Loren. *He wasn't a special agent, he was a goddamn accountant.*

What blew my mind, said Nolan Staple, was how those kids had it all worked out. Watching Hailey and the old bald creep and sneaking food to Ariel. You have to wonder. Here were Hailey and his brother plotting how they were going to set up their own free state and support it with their filthy drug lab, and there were those kids out in the brush, plotting how they were going to stop them. And by the way, Bobby's not the one that got Ariel pregnant.

And now she's got to go through this other helluva thing, said Corey, thinking of the procedure in Coeur d'Alene.

An incest pregnancy, said Ingrid. She's thirteen.

What's the Doggett place look like, asked John.

Like a bomb hit it, said Corey. The camper exploded, and then their ammunition dump, as they called it. The trees around it are pretty scorched. But the fire didn't jump the creek, and they got it out.

Did we get any rain?

A sprinkle, Corey says. She isn't going to tell John about the crackling underbrush, the grass dried to tinder. They were damned lucky to get the Doggett fire out. Everybody on both sides of the gulch had turned out with chain saws and rakes and hoses and shovels and gunnysacks, chasing stray sparks and smolders and ripples of flame while the boys from the county brought in the bulldozers.

Pasture holding out, asks John.

Sure.

Been up to see the mares?

They're doing fine.

John turns on his pillow. It's strange to see him looking so deflated.

You decided what you're going to do, Corey?

Pretty much.

Art school?

Going to give it a try.

Goddamn this bed, I'll be glad to see the last of it. I'm going to sleep in my boots from now on. Corey, I've been thinking. That bunch of mares, I'll buy them from you if you want. Save them from the slaughterhouse for another year. Next year'll be a better year, bound to be, and maybe when I get out of here, I can hire the Tendenning boys to help me halter-break the colts.

You'd do that? That'd be damned nice of you, John.

Like to, if you'll let me. Corey—

What?

You're coming home, aren't you. Eventually?

Ariel curls in the seat of the Volvo, sucking her thumb and pretending to sleep. Maybe she has slept. The sun through the windshield
warms her, drowses her, and she's lost track of time, which is moving
like the flickers cast by pine trees on both sides of the interstate highway as it rises into the mountains. Flicker, flicker, flicker, that's been
her life so far. Flicka flicka flicka. As long as she can pretend to sleep,
she can make time hold still. She can keep this drive from ending, she
can hurtle west forever in the warmth and the soporific drone of the
Volvo's engine. At least she's headed west.

Ariel's got a plan, of sorts. Sleep as much as she can, sleep through
this *procedure* that she's headed for tomorrow, sleep and sleep. But
she's seen what happens to someone who sleeps too deeply and too
long, and as soon as she knows she's Ariel again, she's going to *wake
up*. The details are sketchy, but soon she'll *wake up* and she'll *roll*. Ariel,
whom nobody could make cry, has lately cried a lifetime of tears, but
she doesn't think she'll ever cry again. She'll have a cast-iron coating,
she can feel it already. She may have to wait—she already knows she's
going to have to be looking out for Corey, who doesn't have a clue what
the real world is going to be like, let alone art school, and it's going to
be up to Ariel to see that Corey makes it okay. But that won't take forever. Before forever comes, this *procedure* will be over. Done with.

She doesn't know what Annie Reisenaur could tell her about cast-
iron feelings.

So, Coeur d'Alene by tomorrow, stay over a day for the procedure,
home the next, said Ingrid, who among other favors has broadened
Corey's either-or idea of the sexes.

Guess so. Thanks for the loan of your car.

Think nothing of it. Anything for John.

Corey glances at Ariel, curled under the safety belt in the passenger seat with her hair a dark tangle over her face, and then back at the interstate that rolls over the trail to the west that the old surveyors laid out, a hundred and fifty years ago. The little high-plains towns of Frenchtown and Alberton and then the mountain towns of Superior and St. Regis fall behind as the interstate climbs higher. On the other side of the state line will be Wallace and Kellogg and, eventually, Coeur d'Alene.

Like Ariel, Corey's got a plan, somewhat more detailed than Ariel's, but maybe not by much.

Never knew what made you think you'd be an artist.

Loren, you sound like you're a long way away.

Guess you found out some things you never wanted to know.

The bank statements, yeah. That was the last straw. No wonder you could afford to buy horses.

Hell, girl! You're stuck with the horses. Whatever you do with your fat attorney, you're stuck with my horses.

But I'm not stuck with you, Loren. I've heard enough out of you. You can go back to your grave.

And yet.

What she wouldn't have dared to remember earlier. What made her what she is. Some local rodeo, perhaps, maybe at the Murray County Fair Grounds, when she was ten or so and Loren was—let's see, he was nineteen when she was born, so twenty-nine—so young—swinging her up and setting her in the saddle astride old Barney, his top horse, who had a white star on his long face and a white off hind foot that wouldn't hold a horseshoe and a little whorl of hair on his neck that she liked to put her finger on.

All the cowboys and cowgirls were lining up for the Grand Entry. It was the ritual that used to begin every rodeo, however small, with every contestant mounted, spurred and chapped, and getting ready to parade into the arena and form a single long file of riders facing the grandstand. Corey could hardly breathe. She was gripping Barney with her knees, the stirrups of Loren's saddle way too long for her.

Get out there, Corey, said Loren, and show 'em what you can do. He slapped Barney on the rump, and Barney threw up his head and trotted along with the moving line of riders. As they entered the arena, Corey heard the crowd noise from the grandstand, sun flashing off the brass instruments of the band playing in the bleachers, the static from the loudspeaker mounted over the bucking chutes. Stirrup-to-stirrup with two strange cowboys, blinking in the sun, she wheeled Barney to face the grandstand.

"Ladies and gentlemen, please stand for the Riding of the Colors."

At each end of the line was a cowboy with a flagstaff fitted to his stirrups. A hand signal, silence, and then both color-bearers spurred their horses. The only sounds were hoofbeats and the crackling of flags as, at full gallop the color-bearers circled the line of contestants, passing each other behind the line and in front to take their places again at opposite ends.

Their horses snorted, frothing, and a roar rose from the grandstand as the band struck up the anthem, but Corey had eyes only for Loren. Loren, so young and so straight, the sunlight crowning his fair hair and his eyes blazing blue as the sky above while he held his hat against his chest for the national anthem and faced the rippling flags.

Don't know, says Andreas, whether you can carry all that with you and still be an artist.

Guess I'll have to find out.

In the Flyover Fiction series

Ordinary Genius
Thomas Fox Averill

Jackalope Dreams
Mary Clearman Blew

The Usual Mistakes
Erin Flanagan

The Floor of the Sky
Pamela Carter Joern

Because a Fire Was in My Head
Lynn Stegner

Tin God
Terese Svoboda

The Mover of Bones
Robert Vivian

Skin
Kellie Wells

University of Nebraska Press